ANTIQUE

BLUES

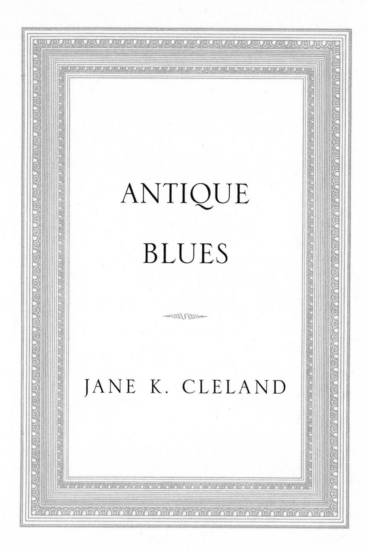

ANTIQUE

BLUES

JANE K. CLELAND

MINOTAUR BOOKS ❧ NEW YORK

ANTIQUE BLUES. Copyright © 2018 by Jane K. Cleland. All rights reserved. Printed in the United States of America. For information, address St. Martin's Press, 175 Fifth Avenue, New York, N.Y. 10010.

www.minotaurbooks.com

Library of Congress Cataloging-in-Publication Data

Names: Cleland, Jane K., author.
Title: Antique blues / Jane K. Cleland.
Description: First edition. | New York : Minotaur Books, 2018. | Series: A Josie Prescott Antiques mystery ; 12
Identifiers: LCCN 2017045721| ISBN 9781250148742 (hardcover) | ISBN 9781250148759 (ebook)
Subjects: LCSH: Prescott, Josie (Fictitious character)—Fiction. | Murder—Investigation—Fiction. | Women detectives—Fiction. | Appraisers—Fiction. | Antiques—Fiction. | GSAFD: Mystery fiction.
Classification: LCC PS3603.L4555 A85 2018 | DDC 813/.6—dc23
LC record available at https://lccn.loc.gov/2017045721

Our books may be purchased in bulk for promotional, educational, or business use. Please contact your local bookseller or the Macmillan Corporate and Premium Sales Department at 1-800-221-7945, extension 5442, or by email at MacmillanSpecialMarkets@macmillan.com.

First Edition: April 2018

10 9 8 7 6 5 4 3 2 1

This is for G.D. Peters.
And of course, for Joe.

AUTHOR'S NOTE

This is a work of fiction. While there is a Seacoast Region in New Hampshire, there is no town called Rocky Point, and many other geographic liberties have been taken.

ANTIQUE

BLUES

CHAPTER ONE

T he makeup didn't quite cover Lydia's black eye."

I paused just outside the study. I knew the voice. Trish Shannon, my friend Mo's mother, was talking about Mo's kid sister.

I was on my way to the loft to spend some time with Mo's just-purchased Japanese woodblock print, but hearing Trish, I peeked through the one-inch gap between the door and the jamb in time to see Trish brush aside tears. Even though she was in her late sixties, Trish's face was unwrinkled, her complexion creamy. When she retired from her pro golf career, she stopped dyeing her hair, and now, twenty years later, it was mostly silvery white peppered with a few streaks of darker-than-night black.

Frank, Mo's dad, a well-regarded blues guitarist, slapped his chair arm. "Son of a bitch."

"We don't know it was Cal."

"Who else? You think Lydia has someone else in her life who hits her?"

"To be fair, we've never seen her with a black eye before. She says she fell down."

"He treats her like dirt, and now he's hitting her? I'll kill him. That's what I'll do, the son of a bitch. Then our baby girl won't have to worry about falling anymore."

Trish smoothed her skirt, then met Frank's eyes. "I'll help."

"Josie?" Mo called from somewhere in back of me, maybe the kitchen.

I scooted to the teak-and-iron spiral staircase that led to the loft. "In here!"

Mo hurried around the corner. Mo's raven-black hair was newly cut into a stylish wedge.

"I know, I know," I said with more composure than I felt. "The party is outside, but I wanted to see the print again, so I thought I'd sneak up to the loft."

Mo flushed. She was a new collector, a bit awed at having taken the leap from admirer to buyer, and the fact that I, the owner of Prescott's Antiques and Auctions, respected her purchase, tickled her.

"I'm thrilled you like it enough to want to see it again. There's no need to sneak, though!"

"Thanks, Mo. Maybe I'll grab Ty. I'd like him to see it, too."

"Mo?" Trish called. "Is that you?"

Mo poked her head into the study.

"Do you have a minute?" Frank asked.

"Sure." Mo turned to me. "Go on ahead. I'll catch up with you."

Mo disappeared into the study, closing the door, and I made my way to the backyard. Garden-party fun swirled around me, the kind of hum and buzz that comes from fifty people clinking glasses, laughing, and walking across the flagstone patio.

I spotted Ty over by the shed chatting with an attractive woman in her late twenties. She had wavy reddish brown hair that fell to below her shoulders, and curves galore. The whitewashed shed was designed to look like a miniature house, complete with dormer and blue shutters. Ty stepped inside, reappearing seconds later carrying an old-style wooden croquet set.

At the woman's direction, Ty delivered the croquet set to a couple standing on the grass. He smiled at something the redhead said, then left her and walked to the bar. By the time I reached him, he was talking to Lydia, Mo's sister. Lydia was wearing oversized sunglasses, all the better to hide a black eye. She was taller than Mo by several inches, and thinner by several pounds. Her hair was as black as Mo's and cut in an easy-to-maintain short bob. As if Ty felt my presence, he turned in my direction, and when our eyes met, he smiled. My heart gave an extra thump. Ty and I had been a couple for ten years, and I still felt the new-love thrill every time I saw his face. I waggled a finger, asking him to join me. Ty said something to Lydia and crossed the patio.

He smiled down at me. "What's up, cutie?"

"I want you to see Mo's print." As we set off for the loft, I added, "Am I interrupting? Were you getting ready to play croquet?"

"No, although I will if you want to."

I took his hand. "I like croquet. We used to play it when I was a kid."

"Let's buy a set."

"That's a great idea. Our first game for our new life together."

He squeezed my hand. "Speaking of which . . . any more thoughts about the wedding?"

"I'm in favor of it."

"Good."

"But I want to disappear on a Friday and reappear on Monday, married, and you want a proper wedding and a big reception. I just hate being the center of attention."

"You're supposed to be the center of attention on your wedding day."

"I don't want to have to perform."

"You're too modest. You give touching toasts. You deliver inspirational speeches."

"Maybe, but I'm never comfortable. I want to enjoy my own wedding."

"Good point."

I didn't know what to do. I didn't want to disappoint Ty, but I didn't want to disappoint myself either.

"Now what?" I asked.

"Now we think." Ty kissed my forehead. "We'll figure it out."

I twirled my engagement ring. We might be struggling a bit with wedding plans, but I was super-excited to be engaged.

When we reached the top of the loft stairs, I blinked, momentarily blinded by the dazzling sunlight streaming in through the wall of windows.

"Nice poster," Ty said.

"It's a Japanese woodblock print, not a poster."

"I was joking."

"Oh." I took a step closer. "It shouldn't be hanging here. The inks break down in sunlight."

"It's holding up fine so far. What's the artist's name again?"

"Utagawa Hiroshige, one of Japan's most revered nineteenth-century artists. This print is called *Meguro Drum Bridge and Sunset Hill.* It comes from the series *One Hundred Famous Views of Edo,* which many experts consider to be his finest work."

The winter scene was rendered in shades of white, blue, and brown, with a touch of coppery orange in the shadows. Faint sparkles glittered across the sky. A dark orange rectangular signature cartouche was positioned on the right side, halfway up. A second rectangular cartouche, also in dark orange, was positioned at the top right, abutting a square poem-card. All three contained black calligraphy. The poem-card featured a subtly gradated orange-and-blue design of what appeared to be a shimmering orange sunset reflected on undulating blue water. The vibrant and bold colors in the print were also gradated, especially the blues in the sky and river. I stepped back to consider the picture itself, not the technique. Snowflakes spun against a steel-blue sky. Five people crossed a lapis river on a snow-covered bridge, none of their faces visible. Some were turned aside. Others were hidden by umbrellas. All were hunched over as they trudged through a storm.

"If it's from a series named *One Hundred Famous Views of Edo*," Ty asked, "how can this one be number one-eleven?"

"I know . . . it's funny. Actually, there are a hundred and eighteen in the series."

"What's Edo?"

"Tokyo. It was renamed in 1868."

"Do you know everything?"

I laughed. "Would that it were so. I looked it up when Mo told me she acquired it. Hiroshige designed it in 1857. Original prints from this series are extremely scarce. Only seven complete sets are known to be extant. No one knows how many sheets were printed from each image in the first place, probably no more than a few hundred, so it's rare to see one, and it's super-rare to see one in such good condition. More than a hundred and fifty years of framing and reframing, packing and moving, exposure to light, curious hands touching and stroking, coffee spills, and so on take their toll."

"You think it's a fake."

"Let's just say that I want to know more about it."

We stood for a while longer, taking in the snow-tipped trees and pristine white hillside, and the people, solitary figures on a snowy bridge.

"I like that," Ty said, pointing to the square poem-card. "He really captured the feeling of moving water."

"The technique is called *bokashi*." I squinted, and the illusion of undulating water strengthened. "The detail is amazing."

"*Bokashi,*" a man said. "The mark of a master."

I turned quickly. Cal and Lydia were climbing the stairs to join us. Lydia still wore her sunglasses.

Ty and I had seen Lydia several times during the dozen-odd years Mo and I had been friends. At thirty, Lydia was the youngest-ever director of Hitchens University's Technology Transfer Department. She traveled the world negotiating private industry's use of university-owned patents and intellectual property. She was articulate and poised, and not the least bit shy about sharing her opinions. To call her direct was like calling the ocean wet—it was true, but missed the point. I didn't warm to her, but I appreciated that I always knew where I stood with her and that her opinions were always informed and thoughtful. I'd met her boyfriend, Cal Lewis, before, but Ty hadn't. Since Cal and I shared an interest in art and antiques, and he was smart, educated, classically handsome, and utterly charming, I couldn't account for the fact that every time I spent any time with him, I felt like I needed a shower.

"Hey, Lydia," I said, smiling. I allowed my smile to fade some. "Cal."

"Josie!" he said.

He kissed my cheek, and I fought an urge to rub the cooties away.

"I don't know if you've ever met my fiancé, Ty Alverez. He used to be police chief back when you were in high school."

Cal extended his hand for a shake. "And now?"

"Homeland Security. How about you?"

"Assistant professor at Hitchens, art history. I'm also the assistant director of the Langdon Art Museum on campus."

I turned to Ty. "We've been there. Do you remember? They specialize in Asian art."

"Last winter. You liked one of the fishbowls."

Cal smiled at me, and I had to stop myself from backing up a step, a visceral reaction.

"If you liked it," Cal said, "it must be special."

"Everything in the museum is special."

"Is that your specialization?" Ty asked. "Asian art?"

"My dissertation was on the nature of kami in Japanese artifacts. I study the sacred energy communicated from artist to art." He laughed. "You can blame it on the navy. I was stationed in Japan, at Yokosuka, and I got interested in the concept that objects like vases and pots have souls."

Lydia pushed up her glasses. "I love that idea . . . pots have souls."

Cal turned to me. "Isn't that why you were attracted to the fishbowl? Because it spoke to you on a subliminal, emotional level?"

"Not really. I'm awed by objects of great beauty and inspired by the artists and makers who create them, but there's nothing mystical about it. The craftsmanship of that fishbowl . . . well, it's breathtaking." I turned to the print. "Same with this woodblock print. The way Hiroshige was able to create the sense of quiet and isolation—the stillness of a snowstorm. It's an astonishing accomplishment. Where did you find it?"

"A Boston gallery. I heard through the grapevine that it was included in an estate sale they acquired. I got there before they even catalogued the collection. They only deal in contemporary art, so I was able to get a great price. I tried to get my museum to buy it."

"They didn't want it? I'm surprised."

"The only Hiroshige they'd consider is an original *The Great Wave off Kanagawa*. Are you ready for their logic? It's the only work famous enough to add clout to their fund-raising, which is, evidently, their sole concern. Absurd!"

"Well, at least you know the print found a good home with Mo."

"That's bull. All fine art should be in museums, not in the hands of greedy and selfish collectors."

My jaw tightened. "Mo doesn't have a greedy or selfish bone in her body."

"All collectors, by definition, are greedy and selfish." He held up a hand like a traffic cop. "I'm not overlooking the fact that I'm the one who sold it, which makes me an accessory to the crime. I get it . . . but Mo's rapaciousness and my complicity are irrelevant. The fact that Mo is a decent woman and I'm a pragmatist aren't germane to the broader point."

"Josie?" Mo called from downstairs.

I leaned over the railing. "Hey, Mo."

"I can't come up now, but I need to talk to you at some point. My insurance company needs an appraisal."

"What about the gallery it came from?"

"Rheingold . . . they're not certified whatevers. You are."

"I'd love to. Thank you, Mo."

Mo's gaze shifted to a spot over my left shoulder, and her expression darkened. I glanced back. Her eyes were searing into Cal's face with such ferocity, I could almost smell the singed flesh.

Cal smiled at me, but his eyes remained cold. "I can make it easy for you, Joz. Type up my statement of authenticity on your letterhead, attach the receipt, and boom—you're done."

"Thanks, but the insurance company needs to know the print's value, not just whether the seller says it's genuine and the sales price."

"I negotiated a fair price. That sets the value."

"Come on, Cal," Lydia said. "You know better than that." She turned to me. "I deal with this issue all the time. Just now, for instance, I have to figure out how to price a promising but unproven compound. Do I consider what it might be worth to a pharmaceutical company hot for a new diabetes medication? Do I look to past sales for comparable compounds? Do I try to gauge the likelihood of success and discount the price accordingly? I have to deal with imperfect information, insufficient evidence, conflicting expert opinions, and plenty of uncertainty. In other words, how much is a compound with no known value worth?"

Cal laughed. "More than a Japanese woodblock print."

"I rely on data," Lydia said, her eyes fixed on my face, ignoring Cal's comment. "How about you?"

"The same. I always say I'm in the research and analysis business."

"Josie?" We all looked down at Mo. "I've got to get back to the party. I'll bring the print to your place Monday after school, if that's all right."

I told her that would be fine and thanked her again. After one more scorching look at Cal, she headed out.

I turned to Cal. "By any chance, do you know how many impressions of the print were made?"

"No. Sorry."

"How did you authenticate it?"

"I was able to verify provenance. You'll read the details in the statement I gave Mo. Here's the one-minute version: A few years after trade opened with

Japan, Abner Barnes went on a fact-finding mission for a Boston merchant, seeking importing or exporting opportunities. That was in 1861. He bought this print for his private collection. It has remained in the Barnes family until now. And, of course, the *bokashi* in the title cartouche proves it's a first edition."

"Why did the Barnes family sell it?"

"Probably the current Barnes is an assistant professor tired of earning a quarter of what his lawyer girlfriend does, so when his dad died, he decided to liquidate the estate." He snickered. "How about you, Ty? I know Josie's at the top of her game. What do you think about having less power and earning less money than Josie?"

Ty glanced down at me and smiled, then turned back to Cal. "Josie and I work in different fields. Each has to be judged on its own merit. As Homeland Security's director of training for the tri-state area, I have plenty of power, and I earn a good living. From what I hear, it's tough to get an assistant professorship, and even tougher to land an assistant director slot in a museum, so it sounds like you're doing well, too."

Cal's mouth twisted into a sardonic grin. "Good deflection, Ty. Sounds like you've had some practice saying it." He winked at me, and I moved closer to Ty. "Speaking of practice, do you play tennis, Ty? Lydia here can't even give me a game."

"No. I never caught the bug."

"How about rock climbing? That's my new favorite hobby. I can get up that wall faster than anyone."

"Which wall?" Ty asked. "I used to climb quarries for fun. I'd love to give it a try."

"Middleton Gym, on Islington. We should meet there someday. I like a good race."

"Not me. I like to take it slow, plan each move, and execute according to the plan."

"You're not a risk taker."

"Not hardly."

"Which makes for a good security analyst," Lydia said. She play-punched Cal's arm. "And good husband material."

"If you don't mind spending life bored." Cal placed his arm around

Lydia's shoulders and squeezed, a little too hard for my taste. "What do you think, baby? You look like you're ready for some champagne."

"Definitely." She raised her hand, a miniwave good-bye. "Nice chatting."

We stood at the railing and watched them return to the party. As soon as they were out of earshot, Ty began laughing.

"I can't help it," I said. "I hate him."

"I know. I think it's funny."

"Poor Lydia."

"She seems to like him."

Lowering my voice even further, I repeated what I'd overheard, that Trish and Frank thought Cal hit her, that he had escalated from generalized nastiness to physical abuse. "I don't understand staying with a man who hits you."

"Maybe she thinks she deserved it."

"Ick."

"Ick?"

"A technical term for dismay." I leaned my head against Ty's shoulder. "I love you."

Ty raised my chin with his index finger, leaned down, and kissed me.

CHAPTER TWO

Gretchen, Prescott's office manager, had hung wind chimes on the inside of our front door years earlier, and they jangled merrily as Mo stepped inside. She held a large red leather portfolio.

After she said hello to everyone, she unzipped the portfolio and lifted out the woodblock print. I placed it on an easel we keep in a corner next to the bank of file cabinets.

Sasha, my chief antiques appraiser, walked toward it slowly, her concentration absolute. "I never thought I'd see a Hiroshige close up."

Fred, my other antiques appraiser, joined her. "Look at the color saturation."

Mo stood nearby beaming like a new mother listening to people coo over her baby.

Following Prescott's protocol, I videotaped the print, front and back, describing it carefully, including its measurements, then uploaded the file to our cloud storage. Gretchen printed a receipt and logged the print into our computer database.

"Do you have time for coffee?" I asked Mo.

She glanced at the clock mounted near the ceiling, a Chessman original. It read 4:35.

"A quick one. My mom's book club meets at the house tomorrow, and I told her I'd make my irresistible chocolate swirl cupcakes before dinner tonight."

"What makes them irresistible?" Cara, our grandmotherly receptionist, asked.

"Sanding sugar. It adds a sweet crunch."

A gleam of interest lit up Cara's eyes. "I've used pearl sugar, but never sanding."

"Pearl is good, too. Sanding is coarser."

"I'm going to try it." Cara looked at me and smiled. "I'll bring up coffee."

I thanked her and pushed open the heavy door to the warehouse.

Mo paused ten steps in, taking in the rows of shelves. A walk-in safe in the corner held our most valuable objects, but our inventory of vintage goods and collectibles was organized by type and stored on open shelving.

"This is incredible, Josie. As long as we've been friends . . . I had no idea."

"Thanks. We sell a lot, so we need to stock a lot."

Hank, Prescott's Maine Coon cat, dashed over and mewed imperatively. He wanted to know where I'd been. "This handsome fellow is Hank." I scooped him up for a cuddle. "Have you been a good boy, Hank?" Angela, the newest addition to our feline family, scampered in our direction. "And this beauty is Angela." She followed us up the stairs. "She's my little angel."

Upstairs, I took one of the yellow brocade Queen Anne wing chairs, and Hank curled up on my lap. I stroked his tummy, activating his purring machine. Mo sat across from me on the matching love seat. She extracted an envelope from her bag and handed it over. I unfolded the documents, the receipt, and Cal's statement of authenticity, which required that I stop petting Hank. Annoyed, he jumped down.

Cal had paid $25,500 to the Rheingold Gallery in Boston for the print, a bargain but not a steal. Stapled to the receipt was a copy of Mo's check to Cal for $28,050, giving him a 10 percent finder's fee, a fair reward for locating the print and negotiating its price.

"Have you purchased anything else through Cal?"

"No. I had no plans to buy anything, but I just fell in love with this print. Besides, between the way Cal found it, you know, just out of the blue, and my godmother leaving me some money, it felt like it was meant to be."

"I know just what you mean. Serendipity. I'm sorry to hear about your godmother, though."

"Thanks. Edith Winslow. She was a dear, one of my mom's golf instructors, and the person who convinced her to go pro. She died about six months ago and left me twenty-five thousand dollars. Wasn't that incredibly generous of her?"

"I bet every time you look at the print, you think of her."

Mo smiled. "Exactly."

I heard the click-clack of Gretchen's heels crossing the concrete and mounting the stairs. Gretchen was the only one among us who wore stilettos every day. She came into the office and lowered the silver tray onto the mahogany butler's table.

"Cara's on the phone, so I deputized myself."

I thanked her and poured from the silver pot into Minton cups.

Mo added a thimbleful of cream to her coffee and stirred. She waited until the sound of Gretchen's heels faded away, then said, "Lydia thinks paying for an appraisal is a waste of money."

"Your insurance company won't issue the rider without it."

"She said that I don't need insurance, that the print isn't valuable enough to worry about. That since I live at home—that's a nice way for her to get in a dig about my divorce—and the house is secured six ways to Sunday, I shouldn't bother. What do you think? If you were me, would you get the appraisal?"

"Yes. Forget the insurance implications. It's the only way to know what an object is truly worth."

"Lydia's smart and sensible, but she doesn't always consider the whole picture. That example she gave yesterday, about what a new compound might be worth to a pharmaceutical company . . . When you rely so heavily on data and expert opinions, you risk forgetting about the people who are sick."

I felt uncomfortable. If I didn't tread carefully, I'd find myself enmeshed in someone else's family feud.

"You know what I like best about teaching first grade?" Mo continued. "It means something. I teach kids to read. I teach them to empathize. I make good citizens. All Lydia makes is money."

"She *does* help bring new medications to market. Anyway, it's not a competition." I smiled. "Anyone who teaches with as much passion as you do is a hero in my book. So is anyone who volunteers as much as you do."

"Thank you, Josie. I don't know why I let Lydia get under my skin. I'm a grown woman. It's about time I start acting like it."

"You're doing great, Mo!"

Mo sipped her coffee. "I had brunch with Steve yesterday."

I leaned back. "Really? That's a surprise."

I liked Mo a lot. She hadn't confided in me about why she and Steve had split up, but from the scuttlebutt that had made its way around New Hampshire Children First!, I gathered that Steve had a roving eye, and Mo got tired of being lied to.

"I know," Mo said. "I called him about a month ago. I don't know where I found the courage. We've gone out a few times since then. Do you think I'm weak?"

"No! Why would you ask that?"

She placed her cup on the tray. "I'm thinking of getting back with him."

"You must love him very much."

"Everyone will laugh at me."

"I'm not laughing. I think it's romantic. Besides, who cares what other people think? It's your life."

"Not everyone is as nonjudgmental as you are."

"I don't know about that—but thank you. Good luck, Mo. I'll be rooting for you both."

"Thanks." She reached for her coffee cup. "Do you know Nora Burke?"

"No. Who is she?"

"A book club friend I saw yesterday." She set her cup down without drinking. "After I left Steve, three people told me they'd seen him with another woman, at a candlelit dinner, all lovey-dovey in the park, that sort of thing. They thought they were doing the right thing."

"What did you think?"

"That they enjoyed it a bit too much."

"That's awful. Why do you ask? Is Steve seeing Nora?"

"What? No. Sorry . . . I was thinking of something else. I don't know who he was seeing—or even if the accusations were true. He denied it then, and he still does. We broke up because of money." She waved it aside. "Never mind. I need to go." She took one last sip and stood. "This is some of the best coffee ever. What's your secret?"

"Arabica beans, freshly ground. Cara tells me it's the single most important factor."

I walked Mo out.

The trees that ringed the parking lot were dressed in their autumn best. Some leaves glowed like topaz. Others glistened like opals. I took in a deep breath of warm, clean air. September in New Hampshire is perfect, with temperatures in the seventies most days. Everywhere you look, you're surrounded by a mural painted in iridescent pinks, incandescent reds, radiant oranges, and glittering golds, as showy as a peacock. October is perfect, too, a little cooler, with the autumn foliage fading but still teeming with color. Then winter sets in.

Mo leaned against her car, an old Saab. She stared off into the woods for a moment, past the white steeple of the Congregational church next door, toward the ocean.

"Are you going to this year's volunteer appreciation luncheon?" I asked.

Mo turned toward me, shielding her eyes from the sun with the side of her hand. "Sure. How about you?"

"I wouldn't miss it."

That's where Mo and I first met. About a year after I moved to New Hampshire, a dozen years ago, I'd joined the fund-raising committee of New Hampshire Children First! Mo had been wrangling horses in the charity's therapeutic horse-riding program for a few years, starting when she was eighteen. That first year, we sat next to one another at the charity's annual volunteer appreciation luncheon. I'd been stunned to receive the Fund-raiser of the Year award. Mo had received the charity's highest honor, Volunteer of the Year.

Mo opened the driver's side door. "Those kids . . . those horses . . . they've gotten me through more than one dark day."

"You've gotten those kids through some dark days, too."

She gave me a quick hug. I stood and watched until she turned left out of the lot, toward the interstate.

Rheingold Gallery was located on Newbury Street in the tony Back Bay section of Boston. I only knew of it from one mention in an industry publication, *Antiques Insights*. Each issue of the magazine included a column called

"Small Victories." The snippet, which I recalled seeing in one of last spring's issues, had compared traditional Japanese art with the hot new Superflat movement. Rheingold had recently acquired some important contemporary works, and the "Small Victories" author had been impressed with Rheingold's catalogue copy, referencing it as an example of how to shrewdly adapt antiques insights to modern-era art. I parked in the garage under Boston Common and walked the few blocks to the address.

Through the plate-glass window, I saw an attractive woman in her forties leaning against a teak desk chatting with a tall man some years younger. She wore a teal-and-beige Chanel tweed suit. Her sandy blond hair was pinned up in a French twist. He wore jeans and an off-white linen shirt, untucked. His hair was long.

The paintings perched on easels in the window were abstracts, some geometric and symmetrical, others comprised of seemingly random slashes of color. I recognized a dramatic Jun Inoue painting, a combination of graffiti and *shodo,* traditional Japanese calligraphy.

I entered the gallery. The woman smiled, then turned her attention back to the man.

A younger woman with waist-long dirty-blond hair and big brown eyes approached me and asked if she could show me anything in particular.

I didn't reply for a few seconds, taking in the gallery's minimalist style, noting the bold colors and the simplicity. "Thanks. I'm interested in learning about a Japanese woodblock print you sold last week."

"Oh, sorry. We only deal in midcentury modern and contemporary art."

"This was part of an estate you bought."

She looked confounded. "That's not possible. I'd know if we bought an entire estate."

"The Barnes estate."

"I'm afraid there's some mistake."

I pulled the receipt from my bag and held it so she could see it.

"This isn't . . . This doesn't make sense."

"Is the owner around? Or a manager?"

She glanced at the older woman. "Sylvia owns the gallery. Sylvia Rheingold. And you are . . . ?"

"Josie Prescott. I'm an antiques appraiser from New Hampshire."

Sylvia patted the man on his upper arm, said something to him, and leaned in for an air kiss. He grinned and left.

"This is Josie Prescott," the young woman said. "She has a receipt . . . You need to look at it."

I held it up.

"Thank you, Heidi, that's all." Sylvia waited until Heidi disappeared behind a partition. "Where did you get this?"

"From a friend who hired me to appraise it."

Her brow creased, and she met my eyes straight on. "This isn't our receipt. It's our logo, but not our format."

"Do you know Cal Lewis?"

"No."

"Cal told me he heard through what he called the grapevine that you bought the Barnes estate, which included a Hiroshige woodblock print."

"I rarely buy estates. I don't have the capacity to catalogue and sell objects that are out of my niche, which, as you can see, is rather narrow."

"Since you didn't sell this print and you don't know Cal Lewis, it seems to me I might have stumbled into a bramble patch."

"Who is Cal Lewis?"

"He's an assistant professor at Hitchens and the assistant director of their on-campus museum. He's a fairly well known expert in Asian artifacts, mostly Japanese vases and pots." I was tempted to add that I had no clue why he would do such a thing—or why he thought he could get away with it—but didn't.

"If he was going to try some kind of con job, why wouldn't he choose a gallery that deals in Japanese art?"

"I don't know."

"Should I expect other appraisers to contact me to ask about sales I didn't make?"

"I don't know that either. I'll ask him and let you know what he says."

From her skeptical look and the derisive twist of her mouth, I could tell she was wondering if I was involved, and I bristled.

"I'm just the messenger," I said, "as upset as you are, maybe more so."

Sylvia's scorn faded. She nodded slowly. "Can I get a copy of this document?"

"I'll ask the owner for permission, and if she says it's all right, I'll email it to you."

I extracted a business card from my tote bag and handed it over.

Sylvia stared at it for a moment, then raised her eyes to mine. "Whatever is going on here . . . it's not good."

I slipped the receipt into my bag. "I'm sorry to drop this Pandora's box on your doorstep. I'll be in touch soon."

CHAPTER THREE

As soon as I reached I-95 on my way back to New Hampshire, I pulled onto the shoulder and called Ellis Hunter, Rocky Point's police chief, and my friend.

I told him what I'd discovered at the Rheingold Gallery. "Given that Cal hits women, or, rather, given that there are allegations that Cal hits women, I'd love for you to keep me company while I talk to him."

"Is this an official request?"

"No. I'm asking as your friend. I don't know what's going on, Ellis. It's possible that Cal was the one who got conned, that he's not the con man. But he's supposed to be an expert in Japanese objects, so that doesn't gel. To make matters more confusing, Cal said he knew the print was a first edition because of the *bokashi* in the signature cartouche. That's not how you determine authenticity."

Ellis asked about *bokashi,* and I explained how it was used in the poemcard.

"Did you tell Mo?"

"No."

"How come?"

"Because I didn't want to upset her. For all I know, he simply misspoke."

"Is the print a fake?"

"Probably."

"What makes you think so?"

"Forget that Cal lied about where he bought it and misrepresented the importance of the *bokashi,* the colors are surprisingly vivid, especially the blues. Without further analysis, there's no way to tell what particular pigment was used in this work, but typically, the inks in traditional Japanese woodblock prints are among the most light-sensitive in the world. Dyes and pigments that fade quickly are called fugitive, and blue, whether indigo or Antwerp or one of the organic pigments, is among the most fugitive of all."

"Couldn't the print have been kept out of the light all these years?"

"Yes. That's why I said probably."

"Let's say it's a fake. Would Cal have known?"

"Most likely, although there's a fair chance that he was merely overconfident and did a cursory job on his authentication, then lied about where and how he acquired the print to give it a loftier pedigree than it deserves. Of course, it's also possible someone lied to him and he fell for it. If so, he got snookered good."

"What does your gut tell you?"

"He seemed resentful that he earns less than Lydia. I could see him trying an end-around to pocket a little extra cash."

"You don't like him."

"What are you? A cop?"

"And a good one. The way you tell it, he's got ethics problems, attitude problems, and a temper. No wonder you want me there when you talk to him."

Ellis and I circled the Shannons' house to meet up with Mo and Cal in the garden. The sound of ocean waves lapping against the boulders that lined the shore lulled me, like always. Sun-tipped sequins darted across the dark blue water. Nothing relaxed me like the sight and sound of the ocean.

As we turned the corner, the soft hum of a guitar caught my attention. Frank sat with his back to us playing a blues tune I knew but didn't know. Frank was tall and fit and loose-limbed. His craggy features and weathered skin made him look like an outdoors man, a rancher maybe. He wore dark blue cargo shorts and a sky-blue polo shirt.

We walked across the flagstones, and Frank, hearing our footsteps, looked over his shoulder. He smiled and stood up, placing his guitar on a thick maroon towel he'd laid on top of a black wrought-iron table.

"Josie. Good to see you."

"You, too, Frank. That was beautiful. What is it?"

" 'I Believe I'll Dust My Broom.' "

"I love it. I don't know if you've ever met Ellis Hunter?"

"Never had the pleasure."

Ellis said, "Nice to meet you."

"I called Mo a little bit ago. She was going to ask Cal to meet us here. I have a couple of questions about Mo's Japanese print." I glanced around. "Have you seen them?"

"Mo, not since breakfast. Cal, not since yesterday." He surveyed Ellis's face, pausing at the dark red scar that ran in a jagged line from his right eyebrow to his eye, a relic, I suspected, from his days as a New York City homicide detective. "Hunter . . . you're the police chief." He turned toward me. "You've brought a police chief to ask Mo questions about her print? That doesn't sound good."

"Ellis is a friend," I said, telling one truth while avoiding another.

"Fair enough." Frank flashed a smile. "Actually, I'm glad to see you. I was going to call. I'm thinking I want to sell this baby." He pointed toward his guitar. "You handle musical instruments, don't you?"

"Sure." I smiled. "It would be an honor."

"Good. It's a 1930 Martin OM-45 Deluxe. They only made fourteen that year, and I think this one was built for Robert Johnson, a pretty famous blues man back in the day."

"Why do you want to sell it?"

"Estate planning. It's hard to believe, but I'm closing in on seventy. If anything happens to me, I don't want Trish to have to deal with it."

"I'll be glad to handle the sale, but if you'd rather not sell right now, we could appraise it for you, so when either of you is ready, you'll have a good idea of its value."

"That sounds like a smart first step. Let's do it."

I smiled. "Excellent!"

"I'll get it cased up, and check on Mo, too. Sometimes she gets working on those lesson plans of hers and loses all track of time."

I found my iPad in my tote bag. "I'll have my office prepare the paperwork. Tell me what it is again."

Frank dictated the model number and Robert Johnson's name, while I typed.

I keep a miniature flashlight attached to my belt, so I'll always have it handy when I need to examine the undersides of tables and insides of drawers, and I used it now to peer into the sound hole to confirm the serial number, 45317, then videotaped the guitar.

When I was done, Frank lifted it clear, bundled up the towel, and went inside.

"You look excited," Ellis said.

I typed a note to Gretchen asking her to prepare the appraisal documents. I looked up. "Want to guess why?"

"Because you're excited."

"I never could get anything past you."

"What do you know about guitars?"

"Nothing."

"And that makes you an ideal choice for appraising them."

I hit the SEND button. "Don't be sassy. I know how to appraise valuable objects. I never know anything about anything until I learn it."

"Too bad everyone doesn't share that attitude. Lots of people think they know things when they don't."

"And most of those people don't hesitate to share their opinions. Except they don't call them opinions. They call them facts."

One corner of Ellis's mouth twitched. "I know you . . . you're talking about someone in particular. Who?"

"Cal. You'll see."

Frank came out with two black guitar cases in hand. "I can't find her. I called her cell, too." He lowered the cases to the table. He patted the one closest to him. "This is my working case. The guitar's in it. The other case is the original, from Martin." He looked around the yard. "Mo said something the other day about playing some game, croquet or badminton, I forget which. She might be in the shed hunting down birdies or wickets. I'll check."

Ellis's phone vibrated. He glanced at the display. "I need to take this."

Ellis sat on a wrought-iron bench while Frank and I crossed the lawn to the shed. Frank opened the door and switched on the light. The left side was full of lawn care equipment, including a riding lawn mower. Tools hung on pegboard hooks. Sports gear was housed on the right. Two kayaks were suspended from the ceiling; three bags of golf clubs rested on a wooden platform; six tennis racquets, four badminton racquets, and a mesh bag of birdies hung from brackets above the croquet set; and a rolled-up badminton net and silver poles leaned against the wall.

Mo wasn't there.

He turned off the light and shut the door. "What time did she say she'd meet you?"

"Five."

He glanced at his watch. "That's now." He stared into the shrubbery that surrounded the shed as though he might spot Mo hiding under a bush. "It's not like her to miss an appointment."

"It's not urgent. I can come back another time."

"I guess."

"Do you have Cal's number?"

"No, but Lydia will. She's in the living room, working. She left work early today. She didn't want to risk getting stuck in traffic and being late for Trish's book club. Sometimes I think Lydia likes the book club more than Trish does."

We walked across the lawn to the patio. Ellis was reading something on his phone.

"We're going to ask Lydia for Cal's phone number," I told him.

He met my eyes and nodded. "Why don't I wait here."

I knew Ellis well enough to understand his unspoken message. He didn't want to spook Lydia into refusing to give me Cal's number.

I followed Frank into the house, through the mudroom, down a corridor, and into the living room.

Frank stopped about ten feet from where Lydia sat in a red leather club chair. Her feet were curled up under her. She was reading from a legal brief. There was a faint purple smudge under her right eye.

Frank cleared his throat. "Lydia?"

She looked at me, then back at Frank. "Is something wrong?"

"Do you know where Cal is?"

"Why?"

"Mo arranged to meet Josie and him. Neither one of them showed up."

"Maybe they got the location wrong." She met my gaze. "Or you did."

"It's possible, I suppose," I said. "Do you have his phone number?"

"Sure."

She called it out, and I entered it into my phone. Frank and Lydia kept their eyes on my face as I waited for the call to connect. It went directly to voice mail. I listened to Cal's voice invite me to leave him a message.

"Hi, Cal. This is Josie. Josie Prescott. I thought you, Mo, and I were going to meet up today at the Shannons' house. At five. In the garden. Did I misunderstand the location? Give me a call, please! I have a few questions about the woodblock print. Thanks!"

Lydia tapped the brief against her leg. "What questions?"

"Technical stuff. Were you with Cal when he bought it?"

"No. We're not joined at the hip."

"So you don't know where he is now?" Frank asked.

"No. What's going on?"

I smiled. "Just a couple of questions. Could Cal be at Hitchens?"

Her shoulders lifted an inch, then dropped. "Maybe. We're not scheduled to get together until tomorrow."

"If you talk to him, ask him to call me, okay?" She said she would, and I turned toward Frank. "Why don't we check the garden again?"

"Sure."

I glanced over my shoulder as we left the room. Lydia was already back at work, flipping pages, shaking her head over some point in the brief.

Ellis stood facing the ocean, his back to us. He was on his phone.

Mo and Cal weren't in sight.

"I wonder where they are," Frank said. "I don't like it. Mo doesn't make mistakes about locations any more than she forgets appointments."

"I know."

"I'll go ask Trish if she knows anything."

"Want to sign the appraisal authorization? Then I'll stow the guitar and meet you back here."

Frank read the agreement, signed the electronic form, and headed into the house.

I opened the modern case to confirm that the guitar was inside, latched it closed, and carried the two cases to my car. I wrapped each of them in protective blankets and secured them in the trunk.

When I got back to the garden, I took another look around. Neither Mo nor Cal had shown up. I walked past Ellis, back on the phone, toward the ocean. When he saw me, he raised his index finger. I gave him a thumbs-up.

Riffles of whitecaps ran along the surface, a light chop. Farther out to sea, the water looked black and deadly. I reached the low fieldstone wall that protected the unsuspecting or the preoccupied from the twenty-foot drop. I looked to the right, south. Instead of the tan thick-grained sand that covered most of New Hampshire's coastline, overlapping eight-foot granite boulders ranged along the bottom of the cliff and stretched ten feet into the ocean. Glossy ribbons of bottle-green seaweed were wedged between some of the boulders.

I glanced at Ellis. He was nodding at something someone was saying. I turned north and watched the frothy waves batter the boulders and the cliff. When the water ebbed, I spotted a heap of clothing lying on a boulder, something pink and flowery. I tried to imagine how it got there, then gasped and tripped, scraping my knee on the rough stone wall. It wasn't a pile of clothing. It was a body.

I spun toward Ellis. He must have seen panic on my face, because he ended his call and started jogging toward me.

I turned back to the rocky shoreline.

"What is it?" Ellis called as he ran.

I could see it was a woman. Her face was turned toward the shore, toward me. I squinted to try to discern her features.

"Oh, God," I whispered, pointing at the boulder, fighting tears, my throat closing.

Ellis stood next to me, and together we stared at Mo's broken body.

CHAPTER FOUR

I sat on the lawn with my back to the stone wall and my head between my knees, waiting for the gold flecks dancing in front of my eyes to disappear. Tears streamed down my cheeks. Ellis was on the phone barking orders. After a few seconds, the specks floated away. I found a tissue in my tote bag and wiped the wetness from my face, then used the wall to hoist myself upright.

A police boat cut its engines fifty feet from shore, glided for a few seconds, then dropped anchor. I recognized the medical examiner, Dr. Graham. I'd seen her before, but I didn't know her. She was petite and about my age, midthirties. From all reports, she was totally by-the-book and as thorough as all get-out.

Two men I didn't know, both in their thirties, and both wearing official Rocky Point police windbreakers, lowered a dinghy. It landed in the water with a loud plop. One of the police officers climbed in, followed by a younger man wearing a Rocky Point Crime Scene Technology jacket. The police officer on the larger boat helped the doctor navigate her way into the dinghy. She stepped down, setting it rocking. He passed two black bags, a big one stamped with the department's gold logo, and a smaller one, more the size of a camera case, to the tech. Once the dinghy settled down, the police officer rowed toward the boulders.

"No!" Trish screeched to the heavens, shattering the stillness.

I spun around. Ellis stood on the patio, his face lined with concern, his hand on Trish's shoulder. Frank kept his eyes on Ellis's face and his arm under Trish's elbow, ready to catch her if she fainted, which from her ashen complexion seemed like a realistic possibility.

"No!" Trish screamed again, her head back, her eyes scrunched closed.

Lydia had a death grip on the back of a wrought-iron chair. She looked as scary-pale as her mother.

Ellis said something I couldn't hear.

Trish shrieked again, and Frank embraced her. She howled again and again, her cries growing louder. Her legs buckled. Frank walked her to a bench.

I hadn't had enough time to process the fact that Mo was dead, that my friend was dead, and witnessing Trish's tortured reaction made the horror worse, more palpable. It felt wrong to watch something so private, so harrowing. I looked away. As Trish's screams faded to whimpers, I fought back a fresh wave of tears. After a few seconds, I had myself under a modicum of control.

The medical examiner was squatting on the boulder, leaning over Mo's body. She wore turquoise plastic booties. The tech did, too. He was video-recording Mo's corpse and the craggy rocks. The dinghy was moored ten feet away, roiling in the increasingly choppy water. The police officer who'd rowed the doctor and technician in sat in the boat watching them work.

On the lawn overlooking the crime scene, Ellis was listening to Claire Brownley, a detective I'd known for years.

Lydia, ignoring Detective Brownley, spoke to Ellis, and Ellis nodded.

"Daryl!" Ellis called, and a young police officer hustled over, listened for a moment, then ran ahead and opened the kitchen door.

Lydia whispered something to Frank. He helped Trish stand and placed his arm around her shoulders, said something to her, and led her into the house. Lydia dragged along behind, her shoulders bowed.

Ellis resumed his conversation with the detective. I was curious about what they were discussing. No one was paying any attention to me. Keeping my eyes on the ocean, I sidestepped past beds of late-blooming roses until I was partially hidden by clusters of tall grass. I walked backward past the rosebushes, then turned inland. I skirted the patio by staying on the far side of the hedges and bushes. I paused behind a tall lilac bush, close enough to hear but not so close as to intrude.

Frank burst out of the kitchen and headed straight to Ellis with Lydia on his heels.

"I heard Cal's name on that police officer's radio," Frank told Ellis, his tone so sharp it could have poked a hole in iron, "and I came on the fly. Have you located him?"

"Not yet," Ellis said. "He told the Art Department secretary that he'd be back for a student conference. He didn't show up."

"That son of a bitch."

"Daddy, please."

"Enough. Your sister's dead." He froze her with an icy stare. He turned to Ellis. "I need to get back to Trish. So he's on the run. Now what?"

"Now we find him."

"Whatever you need, you just let me know. You name it, you got it."

"Thank you."

Frank met Lydia's stony gaze. "Stay and tell him everything you know about Cal."

"Of course." She turned toward Ellis. "Cal had nothing to do with what happened to Mo."

Ellis waited until Frank was back inside. "Are you all right to talk? We can wait a little."

Lydia lifted her chin. "I'm fine. Upset, of course, but I can talk."

A boat engine revved high, then quieted, and we all turned toward the ocean. A second police boat pulled up beside the first one.

"I appreciate your cooperation," Ellis said. "Do you know where Cal is?"

"No."

"When did you last talk to him?"

"This morning. I stayed at his place. We're not scheduled to see each other again today because tonight is my mom's book club. Oh!" She touched her mouth. "I need to call everyone to cancel."

"We'll talk to them as they arrive. To be sure I understand—Cal isn't expecting you back at his apartment later?"

"No. On book club nights, unless Cal attends, I stay here." She shook her head, a small, sad motion. "My mom's pals can toss back wine with the best of 'em. I try to keep up, so I never drive afterward. I called Cal earlier and left a message. I told him what happened and asked him to come over, to help me." She glanced at the side of the house that led to the driveway. "I'm sure he'll be here any minute." She closed her eyes for a moment. "I can't believe this is happening . . . I just can't believe it."

"Why don't you go see how your folks are doing? I'll catch up with you later."

Lydia took in a deep breath. "I'll go in when we're done. Daddy's right—if I can help, I want to. What else can I tell you?"

"When did you last see Mo?"

"Let me think." Lydia rubbed her forehead. "Yesterday, maybe."

"Last night?"

"No. I was with Cal from after work until this morning. I stayed here the night before, so I would have seen Mo at breakfast."

"Do you have your own home?"

"I keep a studio apartment near campus. I don't use it much."

"How was Mo feeling yesterday?"

"About what?"

"In general. Did she seem the same as always?"

"I guess. I didn't notice anything in particular, and I think I would have if something was different."

"Was Mo dating anyone?"

"Not that I know of. She's recovering—she *was* recovering from a bruising divorce. It was final last October, and she's been slow to bounce back."

"Why was it bruising?"

Lydia snorted, half harrumph, half derisive chortle. "Her ex, Steven Jullison. He calls himself Stevie, and that tells you just about everything you need to know about him. He's a first-grade teacher, which feels right since he acts about six most of the time. The precipitating event that made Mo finally toss him out was that she found out he was going on overnight playdates with some hottie."

"Who?"

"I don't know."

"Do you know where Mr. Jullison lives now?"

"No. As far as I know, though, he's still teaching at Rice Dixon Elementary School."

Ellis extracted a notebook from his pocket and flipped to an empty page. He wrote something, then asked, "He didn't want the divorce?"

"I don't know, but I doubt it. If they got divorced, the hottie would expect Stevie to marry her, and he was chronically responsibility averse. Also, Mo supplemented their modest incomes by drawing from her trust fund. Stevie wouldn't like the idea of having to live on his own income. The divorce was her idea, but she took it hard. She was heartbroken."

"Was she depressed?"

"Sure. Isn't that a symptom of heartbreak? That and feeling like a rusty used car in a new-car lot."

"How did the depression manifest itself?"

"She cried a lot."

I felt a stab of sadness. Poor Mo.

"Would you say that she was beginning to find her footing, or was she still running low to the ground?"

"What are you suggesting? That Mo killed herself?"

"I'm not suggesting anything. Was she beginning to be more like her old self?"

"Not noticeably."

"What did Mo do for work?"

"She was a teacher, too. Third grade."

"At the same school?"

"Yes." Lydia pointed at the low stone wall. "Look at that wall. I told Daddy to make it higher, but Mom liked the view."

"You think it was an accident."

"Mo always was a little klutzy. She had two left feet."

"Who were her best friends?"

"I don't think she had best friends, not in the way you mean. She didn't do a lot of girly things, like go shopping or have spa days or anything like that. She spent a lot of time at New Hampshire Children First!, volunteering." She glanced around and walked to one of the tables. "I'm okay to keep talking, but I need to sit."

Ellis pulled out the chair opposite her. I stepped back from the lilac bush and took a few careful steps toward a boxwood hedge. By separating some eye-level branches, I could keep them both in view.

"How did she and Cal get along?" Ellis asked.

Lydia stiffened. "Mo could be a complete bitch, excuse my French."

I was so appalled at Lydia's heartlessness, I stumbled into the hedge. A twig scraped my ear, a small scratch.

"She didn't like him?" Ellis asked.

I righted myself and resumed my observation. Lydia was sitting with her hands clasped in her lap. I wondered if she truly believed what she was saying or if she had a secret motive for bad-mouthing her just-dead sister.

"She couldn't stand him. She acted like she was the grown-up and I was just a little kid."

"That sounds annoying."

"And then some."

"Were the hostilities open?"

"Cal wasn't hostile. Mo tried hard to bring out his bad side, thinking I'd wise up, but he doesn't have a bad side. He's a good guy, funny and witty. Ask anyone—he's charming and smart." She waved her hand dismissively. "Mo didn't want to believe that he was good to me or good for me. She thought his sarcasm was just mean."

"How did you get that shiner?"

Lydia touched her bruised cheek. "I fell. I guess clumsiness runs in the family."

"It sounds like Mo was out to derail your relationship. How come?"

"Jealousy, maybe."

"What can you tell me about the Japanese woodblock print?"

"Nothing. I mean, I don't know much about art. Mo was thrilled with the purchase."

"Thank you." Ellis closed his notebook. "Can you think of anyone else I should talk to?"

"Josie Prescott. Mo thought the world of her."

Tears welled when she spoke my name.

"Her colleagues at her school," Lydia continued. "The people she volunteered with. I don't know who else."

Ellis thanked her again and slipped the notebook into his pocket. A uniformed officer waited on the grass. I knew him. Griff was close to retirement, and laid-back. The other officer, Daryl, who was still in with the family, was younger, in his early thirties, and earnest. Ellis caught Griff's eye, and the older man hurried toward him.

"Walk Ms. Shannon inside, Griff, and stay with the family. If anyone thinks of anything that might help, call me immediately. Send Daryl out."

Lydia walked into the house without saying another word, and Griff followed.

I came out from behind the bush.

Ellis spotted me and took a few steps in my direction. "Let's walk to the wall." When we reached it, he asked, "Were you able to hear?"

"Yes."

"Did everything gel with what you know?"

"Mostly."

"What's off?"

"Mo introduced her ex to me as Steve, not Stevie, and that's what she called him every time I was with them. And Mo wasn't the least bit klutzy." I blinked away tears. "I've seen her ride horses a dozen times. She was graceful and confident, a natural athlete. Why would Lydia lie about those things?"

"What do you think happened to Mo?" Ellis asked, pretending he hadn't heard my question.

"She grew up here. She wouldn't have misjudged the wall."

"Was she a drinker?"

"No. I've never seen her have more than a glass of something, wine or beer, usually."

"What does 'usually' mean?"

I smiled. "I saw her down half a margarita once."

"Did she do drugs?"

"Not that I ever saw."

Ellis's phone vibrated. He pulled it from his pocket and glanced at the display. "It's the medical examiner. Thank you, Josie. You don't need to stay. I'll be in touch later." He called to Daryl, waiting on the patio. "Make sure Josie gets to her car without being overrun by reporters." He turned away and answered his phone with a crisp "Hunter."

I didn't want to leave. I wanted to know what the medical examiner was telling Ellis, what other questions he'd ask Mo's family, and whether Cal would finally show up as Lydia expected, and if not, how Ellis planned to track him down. I scanned the ocean starting from the south, my eyes moving slowly north, wanting to capture one last mental picture of the crime scene.

I felt queasy, imagining Mo's terror as she plummeted onto the boulders. Shivers of fear and upset pricked at me. Mo hadn't tumbled off the wall. She hadn't killed herself. That left murder. The second police boat turned on its side lamps, and streaks of white light shimmied across the midnight-blue water. Twilight was closing in. Where was Cal? Had he witnessed Mo's fall and slunk away like a coward? That sounded like Cal. He was a bully, all bluster and no action. The medical examiner sat in the dinghy, her back to me, her phone to her ear. The police officer rowed her back to the mother boat, his oars cleaving the water as if it took no effort at all.

Daryl cleared his throat. "Josie?"

I stood for a moment longer, fighting tears, staring at the ocean, watching the remaining sliver of orange sun disappear below the horizon.

I turned toward Daryl. "I'm ready."

Yellow-and-black police tape separated the driveway from the street. Daryl raised it for me, then followed me to the road.

Reporters, some new to me, others I'd seen on TV or in person, called out questions, asking what I'd seen and what I knew. I ignored them all. Wes Smith, a reporter for Rocky Point's hometown newspaper, the *Seacoast Star,* stood apart from the group, near his newish red Ford Focus, surveying the scene with unrelenting intensity. Three women and one man stood off to the side, talking quietly among themselves. I recognized two of them, a stately woman Trish's age named Abby Young and the redhead who'd organized croquet at Mo's garden party. Abby was a frequent visitor at the tag sale, cruising the aisles seeking out objects that featured the letter *Y.* A petite blonde in her early thirties nodded in agreement to whatever Abby was saying. One of the men kept his hand on the blonde's shoulder. He was tall and lanky with bushy brown hair, a thick mustache, and a pointy chin. I gathered that members of the book club had arrived and didn't want to leave.

Daryl walked me to my car. He opened my door. "You okay?"

"Not really. Mo was my friend."

"I'm sorry for your loss."

"Thank you."

I tilted my head toward Abby and the others. "Those folks are all in the book club."

Daryl half turned to see whom I was referring to. "Yes."

I slid behind the wheel.

"Would you like an escort home?" he asked.

"Thank you, Daryl. I'll be all right."

He shut my door and stepped back.

I'm good in a crisis—rational, methodical, and careful. It's after the crisis has passed that I fall apart. *Oh, Mo,* I thought, fighting more tears. I didn't want to cry. My phone vibrated. It was a text from Wes: *Meet me in Tiller's lot. Now.* Since Wes's web of contacts was legendary, remarkable in both depth and breadth, there was a chance he had already garnered facts I could use in trying to understand what had happened to Mo. Wes ran a tight ship, though: If I wanted information, I'd have to give information. And I would. I glanced at the rearview mirror. Daryl hadn't moved, and when he caught my eye, he semisaluted. I raised a hand in response. Wes's car was nowhere in sight.

I turned onto Main Street, drove into Tiller's Shopping Plaza's parking lot about three miles down the road, and parked facing the street next to Wes's Focus.

"What's going on?" he demanded. "All I know is what I heard on my police scanner—that someone is dead. Who is it?"

"Oh, God, Wes . . . it's Mo. Did you know her? Mo Shannon?"

"No. Did she fall? Or was she pushed?"

"I have no idea."

"How do you know her?"

"She's a friend. We volunteered together for years."

"Why were you there today?"

"An antiques thing." My eyes filled again, and I gulped.

Wes peppered me with questions I couldn't answer, until finally he gave up. His tone turned stern. "You hear something . . . you call me."

"You, too, Wes. Please. Mo was a good friend."

I watched him zip away, back in the direction of the Shannon house.

Ty had left me a voice mail about an hour earlier. "I just got called down to Washington, God only knows why. Urgent, but no details. I'm at my house right now, packing. I'm hoping to make the eight o'clock shuttle so I can be at the office first thing in the morning. I'll talk to you soon. Love you."

I called him back and got him in the car.

"Traffic is horrendous," he said, "so I shouldn't stay on the line long."

"That's okay. We can talk later." I gave him a thirty-second rundown on Mo. "I'm stunned and so, so sad, and completely confused about what could have happened to her. And now you're leaving town. Do you know when you'll be back?"

"No. I don't even know why I'm going. I'm so sorry, babe. I know how much you liked Mo. Me, too. Let me pull over and check—maybe I can delay going down there for a day or two."

"No . . . you take care of business."

"Are you sure?"

"Yes. I'll be fine."

"You should call Zoë and see if she's around."

"Good idea. Do you think you're in trouble?"

"Why would I be in trouble?"

"What else could it be if it's urgent, without information?"

"I can think of four thousand two hundred and twelve reasons, and that's just offhand. I better go . . . I'll call you at bedtime."

We said our good-byes, and I slid my phone into my tote bag.

I sat for a minute, watching nothing in particular, allowing the anguish I'd been quelling to sweep over me, and then the tears came. I leaned against my steering wheel and sobbed. I cried until I ran out of tears. I patted my eyes dry with another tissue and blew my nose. I sat until I felt less shaky, then tapped the radio button. I wanted to listen to something so I wouldn't have to think. The radio was set to the Hitchens University station, which played classical music and broadcast professors' lectures.

I recognized the student host. His name was Greg Lindsay, and he was a regular.

"According to a tweet just sent by Wes Smith, a reporter with the *Seacoast Star,* a source within Rocky Point's medical examiner's office says that it looks like Mo Shannon's death was a homicide. We've reached out to Wes for more details, and will bring you updates about this shocking development as soon as we get them."

My throat closed. *Someone killed Mo.* I'd known it, yet somehow I simply couldn't comprehend it. I coughed, choking, then sipped some water. Mo had spent her life doing the right thing, and all it got her was killed. Crisis-calm descended on me yet again. My throat opened, and in one savage surge, anger supplanted sorrow. Anger was easier to deal with than grief. Anger inspired action. Grief was debilitating. My hands curled into fists.

I had no doubt that if Mo's print could talk, we'd learn who murdered her.

CHAPTER FIVE

Zoë, my landlady, neighbor, and friend, was the soup queen. She could take any mélange of fresh or leftover ingredients and make a delicious soup. I'd never been in her house when soup wasn't in the fridge or simmering on the stove.

It was almost eight when I called to tell her about Mo and ask if I could come over for dinner. "I know it's late. We can order pizza. My treat."

"I'm so sorry, Josie. What a terrible thing. Of course come over. We've already eaten, but I can offer you leftover roast chicken and just-made chicken soup."

"Even better. I'll bring the fixings for martinis."

"Good. Come whenever."

After a hot bath and a cold martini, I walked across our shared driveway. As soon as I opened the door, I was enveloped by the aroma of bay leaves and thyme. Zoë's chicken noodle soup. My favorite.

Zoë was tall, close to six feet, and willowy. She had short near-black hair and big brown expressive eyes. She wore a white fitted T-shirt and low-cut jeans. She could have just walked off the pages of a trendy fashion magazine.

As Zoë served up a portion of salad, I poured martinis from my silver bullet-shaped shaker—gin, of course, the good stuff, Bombay Sapphire, which I kept in the freezer, shaken with a capful of Limoncello, a concoction of my dad's creation. I used an atomizer to spray vermouth inside chilled glasses, another trick I learned from my dad. I filled them nearly to the top with the frozen liquor. I rimmed the lip of my glass with a curlicue of lemon rind, then tossed it in. I slid two oversized green olives into Zoë's drink. They spiraled to the bottom.

Zoë sipped her martini. "Yum." She stirred the soup. "Ellis called. He hopes to be home by nine."

I glanced at the wall clock. It read 8:50. "Home?"

Zoë's olive skin took on a rosy hue. "It's official. He's moving in this weekend."

"That's wonderful!"

"Thanks."

I wanted to ask why she'd changed her mind about living with Ellis, but I didn't. Yes, she'd worried for years that her kids would grow attached to him, and then he'd leave, but her announcement had a flavor of celebration, and I didn't want to say anything or ask anything that smacked of criticism.

As if she could read my mind, she said, "The kids adore him. They're older now, and he's been in their lives for as long as they can remember."

"Are you thinking of getting married?"

"Not now. You know I'm seriously gun-shy. I married a man everyone but me knew was a loser, which to this day makes me question my judgment. Ellis comes with his own baggage. He gave his heart and soul to his wife. When she died, he lost more than the love of his life. He lost his footing. Our solution is to proceed by baby steps."

"You're so sensible."

"And I make a mean chicken soup." She stirred the pot. "How are you doing?"

"Not good. You met Mo—you know."

"Lots of times. She was lovely."

"I just can't—" I broke off as Ellis walked in through the back door. He looked all in.

"Hey, Josie."

"Hey."

He turned to Zoë and opened his arms. She slipped into his embrace, resting her head on his shoulder for a moment.

She smoothed his hair. "Hungry?"

"Starving. First, though, a beer."

He kissed her and walked to the fridge. Zoë got a bowl from the cupboard.

"Any news?" I asked Ellis.

He found a Redhook pale ale and took a long draw before he answered. "I don't know about news, but I know who I want to talk to. Cal Lewis. He hasn't surfaced. You haven't had a callback, have you?"

"No."

"Neither has Lydia."

"Why not ask Wes to run an article about the situation?"

He drank some more. "Too risky. If Cal saw his name in the paper associated with murder, he might panic."

"I heard the headline that it was murder, but I didn't really think . . . I mean, I knew . . . I just can't fathom . . ." I stopped speaking and closed my eyes for a moment. I couldn't speak for several seconds, and when I did, my voice sounded harsh, unlike my own. "Is it official?"

"Not yet, but it will be by morning. The ME found contusions on Mo's neck that aren't consistent with a fall."

My anger bubbled just below the surface. "Cal's not stupid. Once he hears that Mo is dead, he'll know I told you he was supposed to meet us."

He finished his beer and tossed the bottle into the recycling bin. "As far as I know, Cal is a family friend who might have insights into what happened to Mo, nothing more."

"In other words, he's a person of interest, but you don't want him to know it."

Ellis smiled. "Wes will hear from someone, not me, that Cal is a family friend who might have insights into what happened to Mo."

"There must be an echo in here."

Ellis walked to the stove. "This soup sure smells good."

I could take a hint, so I let it go.

The soup was as soothing and satisfying as always. The reheated chicken was moist because Zoë had long since adapted my mom's technique—she warmed it in gently simmering poaching liquid, a combination of white wine, lemon juice, Dijon mustard, and minced garlic, with a dash of hot sauce and more than a dash of onion powder.

I texted Wes as soon as I got home: *Where's Cal Lewis? Do you know? As you ask around, make it clear that Cal is a family friend who might have insights into what happened to Mo. He's not a suspect or even a person of interest.*

I was glad to sow the seed Ellis planted, not only to help him but because I wanted to know, too. I trudged up to bed, exhausted, angry, and sad.

The next morning, I stopped at my favorite bakery, Sweet Treats Bakery & Tea Shoppe, en route to work. I wanted a blueberry muffin, and no one made them like Sweet Treats. The owner, a woman named Noeleen McLoughlin, told me that they flash-froze blueberries picked locally in July. Maybe that was the trick. I got in line, and with one whiff of the cinnamon and vanilla wafting throughout the shop, I was transported back to my mother's kitchen, to before she died when I was only thirteen. Sweet Treats smelled like love. I unzipped my jacket. The bakery was deliciously warm, a welcome respite from the morning chill.

I checked my iPhone as I waited my turn. Wes had texted an urgent request to meet. I replied that anytime after ten worked for me. That would give me ample time to get updates from my staff. When my turn came, I ordered a dozen blueberry muffins because everyone loved them as much as I did, then spotted a honey-dipped doughnut, golden brown and dripping with sticky glaze, and ordered a dozen of those, too.

Just before I reached my car, with ideas for authenticating Mo's print whirling in my head, I stopped short. I hadn't thought of it until now, but with Mo dead, I didn't know who owned the Japanese woodblock print. We'd need to put our appraisal on hold unless Ellis asked us to continue as part of his investigation. Frustrated at the thought of anything slowing me down in my effort to help find Mo's killer, I called Ellis and explained my concern.

"Do you know Theo Caswell?" he asked.

"Not well, just to say hello to at Chamber of Commerce meetings and summer concerts on the green, that sort of thing, but he seems like a good guy. Family law, right?"

"He's Mo's lawyer. I'm meeting him at noon. I'll call you afterward and let you know what he says. If the heir doesn't want to go forward with the appraisal for some reason, I'll get a court order."

"Maybe I should come with you, in case either of you has questions about the antique."

"Sure, if you don't mind hanging out in his reception area until and unless."

I assured him that I didn't mind a bit. "On a different topic . . . Zoë told me you're moving in. Congratulations!"

"Thanks. I'm psyched. Zoë's a catch."

I smiled. I loved a man who told the truth.

As soon as I walked into my company's front office, Gretchen said, "Oh, Josie . . . I was so sorry to hear about Mo. It's shocking."

"Thank you, Gretchen." I made eye contact with my staff, one at a time. "I'm not going to pretend I'm feeling fine. I'm not. Mo's death is a terrible loss. She was a good friend and a truly remarkable woman. I'm pretty shaken up."

Gretchen's beautiful emerald eyes moistened. "What happened?"

"I wish I knew, but I don't." I turned toward Sasha. "We need to hold off on appraising Mo's print. I hope to learn who inherited it soon."

"Of course."

"I'm assuming it's in the safe." She nodded. "Where are you with the appraisal?"

"All I've done so far is reach out to museums that have Hiroshige prints in their collections. I want to hear how they approached authentication."

"Good. If you hear back from anyone you've already contacted, go ahead and talk to them, but keep our interest vague."

She tucked her baby-fine brown hair behind her ears. "All right."

I turned to Fred. His black square-framed glasses sat on his desk. He was experimenting with contacts.

"Talk to me about Frank's guitar."

"I doubt it's real."

I leaned against the guest table. "I'm sorry to hear that."

"Martin is one of the most highly respected guitar brands in the world, which makes it among the most copied."

"Copied, sure. But counterfeited?"

"Yup." He tapped a paper on his desk. "Martin is aggressive in quashing illegal copies, so if you're going in that direction, you need to counterfeit. So far, I've located three guitars that made their way into reputable antiques auctions and were later revealed to be fakes."

"Like Matisse—he said he painted fifteen hundred canvases, and twenty-five hundred of them were sold in America."

"I think that's a perfect analogy. I've verified that only fourteen OM-45 Deluxe guitars were produced by Martin in 1930 because the economy tanked in '29. Before then, in the mid-1920s, the guitar market was booming, and Martin employed the most innovative designers and the finest craftsmen in the world. The minute the stock market crashed, demand for high-quality guitars plummeted. Martin laid off all but its most skilled workers, which explains both why there were only fourteen built that year, and why the quality is so high. For this appraisal, I think we need to locate every one of those fourteen."

"Can you?"

"Probably not. Martin keeps good records. All the inventory was sold to various shops around the country, but every one of those stores is out of business. None of the owners or their heirs is popping up in any search, including those done by the security company that does our background checks. I'll keep plugging away, but I'm ninety percent sure tracking sales from Martin is a nonstarter."

"That's terrific work, Fred. And impressively fast. What's your plan B?"

"I'll start by posting a request for information on guitar forums and blogs. The online community is large and enthusiastic."

"Excellent."

"Also, we need to ask Mr. Shannon where he bought it and whether he has a receipt or a prior appraisal. For obvious reasons, I didn't want to bother him."

"Agreed. Do you have any context yet for determining value?"

"Oh, yeah." He grinned. "Get ready to have your mouth water. One of the fourteen sold at auction a few years ago for three hundred and sixty-six thousand dollars. If we can confirm that Robert Johnson, one of the first inductees in the Rock and Roll Hall of Fame, had owned and used Frank's guitar, its price will skyrocket."

"Let's get Davy up here to examine the instrument itself, but since this is a private appraisal, not preparation for a sale, keep it on the qt."

Davy Morse was our go-to expert on plucked or strummed string instruments. Based in New York, he was an expert's expert: experienced, knowledgeable, insightful, and ethical. He was a Juilliard-trained guitar player, and he'd gone on to earn a certificate in sound engineering. After spending eight years touring nationally with two Broadway shows, he'd hung out his shingle as a consultant. His projects varied from serving as a guest curator to designing a guitar for wheelchair players and from appraising vintage instruments to helping video game designers get the music right.

I smiled at Sasha to include her in my comment. "Good job, both of you."

I left them to their work and pushed through the heavy door into the warehouse. Angela came romping up the center aisle to say hello, and I gathered her up. As I kissed the top of her furry little head, I thought, not for the first time, that there was no greater solace than cuddling a cat.

Wes stood on top of the dune with his back to the street. I drove onto the sandy shoulder and rolled to a stop. At the sound of my door closing, Wes turned around. He watched me crab-walk up the shifting sand.

"How come you asked about Cal Lewis?" Wes asked, skipping hello, as always.

"Hi, Wes. Nice to see you."

"You, too. So what gives?"

"You're welcome."

Wes grinned. "Thanks for the tip."

"Did you find him?"

"Not yet. I've only been working on it a few hours, but I reached enough people who should have seen him to be able to report that he disappeared around four thirty yesterday."

"Disappeared?"

"So it seems. He left Hitchens just after his three o'clock class. That's around four fifteen. He told the department secretary that he was going to grab some sushi but would be back in time to meet with a student. No one on campus has seen him since. Do you think he killed Mo?"

"I don't know. He overheard Mo hire me to appraise the woodblock print he sold her. If he was aware it was a fake, he'd know that meant the jig was up."

"Did he really think Mo wouldn't get it appraised?"

"Never underrate the power of arrogance. Cal thought his stamp of approval would be sufficient. Mo's sister, Lydia, told her the print wasn't worth appraising. I haven't asked her, but I bet he primed her naysaying pump."

"What a doofus."

"Did the police figure out where he went for sushi?"

"Not yet, but I learned that he was a regular at Little Tokyo, in Durham, about ten minutes from campus."

"I'll bet he didn't go there yesterday."

"No bet."

"Even assuming the print is a fake, why would he disappear? If he got called out on it, all he'd have to say is sorry, I screwed up, and return the money."

"How much money are we talking?"

"Twenty-eight thousand, more or less."

"Then I know why he took off—he's broke. He has thirty-one dollars in his checking account."

"How can you possibly know that? Banking information is confidential."

"Thanks," Wes said as if I'd given him a compliment.

I didn't push it. "Maybe he has another account."

"I'll keep digging, but he uses direct deposit for his paychecks, and this account is where they go."

"Then he must have planned his escape."

Wes pulled a spiral-bound notebook from his pocket and flipped it open. He tapped a minipen out of the wire casing and scrawled something. "I'll check on withdrawals and whether he has other accounts. Why would he kill Mo? Just because he couldn't refund her money?"

"Not exactly. Because it would have been humiliating to admit he didn't have the money."

"Money's the root of all evil."

"Not according to the Bible. The *love* of money is the root of all evil, not money itself, and that's exactly what I'm saying about Cal."

"You used the word 'escape' earlier. Did Cal escape or flee? Is there any chance he's a victim here?"

"What kind of victim?"

"I don't know. I'm just asking."

"I don't know either, but it's a good question, Wes. What about the Shannons' neighbors? Did anyone see anything?"

"Nope. We've got us a big fat doughnut hole. Everyone was at work or otherwise occupied. One guy is out of the country on a business trip to Brazil—he left the night Mo died. I'll follow up when he gets back. A few of them have security cameras, but they're all aimed at their own houses, not the street. Then there's Mo's phone. According to my police source, three calls came from the faculty lounge the day Mo died, one at three ten, one at three eighteen, and one at three twenty-four. The first one came from Edna Fields, Mo's principal. She says that she wanted to give Mo a heads-up about a new student transferring in the next day. When she learned Mo had already skedaddled, she decided to call her. She left Mo a message. Steve Jullison, Mo's ex-husband, made the second call. He volunteered that he called to ask about a lesson plan—Mo had mentioned a nifty new exercise she'd come up with, and she'd offered to share it with him. They spoke for about three minutes. The third call lasted only one minute, but no one is admitting making it. I figure Steve called her twice. He didn't call about any lesson plan—paleeze! He was trying for a little nookie with the missus. She agreed, but he had to check his calendar. He did so, then called her right back to confirm the date. What do you think?"

"Where is that coming from, Wes?"

"Logic. Why else wouldn't someone admit calling her?"

"I have no idea. Neither do you."

Wes chuckled.

"God, Wes, you're something like something I've never seen. Why did the principal call Mo from the faculty lounge, not her office?"

"When she didn't find Mo in the lounge, she decided to cross that item off her to-do list then and there. There's a faculty phone listing tacked to the wall, so it was easy to do."

"I can't believe your police source gave you all this detail. Or that they got it so quickly."

"They can move fast when they need to. And why wouldn't they give it to me? They're trying to nail a killer, and they know media exposure can help." Wes wiggled the pen back into place. "What else you got?"

"Nothing. You?"

He pocketed his notebook. "Nada. Catch ya later!"

Wes jiffled down the dune, hopped in his car, and drove off, traveling north, toward the town center.

I stood a while longer, thinking about family dynamics. There was some weirdness between Mo and Lydia.

The sun disappeared behind a tendril of fast-moving gray clouds, and I shivered as a blast of unexpectedly cold air blew in off the ocean. Time to go.

CHAPTER SIX

T heo Caswell was in his late thirties. He was movie-star hand-some, with longish brown hair and penetrating brown eyes. His office was in a new, all-glass building on Ocean Avenue, not far from Rocky Point's police station.

Theo stood behind his mahogany desk, which was angled to provide a sweeping view of the ocean.

He smiled at me. "Josie! This is a surprise. A good one, but a surprise."

Ellis offered his hand for a shake. "Thanks for meeting with me so promptly. I asked Josie to join me in case a question came up about any antiques. She'll wait outside."

"Josie's welcome to stay. Mo's beneficiary has already informed me that she plans on making the contents of the will public. Have a seat."

Ellis and I got ourselves settled in matching blue guest chairs; then Theo sat down behind his desk.

"Mo's will isn't complicated. She bequeathed all her clothing to Good-will, and all her jewelry, financial assets, and household goods to New Hamp-shire Children First! She estimated that her jewelry was worth about ten thousand dollars. She had around fifty thousand in cash and mutual funds. She thought her household goods would sell for a few thousand dollars. A trust that had been set up by her mother when she was a child provided a monthly income of roughly three thousand dollars. That income was also willed to New Hampshire Children First! Should the organization cease operations or fail to meet certain ethical metrics, the income would revert to her sister, Lydia Shannon, or Ms. Shannon's heirs."

Ellis rubbed the side of his nose. "Who assesses the ethical metrics?"

"I do."

"So there's some arrangement for ongoing compensation for you."

"Yes. A token amount for what is expected to be minimal work—a yearly look at their tax filings and annual report, and a review of whether any complaints had been filed against the organization. I don't anticipate any problems. New Hampshire Children First! has been in existence since 1922. It's well funded by multiple sources. There haven't been any complaints filed, ever. There's no reason to expect this record of excellence to change." Theo crossed his legs. "Mo called me last Friday to tell me she'd acquired an antique print, planned to ask Josie to appraise it, and would send me a copy of the appraisal when it was done. I explained that there was no urgency, from my perspective, since the print would be included in the category of household goods." He swiveled to face me. "How much is it worth?"

"I don't know. Mo asked us to appraise it, but I put it on hold when she died. It's in our safe. If it's real, it's worth around twenty-five to thirty thousand dollars, maybe more because it's in remarkable condition. Christie's sold the same print a few years ago for a little more than ten thousand dollars, but it was quite faded."

"*If* it's real?"

"It hasn't been properly authenticated, so there's no way to tell."

"I'll alert New Hampshire Children First! that it's in your possession."

"I know the director well. Helene Roberts. I'd be glad to talk to her about the appraisal."

"I'll let her know to expect your call."

"When did Mo prepare the will?" Ellis asked.

"She revised her will the same day her divorce was final, last October."

"Was the divorce contested?"

"Nominally. They filed jointly based on irreconcilable differences, but there were some skirmishes."

"What about?"

"I got the impression that her ex would have been glad to reconcile."

"Mo wasn't interested?"

"No way, no how."

"Was adultery involved?"

"So Mo claimed. Steve denied it."

"Did you believe him?"

Theo flipped his palms up, a "who knows" gesture. "I gave up long ago trying to get a handle on other people's relationships. My impression, for what it's worth, was that Mo adored him."

"Then why wouldn't she reconcile?"

"Pride, probably. That's usually the reason. She quoted her sister a lot. 'Lydia says I'm a fool,' that sort of thing."

Ellis asked a few more questions: who Steve's lawyer had been, did Theo know any of Mo's friends, and did Mo have any enemies. All he got for his effort, though, was the name of the lawyer. When Ellis was done, he stood, so I did, too. He thanked Theo for his time and asked for a copy of the will, which Theo had already prepared for him.

When Ellis and I reached the street, he asked if I'd heard anything or thought of anything that might help in the investigation.

"The German word for a mixing spoon is *Kochlöffel*. When someone was a busybody, you know, always sticking their noses in other people's business, my dad called them a *Kochlöffel*. Mo told me Lydia tried to convince her not to waste money having the print appraised, that it wasn't valuable enough to bother with. Mo told Theo Lydia thought Steve was a loser, that Mo shouldn't get back with him. If my dad were here, he'd say that Lydia was a *Kochlöffel*, always wanting to stir the pot. Are you surprised that you can't find Cal?"

"Are you?"

"Yes. It's not so easy to disappear nowadays, what with computers tracking our every purchase and security cameras everywhere." I waited a moment for him to comment, but he didn't. "Do you think he's on the run?"

"I think it's too early to say."

"Is Mo's death going to be ruled a homicide?"

"It looks that way."

"It's possible that whoever killed Mo killed him, too."

"What makes you think so?"

"Nothing. I mean, nothing specific. It's logical, though, isn't it?" My phone vibrated. I rustled around in my tote bag until I found it, then glanced at the display. I didn't recognize the number. "I should take this."

"Sure."

With my eyes steady on the pink rambling roses that grew in the sandy soil near the dunes, I answered the call. It was Theo Caswell, and he wanted me to know that Helene Roberts looked forward to talking to me. I thanked him, and that was that. I repeated his message to Ellis, promised I would keep him posted, and we headed for our cars.

Helene Roberts had taken the reins of New Hampshire Children First! nearly two decades earlier, when she was in her late thirties, and she had transformed it from a one-program charity into a leading medical research and treatment institution. The nonprofit's mission to help children with emotional, physical, and learning disabilities hadn't changed; the vision of how to achieve it had, and both the overarching strategy and the detailed tactics had been designed and implemented by Helene. I admired her as much as anyone I'd ever known. She was a leader and a mentor, and good through and through.

I arrived at Helene's office around two. The administration building was housed in an old farmhouse. Jasper Jackson, the last survivor of his family, had donated the thirty-five-acre property to New Hampshire Children First! in the 1970s.

Helene met me in her private study, which had originally been the back parlor. She looked the same as always—polished and professional. Her light brown hair was cut short. Her blue eyes radiated intelligence and kindness. She wore a blue-and-white checked blouse, with the sleeves rolled up to her elbows and navy-blue slacks. Her only jewelry was a simple pearl pendant with matching earrings and a gold wedding band. Blue plastic-framed reading glasses hung from a thin black nylon lanyard around her neck.

Helene placed her hands on her old-fashioned green leather desk blotter. "I'm devastated about Mo. Just devastated."

"Me, too. It's beyond awful."

"I couldn't believe it when Mr. Caswell told me we were her beneficiary. I've already asked the board to begin brainstorming ideas—I want to come up with a special way to acknowledge her generosity, maybe renaming the horse-training grounds for her."

"That's a lovely idea."

"And I understand we're now the owners of an important Japanese woodblock print. Would you recommend we sell it?"

"It hasn't been appraised, so I don't know its value. If you'd like, I'll complete the appraisal, pro bono, of course. Then I can make a recommendation."

"That's wonderful of you, Josie. Please do."

I explained I'd need her to sign the authorization, then called Gretchen to explain how to word it. Twenty minutes later, the form had been signed, and I was on my way back to my office.

As soon as I stepped inside, Gretchen told me that she'd read on the *Seacoast Star* blog that Mo's funeral was scheduled for Tuesday at two, and I asked Cara to put it into my calendar.

"Why the delay?" I asked.

"The teachers at Mo's school get out early on Tuesdays. This way, they can attend the service."

"That's sensible and thoughtful." I shook my head. "You all know how much I cared about Mo, so you can understand how I'm feeling right now. I understand that life goes on and work needs to continue. I appreciate your patience if I'm scattered for the next little while."

"Of course," Gretchen said.

There were other sympathetic reactions, too, and I acknowledged them all, grateful for their support.

After a moment, I caught Sasha's eye. "So . . . we're back on with the Hiroshige print. Have you heard anything from those curators you contacted?"

"Yes," she said, "and it's about what I expected. There's no master list, so tracing a print's history is nearly impossible. Since we have no information except Cal's statement, which seems to have no backup, we're in a tricky spot. I'll start researching the Barnes family now. It's possible someone will know something. Fred and I are talking about various digital analyses options. Other than that, I suspect we'll need to test the materials."

The phone rang, and we all turned toward Cara.

She put the call on hold. "It's Frank Shannon, Josie."

"I'll take it upstairs." I jogged through the warehouse and dashed up the steps.

"I hope this isn't a bad time," he said.

"Not at all. How are you?"

"Worse than you can imagine. You always hear that the death of a child is a parent's worst nightmare, but that's not the half of it. It's a nightmare you can't wake up from. I need to think about something other than my darling daughter for a bit, so I was hoping that maybe I could tell you some about the guitar's history. I know it would help me to get out of my own head."

"Oh, Frank, I'm so sorry. I wish I could do more. It was on our list to ask you about the guitar, but we planned to wait until after the funeral to schedule a time. Are you sure you're ready? We can put it on hold for a week or so."

"Like I said, I'm a hot mess, and doing nothing makes it worse. If you have the time, I'd like to do it today."

"I can come to the house now, if you'd like."

"Nah. Let's go out. If Trish sees me doing business, she'll get upset. She has her way of grieving, and I have mine, and that's that. To tell you the truth, I could use a drink. Do you have a favorite watering hole?"

"The Blue Dolphin lounge is a good place to talk. Do you know it?"

"Sure. Trish is a fan of the restaurant. Four thirty work for you?"

I told him it did, and I felt a familiar rush of adrenaline, the one I always felt at the start of a complex appraisal. I hoped Frank had juicy secrets to share.

CHAPTER SEVEN

T he Blue Dolphin was my favorite restaurant. The three-story brick building had been designed in the mid-eighteenth century to fit into the slender, rounded corner lot. I pushed open the heavy wooden door and greeted Frieda, the hostess.

I paused at the arched entry to the lounge. Frank wasn't there. The lounge was a wood-paneled room with an oversized fireplace and bay windows overlooking the Piscataqua River. I nabbed my favorite table, a small one in the corner. From where I sat, I could see clear across to Maine. A light breeze was blowing, and in the glare of the late-afternoon sun, the burnt-sienna and gold leaves blazed like fire.

Jimmy, the bartender, greeted me by name and called that he'd be right over.

Jimmy had red hair and freckles, and he smiled a lot. He was just that kind of guy. He'd been one of the first people I'd met when I'd moved to Rocky Point, and one of the most welcoming.* Frank's reflection appeared in the window, and I looked over my shoulder, smiled, and waved. He wore black Dockers and a white linen shirt, very urbane, but he walked with the rolling gait of a country man.

Jimmy came out from behind the bar, said hello to Frank like he knew him well, flicked cocktail napkins toward us as if he were skipping rocks on the surf, and took our order: a dry martini, Bombay Sapphire, up with a twist, for me; a double Johnnie Walker Green on the rocks with a splash for Frank.

---

* Please see *Deadly Appraisal*.

Frank's eyes followed Jimmy as he walked back to the bar. "Thanks for meeting me on such short notice."

"I'm glad it worked out."

Frank reached a hand up and massaged the back of his neck. "I'm stiff from not sleeping."

"It's horrible losing someone you love, but it's worse when it's unexpected, I think."

"Sounds like you have experience. Who'd you lose without notice?"

"My dad." I looked out the window. The sun was sinking fast. I could make out the trees across the river, but barely. I didn't want to talk about my dad. He'd died the year before I moved to New Hampshire, and despite the passage of time, or maybe because of it, since no one I knew now had known him, the wound still festered. "It was a long time ago."

Jimmy arrived with our drinks.

Frank raised his glass. "May the road rise up to meet you."

I touched my glass to his. "May the sun shine warm upon your face."

"God help me. God help us all." He took a healthy swallow. "I never thought I'd have to bury one of my daughters." He drank some more. "I adored Mo. She never said a bad word about anything or anyone, including Lydia. Not one. And Lydia gave her plenty of cause." He jiggled his glass, propelling the ice into a ferocious whirlpool. "They never got along, not really, not like sisters." He drank some more. "Sorry to be maudlin. Hell, look at me, using a word like 'maudlin.' The first time I heard that word was when Tommy Gale died. Tommy was my bass player, best in the business, and he died in his sleep at age thirty-one. Whoever heard of that? He had some kind of heart condition no one knew about. After a week or so, I was still moping about, and Trish told me to stop being maudlin. I waited until she went in the other room and looked it up. Foolishly sentimental. That's what it means. Foolishly sentimental." He shook his ice again. "The next day I drank a toast to Tommy and hired a new bass player." He tilted his glass toward me. "To Tommy."

I clinked. "To silver light in the dark of night."

He clinked. "Hear, hear."

"Tell me about the guitar. How did you come to own it?"

"It came from Abbot's Musical Instruments in Jackson, Mississippi. Man, I wanted that guitar. Looking at it through the window, I could tell it was the best I'd ever play, and I was right. I tried it out and knew I had to have it. It was Ricky Joe who bought it, though, 'cause he had the cash beans. My career took off the day I got hold of it. When you play the blues with a guitar like that, work finds you."

"When was that?"

"Nineteen seventy-three."

"Do you have a receipt?"

Frank finished his drink. "Well, now we're getting down to it."

I waited. Waiting was an important part of listening.

He finished his drink and set it down. "You ready for another?"

"No, thanks. I'm good."

He raised his glass to catch Jimmy's attention, pointed to his chest, indicating he was the only one ordering a refill, then focused on me. "No, I don't have a receipt."

"How much did you pay?"

"It was priced at twenty-eight thousand dollars, a fortune at the time."

"You didn't buy it, did you?"

"You got good ears."

"I noticed how you worded it, if that's what you mean. Was it a gift? From a woman you don't want Trish to know about?"

"Let's just leave it that I got it from Abbot's in the seventies. Can't you appraise it without a receipt?"

"Sure, but it's completely possible that Abbot's records go back that far." I sipped some of my martini. "We can call them."

"Maybe it's best you don't."

"Why?"

"Let's let it lay and talk about what you can do, not what you can't."

"Come on, Frank."

"I never got in trouble keeping my mouth shut."

"If I can't confirm provenance you'll never be able to sell your guitar for top dollar—or insure it for fair market value."

"Explain to me about provenance. What do you need, and why does it matter?"

"In the antiques world, provenance means that we can document a clear trail of ownership from the moment of creation to now. There's two options.

Go from the producer forward or from the current owner backward. From what we've learned so far, it looks like the first option is closed to us. That leaves only the second approach: to work from the current owner—you—backward."

"I don't like it."

"Without clear title, you're leaving money on the table. You'll lose half the value, maybe more. Plus, the Robert Johnson association probably goes down the tubes."

Jimmy swung by with Frank's drink. Frank thanked him and swallowed a third of it in one long gulp.

"Did you steal it, Frank?"

His eyes shot daggers at me. "Hell, no!"

"You can tell me—the statute of limitations has long passed."

"I've never stolen nothing in my life."

"Then what's the big secret?"

"Trish can't know. Not ever."

"I can create a side document for the appraisal, but if you ever want to sell it, the world will have to know."

"Give me a minute to think on this."

Frank stood, took another long slug of whiskey, and walked out of the lounge with an unconscious swagger. Two middle-aged women sitting at a table near the front pointed and whispered. It wasn't every day you saw a local celebrity strut by.

While I waited for Frank to return, I checked messages. Wes had emailed asking if I had any new information. Ty had texted that he missed me and would call just before bed. Given that a lot of Ty's work was top secret, I hoped he'd be able to tell me why he'd been called down to Washington, but I wouldn't be surprised if he couldn't say a word. I opened my photo management app and scrolled through the images until I found some from last summer's New Hampshire Children First! volunteer picnic. My eyes filled, and I closed them for a few seconds. I understood the term "heartache." Frank came back into the lounge. I slid my phone into my bag.

One of the women at the table near the front, a full-figured brunette, reached out an arm to touch Frank's hand and said something. Frank paused to chat, smiling and laughing. He'd been a professional charmer for a lot of years, and he still was, despite the fact that his daughter had just died. It took a certain kind of man to steel himself like that. I'd learned the hard way that most people who use charm as currency do so because they have nothing else of substance to offer. Charm disarms and can minimize a multitude of sins. Watching his performance made me wonder if I could trust him.

Frank sat down and drank some whiskey, a sip this time. "There are only three people in the world who know how I came to own this guitar: Ricky Joe McElroy, C. K. Flint, and me. I'm telling you because I want to know the truth about the guitar's value. I'm trusting you to keep the information private until and unless I pull the trigger."

"We'll need to contact the store and those two people, and maybe others, but I can absolutely promise we won't release the information to the public without your okay."

"You trust your staff that much?"

"It's what we do, Frank. We keep secrets for a living."

"I'm probably being silly, anyway. For all I know those boys spread the story all over Mississippi." He finished his drink in two long swallows and slapped the glass on the table. "It's more than forty years ago, but a lie started has to be maintained. I promised Trish the year before I'd never gamble again. That was after I got into some trouble, it doesn't matter what kind, and got roughed up some. She told me she wanted no part of a gambler, period, end of story, and I promised her that my gambling days were over. I kept that promise for a while, a few months, I guess. I told Trish I bought the guitar at Abbot's for a hundred and twenty bucks, all I had and then some, that the owner was dumb as a doornail and didn't know what he had, that it was probably worth double what I paid. If Trish knew I'd been lying to her for all our lives, there'd be hell to pay. Maybe worse than hell. Here we go, then—I won the guitar fair and square in a poker game on June fifth, 1973. That's a date I'll never forget. My life got changed that day. Ricky Joe's family owned McElroy Rubber Corporation. Mostly, they made tires. About two months later, Ricky Joe took himself off to Idaho to go hunting and never came back. Last I heard, he married a girl from Boise and they're living the good life on the trust fund his granddaddy set up. C. K. was a good guy, not too bright, but a hard worker. He got himself a job at the local lumberyard right out of high school, and as far as I know, he's still there. I came from the other side of the ditch. I got myself licensed as an electrician, but I hated the work. All I ever wanted was to play the blues and get out of Mississippi. That night, I was down thirteen thousand, can you believe it? I didn't have a pot to piss in, but I was drunk, and I had the gambling fever on me. Ricky Joe offered me double or nothing. C. K. wasn't playing. He was sitting in a corner shaking, just hearing the numbers we were tossing about. I said I wouldn't do double or nothing, but I'd do double or give me that Martin guitar you just bought at Abbot's for twenty-eight thousand dollars. Ricky Joe said done. When I won, Ricky Joe cried like a baby, pissin' and moanin' about how he didn't mean it, how he couldn't do it, how his daddy would skin him alive, how he'd give me thirty thousand, thirty-five thousand, but I wasn't having any of it. I wanted that guitar so bad I could feel the strings under my fingers. I'll tell you this, though—the thought that I might have lost sobered me up and straightened me out. I made Ricky Joe take me to his house there and then, and he made C. K. come as a witness. I grabbed that guitar and the case it came in, and told both those boys sayonara. I went home, convinced Trish that our future was waiting for us out west, and we caught the next bus to L.A. That was an easy sell because Trish was starting to think she had a future in golf, and L.A. was a happening place back then for that dream. And that's the end of that tall tale."

"That's quite a story."

"It's the truth, so help me God."

"So Ricky Joe has the receipt."

"I guess. He probably had it back then. God knows whether he kept it."

"Abbot's must have a record of the sale."

"Or they don't."

"C. K. can verify you won it like you said."

"If he remembers."

"I'll need to verify the events somehow, Frank."

"Sure. Just don't tell Trish." He gave the ice one last spin and downed the rest of his drink. "The owner of the store is the one who told Ricky Joe about the Robert Johnson connection, unless he made it up."

"What's his name? Abbot's owner?"

"I don't recall, if I ever knew it, which I doubt I did."

"What did Ricky Joe tell you about the history of the guitar?"

"That Abbot's bought the guitar off some gal who was somehow connected to one of Johnson's girlfriends. Johnson was quite the ladies' man."

"You don't make things easy, Frank."

"Nothing worth a damn is easy."

I clinked his empty glass with mine. "Words to live by."

My phone vibrated. It was a text from Wes: *Urgent. Call now.*

CHAPTER EIGHT

W hen Wes said something was urgent, usually it signaled nothing more than his eagerness to be first in line. Usually wasn't always, though, so I pushed my half-full drink aside and assured Frank his secret was safe. He stood when I did and insisted on paying, a gentleman. I offered condolences again, and he got misty-eyed and hugged me.

I sat in my car and called Wes. He answered before I even heard a ring.

"I need some info pronto."

"I'm fine, Wes. How are you?"

"Good, good. You were right. Cal didn't go to Little Tokyo. My police source tells me they have him driving down Market Street at four thirty-five."

"What do you mean they 'have him'?"

"On security camera footage. From Harrison Foodmart's parking lot cameras. He whizzed by."

"To get to the Shannons' from Market, you need to take either the interstate or Route 1. If he took I-95, he'd have to pay a toll. What about tollbooth cameras or E-ZPass?"

"Nothing."

"So if he went to Mo's, he took Route 1, which is lined with stores and restaurants and doctors' offices. Surely there are a bunch of security cameras."

"You'd think. They're still checking, but they've got nothing at this point. He might have taken back roads in order to avoid the cameras."

"I suppose it's possible. It's also possible he didn't go to Mo's. For all we know, he's en route to Vegas."

"Good one, Joz! Where do you think he is for real?"

"Have you checked for out-of-state family?"

"He has a sister in Wyoming, and his mom is in an assisted living facility down in Myrtle Beach, but he's not close to either of them. The reason I called . . . Cal hasn't used a credit card or his cell phone . . . how would you find him?"

"You said in your message that it was urgent. What's urgent about that?"

"Don't you want to know what he's up to?" Wes sounded staggered. "I thought you'd be flattered. Every once in a while you come up with a smart idea."

Talk about damning with faint praise. I decided to ignore it. "If I were looking for Cal, I'd ask Lydia who his friends are. I'd talk to people at Hitchens and at the campus museum. I'd look through his desk and his computer. I'd see who contacted him, say in the last three months, and vice versa."

"These are stock approaches. The police and I are tripping over one another. I need a new approach. Give me an idea that's smokin'."

"What about Lydia? If Cal is in touch with anyone, it would be her. Can you tell if he's called her cell or sent her email? Or maybe she's taken out a bigger-than-usual withdrawal to sneak him cash."

"The police are all over it. I don't call that a smokin' hot idea."

"We could—" I stopped myself as an idea rattled me.

"We could what?" Wes prodded.

"I need to go. Sorry." I hit the END CALL button.

Much to my surprise, I had come up with a smokin' hot idea, and I was keeping it for myself.

Sitting in my home office, I reread the document I'd just created and smiled, satisfied. It was good. I emailed it to myself for safekeeping, then printed two copies, slid them into a clear plastic sleeve, and left them by the front door. I crossed the driveway, climbed the steps to Zoë's porch, and rang the bell.

The porch light came on, and I stood in a seashell-pink circle of light. All Zoë's outside bulbs were pink. Ellis opened the door.

"Just the man I want to see." I stepped inside. "Got a sec?"

"Sure."

I spoke to his back as he walked down the hall toward the kitchen. "I need to run something by you."

Ellis stopped. "Privately?"

"Kind of."

"Is that you, Josie?" Zoë called.

"Hey, Zoë! I need to talk to Ellis for a minute. I'll come say hello after."

"Anything wrong?"

"Nope. Just a little business."

Ellis led the way into a parlor off the living room. Zoë called it her thinking room. He slid the pocket door closed. We sat across from one another on matching ladder-back chairs fitted with traditional blue-and-white toile cushions.

I handed him a copy of my flyer and watched him read it. It didn't take him long since most of the space was taken up by photographs. One was a shot of Mo's Japanese woodblock print. The other was a photo of Cal Lewis I'd nabbed from Hitchens University's faculty page. In the photograph, Cal sat in front of a haphazardly filled bookshelf, his chin resting on his hands, his elbows on his paper-strewn desk, a scholar hard at work, or a man wanting to create that impression.

When he looked up, I said, "I think I'd like to post this online. What do you think?"

"This flyer implies Cal has knowledge about the print."

"But not necessarily that he did something wrong. I worded it carefully." I read the headline aloud: "Did you sell this man this Japanese woodblock print?"

"It'll make him rabbit. Just do a regular call for sightings, for the print, not the man."

"The print is a dime a dozen. Everyone and her mother has sold one of these."

"Then we'll have a lot of sifting to do." He leaned back, refusing to be hurried, recognizing my impatience because he'd seen it before. "When we know more about what we're dealing with, then we can talk about publishing someone's photo. It's premature and is likely to do more harm than good. For now, I'm going to ask you to hold off."

Meeting his unrelenting scrutiny, I could hear the last faint sizzle of my smokin' hot idea fizzling out.

Ellis and I walked into the kitchen. He poured himself a cup of tea from the art deco Clarice Cliff ceramic teapot I'd given Zoë last Christmas. He raised a cup in my direction, silently asking if I wanted some.

"No, thanks."

Zoë sat at her kitchen table with her feet up on a chair, flipping through an L.L.Bean catalogue.

I slid into another chair and pointed at the catalogue. "What are you looking for?"

She grinned. "Nothing, but I'll know it when I see it. Any news on why Ty was called to D.C.?"

"Not yet. I hope he'll be able to tell me something when I talk to him later."

"Give him my love."

"I will."

She tossed the catalogue aside. "The kids want to go on a hayride. Want to come? I'm thinking Sunday, around three."

"Great! Let's plan on dinner at my place afterward."

"Sold!"

I revised the flyer, eliminating all references to Cal, and emailed the new version to Wes. My cover note read:

Hey, Wes!

I'm giving you a head start. I'll be mailing this flyer to my entire list in an hour.

You're welcome.

Josie

Two seconds after I hit SEND, Ty called.

"Hey, cutie. How's my best girl?"

"Saying I'm the best implies that you have other girls and they aren't quite up to snuff."

He laughed, a deep rumble. I smiled. I loved Ty's laugh.

"What makes you think I'm joking?" I asked.

He laughed harder. Ty's laugh was infectious, and I caught it. I walked into the living room and plunked down on the couch. After a moment we both quieted down.

"What's so funny?" I asked.

"Stop. Don't start me off again."

"Okay. Are you all right? You sound beat."

"I am. It's been a day. All good, but a lot coming at me from a lot of different directions, leaving me with too many balls to juggle and too much to think about. I'm a single-minded man—give me a task, no one does it better. Give me politics, and I'll go fishing. The executive committee brought me down to Washington because they wanted my opinion on a reorg idea. It looks like all training will be under the purview of a national director, a new position. They want to assess best practices on a local level, sift all the findings through one assessment model, come up with a unified program, and roll it out nationally. Instead of eighteen local directors reporting to five regional managers, the eighteen will report to three regional managers, organized geographically East, West, and Central. Those three regional managers will report to the new national director."

"But different areas have different needs."

"That's a concern I raised. And they agree. They think this approach will translate into quicker decision-making."

"What do you think?"

"I think it's a gamble."

"They want you for East."

"Yes. I'd be based in Rocky Point. They nosed around some about whether I might be interested in the national director position."

My heart stopped, then started again, a slow drumbeat, the kind of low, steady thumping that signals danger. I hate change. Any change. I forced myself to think about Ty, not myself. He was brilliant. Responsible. Experienced. Wise.

"Congratulations."

"Thanks."

"What did you say?"

"I kept it vague . . . you know . . . 'That's something to think about,' that sort of thing. They were just putting out feelers. Nothing was offered."

My pulse quieted, just a bit. "Why wouldn't you leap at the opportunity?"

"Because the director will have to be based in D.C. My home is wherever you are, and you need to be based in Rocky Point."

"Wow. That's like the most romantic thing I've ever heard. Say it again."

"My home is wherever you are. Not to sound cheesy or anything, but you are my heart. I love you."

Outside, a car drove by, and in the glare of its headlights, I spotted a deer in the forest across the street. It froze for a second, then turned tail and fled, disappearing into the night.

"No, I don't."

"You don't love me?"

I laughed. "I see you're not a mind reader. I adore you, Ty, and you know it. I don't need to be based in Rocky Point. I'm Prescott's owner. I can be based wherever I want."

"You're a little bit of a control freak. How could you possibly move to Washington?"

"I'd open a second venue and leave my staff in charge of the flagship location."

"That's crazy."

"Why?"

"Because you don't know anything about the D.C. market."

"I'm a quick learner. And where you go, I go."

"I don't have to go."

"Don't you want a promotion?"

"Sure."

"Then apply. We'll figure it out."

"Why can't we do this with our wedding plans?"

"We will."

CHAPTER NINE

T hursday morning, I woke to pelting rain just before six. I rolled over and pulled the blanket over my head, trying to recapture the slow, dreamy haven of sleep, but it was gone.

I took my coffee to my study and booted up my computer. I wanted to see which media outlets had picked up my call for sightings. The Portsmouth newspaper had a short article on page 8. Two local blogs, one with a newsy bent; the other one, antiques focused, ran it as a major story. All the major antiques sites and publications highlighted it. It was the lead story on the *Seacoast Star*'s home page. Wes featured the photograph of Mo's Japanese woodblock print alongside the headline.

HELP SOLVE A MURDER
HAVE YOU SEEN THIS ANTIQUE JAPANESE
WOODBLOCK PRINT?

Next to it, a secondary article discussed the mysterious disappearance of Cal Lewis, stating he hadn't used any of his credit cards or withdrawn any money from his bank account. There was no direct inference that Cal's absence was related to the call for sightings, but the implication was clear: Cal bought the print somewhere and sold it to Mo. Mo was killed. Cal went missing. Learning where Cal bought the print might help track down Mo's murderer. I was glad Wes did it, but I was also glad that it would be Wes, not me, who had to explain the placement to Ellis.

The article about Mo's print ended with an instruction to contact me with information. I texted Wes: *Great story. I'll let you know if I hear from anyone.*

Fred was at his desk when I arrived around seven thirty, a rare occurrence. Fred was a night owl, often coming in close to noon and staying late into the evening. Since his wife, Suzanne, the general manager at the Blue Dolphin,* almost always worked the dinner shift, his proclivity suited their schedules. Protected by the overhang, I straddled the threshold and shook out my umbrella before stuffing it into the chinoiserie umbrella stand.

I staggered and pressed my palm against my chest. "Call a doctor! I'm seeing a mirage."

"Ha, ha. I can't believe I'm here either, but duty calls. I have an eight A.M. call to Monsieur Pierre Gagnon in Paris. Evidently, he's the owner of one of those fourteen Martin guitars."

"Great work. Speaking of the guitar, I have an update." I sat down. "I spoke to Frank Shannon, and there are aspects of the situation he doesn't want known." I filled him in. "You reach out to Abbot's and go backward from there. I'll work to connect the dots between Frank and Ricky Joe and C. K. Keep written records as usual, but report only to me."

"Got it. And I'll continue tracing the guitars."

"Good. Any news from Davy?"

"He's due up tomorrow at ten."

"Perfect."

Gretchen's wind chimes jingled, and Fred and I looked up.

Trish straddled the threshold. She shook out her umbrella, then placed it in the holder. She looked amazingly put-together considering the ordeal she'd endured the last few days. Her eyes were clear. Her hair was neatly styled. She wore a hint of blue-gray eye shadow, and her lips shone with a rosy gloss.

"I hope I'm not too early," she said. "I saw cars in the parking lot and thought I'd take a chance that you were here."

"I'm glad you did. Trish, I don't know if you've ever met Fred, one of Prescott's antiques appraisers. Fred, Trish Shannon, Mo's mom."

---

* Please see *Lethal Treasure*.

Fred stood and stepped around his desk. He looked as stylish as ever in his slim-fit, perfectly tailored Italian-made suit.

"I'm so sorry for your loss, Ms. Shannon. Josie's told me wonderful things about Mo."

Trish's eyes moistened as she shook Fred's hand. "Thank you."

I walked to the coffee machine. "I see Fred made a pot of coffee. Would you like a cup? We can take it to my office."

She accepted the offer, and I balanced everything on a tray. Fred opened the warehouse door. Upstairs, I used my elbow to flip on the overhead light in my office, then slid the tray onto the butler's table. Trish sat on the love seat. I poured her a cup, and she grasped it as if she needed the warmth.

"I saw this morning's *Seacoast Star*. Reading that article about Cal, positioned as it was, directly next to the call for sightings . . . well, it was upsetting." She lowered her cup to the tray. She hadn't taken a sip. "I thought you might know something. The police aren't telling us anything."

"No . . . I'm sorry."

"Never mind. The real reason I stopped by . . . I wanted to let you know that Mo's funeral is next Tuesday."

"I heard."

"Will you be there?"

"Yes, of course."

She paused for a moment. "Mo left instructions that she wanted to be cremated and have her ashes scattered on the beach. We'll do that privately. The service, though, is public, and I was hoping . . . *we* were hoping that you'd deliver one of the eulogies. Her principal is going to talk about her work with the children. Helene will talk about her volunteer efforts. And our minister, of course." She must have seen my surprised expression, because she added, "Whenever Mo spent time with you, she mentioned it, recounting things you said that stuck with her, reporting on your accomplishments . . . Mo didn't have close friends, not in the conventional sense. She was too busy helping other people. Please . . . will you give the eulogy, as her friend?"

There was only one possible reply. "I'd be honored."

"Thank you." She closed her eyes, just for a second. "May I ask one more thing? As Mo's friend, you might know more than me . . . Did she ever mention Steve? Her ex? I mean lately. Did she?"

"Why do you ask?"

"Lydia told me that Mo was thinking of getting back together with him. I couldn't believe it. I still can't. But Lydia would know more about that than I would. Daughters don't always confide in their mothers, not when they think their mothers would disapprove. Lydia says Mo wouldn't have told me her plans because she was ashamed of her weakness. Loving a man who treated her so poorly."

"That seems a bit strong. I don't know any specifics, but it seems to me that loving someone, flaws and all, doesn't make Mo weak. It makes her loving."

"I agree, theoretically, at least." Trish smoothed her skirt and drank some coffee. "My only concern for my children has always been their ultimate happiness. I know that's trite, to say, 'I only want you to be happy,' but it's true. That's all I've ever wanted for my girls."

"You've had your doubts about Steve."

"Of course. If a man cheats once, he's likely to do so again."

"I hear that Steve denied he cheated."

"Wouldn't you?"

"I don't know. Regardless, people change."

Trish placed her cup on the tray and stood. "Do you believe that?"

I stood, too, and led the way to the door. "Yes. We get better. Stronger. More capable. At least, we do if we want to. Wisdom, you know? Think about yourself. Aren't you different now than you were when you were twenty?"

"Dramatically, but I've never thought of myself as wise. Just road weary."

"Mo did. Besides loving you, she admired you." That was true, and I would repeat it in my eulogy.

"Thank you, Josie. That's nice of you to say."

She paused halfway across the warehouse and touched my elbow. "Your speaking on Tuesday means a great deal to me. And to Frank."

"Thank you for asking me."

I walked her out and watched her drive away.

I took Mo's print from our mammoth walk-in safe and brought it up to my office, hoping it would inspire me to write the perfect eulogy. I set it on a burled walnut easel next to the display case that housed my rooster collection.

The colors in the print, while vibrant in tone, were muted in hue, like my mood. The people on the bridge were anonymous, interchangeable. It depicted existential isolation. Or, I supposed, if I wanted to put a positive spin on it, it portrayed self-sufficiency. Mo was self-sufficient, but she didn't see herself that way. I was aware that there is often a gap between how people view us and how we view ourselves. Hiroshige portrayed Edo as cold and lonely. Mo was warm and personable. Perception. What we see. What we believe. It didn't matter to Mo whether people saw themselves as weak or bad; she saw their strength and goodness, no matter how deeply those qualities were hidden. She truly believed that people were essentially decent, and she had a knack for getting people to believe in their own capabilities. That's what I would talk about in Mo's eulogy. I sat at my desk jotting notes about Mo, recalling examples of her generosity and grace, picturing her gentling the horses and laughing with the children.

I turned toward the window beside my desk. My old maple was in full autumn regalia. Even the steady rain couldn't diminish the brightness of the burnished-gold and dusty-pink leaves. I thought again about Steve. If they'd really been close to reuniting, he might have insights he could share, anecdotes that would bring my eulogy to life. If nothing else, the eulogy provided a good excuse for asking how he was doing.

There was no phone listing for Ricky, Rick, Rich, Dick, Richard, or R. J. McElroy in Boise, Idaho, which meant nothing. He could be one of the nearly 50 percent of the population who no longer used a landline. He might have moved. The phone could be listed in his girlfriend's or wife's name. I Googled additional variations of Ricky Joe's name and came up dry.

I bit the corner of my lip as I ran through the options. It only took a minute to settle on a plan. I decided to call all the McElroys in Boise whose phone numbers were listed in the white pages, then, if that didn't pan out, call the McElroy Rubber Company, which was still in business, and try to sweet-talk Ricky Joe's contact information out of someone.

The first two calls were duds. The third number was listed to an S. McElroy. My call went to voice mail.

"This is Sandy! Ricky Joe and I aren't home, but we'd love to call you back. Leave us a message!"

"My name is Josie Prescott, calling for Ricky Joe." I gave my phone number. "It's important that we talk. This relates to something that happened in Mississippi in the early seventies. There's no problem. I'm not selling anything. I'm an antiques appraiser, and I simply need to verify a date." I repeated my phone number and hung up.

I toyed with calling C. K. Flint, the man who'd sat in a corner shaking while Frank won himself a guitar, but I didn't. It would be better to talk to Ricky Joe first. But there was no harm in seeing if C. K. had a listed phone. He did. He still lived in Jackson, and the phone was listed under his name.

I swung back to my computer and brought up a browser. Rice Dixon Elementary School, where Mo had taught and Steve still did, started its day at 7:50. Classes ended at 3:00. I glanced at the clock on the monitor. It read 9:27.

I had plenty of time to think how to phrase my question to Steve.

CHAPTER TEN

J anson's Antiques Mall was an antiques lover's dream. Two dozen independent antiques and collectibles dealers rented space in a big old red barn set in a five-acre field on the far western edge of Rocky Point. Matt Janson, the owner, was an entrepreneur, not an antiques dealer, and I admired the heck out of his business acumen. Matt told me that the barn was about a hundred years old and had been a bear to renovate. While he was bringing the building up to code, he'd expanded its footprint, nearly tripling the usable space. He'd laid blacktop over a chunk of land for a parking lot and started advertising in local papers and offering discounts to tourists if tour operators made his mall an official stop on their bus tours.

I made a point of stopping by every few weeks. Because we carry some of this and some of that, I know a little bit about a lot of things and am eager to buy anything I can resell at a profit, including things we need to clean, repair, or otherwise refurbish. I often found bargains at Janson's because dealers who specialize usually don't bother to research objects outside their sphere of interest, and I have a nose for value.

I parked near one of three chartered buses. This time of year, we call the tourists who travel through our neck of the woods leaf peepers. Whenever I overhear their oohs and ahs as they realize the colors really are as spectacular as they look in the movies, I always feel a little jolt of pride, as if I had done something to earn their delight.

I pushed open one of a pair of heavy plank doors and entered another world. Matt used reclaimed wood, recessed lighting, and cinnamon-scented incense to create the aura of an idealized country home. Each of the twenty-four vendors had his or her own separate shop, closed in on three sides and open to the central corridors, except at night, of course, when individual pocket doors provided security. The dividing walls were eight feet high, tall enough to create a real feeling of separation, but with the ceiling soaring to thirty feet at the apex, nothing felt closed in. Six units ran along the two long outside walls. Eight more units filled the center, back-to-back, four facing east and four facing west. Two more units ran along the back wall, sharing the space with a corridor that led to public restrooms and a private dealers' room, outfitted with a kitchen and individual lockers. The final two spots took up the space on either side of the entry doors.

I checked my coat and dripping umbrella in the coat room, then faced the information booth, deciding where to start. The place was jam-packed, typical for a rainy Thursday in September.

Matt spotted me and came out from behind the information desk. He was a big man, about six-three, and fit. He was around fifty. His hair was dirty blond, showing a little gray around his temples. He wore it long, gathered at the back of his neck in a ponytail. He moved to New Hampshire because he fell in love with a woman from Rocky Point named Fay. That was twenty-five years ago. He and Fay just had their first grandchild, a girl named Joy.

"Good to see you, Josie. Weren't you here last week?"

"You have a good memory."

"And a knack for deductive reasoning. When something breaks a pattern, it catches my attention."

"I didn't know I was so predictable."

"Sure you did. You cruise through hoping for bargains every few weeks, not every week. So what's up?"

I handed him a copy of the flyer asking for information about Mo's print. "I need to know who sold this Japanese woodblock print."

He stared at the image, taking in the tranquility, the snow, the colors. "It's beautiful. Quiet." He raised his eyes. "It was owned by that girl who was killed. What makes you think the print was sold here?"

"Nothing. I'm checking everywhere. You have a couple of folks who specialize in art prints, and others who sell whatever comes their way, so I thought it couldn't do any harm to ask."

"And you get antsy sitting behind a desk."

"Don't you know it. How's Joy?"

"Perfect. Gorgeous. She just turned three months old."

"Do you have a picture?"

"Is snow white?" Matt slid his phone from a case attached to his belt, tapped, swiped, and handed it over.

The photo showed Joy cooing in Matt's arms. In the photo, Matt was looking at Joy with awe, as if he were holding a twinkling star in his hands.

"Oh, Matt! What a wonderful photo." I handed back the phone. "Congratulations."

"Thanks. I've got a bad case of PGS—Proud Grandfather Syndrome." He grinned. "Luckily, there's no cure."

"You're completely adorable, you know that, don't you?"

"In an embarrassing sort of way."

I scanned the room. "I'm glad to see you're so busy, Matt. You're going to have to build an annex."

"Nope. A second location."

"Where?"

"That depends on you."

"Me?"

"Any chance you're free for lunch on Monday?"

I met his eyes and felt a trill of excitement rush through my veins. "Sure." I dug my phone out of my bag and brought up my calendar. "Where and when?"

"What's your favorite restaurant?"

"The Blue Dolphin."

"Sold. When do you like to eat lunch?"

"Twelve thirty."

"Sold again."

Matt extended a hand, his expression hard to read, somewhere between solemn and exhilarated. We shook.

A middle-aged clerk behind the information booth spoke the words "Christmas ornaments" as she typed them into a computer while a young woman wearing a red beret looked on.

"Do you really have all the dealers' inventories?"

Matt grinned. "Yup."

To get twenty-four independent dealers to trust him with their inventory records was akin to completing a jigsaw puzzle in the dark—until you'd tried it, you couldn't fully appreciate the patience and imagination required.

"How on God's earth did you get them to agree?"

He laughed. "It's in the contract. I won't lease to anyone who doesn't want to participate. It's all upside from their perspective. They enter a one-sentence description of an object, the date it's offered for sale, and its asking price, and we send them customers."

"What happens when the piece is sold?"

"The listing automatically transfers to the archives at the moment of sale."

"So you know how long it took for an object to sell."

"Right."

"Can the archive be searched?"

"Sure. Dealers do it all the time. We also maintain a second archive comprised of all that information, plus the actual sales price. As you know, most dealers offer discounts, but they don't want their competition to know about it. By creating a second archive, we were able to build a Chinese wall separating the information we collect and make available to all leaseholders from the information most of them want to keep confidential. The dealers can search their own records, but no one else's."

"Except you."

He grinned again. "I'm a big believer in squirreling away data. Just because I don't know the information's value today doesn't mean I won't figure it out tomorrow."

"You're a smart man."

"The harder I work, the smarter I get."

"Amen to that." I pointed to the flyer. "Could you search for sales of this print in the archives?"

"Sure. Follow me." He leaned over the information booth counter and pulled an iPad from a lower shelf. He entered the query. Seconds later he had the answer. "A Hiroshige woodblock print was sold on September second at ten after one. No others this year. The name of the print isn't listed. The asking price was fifty dollars." Matt looked up. "Do you need me to go back further than a year?"

"No. Not at this point anyway." I did a quick calculation. "September second . . . that was the Sunday of Labor Day weekend. Who sold it?"

"Rose's Treasures. Number seventeen." He slid his iPad back onto the shelf. "So what do you think? Do you like my software?"

"I love it. Is it proprietary, or did you tweak an off-the-shelf package?"

"A hundred percent proprietary."

My dad always said that contrary to popular belief, it wasn't the devil who lurked in details—it was God. In other words, he explained, talk is cheap. I'd just learned that Matt was more than a dreamer; he was a doer, a rare breed.

"I'm seriously impressed, Matt."

He smiled like he meant it and presented his knuckles for a fist bump.

I'd known Rose Mayhew, the owner of Rose's Treasures, for years, having chatted with her frequently during my periodic buying trips. She was tall and thin, with shoulder-length wavy gray hair and gray-blue eyes. She dealt exclusively in sterling silver, from refined Edwardian coffeepots and hanging decanter labels to utilitarian sets of flatware and miscellaneous objects like antique candle snuffers and vintage key rings. The only items I'd bought from her were outside her area of specialization, including a hand-colored nineteenth-century map of Florida she'd priced at twenty dollars and a pair of brass hurricane lamps I'd found for ten dollars.

Rose was ringing up sales. Three people waited in line. I stepped to the side. When she was done, she glanced around, deciding where to go next. She spotted me and came over to where I was standing just outside her booth.

"Can I help you with something, Josie?"

"Sorry to bother you while you're so busy." I held up the flyer. "I'm trying to find out where this print came from. According to the inventory database, you sold a Hiroshige on September second."

"I did?" she asked, her eyes on the flyer. "Let me think . . . I remember finding a few prints in a box of silver pieces last summer, but I don't recall selling any of them." She raised her eyes to my face. "You know me. If it's not made of silver, I don't pay attention."

"I'm trying to confirm its provenance. Can you tell me where you bought that box?"

Her lips compressed into one thin line.

It's much harder to buy good quality items than it is to sell them, so if you have a reliable source, you never reveal it. If your purchase came from a one-off situation, a garage or moving sale, for example, you might be willing to share that information to someone you trust, like me.

"Sorry."

If it turned out that her Hiroshige print was actually the one Mo purchased, I could revisit my request for information, couching it in terms of ethics and promising to mention her shop by name in any articles we wrote on the subject, a rare promotional opportunity for a small business. Now, though, since I had no reason to think Mo's print came from her shop, I could let it slide.

"I understand. September second was the Sunday of Labor Day. Did you have help that day? Someone who might have made the sale?"

"Yes, Artie helps out every Sunday. He's here today, too—leaf peepers." A customer standing by a locked display case was glancing around, looking for help. "I need to get back to work. I'll ask Artie to step out to talk to you."

I thanked her. I was tempted to ask her to check whether the sale was made with a credit card, but if I could avoid bothering her again, I would. While I waited for Artie, I examined the ceiling. Matt had installed security cameras at strategic points around the perimeter. If Artie couldn't help, maybe the cameras could.

Artie couldn't. Artie was long retired, with a soldier's stance, straight and proud. His hair was white and cut short. He studied the flyer for a moment, then shook his head.

"I used to be a whiz at connecting the objects I sold with their buyers. Not anymore. I don't even remember selling it. Sorry."

I thanked him and returned to the information booth. I explained what I needed to Matt. A few taps later, he swung his iPad around so I could see it.

"This is the camera closest to booth seventeen. The camera takes photos every three seconds. Here's the record starting at eight minutes after one."

I clicked through the photos. At ten past one, I saw Rose hand a plastic-sheathed art print to a dealer I recognized, Jonathan Newson. Jonathan was the owner of Newson's Rare and Vintage Art, booth two. I thanked Matt and darted through the crowd to Jonathan's booth.

Jonathan was about forty. He was short and stout, with a few strands of brown hair artfully arranged over his bald pate.

I eased into his booth and sidestepped to the bin of prints labeled BY ARTIST, G–K. I flipped through and found a faded copy of Hiroshige's *Meguro Drum Bridge and Sunset Hill*. The print was encased in a clear plastic envelope. A diamond-shaped white sticker near the top read *$130/918*.

Jonathan stood near a framed copy of Van Gogh's *Starry Night* mounted on the back wall. He was talking to an older man, pointing to a starlit swirl, then the church steeple. The older man said something. Jonathan waved over a middle-aged woman leaning against the front counter. He left her to finish the sale, and I swooped in.

After we exchanged a quick hello, I showed him the flyer. "Have you sold a *Meguro Drum Bridge and Sunset Hill* lately?"

"No. It's weird that you ask, though, since I just bought one."

"The one in the bin. I saw it."

"I thought it might be genuine. It had the look, you know? Fugitive blues."

"How did you determine it wasn't real?"

"I removed the backing and found 'Morty's Art Prints' stamped on the back."

"Ouch. Does the number 918 mean you bought this print this month?"

"That's right. September 2018. It's my old-fashioned inventory system."

"What do you think of Matt's computerized system?"

"It's terrific. We get a lot of referrals from the information booth. I don't care about the reports, though. I'm a Luddite. I like being able to rifle through the bins myself and see how long prints take to sell, refamiliarize myself with the inventory . . . you know. I'm an art lover, which means I'm visual. I'm in the business because of the objects, not the reports. But those referrals—that's worth the price of admission." Jonathan tapped the flyer. "Is this about that dead girl?"

"Mo Shannon," I said, wanting to speak her name aloud, wanting Jonathan to hear it. "I don't know. At this point, I'm just trying to track the print. Have you heard of any sales?"

"Just hers."

Jonathan's assistant came up. "Excuse me for interrupting. Mr. Donovan has a question."

I thanked him again and slipped away.

Appraising an antique is like any other detective work—you follow leads and rely on luck and experience to help you navigate unknown terrain, and you expect most of your efforts to fail. While I was used to running into brick walls, I never liked it, and today was no exception. As I walked to my car through the driving rain, I tried to put a positive spin on the situation. I'd moved forward—I now knew where Mo's Hiroshige *hadn't* been purchased. You go through enough false starts, all that's left is the truth.

CHAPTER ELEVEN

I reached the Rice Dixon Elementary School at a quarter to three and parked in an empty spot near the rear of the ungated employee parking lot. The rain had slowed to a drizzle, but the sky remained dark. A line of idling cars ran along Bracebridge Road, parents waiting to pick up their kids. I used the time to call work and check my email. Everything was under control. I texted Ty that I loved him, then checked the *Seacoast Star*'s website for breaking news. Wes had posted an update about the medical examiner's findings.

Mo had been strangled, then tossed or pushed off the cliff. From the angle of the contusions on Mo's neck, Dr. Graham stated that whoever had strangled her had stood in front of her and that he or she was taller than Mo. Or, the doctor added, the killer was standing above her, on an incline, for example. *Or a low wall,* I thought.

At three, kids started pouring out of the front doors. Two minutes later, the teachers started exiting from a side door. Steve came out about three ten, a large army-green backpack slung over one shoulder. He held the door for the pretty redhead I'd seen at Mo's garden party and standing behind the police line the evening Mo died. She was laughing at something Steve said. She replied, he nodded, and she walked to a blue Toyota.

I got out of my car and stepped into the traffic lane so Steve would be sure to see me. The drizzle had softened into mist. Steve spotted me and stopped short. His brows raised in surprise, and he smiled.

Steve was just as handsome as the last time I'd seen him, with the same jaunty stride and open demeanor. He looked like the kind of guy it would be easy to talk to, who you wanted to talk to. He was just shy of six feet with nicely trimmed brown hair and brown eyes. He'd played Double-A baseball for the Frisco RoughRiders for two years right out of college and was on his way to the big leagues when he blew out his knee sliding into home.

"Hey, Steve. Long time, no see."

"I'll say."

"You've heard about Mo."

"Sure." He glanced around, maybe checking for stragglers who might be tempted to listen in. "I'm pretty broken up about it, to tell you the truth. You get divorced, everyone thinks you don't have feelings for your ex anymore. Not true."

"Mo said you were back in touch. She was excited about it."

He met my gaze, but he didn't reply.

I took a step closer. "It must be awful, not being able to talk about her."

He ran his fingers through his hair. "You got that right."

"Do you have a few minutes now?"

"I can't." He saw my disappointment and glanced at his watch. "I'd love to talk with you, Josie. I just meant I can't now. I'm on my way to a meeting. It's the Cub Scouts. Can you believe I'm a Cub Scout leader?"

"Yes. I bet you're great at it. How'd you get involved?"

"I got drafted. A friend of mine has a seven-year-old son, and their troop leader got a new job in Arkansas." He looked around again. "I've got to go."

"Trish asked me to give one of the eulogies."

"Good. Mo deserves the best."

"Can you talk later?"

He held my gaze for two seconds. "How's coffee in the morning?"

"Perfect."

"I need to be to school by seven thirty. Can you meet at Sweet Treats at quarter to seven?"

I told him quarter to seven was great, and he walked to his car. I stood on sodden leaves until he drove to the exit and paused at the top of the driveway before turning. I saw his eyes in his rearview mirror. I waved good-bye, and he waved back. He turned right. A minute later, the redhead in the Toyota drove by. She stared at me as she passed, and I felt the fervor of her curiosity. She turned left out of the exit.

I was glad to get back inside my car. At first the mist had felt refreshing. Now it just felt cold.

The rain had started up again by the time I got back to my office around quarter to four.

Fred reported that Abbot's no longer existed. The store was sold after the owner died in the mid-1980s, and the buyer changed the name. He didn't keep any of Abbot's business records.

"Who inherited?" I asked.

"Abbot's sister, Gertrude Joan Mays."

I offered to call Ms. Mays so Fred could continue tracking guitars, and he agreed.

Gertrude Joan Mays lived in Florence, Mississippi, a nice suburb south of Jackson. I got her number from information and dialed. The man who picked up the phone was laughing so hard, he barely got "Hello" out.

"Ms. Mays, please."

"Hold on." I heard a televised laugh track followed by a clatter as the receiver hit a table, then scraping sounds, as if a chair were being dragged across a tile floor, then a shout. "Gertie Joan! Telephone!"

"What's so funny?" a woman asked him.

"Those sports bloopers. I can't see straight, I'm laughing so hard."

"Hello?" she said into the phone.

"Ms. Mays?"

"This is Gertie Joan Mays."

I explained my reason for calling.

"Abbot's Musical Instruments. That was my brother's business."

"The new owner said he didn't have the sales records. Do you?"

"I haven't touched those boxes in nearly thirty-five years."

I sat up. "Are they organized by date?"

"I don't know. I had the manager empty the file cabinets and deliver the boxes here."

"How many boxes are there?"

"Two dozen. Maybe more. How about if I take a gander and see what I've got there?"

"That would be fantastic."

"Tell me exactly what I'm looking for."

"Two things. First, information about how and when Abbot's acquired a 1930 Martin OM-45 Deluxe guitar. Probably there's a record that Abbot's bought it from an individual. Second, the sale of that guitar in late May or early June 1973. I don't know when Abbot's acquired it except that it had to be before then. The buyer was a man named Ricky Joe McElroy."

"McElroy Rubber?"

"That's the family."

"I didn't know Ricky Joe played guitar. It was Frank Shannon, Ricky Joe's best friend, who was the guitar player in that crew."

I felt the ice crack beneath my feet. Every town was a small town, and the Jackson metro area was no exception—and I'd just given Gertie Joan a nifty tidbit to share. I needed to cram the genie back in the bottle.

"Gertie Joan! May I call you Gertie Joan?"

"Of course, hon."

"Gertie Joan, surely you remember what it was like in the early seventies. Everyone was a guitar player back then."

"Ain't that the truth! My boy, Charlie Craig, among them. Now he's a banker. I heard Ricky Joe moved out west somewhere, I don't know where. Tell me again why you need those receipts?"

"The current owner wants to know what the guitar is worth in case he ever wants to sell it. Without clear title, it's hard to sell a valuable object for top dollar."

"I'm on it. It'll give me something to do besides listen to my husband laugh at ridiculous volleyball bloopers."

CHAPTER TWELVE

S asha asked me to come downstairs, saying she wanted to show me something.

I met her at the worktable housing Mo's print. She handed me a loupe.

"Look at the woodgrain in the sky behind the snowflakes, on the left."

I eased the loupe into place and examined the print. "Got it . . . it whorls to the right, then to the left." I removed the loupe. "Since woodgrain is like a fingerprint, if you can verify a documented original has woodgrain that matches this pattern, we're well on our way to authenticating Mo's print."

Sasha smiled. "I've contacted three museums that have documented originals."

"Great job, Sasha!" We walked back to the office. "Have there been any responses to our call for sightings?"

"Only fakes or restrikings so far."

"I'll keep cruising around asking dealers. Let's all keep our fingers crossed that—" I broke off when Cara's voice came over the intercom.

"Josie, it's a Mr. McElroy from Idaho."

I grabbed the phone. "Thanks, Cara. I'll take it upstairs. Tell him I'll be with him in a minute."

I thanked Sasha for the update and ran for the staircase.

Upstairs, I pushed the flashing button. "Thanks for holding, and thanks for calling back."

"Your message was pretty mysterious. What gives?"

"Did you buy a guitar from Abbot's in May or June 1973?"

"Tell me again who you are."

I did so, adding in a bit about the importance of provenance.

"You're working for Frank Shannon. I can't believe it. I didn't think Frank would ever sell that thing."

"My client, whom I can't name, isn't selling the guitar. Lots of people want objects appraised for reasons that have nothing to do with selling them, for instance, estate planning purposes or insurance. What can you tell me about the purchase?"

"It cost me two arms and a leg, broke my heart, and got me out of Mississippi. I lost it in a poker game to Frank Shannon and woke up in the real world. You should have heard my daddy on the subject. I haven't gambled since, not even on lotto."

"Did you buy it at Abbot's Musical Instruments?"

"Yup. That's the place."

"Do you have the receipt?"

"Hell, no. I burned that sucker. Last I heard about Frank, he made it to L.A., married Trish, and scored a big-time record deal. I follow his tour schedule some, thinking that if he ever got to Boise, I'd stop by and give him hell. How are they doing?"

"I'm sorry. As I said, I can't reveal a client's name. Do you recall anything about the guitar—for instance, the brand?"

"Yup. It was a Martin OM-45 Deluxe. I dream about it sometimes."

"Do you know where Abbot's got it from?"

"You're asking about the Robert Johnson connection. I don't know anything other than what I heard from the owner, that Robert Johnson gave it to some girlfriend, and that woman's heir sold it to him. I always thought it was just sales hype myself, but Frank sure took it to heart."

"Thank you, Ricky Joe. You've been very helpful."

"Tell Frank I said hey, no hard feelings."

"Thanks again. Bye." I pressed the END CALL button and dialed C. K. Flint's number. If he was still at the lumberyard, there was a good chance he worked the seven-to-three shift. If so, given the different time zone, he might be at home.

He was. I explained who I was and why I was calling.

"I never was at that store. I don't know nothing about it."

"It's okay, C. K. Everything was on the up-and-up. I just need to confirm what I've heard."

"I don't remember nothing." He slammed the phone down.

I stared at the receiver for a moment before I lowered it into the cradle.

C. K. was scared. It didn't matter why. What mattered was that he hadn't verified Frank and Ricky Joe's story. I sure hoped Gertie Joan came through.

I walked downstairs to get a cup of coffee.

"Sasha, are you done with Mo's print for now?"

"Yes. Should I put it back in the safe?"

"Actually, it reminds me of Mo . . . I'm working on her eulogy. I'll take it back upstairs."

Her eyes softened. "I understand."

A woman stepped into the office. I recognized her as the petite blonde I'd seen standing with the book club members the day Mo died. Her complexion was creamy. Her eyes were hazel, changing from amber to moss green to cocoa as she moved from shadow to light.

"Josie?" she said. "I've seen your photo in the paper. I'm Nora Burke."

"Nice to meet you." Mo had asked if I knew Nora, and once again, I wondered why. "I've heard your name. You're in Trish's book club."

"For longer than I care to remember. I hope it's okay that I'm here . . . I need a birthday gift for my dad. A friend said you're fabulous at honing in on just the right thing."

"We try, that's for sure. Have a seat. Would you like some coffee? Or a cold drink?"

She sat at the guest table. "No, thanks."

I took the chair across from her. "So tell me about your father. What does he do for a living?"

"He's an architect. Very cerebral."

"Any hobbies?"

She flushed. "He writes poetry. I know . . . weird, huh?"

"I think it's wonderful. The world would be a better place if more people wrote poetry."

The phone rang, and Cara picked up. The second line chimed in almost immediately. Gretchen answered that one. Eric walked into the office from the warehouse, reading something from a clipboard. He looked up, saw Nora, and his brow wrinkled. He glanced at the clock. Eric lived with the fear that he'd done something wrong or forgotten to do something or had otherwise let someone down.

Eric took a step toward us. "Am I late? Are you Melissa Sayers?"

"No. I'm Nora Burke, here to see Josie."

"Sorry." From his sheepish demeanor, I knew he was afraid I was mad at him for interrupting my conversation with Nora. "Gretchen and I have some interviews scheduled for part-timers."

I stood up and smiled. "That's good to hear. We always need reliable workers." I turned to Nora. "Let's go to my office."

Nora followed me into the warehouse, pausing to take in the rows of shelves, the worktables spaced along the perimeter, the walk-in safe, and the loading dock at the back. She smiled when she noticed the kitty domain delineated by the comfy rugs abutting the wall not far from the spiral stairs that led to my office.

"This place needs its own zip code."

I smiled. "We get a lot of work done here, that's for sure. I was going to bring something upstairs. Let me just grab it."

"Sure."

I slipped on gloves and picked up Mo's print. Upstairs, I placed it on the easel, then tucked the gloves behind it.

Nora stood by the love seat, considering it. "This is Mo's Japanese woodblock print. I saw the picture in the *Seacoast Star*."

"Yes."

"I'm surprised Mo liked it. It looks so, I don't know . . . lonely."

"That's how some people react to it. Mo saw it as quiet, peaceful. To me, and I think to Mo, it communicates serenity, not isolation."

"To each his own. I guess. I'm more a Renoir sort of girl myself."

"Moments of joy. Lots of music. Lighthearted pleasure on beautiful days."

"Exactly."

"That's why they make both chocolate and vanilla ice cream—people have different tastes." I stood in front of the wing chair. "Have a seat."

When Nora sat down, I did, too.

"Back to your dad . . . Does he write on a computer or longhand?"

"Longhand. He has a leather-bound journal. When he fills one up, he buys another."

"A traditional man who values traditional things. Let me show you some options." I reached for the phone and dialed Gretchen's extension. "Gretchen, would you bring me the Parker and Conklin fountain pens and the rosewood lap desk?"

"Sure! I'll be up in a flash."

I cradled the receiver and turned back to Nora. "These pens are more than gorgeous. They're truly rare. And the lap desk . . . Well, you'll see. Just touching it makes you want to write something!"

"Thanks." She looked at her feet for a moment, then raised her eyes. "That friend I mentioned who recommended Prescott's . . . it was Mo. She talked about you all the time. She thought you were so smart."

I winked away an unexpected tear. "I admired her, too."

"Have you learned anything about the print?"

"Not yet."

"How about her murder? Have you heard whether the police are close to catching the killer?"

"No, but I think they're following up on some leads."

"Like what?"

"I wish I knew. Have you heard anything?"

"Me? No."

"Do you know Cal Lewis?"

"I've met him a couple of times at book club meetings."

"Somehow I just can't picture Cal participating in a book club."

Nora laughed. "I see you know him. He comes for the cocktails and nibblies. He likes to correct our wrong opinions."

"I can hear him now. If you saw the *Seacoast Star,* you must have read that Cal is missing."

"I did. The whole situation is so upsetting and confusing. What do you think is going on?"

I leaned back, resting my head on a side wing. "I think Cal is in trouble."

Nora leaned forward. "What kind of trouble?"

"I have no idea, not specifically. It's possible that Cal went missing on purpose, which suggests that he has some involvement with the print he doesn't want to acknowledge, or maybe even that he knows what happened to Mo. The only other possibility is that something happened to him and he's unable to communicate with his employer or his girlfriend or the police. Either way—the way I see it, he's in trouble."

"Maybe he just got fed up with the day-to-day and decided to start over somewhere else. I feel like that sometimes."

"What do you do?"

"I'm an accountant. I love numbers. It's people I struggle with. If they don't like the results, they blame the messenger. Some days I wish I'd gone into construction like my husband. Nails and hammers don't talk back."

"But the people who hire the contractors do. I'm not sure you can ever get away from people, with all their foibles, unless you go off the grid completely." I laughed. "Somehow I can't picture Cal living off the land, and if all he wanted was to start over somewhere new, why hasn't he used his credit cards or withdrawn money from his bank account?"

"Because he doesn't want to be found."

"That's possible, I suppose. Unusual, but not unheard-of. A guy goes out for a pack of cigarettes and just keeps on truckin'. It's harder nowadays to disappear, though."

"Whatever is going on, Lydia must be beside herself."

I heard the familiar click-clack of Gretchen's heels as she walked across the concrete floor and came up the stairs. She lowered a black-velvet-covered tray to the butler's table. Each fountain pen rested on its own black velvet pillow beside the lap desk.

"Can I get you anything else?" Gretchen asked. "Coffee?"

Nora still didn't want anything to drink.

I thanked Gretchen, and as her steps receded, I picked up the Parker pen. "This pen works perfectly, from accepting a full supply of ink to writing evenly, without sputtering."

Nora leaned forward. I moved the pen a bit to catch the light, and the ornate gold filigree barrel and mother-of-pearl insets glimmered.

"Because of its scarcity and superb condition, this one is pricey—two thousand dollars." I laid it down and picked up the Conklin. "This one has an uncommonly large black hard-rubber crescent-filler and a gold trefoil filigree overlay. It works, too, and it's also rare. It's priced at a thousand dollars."

"I had no idea. Thousands of dollars for a pen?"

"I know. It's amazing. They'll probably sell to collectors, not users. Which is why I think this lap desk might be exactly right for your dad. It's only ninety dollars, because it has no pedigree. It's handmade of oak." I lifted the lid. "There's room inside for papers, or your dad's current journal. It's simple, and I think it's gorgeous, but that's an issue of taste and opinion. Go ahead and pick it up. Place it on your lap and see what you think."

She used two hands to lift it. "Oh! It's light. It looks so substantial, I thought it would be much heavier." She lifted the lid and lowered it. "I think my dad would love it. You said the price is ninety dollars? Is there any way you can do better?"

"I'm sorry, no. We work hard to price our objects properly, and we never discount them."

"Ninety dollars seems fair . . . It's just that it's more than we typically spend on birthday gifts." She returned the lap desk to the tray. "The pens are fabulous, too." She stood. "I can't thank you enough for taking the time to show me these. I'm going to talk to my sister about the lap desk and see what she thinks."

I stood, too. "Good idea."

I walked Nora downstairs and opened the front door. Puddles dotted the asphalt. Water dripped from the eaves and trees. The sky remained leaden. I watched her walk to her car, sidestepping to avoid pools of water.

A puff of exhaust caught my eye. A black sedan, mostly hidden by chest-high brush, was idling on the shoulder of Ellerton, just beyond our parking lot. Nora got behind the wheel of her white Chevrolet Cruze, and three seconds later, prisms appeared in the puddles as light glinted off the metal parts of her phone. She rested it against the steering wheel. The black car was hard to spot. Evidently, Nora hadn't noticed it.

It looked like someone was following Nora. Why? She had asked a lot of questions about Cal, but still . . .

She backed out of the space and drove up to the exit, her left-turn light flashing, waiting for a break in the traffic. The black car edged forward.

I was too far away and the foliage was too thick to see who was in the black car, but one thing was clear—someone actually was following Nora, and it looked like she didn't know it.

I ran for the warehouse door, sprinted across the open area, charged up the steps to my office, grabbed my tote bag, and raced downstairs.

"I'll see you all later!" I called as I dashed out the door.

CHAPTER THIRTEEN

By the time I got to my car, both Nora's Chevy and the black sedan were gone. I turned left, toward the interstate, and on a long stretch of straightaway, I spotted the black car. I sped up. At a curve in the road half a mile farther down the road, I recognized Nora's Chevy, four cars in front of the black vehicle, a Lexus, which was now three cars ahead of mine.

We sailed past the entry ramp for the interstate. Nora turned right onto Main Street, the most direct route to Rocky Point's central business district. She parked in front of Sweet Treats bakery. The black sedan and I continued on.

As we circled the village green, I tried to read the Lexus's license plate, but it was streaked with mud, no surprise on this rainy day. I could see two men, one behind the wheel and one in the rear, but I couldn't discern enough of their faces to identify individual features.

When the Lexus rolled to the curb, I did, too, keeping my distance.

Five minutes later, Nora, carrying a white box tied with red string, got back into her car.

Nora headed toward the ocean, making what seemed like random turns. The Lexus closed up. I hung back.

A few minutes later, Nora turned onto Old Mill Pond Road, then spun into the entry road of the Pond View condominium complex, a gated community overlooking the pond.

The Lexus continued down Old Mill Pond Road. So did I. As I passed the entry, I slowed to a crawl so I could see what Nora was doing. She'd reached the ornate black iron gate, and the two sections were moving sideways. I was in time to see her raise her visor—she'd used a remote clipped to it to open the gate.

The Lexus was far ahead now. It turned onto Market Street, which led back to Rocky Point's town center. I turned, too. A half mile farther along, it turned left onto a short road called Langley Lane. I'd passed it a hundred times, but I'd never been on it. I thought it probably connected to Main Street, which ran parallel to Market. Only after I followed the Lexus onto Langley did I discover my mistake. Langley was a curvy road that ended at a dense thicket. The Lexus had already turned around and was driving back the way we'd come. I U-turned at the dead end. Around the first curve on my way back, I gasped and slammed on the brakes—the Lexus sat sideways across the road, trapping me. I plunged forward, then, thanks to my seat belt, jerked back. My head whacked into the headrest.

The driver got out of the car and stood for a moment, facing me. I pushed the door-lock button and felt around in my tote bag for my phone, keeping my eyes on his long, bony face. I took two photos in quick succession, one of the man, the other of the vehicle, then tapped 9-1-1, keeping my hand on the SEND CALL button, but not pushing it.

The driver wore a gray suit that needed pressing. His hair was brown and cut short. He had deep-set eyes that even from this distance seemed hard enough to crack the windshield. The back passenger window lowered, and the occupant turned to watch. At this distance, I could only discern that it was a man.

The driver said something to the passenger, then walked toward me. My pulse speeded up, and my mouth went dry.

I lowered my window two inches as he approached.

The air was thick, damp, and cold. I shivered.

He leaned down to meet my eyes. "You're following us."

"No, I'm not."

"If you're not following us, you're following Nora Burke. Why?"

"I'm not doing anything wrong."

He spun toward the thicket as if he'd heard something. I kept my eyes on his face. He exuded power. After a minute, he turned back to me.

"My boss wants to talk to you. Come sit in his car."

"Who's your boss?"

"Chester Randall."

"I don't know him."

"He knows you. You're Josie Prescott, a local businesswoman. He's a local businessman. He thinks you might have a lot in common."

"What kind of business?"

"Entertainment."

"Who are you?"

"Mr. Randall's driver."

"What's your name?"

"Come on. Mr. Randall's waiting."

"Why were you following Nora?"

"Ask Mr. Randall."

"I'm not comfortable getting into his car, but if he wants to meet at Rocky Point Diner, I'll be glad to talk to him there. I have time now."

"You have nothing to worry about."

He tried to open my door. When he couldn't, his brows drew together and he stared at me. I was glad the glass separated us. I couldn't tell if his eyes were super-dark brown or black. They were cold and emotionless. I didn't reply.

"I'll ask."

He walked back to the car, opened the driver's side door, and leaned in. Entertainment covered a vast spectrum of activities. Somehow I didn't think Chester Randall owned Pirate's Cove Miniature Golf. A minute later the driver returned.

"Okay. We'll follow you."

I exhaled, and only then did I realize I'd been holding my breath.

I drove directly to Rocky Point Diner. The parking lot was half full, and since I was a regular, I knew that most of the people inside would be older folks out for the early bird special and families taking advantage of the weekday kids-eat-free offer. I parked as close to the front door as I could.

I grabbed my iPad, brought up a browser, and Googled "Chester Randall Rocky Point NH."

Chester Randall owned the Colonial Twist, some kind of restaurant, on Ocean Terrace, a short street that ran between Ocean Avenue and Warren, forming a T at both ends, serving as a nifty shortcut from the beach to the village. His signage must be minuscule and his building undistinguished. His photo showed a portly man in his sixties, with a welcoming smile and a full head of brown hair. I checked for restaurant reviews and didn't find any, but at least I knew that Chester Randall was for real. I got out of my car, wishing I'd grabbed my coat when I'd left the office. It was get-in-your-bones cold, more like November than September.

I stood near the hostess stand, watching Chester Randall walk toward the door. He was tall and broad, and big all over.

He stepped inside and extended his hand for a shake. "You run a good business, Josie Prescott. I'm glad to know you."

I shook his hand. He had a firm grip. "Thanks."

He took charge, asking the hostess for a quiet booth in the back, then stepping aside, so I could follow her. The hostess dropped two menus on the table and told us our server would be with us soon. I slid onto the banquette.

Chester took off his raincoat, hung it neatly on a hook by our booth, and sat across from me. He wore a brown suit, a yellow shirt, and a tan tie with fine brown stripes.

He picked up a menu. "I tend to eat late, so maybe I should have a little snack, just to hold me over. How about you?"

"I'll just have coffee. Thanks. You want to tell me why you blocked the road, trapping me?"

"In a minute . . . Let me order first."

The waitress came over. Her name tag read PHYL. She wore a pink uniform with a white frilly apron and sensible white tie-up shoes.

Chester looked up from the menu. "Is the chicken soup any good, Phyl?"

"People seem to like it."

"Not for nothing, Chester, but I love it."

"Good. The lady will have a coffee. I'll have a Coke and a bowl of chicken noodle soup, with extra crackers."

Phyl took the menus away.

Chester shook his head. "You're not wearing a coat." I could almost hear him tut-tut. "This weather . . . You're going to catch cold."

"My mother always said you catch a cold from germs, not bad weather."

"Yes, but in bad weather, germs have an easier time getting in, so you wear a coat to help keep them out."

"Chester, you're very persuasive." For some reason, his concern touched me. As the only child of only children, I'd grown up without an extended family. I had a fleeting thought: If I'd been lucky enough to know one of my grandfathers, I bet he would have been a lot like Chester. "And very sweet."

"Shhh. That's the kind of thing you don't want getting around."

Phyl came back with our drinks. She dropped a paper-covered straw next to Chester's Coke and set down a shallow bowl filled with tubs of half-and-half. I took one, gave it a little shake, and poured it in. Chester picked up his straw and examined it as if he'd never seen one before. He began to pick at the end with a fingernail. I was a ripper, tearing into Christmas gifts—and paper-covered straws—with abandon. When he'd separated the end bits, he scooched the wrapper down enough to extract the straw. Chester was a patient and meticulous man.

We each took a sip of our drinks. Chester smoothed out his straw wrapper. When he raised his eyes to mine, his manner had changed from grandpa to all business.

"So, why I blocked the road." He folded his fingers on the table. "Do you know Cal Lewis?"

"Why?"

"That's no answer."

"That's the only answer you'll get until you tell me why you want to know."

"I need to talk to him about a business thing. How well do you know him?"

"What is this, Chester? The third degree?"

"You're a little cagey, huh?"

"Circumspect."

"Careful. I like that."

Phyl brought Chester's soup and a saucer piled high with cellophane-wrapped packages of saltines.

Chester thanked her. He shook some pepper onto his soup. "So where's Cal?"

"I don't know. Does Nora?"

"I think so. I think they're an item."

"Get out of town."

He blew on a spoonful of soup. "For real."

Ideas and contradictions ricocheted through my brain. Cal was with Lydia. Nora was married. Chester was following Nora, who had nothing to do with Cal. Except maybe she did. Maybe that was why Mo had asked if I knew her—Mo had resented her so-called friends for passing along sightings of Steve with another woman, and here she was facing the same dilemma, debating whether to tell Lydia that she'd seen Cal with Nora. Chester probably read the *Seacoast Star,* like everyone else in Rocky Point, so he knew I was interested in Cal. Nothing made any sense. Unless Nora really was involved with Cal, or Chester genuinely thought she was. There was only one reason I could think of why Chester would care if Nora and Cal were an item.

I drank some coffee. "You're involved with Nora. You're following her because you think she's two-timing you with Cal. Three-timing, really, since she's married."

"You were right. This is delicious." He tore open a packet of crackers. "I've been happily married to the love of my life for forty-two years. I'm not involved with Nora. I'm pretty sure she's involved with Cal, though."

"Why do you care?"

"Business."

"What business?"

"Mine. What's Cal to you?"

"Nothing. Cal is Lydia's boyfriend. Lydia is Mo's sister. Mo Shannon. I'm sure you've read about her . . . She was murdered. Mo was my friend."

Chester blew on another spoonful of soup. "My condolences."

"Thank you."

"Is Cal involved in Mo's death?"

"I don't know. He's MIA, that's for sure."

"I assumed he went missing to avoid me."

"Why would he want to avoid you?"

"He owes me money."

I lowered my cup so quickly it clattered on the saucer. "He does?"

"Do you know my restaurant, the Colonial Twist?"

"I didn't even know there was such a place until I Googled you just now. You don't have any Yelp reviews."

"My customers prefer it that way."

"You let Cal run a tab?"

Chester placed his spoon on a napkin beside the bowl, lining it up. "Do you have a few more minutes? I want to show you the Colonial Twist. I think you'll be interested."

I agreed.

Chester caught Phyl's eye and drew a few lines of text in the air. Phyl delivered the check on the run.

I reached for my wallet.

He held up a hand to stop me. "Allow me. Please."

"I invited you."

He smiled and placed three dollar bills under the salt shaker. "Next time."

"Thank you, Chester."

Two minutes later, we were in our cars, traveling toward a restaurant I'd never heard of and knew nothing about. Before heading out, I texted Cara to tell her where I was going, just in case.

CHAPTER FOURTEEN

Chester led the way to Ocean Terrace. Halfway down the block, he turned into a long driveway, passing eight-foot-high fieldstone columns. He wound his way around a Tudor-style mansion and parked in a roomy lot at the rear. There were about twenty cars scattered throughout the space. If the name Colonial Twist appeared anywhere, I couldn't see it.

I got out, locked my car, and leaned against the still-damp hood.

"I don't care if you're having the party of the year, I'm not going home with you, Chester."

He smiled. "This isn't my home. This is my restaurant. Come on in."

"You don't believe in signage?"

"Adds to the allure. If you don't know it's here, you're not in the know."

"How does anyone know it's here?"

"Word of mouth. I opened with the support of some important customers, and they spread the news."

"I go out for an occasional cocktail and dinner, and I didn't know about it."

"You're not my target customer."

"Why not?"

"You're too wholesome."

I laughed. "You're not bringing me to a strip club, are you?"

"Where the girls wear go-go boots like back in the sixties and do the Twist?"

I laughed louder. "While wearing skimpy Revolutionary War–era clothing. The Colonial Twist, get it?"

He guffawed. "You have quite an imagination, Josie. No, we're just a fancy white-tablecloth joint."

"Just because I'm a regular at a diner doesn't mean I don't like to get dressed up now and again."

"I'm glad to hear it. You're welcome anytime."

The door was impressive. It was made of walnut and was ten feet high, with a hammered pewter handle. Chester pushed a square silver metal panel affixed to the wall, and the heavy door swung out. Inside, a middle-aged man wearing a twentieth-century British uniform welcomed us. His helmet was white with red feathers. His jacket was red with epaulets and black insets at the wrist. His slacks were black. An attractive woman in her twenties smiled as we stepped over the threshold. She wore a knee-length black long-sleeved sheath, conservative pumps, and pearls. She took Chester's coat and handed him a chit.

The entryway was paneled in dark wood with dentil crown molding and box molding below a marquetry chair rail. The ceiling was painted sky blue. Three ceiling fans kept the air moving. The blades were shaped like palm fronds, constructed of a tan grassy material. I felt as if I'd stepped through the looking glass.

The doorman opened a second door located at the end of the entryway, and Chester gestured that I should precede him. We crossed into a beautifully appointed lounge. The room featured the same wood paneling as the entryway. Oversized black leather couches and beige corner chairs with tufted upholstery were grouped into conversation areas. Red-and-blue Oriental rugs covered the hardwood floor. A gas fire blazed in a fieldstone-enclosed fireplace. Nineteenth-century paintings hung on the walls, including a still life depicting a bountiful harvest, a landscape of rolling hills and a meandering stream, and a hunting scene, the hounds frisking around the horses. On the right, a bar ran half the length of the room. Two men sat on leather stools at the far end. Beyond the bar was the restaurant. Heavy wine-colored velvet drapes covered the windows. Vivaldi's *Four Seasons* played softly in the background.

I turned slowly, taking it all in. "I'm gobsmacked, Chester. I can't wait to come back for drinks with my fiancé."

"Wonderful! I want to show you something else, but first, let's toast to our new friendship. What's your pleasure?"

The bartender, a man in his fifties with wavy brown hair, strolled toward us. He wore a long-sleeved white shirt under a tartan plaid vest and black slacks.

"I'm not speechless often, but seeing this place . . . well . . . I think a Bombay Sapphire on the rocks with a twist is in order."

"Maker's Mark for me, Jeremy."

Chester pulled out a stool for me. I climbed up, and he followed.

The bar railing was cylindrical, made of brass, with foot-high elephant heads mounted on the braces that attached the railing to the bar.

I pointed to an elephant head. "That's fabulous."

"I had it made by a retired ironworker. I described what I wanted, and he did the rest."

Chester swiveled to face me. "The Colonial Twist is a profit-making enterprise. We offer a full bar but a limited menu, only four items: a ribeye steak, a grilled chicken Caesar salad, my mother's lasagna, and lobster alfredo primavera. I also run the Colonial Club, a nonprofit social club. The proceeds from the club are used to teach ex-cons to cook. We then help them get internships and jobs."

"You have convicts working here?"

"No. That program is run out of a different facility over in Durham. We have a stellar track record, and I'm proud of it. More than ninety percent of our students never go back to prison."

Jeremy placed a linen cocktail napkin in front of me. Real linen, winter white and crisply ironed. He centered my heavy cut-crystal glass on the napkin.

"That's terrific, Chester."

He touched the rim of his glass to mine. "To new friends."

I raised my glass. "To new friends."

"We also partner with other local nonprofit organizations to help them do their good works—the Rocky Point Computer Literacy Foundation, New Hampshire Children First!, and the Harmonics Glee Club, among a dozen others."

"I'm involved with New Hampshire Children First! myself. It's a fabulous organization."

"You see . . . I knew we'd get along." He slid off his stool and picked up his drink. "Follow me. You can bring your drink."

He set off for the end of the bar. I carried my drink, wrapped in the napkin, and trailed along.

At the end of the bar, another uniformed doorman stood by a door on the right. He pushed it open, and we passed through into a square, windowless room. An older woman, wearing the same style of black sheath as the younger woman at the front, stood behind an ornately carved hostess stand. She smiled at us but didn't speak. To her right was a double set of doors. A security camera was mounted overhead.

"You have ID on you?" Chester asked me.

"Sure. Why?"

"Because everybody has to sign in."

I met his eyes across the top of my glass. I swallowed some gin, then went up on tiptoe and leaned in close so he could catch my whisper. "This sounds like a setup."

"What kind of setup?" he whispered back.

"You're making a porn movie. You've got Cal tied up in there. You plan on holding me for ransom." I drank some more gin. "And that's just off the top of my head."

He guffawed again. "I love your imagination, Josie Prescott! It's not a setup. No porn. No Cal. No kidnapping."

"I don't want to sign in."

"Rules are rules."

"Let's go back to the bar."

"You need to see this."

"Then show me." I drank some more. "I'm kind of a privacy fiend, Chester. I show my ID to my banker and at the airport when I want to board a plane. Nowhere else." I lifted my head to the security camera and waved. "Plus, you've already got me on film."

Chester considered my request for ten seconds. "Why not? I can make an exception."

Chester made a whirling motion with his hand, and the doorman sprang forward and pulled open the doors, revealing a casino, all glitz and glam, mirrors, and gilt.

My mouth opened, then shut. "You're kidding me."

"Nope. The nonprofit Colonial Club runs the casino. The earnings pay for the good works."

I began a slow inspection. The place was about a quarter full, more men than women, most of them in their fifties or older, all of them well dressed, well kempt, and totally absorbed with the action. Ice clinked in glasses, chimes and bells rang out from the slots, conversation purred softly, riddled with occasional exclamations of pleasure or dismay, and the dealers calling out the odds and the bets and the winning combinations spoke in well-modulated tones. All the dealers, both men and women, were dressed like Jeremy. Women in black sheaths and pearls and men in tuxedos walked the floor serving drinks, clearing empties, pushing in chairs, and picking up any stray bits of litter. The ceiling was mirrored. Security cameras were mounted everywhere, in the light fixtures, above the paintings hanging on the walls, and over every doorway. I counted three blackjack tables, two roulette wheels, a craps table, and half a dozen rows of slot machines. Four oval felt-covered poker tables were positioned behind a brass railing. To my left was a booth labeled TICKETS. Next to it was another booth, the sign reading CHIPS.

I turned to face Chester. "Is this legal?"

"Hell, yes. We use tickets and chips, not cash."

"People buy tickets at one booth and redeem them for chips at a second."

"Exactly. It's on the up-and-up."

"If I have winnings, I reverse the process."

"And pay out we do. We have a payout rate of nearly ninety-seven percent."

"I don't know the industry, but that sounds impressive."

"It is."

Six people sat at a roulette table. No one was talking. Everyone's eyes were fixed on the spinning red-and-black wheel.

"That's why Cal owes you money. He lost."

"Big-time. Sixty-two thousand dollars."

"My God! That's probably more than he earns in a year!"

"It's a problem."

"You let people play on tick?"

"Only when I know them. He's never stiffed me before."

"Has he lost that much before?"

"Not that much, no. But he's lost over twenty grand before. More than once."

"He lives on his salary. How did he raise the money?"

"He took to dealing art."

"Japanese woodblock prints."

"I don't know the specifics. What I do know is that he has a reliable source, or so he told me. He was cautious about it. He didn't want to flood the market and make a stir."

"Counterfeits." The roulette wheel slowed to a stop, and the dealer slid piles of chips to the winners. "Why are you showing this to me?"

"Maybe you're a gambler. I need new blood."

I laughed. "You're a piece of work, Chester Randall. I'm sorry to disappoint you, but I don't gamble. Not the way you mean."

"No harm in trying."

"I can tell when someone's pulling my leg." I shook my glass a bit, spinning the ice, then drank some gin. "What do you do with people who don't pay their debts?"

"I don't break kneecaps, if that's what you're asking. I work out a payment plan."

"How did you get onto Nora?"

"He brought her here a couple of times. They seemed pretty simpatico, if you catch my drift. When it became clear he wasn't going to pay up, I got her name from the door. Unlike some people I could name, Nora had no problem signing in. Nora is a lively girl."

"Lively? That's a word with multiple meanings. Which one do you intend?"

"The tight-skirt-cling-to-your-man-bat-your-lashes-drink-oodles-of-champagne kind of lively."

"That's a very colorful description, and paints a profoundly different picture than the straight-arrow young woman I know. Did you research her at all?"

"She's been married to a man named Kevin Burke for seven years, and she works at Hitchens University, in financial aid."

"Why haven't you approached her directly?"

Chester laughed again. "I can tell you've never had an affair. I've seen how she looks at Cal. She'd never give him up."

"That condo complex she turned into—is that where she lives?"

"Yes. I was hoping she'd go to Cal's hidey-hole for a little canoodle before going home."

"What makes you think he hasn't taken off for California or Bali or somewhere?"

"Same reason I think he's alive. If he'd left town or died, she'd be upset. Instead, she glows like a girl in love. He's safe and sound, and she knows where."

"You should be a detective. Have you shared these insights with the police?"

"Nah. If I had any evidence . . ."

"Why are you telling me, Chester?"

"Two reasons. First, I admire you. I have for years. I read the papers. I know who you are and what you've accomplished. Your TV show is one of my wife's favorites. She says she wishes she had a daughter like you. We have three sons, wonderful boys, all of them, and she loves them like nobody's business, but a woman wants a daughter, too, and if she had her pick, that daughter would be you."

I looked away, embarrassed at the tears that sprang to my eyes. After a moment, I turned back. "Please thank your wife for me. That's one of the nicest compliments I've ever received."

"I will. She'll be pleased. Second, I think you're going to find Cal, and when you do, now that we know each other and you see I'm a good guy, I think you'll tell me where he is."

"What makes you think I can find him?"

"Because you'll know how to trace him through the art he's selling. I wouldn't even know where to start."

"You've given me an idea, Chester. I may actually be able to help." I looked around some more. "Why all the cloak-and-dagger if the casino is on the up-and-up?"

"This is a private club, and I think you'll agree that I've created a nice atmosphere, different from what you find in public casinos. Tourists in droopy shorts and sandy flip-flops don't fit."

" 'Nice' isn't the word I'd use to describe this place. 'Sophisticated,' maybe. Not 'nice.' "

"I'm modest."

I smiled. "Is there an initiation fee?"

"Sure. Ten thousand."

My eyes widened. "Ten thousand dollars? Are you telling me Cal paid you ten thousand dollars?"

"No, his other girlfriend did. Lydia Shannon. She bought him a membership."

"Lydia's a gambler?"

"She likes a game or two. Blackjack, mostly. She came the first time as her father's guest."

Frank still gambled, and that meant he'd lied to Trish. I knew it wasn't any of my business, but I felt disappointed nonetheless. "Does Lydia lose?"

"All gamblers lose."

"Does she lose so much she needs to run on tick?"

"No."

"How about Frank?"

"He's a disciplined player. If he loses a thousand, he shrugs it off. If he wins a thousand, he tips the dealers big and walks away. Usually."

"Usually?"

"He's had his moments."

"How bad?"

"Why?"

"I'm trying to get a feel for the situation."

"He lost upwards of a hundred thousand about a year ago, but we've worked it out."

"That's a big number." I watched the poker players for a few seconds. Three men, all wearing sport coats and ties, and a woman wearing a red turtleneck dress were examining their cards. They all had piles of chips in front of them. Four cards sat faceup in the middle of the table. I could almost feel the intensity of their deliberation as they weighed their options. "That looks like Texas Hold'em."

"It is."

I finished my drink. "If I find Cal before you do, I'll let you know."

"Thank you. And vice versa."

We shook on the deal, and Chester walked me out.

"It was a pleasure meeting you, Josie Prescott."

"You, too, Chester Randall."

I turned left out of Chester's Tudor enclave toward Ocean Avenue. When I reached Ocean, I pulled onto the sandy shoulder and called Wes.

He answered on the first ring, sounding out of breath, which he probably was. Wes always moved at warp speed.

"Whatcha got?"

"Do you know the Colonial Twist?"

"No. What is it, a dance?"

"A restaurant and bar. High end. The owner is Chester Randall. He also runs a nonprofit social club called the Colonial Club."

"Here in Rocky Point?"

"Yes. Can you find out about them—and him?"

"Is this connected with Mo?"

"I don't know. Maybe."

"Tell me the names again."

I did so. "Thank you, Wes."

"You owe me, big-time."

"You know I give you what I can as soon as I can."

"See that you do." Wes's tone morphed from pugnacious pit bull to kid brother in the snap of a finger. "Listen, I need a favor."

"Sure. What?"

"I'm applying to be a justice of the peace. I need references who'll attest to my good moral character. I know, it's stupid, but what can I say . . . it was Maggie's idea. She transferred into her bank's compliance division, and she works with lawyers all the time. It turns out justices of the peace can take depositions, and she thinks that since I ask questions for a living as a reporter, I might be pretty good at it. I don't know. I think it sounds pretty lame."

"I think it's a great idea, Wes. I bet you'll be applying to law school within a year."

"No way."

"Never say never. And of course I'll write you a reference."

"Thanks. I'll send you the paperwork. The thing is . . . I'm doing it because we can use the extra money. I mean . . . well . . . Maggie is pregnant."

My eyes filled. I was as excited for Wes as if he'd been my brother for real. "Oh, Wes!"

"Can you believe it? I'm going to be a father."

"You'll be a wonderful father. How is Maggie feeling?"

"Better than ever. She says she loves being pregnant. Don't tell anyone, okay? She's only three months along. She wants to hit four months before we spread the word."

"All right. Give her my love."

"Will do, and I'll get you the skinny on the Colonial duo. Also, do you remember how you asked about Lydia, whether she'd been in touch with Cal? I don't have any information—yet. As to Cal or Lydia withdrawing an out-of-whack amount of money, nope. And he doesn't have any other accounts, not even a savings account. He's always short, and she always has plenty of cash, with no unusual transactions between them. You got anything for me?"

"No."

"Catch ya later."

After he hung up, I texted Ellis: *Chester Randall at the Colonial Club knows Cal.*

I sat for a minute longer, then drove home.

CHAPTER FIFTEEN

Ty called while I was sitting in the living room, doing nothing. It was about ten.

"I had a good day," he said. "How about you?"

His voice had pep in it, and a secret.

"You sound very cheery. What's going on?"

"The powers that be asked me to head an ad hoc committee to begin to think about the new training strategies."

"Congratulations! Who's on the committee?"

"That's the best part. I get to choose my own team, and our meetings will all be conducted via videoconference from my office in Rocky Point."

I pulled a creamy white wool afghan up over my thighs. My mother had crocheted it about a year before she died.

"They're letting you work on a national project from New Hampshire? No wonder you're excited."

"Sean, you know, my boss's boss, took me aside and said he was eager to see how it worked, that if there were no glitches or delays, it could help make the case for more remote assignments."

"Oh, Ty. This is such fabulous news! How will you decide who should be on your committee?"

"A little of this and a little of that. I want representation from each geographic region and area of expertise. I'll tell you more about it tomorrow. I should be home by noon."

The next morning, I was up and out by six. I checked the thermostat I'd mounted outside my kitchen window. It was sunny, but only forty-two degrees. I put on my Thinsulate vest. I could see my breath as soon as I stepped onto the porch.

I walked along the street for a quarter mile until I reached the spinney and turned in. A hundred yards down the path, I came to a fork. The right tine wended its way through the trees to the meadow beyond. The left tine swung hard for fifty feet to an old stone wall, then turned north and ran along it for two miles. I turned left.

The path was thick with fallen leaves, and where the sun broke through the leafy canopy, deep shadows and bright swaths of light dappled the ground. I loved crunching through the woods in fall.

I knew a few divorced couples who stayed in touch, but I knew more who didn't. I had no idea where Steve and Mo fell on the spectrum of affinity. Mo seemed to think that the fire between them still smoldered, but I had no way of knowing if she'd been in dreamland on that front. From my brief conversation with Steve yesterday, I'd sensed genuine grief, but I might have misread his reaction. If their divorce had been as acrimonious as Lydia implied, there was no reason to think that Steve would be receptive to helping me with her eulogy. So my task was simple, though unpleasant: Before I did anything else, I needed to feel him out about Mo.

I walked for more than a mile before turning back. I spent most of it thinking about Steve, wondering how Mo's death was affecting him. He said that he still cared about her, and that made sense to me. Even after a breakup, if you've loved someone, her death had to hit you like the flu. If they were thinking about a do-over, it had to be worse, like something inside of you died, too.

When I arrived at Sweet Treats, at twenty minutes to seven, the takeout line stretched to the door, but three of the eight tables were empty. I grabbed one by the side wall. A moment later, Steve stepped inside, and I raised a hand to catch his attention.

Noeleen, the owner, was working the front and stopped to greet us.

She was short, about my height, and full-figured, and she was always cheerful and kind. Her hair was ash blond. Her eyes were dark blue.

"So good to see you, Josie! Steve! What can I bring you to drink?"

"Tea, please. Irish Breakfast. With milk."

"Steve? Coffee?"

"You better believe it. Thanks, Noeleen."

Steve swung his backpack to the side, tossed his coat on the back of the chair, and sat down.

"You're a regular here," I said.

"As is everyone who's ever eaten Noeleen's cinnamon buns."

"True. The doughnuts wipe me out, too. And her muffins."

Noeleen returned with our drinks, a mug of coffee for Steve, and a gilt-edged white porcelain teapot for me. The cup and saucer matched the teapot. We ordered food. Steve chose an egg-and-sausage scramble on a cinnamon bun. I went with an order of three honey-glazed doughnut holes and a fruit salad.

I watched Noeleen chat her way to the back, then turned to Steve. "May I ask you something that's totally none of my business?"

He leaned back. "That's a heck of a question to spring on a man before he's finished his first cup of coffee."

I stirred some sugar into my tea.

He drank some coffee, his eyes on my face. "What the heck. Shoot."

"Were you and Mo getting back together?"

"Maybe. We were in touch. Why?"

"As I told you, I'm giving one of the eulogies. I was hoping you might help me, but I need to know what I'm stepping into before I ask. I like you, Steve, and I don't want to put you in an uncomfortable position. Who initiated getting back in touch?"

"She did. I might have if she hadn't." He shook his head. "The breakup is all on me, and so is our not getting back together right away. You know that I've been living with a woman named Kimberly Larson?"

"No, I didn't. I heard you denied playing around."

"Any lies told in the course of divorce proceedings don't count."

"Situational ethics."

"A branch of philosophy I know well."

"Was Kimberly the woman you got involved with while you were still married to Mo?"

"Yes."

"I bet Kimberly has a seven-year-old son, a Cub Scout."

"Ryan. He's a good kid, which makes the whole situation pretty much a nightmare."

Noeleen brought our food, and the sweet aroma of vanilla enveloped me. She refilled Steve's coffee and asked if we needed anything else. We didn't. I poured more tea and stirred a few drops of milk into the mahogany brew.

"Mo wanted me to leave Kimberly before we got back together. I wanted to see if our reconciliation was for real first. Hedging my bets, I guess you could say. She didn't want any part of that plan. She said she didn't trust me, and if I wanted her to, I had to earn it. We were dickering over the terms when she died. We had plans to meet for dinner that night."

"Really? Do the police know?"

"No, and I hope they never find out. I didn't kill her. I didn't see her. I don't know anything."

"Where were you supposed to meet?"

"Abitino's. Do you know it?"

"Yes. I love it. When did you make plans?"

"That afternoon. I called her from the faculty lounge."

"So Kimberly wouldn't see Mo's number on your cell phone."

"Makes me sound like a jerk, doesn't it?"

I smiled to take the sting out of my words. "Pretty much."

"It gets worse. I nearly got caught. Kimberly walked into the lounge just as I was hanging up. I had to lie about the call. I said I called the car dealership to schedule a tune-up."

"What did you say when she asked why you didn't use your own phone?"

"My cell was in my briefcase in my classroom, and I'm lazy. The phone was right there, so I used it."

"You're quick on your feet."

"Liars have to be."

"You really do sound like a jerk, Steve. I wonder why I like you so much."

"I'm a lot of fun to be around, quick-witted, and I don't lie to you."

I laughed. "I knew there was a reason. Now I see there are three. Did you get a tune-up?"

"No, as I explained to Kimberly the next day, I got the date wrong. The car's not due for service until December. Slick, wouldn't you say?"

"Super slick. What time were you supposed to meet Mo for dinner?"

"Eight. She was doing some baking for her mother first. I waited until eight thirty, then called her from the restaurant phone. I told the hostess I forgot my cell. I didn't leave a message. I figured I'd see her at school the next day and find out what went wrong."

"I'm surprised the police haven't asked you about it."

"Why? The restaurant was packed, the hostess was a high-school kid who was just trying to keep up, and I made the reservation using the name Baker."

"Why Baker?"

"It's easy to spell, easy to remember, and common."

"What did Mo think about your using a made-up name?"

"She didn't know. I made a point to always get there first."

"What did you tell Kimberly about where you were going?"

"To a Cub Scout training session."

"Was there one scheduled?"

"Yup. And my buddy Don promised to cover for me."

"Oh, what tangled webs we weave . . ."

"No joke, Josie. It was a mess and getting messier by the day. The only good news is that almost no one knows Kimberly and I are involved. I insisted on that. Talk about awkward. My ex-wife teaches in the classroom next to my current girlfriend, the 'other woman' who broke up my marriage, and she doesn't know we're living together."

"And Kimberly is putting pressure on you to marry her."

"Like a vise."

Hearing so many sordid details, I was almost sorry I'd asked Steve for help. I was glad he was only a casual friend. "What are you going to do?"

"Punt."

The attractive redhead I'd seen organizing croquet with Ty, standing with the book club members, and walking with Steve in the school parking lot entered the shop, glanced around, and beelined for our table, brushing past people waiting for takeout. She was even prettier close up under Sweet Treats's golden recessed lighting than she'd been in harsh sunlight or fading twilight, or under a cheerless gray sky. She looked less chunky and more like an athlete, big-boned and curvy, but sinewy and powerful, too. Her hair was a rich coppery red warmed with glints of gold. Her eyes were green, more olive than Gretchen's startlingly bright emerald.

"I thought I'd find you here!"

Steve lumbered to his feet. "Kimberly!" He kissed her cheek. "Josie, this is Kimberly Larson. Kimberly, this is Josie Prescott, an old friend."

I smiled. "Hi."

She smiled, too, but hers seemed pasted on. "It's so nice to meet you. Steve loves this place for breakfast."

I smiled some more, aware of her unspoken message: She was alerting me that she knew Steve's preferences, and that I'd better not encroach.

I felt like waving my engagement ring under her nose but settled for a verbal cue instead. "I saw you at Mo's party. My fiancé helped you carry the croquet set. Ty."

"I thought you looked familiar!" Her stiffness relaxed a notch. "Ty was a doll to do the heavy lifting for me." She turned to Steve. "Can I join you for a quick cup of coffee? I know we don't have much time."

Steve squeezed her shoulder. "Josie and I were in the middle of something. I'll catch up with you at school, okay?"

Kimberly's cheeks flushed. "Oh, sure. Sorry."

She left without a final glance at me. I wasn't her issue; Steve was. I watched to see which way she turned once she hit the sidewalk. She walked diagonally across the street and entered the central parking garage.

I looked back at Steve as he sat down again. "She didn't just happen to be walking by. She parked in the garage."

"She tried to get me to tell her why I was leaving so early this morning. She must have followed me. Jeez . . . I don't have a girlfriend, I have a stalker."

"Given your track record, who can blame her?"

"Touché. One way or the other, I expect I'll get an earful later. I need to go in a minute. School bells stop for no man. You said you were going to ask for my help with the eulogy. Specifically, what can I do for you?"

"I'd love an anecdote . . . something that explains Mo's specialness. I feel as if all I have at hand is a collection of banal generalities."

I'd always heard that eyes are windows to the soul, but Steve's weren't. His revealed nothing. He could have been deciding whether he wanted a refill on his coffee.

"You're doing this for me, to give me a chance to grieve, to share how much I loved her."

"For both of us. And for Mo."

He nodded. "Thank you for asking. I'd like to help. Very much."

I dug around in my tote bag for my card case and handed over a business card.

He stood and slipped the card into his shirt pocket. "I'll email you today, or tomorrow at the latest." He glanced around, caught Noeleen's eye, and scribbled in the air.

"This is on me," I said.

He grinned, and the boyish charm I remembered was writ large upon his face. He was cute as a bug.

"Thanks."

"One last question: What do you think about Lydia?"

He reached for his backpack. "From the top of Lydia's world-class brain to the bottom of her empty heart, she is certain she knows what's best for everyone, in every case, all the time." He slung the backpack over his shoulder. "That kind of arrogance really doesn't work for me. We butted heads a lot."

"I appreciate your candor, Steve."

Noeleen brought the check and thanked us for coming.

I left the tip on the table and walked Steve to the door before joining the line at the cash register. He repeated his promise to be in touch soon, then left, heading away from the garage. Evidently he'd found on-street parking. His gait as he walked away didn't match his nonchalance. He'd seemed weighed down, maybe from guilt, or possibly because his lies had finally caught up with him.

I could see why Mo wanted to get back with him, though. He was smart and quick, up to her intellectual weight. He had an unusual magnetism, too. When he talked to you, his focus was white-hot, and Mo would have melted under the heat of his attention.

"Fancy meeting you here."

I switched gears. Lydia was in line waiting to order. I hadn't seen her arrive. Her shoulders drooped. She had new wrinkles around her mouth and eyes. She'd ditched the sunglasses, and her makeup did a good job of covering whatever remnants of the bruise remained.

"Lydia. How are you doing?"

"It's tough. My mother does nothing but cry. My father paces around like a big cat in a small cage. And Cal is still missing." She moved forward one step. "I've been locked up at home . . . Have you heard anything?"

"No."

The line crept forward again.

"I saw you with Stevie just now. Giving comfort to the enemy?"

"Why is he the enemy?"

"That's good. If you don't want to answer a question, ask one instead."

Lydia was exhausting. "I wasn't avoiding the question. Even though Mo and Steve were divorced, I thought he might be upset, and I wanted to offer my condolences. I like him. I always have, so naturally I don't consider him an enemy, but I was curious why you did. If you don't want to tell me, that's fine."

The line edged ahead. In another minute, it would be her turn.

Lydia kept her eyes on the man in front of her. "Is he all broken up about Mo's death?"

"Yes."

"Yeah, right. I hear from Mo's lawyer that she donated that Japanese woodblock print to New Hampshire Children First! What do you think they'll do with it? Sell it? Or make it the centerpiece of a shrine for Mo?"

I told myself that Lydia must be awash in a sea of misery, that no one could possibly be so mean-spirited unless they themselves were suffering unendurable pain. These rational musings didn't affect my emotional reaction, though. I fought an instinct to flee without speaking another word, to escape the bitterness that seemed to envelop her like a shroud.

"I don't think they've decided yet. I'll see you on Tuesday, Lydia. Again, my condolences."

I walked to the cash register and paid the bill, relieved to get away.

CHAPTER SIXTEEN

Davy Morse's vintage Mustang swung into our lot about ten fifteen. Davy was around sixty. He was shorter than most men, about five-four, and thin, with a full head of close-cut gray hair. He wore a blue baseball cap backward with some writing stitched on it. I couldn't make out the words. He spotted me looking out the window and waved. I waved back and opened the front door.

"Hey, Davy! Long time, no see."

He spread his arms wide. "You sure called me up here at the right time of year. These colors are bitchin'. You hear about the foliage, but man, this is something."

"When I first moved here, I thought it looked like a tapestry." I took a step toward him. "It's good to see you, Davy. How's Ruby?"

"Good, good. She sends regards. What's it been since I looked at that mandolin for you? Three years? Four? It was winter, I remember that. Ruby was with me, and she still talks about freezing her bippy off."

As he stepped inside, I read the words on his cap: METAL FOREVER. He wore a leather bomber jacket over a light blue denim work shirt, jeans, and Frye boots.

"Everyone! You remember Davy Morse."

Fred stood and walked around his desk to greet him.

Sasha, on the phone, smiled, and her eyes lit up.

Gretchen, a celebrity-gossip junkie, smiled at Davy as if he were a rock star.

Cara stood and fussed at him. "You must be tired after your long drive."

"Heck, Cara, I'm not tired. I'm hungry. Do you have any of those ginger-snaps of yours?"

"I brought in a fresh batch today!"

"Bless you." He kissed her cheek.

Cara laughed. She brought the tin of cookies to the guest table. Davy rubbed his hands together and pried open the lid. He took a cookie and popped it in his mouth. He made yum sounds, his eyes half-closed.

"Even better than I remembered. You're a wizard, Cara!"

Davy ate gingersnaps and chatted with every member of the staff. I stood by the wall and watched their interactions, appreciating Davy's deft control of the content. He had a gift for making people feel comfortable. When the conversations began to wane, I stepped forward.

"Davy? Sorry to interrupt. What do you say we go to my office and I fill you in?"

"Sounds like a plan."

"Fred, did you set up a studio?"

"This afternoon at four. We should leave here around three forty."

"Good."

I pushed open the door and entered the warehouse. Davy followed. Up-stairs, we got settled in the seating area, with Davy on the love seat.

"We're appraising a 1930 Martin OM-45 Deluxe guitar. Right now, I'm working on the provenance, while Fred is tracking down the fourteen made that year. We need you to authenticate this particular instrument. Fred told me we need to worry that this one might be a counterfeit."

"He's right, and no one knows how many forgeries are out there. To complicate the issue, Martin makes its own authentic replicas, which sell for seventy thousand, by the way, so there's serious motivation to create fakes."

"If ours is real and we can verify provenance, what are we looking at?"

"Four hundred thousand. Maybe more depending on who owns it, condition, and so on. Whose is it?"

"I can't tell you."

"Is it for sale?"

"No."

"I'll play it, and I'll know."

"Fred said you'll only need two days to know if it's authentic."

"With any luck, I'll only need an hour, but to make it official, I'll use my fifty-one-point checklist."

"Let's get you started."

I used my desk phone to call Fred and ask him to bring the guitar and both cases to station three, the worktable closest to Hank and Angela, then led the way downstairs.

Halfway down, I paused and turned to look at him. "Ty and I are getting married in June. Will you and Ruby come up?"

"Yes."

"Really?"

"Don't sound so surprised!" He took my hand and squeezed it. "You're the real deal, Josie. I'm your friend."

I squeezed back. "What a nice thing to say. Do you think there's any chance you can bring Shelley with you?"

"Never say never."

Shelley was a friend from my days working at Frisco's in New York City. After I got caught up in the big price-fixing scandal that rocked the high-end antiques auction world, my so-called friends fled as if I had a contagious disease, all except Shelley.

We reached the table before Fred.

Davy squatted beside Angela, sleeping in Hank's basket.

"Who's this beauty?" he whispered. "I haven't met her before."

"She's our newest baby. Her name is Angela. Isn't she a doll? She's a complete love bunny."

He eased a finger under her chin and stroked gently. I could hear her sleepy-time purr from where I stood.

Fred came up, giving Angela a wide berth so as not to disturb her. He hoisted the case containing the guitar onto the worktable and placed the original case next to it. Fred unlatched the working case.

"See ya later!" Davy whispered to Angela.

Davy stood five feet from the guitar and examined it with laserlike intensity. He walked to the table and lifted the guitar from the case, setting it in the center of the worktable. He adjusted the light and leaned in close, studying it. Fred was observing Davy's technique like a disciple.

When he was done, Davy carried the guitar to a nearby stool. He began strumming a bluesy number I didn't recognize.

I moved to stand beside Fred. "Do you know what he's playing? It's beautiful."

Davy looked up. "'Devil Got My Woman,' a Skip James tune."

After a few more seconds, I touched Fred's arm. "I'm going to leave you to your work."

Fred nodded, but I wasn't certain he heard me.

As soon as Ty and I were seated at the Blue Dolphin's best table, a big one by the window, I reached across the snowy-white linen tablecloth and took Ty's hand in mine. "So I have an idea. Let's get married on the beach, just the two of us. Plus witnesses, of course. By a judge. Max can hook us up with a judge. Or Ellis can."

"Okay."

I laughed. "Just like that? You agree?"

"Sure. Then we'll have a blowout party."

"Yes. This way, we each get what we want most."

"Sold."

"This was so easy."

He kissed my hand. "I knew we'd figure it out. When?"

"June twenty-first. It's a Thursday. We get married on the beach in the morning, then disappear, just the two of us. We'll check into Wentworth by the Sea. On Saturday, the twenty-third, we have a party, maybe here at the Blue Dolphin. I won't get stressed. Everything will be perfect."

"Done. Except we may have more people than the restaurant can hold."

"We'll put up a big tent in the back, and the Blue Dolphin can cater it."

"Good. I'll think about the invite list. I have a feeling some folks may come up from D.C."

"Davy said he and Ruby would come from New York and that he might be able to convince Shelley to come, too."

"I want a conga line."

I laughed. "You've got it."

"We're getting married in June."

"I always wanted a June wedding. We need to book the honeymoon suite at the hotel."

"I hope it's available. June weddings are so popular, we may be too late."

"Call me Ms. Flexible. I don't care if we get a suite. Any room will do."

"Let's check out the options now. Today."

"Really? Today?"

He took my hand and kissed it again. "Yes, today. Eat fast."

Ty turned onto Bow Street while I called Wentworth by the Sea. I clicked through their interactive phone system until I reached Sarah Collins, an event planner. She could see us at five. I made the appointment.

The dash clock read 2:47. "I'd like to stop by my office for a few minutes. How should we coordinate?"

"I'll go home and unpack and check in with my team. How about if you drive yourself home? You can leave your car there, and we'll go to Wentworth together."

"That'll work! I'll be home by four thirty at the latest."

Ty rolled to a stop at Prescott's front door.

I paused, my hand on the door handle. "I'm excited, Ty. We're making plans for our wedding."

"Me, too."

"It's really happening. June will be here before we know it."

He stroked my cheek with his index finger, and I closed my eyes, relishing the moment.

I sat at the guest table and stretched out my legs. When Gretchen was off the phone, I asked, "How did the interviews for a new part-timer go?"

"Great. We've identified two solid candidates." She smiled, her eyes twinkling like sparklers on the Fourth of July. "Eric has a flair for asking just the right questions worded in just the right way."

"That's good to hear. Will you bring them both in for training?"

"Assuming their references check out."

"Let me know if and when they come in. I want to welcome them and—" I broke off as the wind chimes tinkled. Steve Jullison opened the door. I stood up. "Steve!"

He closed the door behind him. "Do you have a minute to talk?" His eyes communicated urgency.

"Sure. Come to my office."

Upstairs, Steve stopped at the end of the love seat to assess Mo's wood-block print. He didn't approach the easel. He didn't speak. After a few seconds, he angled his head to the side. After a minute more, he turned to face me.

"I don't have long—I came straight from school, and I'm meeting Kimberly and Ryan at four. I thought of something you might be able to use in your eulogy, but I don't want Kimberly, Frank, Trish, or anyone to know I talked to you."

"I'm good at keeping secrets, but why? What's wrong with the world knowing Mo married a man classy enough to be able to talk about her good points even if their marriage didn't work out?"

"None of them would see it as classy. They'd see it as smarmy." He flipped a palm, dismissing his thorny breakup and possible reconciliation from our conversation. "When Mo and I were first married, I asked her what it was about Japanese woodblock prints that spoke to her. She said it was the dual-ity. Muted colors that communicate vibrancy. Isolated settings packed with life. Two dimensions communicating a three-dimensional narrative. Here's the thing, Josie . . . this duality can be seen in Mo herself. You know—she was kind of reserved, a loner, yet she loved being around people, that sort of thing."

"Oh, Steve, that's so beautiful. And so true. That describes Mo to a T."

"Use it. Just pretend you asked her the question, not me."

"But you're the one who—"

He held up a hand to stop my objection. "Do it, Josie. Do it for her folks."

I smiled. "All right. I will."

I walked him out, then ran back upstairs to write it down. When I delivered Mo's eulogy, I wouldn't speak Steve's name aloud, but I'd be thinking it.

I had almost an hour before I needed to go home, so I decided to make another stop to ask about Mo's print.

Murphy's Interiors was Rocky Point's oldest furniture store. It was known for the quality of its offerings and the knowledge of its salespeople. About five years ago, Murphy's integrated boutiques within the store, similar to how department stores invited fashion designers to open branded mini retail shops inside their walls. One of the boutiques was an interior design firm named Branson Wills.

Anita Wills was a licensed interior designer, a favorite of architects. Anita was Chinese American, in her forties. She wore a purple sweater dress and black ankle-high boots. She and Sasha had been classmates at Hitchens, earning their Ph.D.'s in art history the same year. Eli Branson, her business partner, spent most of his time overseas, hunting for unique pieces. They often carried antiques, one-of-a-kind objects. I rarely found bargains in their shop, but I often found inspiration.

Branson Wills occupied a spot about halfway back on the left, just after Quentin's Spy Shop. I threaded my way through an array of opulent and utilitarian offerings from Biddington Silk Flowers, Seacoast Living Home & Hearth, French Heart Linens, and Rocky Point Gardens and Patio Furniture.

Anita stood under a teak pergola talking to a couple I didn't know. My phone vibrated, startling me. It was Wes. I stepped aside to answer the call.

"Where are you?" he demanded, as brusque as ever.

"I'm fine, Wes. Thanks. How are you?"

"Good, good. So you asked about Chester Randall, the Colonial Twist, and the Colonial Club. I couldn't find any dirt." Wes sounded disappointed. "He's active in Rotary International and at St. Teresa's Catholic Church. His business is solvent. His charity's paperwork is up-to-date. People like him. You're supposed to be giving me leads, not busywork."

"Some leads don't pan out, you know that. I'm glad to hear Chester's on the up-and-up."

"You owe me, Josie. Pay up."

I was tempted to wriggle out of answering, but I didn't. Our relationship chugged along nicely because we honored our unspoken quid-pro-quo arrangement. If I didn't give Wes some quid pretty darn soon, it wouldn't be long before he stopped providing the pro quo.

I told him what I'd learned from Chester about Nora and Cal. "The thing is . . . she's married."

"That adds a lump of coal in the stocking, doesn't it? Maybe her husband killed Cal."

"I don't know anything about Nora's husband, except that he works in construction and his name is Kevin Burke."

"I'll find out. What do you know about her?"

I filled him in about what little I'd gleaned, and he said, "Talk soon," and hung up.

I still owed Wes, but I was catching up.

I turned back toward Anita. She was sitting at her desk. The couple sat across from her in matching Louis XVI eighteenth-century-style chairs. She placed a book of design options—an idea book—on the desk, facing them, and they began flipping pages, pausing occasionally to comment on various design styles. Anita sat, listening, gathering data for her custom design. I walked toward her, staying far enough away so my approach wouldn't feel intrusive, but not so distant that she wouldn't notice me.

Anita spotted me, smiled, said something to her clients, and stood to greet me.

"Josie, it's so good to see you."

"And you, Anita. I'm sorry to bother you. I see you're with clients, so I'll only take a minute. I'm hoping you can help me with an appraisal I'm working on—a print from Hiroshige's 'One Hundred Famous Views of Edo.' Have you sold any in the last few months?"

"Josie, you know how much I respect and admire you, but we don't share sales data."

"Let me ask you this—did you ever meet Mo Shannon?"

"The name doesn't ring a bell."

"You must have read about her murder. Or heard about it."

"I don't follow the news. I get too upset."

"I understand, and I'm sorry to have to mention it, but Mo Shannon was a friend of mine. Shortly before she was killed, she bought what is purported to be an original *Meguro Drum Bridge and Sunset Hill*. She asked me to appraise it. She acquired it through a private sale facilitated by a man named Cal Lewis."

Anita's brows drew together. "I don't know anyone by that name."

"How about Nora Burke?"

"I'm sorry. No."

"But you sold one, didn't you?"

She met my eyes for a moment. "It's true that we acquired a portfolio of 'One Hundred Famous Views of Edo.' Several images have sold. I'd have to research whether that was one of them."

"Is there any way you can look it up now?"

She glanced at the couple. They were chatting softly.

"I'm sorry, Josie, but I can't. I need to get back to them."

I lowered my eyes to the time display on my phone. Ty was waiting for me. My impatience would have to be contained. I asked if I could come back at ten tomorrow morning for the answer, and she agreed. I thanked her, and we shook on it.

CHAPTER SEVENTEEN

s soon as Ty turned onto Route 1B, he asked, "Do you really like the idea of holding our wedding reception in a tent?"

"It'll be a really nice tent."

"I was thinking of something more elegant."

"We can make the tent elegant, lots of candles and fancy china."

"Okay, then."

"Then on Sunday, we can change out the decorations and have a hoedown, you know, country music and a barbecue, a brunch kind of thing for out-of-towners and our closest friends. We could schedule it for eleven, so people who needed to leave by two or three would still have time to party."

"I like it. We'll have a grand affair to mark the propitious occasion of our marriage, then go back to our jeans and country-dancing roots."

"Yee-haw."

"We have one more major decision—where do you want to go for our honeymoon? I was thinking Paris."

"I want somewhere quiet, where I can just gel. How about St. John?"

Ty began laughing.

I joined in, cackling until my sides hurt. We laughed all the way across the bridge and didn't stop until the sprawling resort appeared in the distance.

"Now what?" I asked when I could talk again.

Ty touched my hand. "We'll figure it out."

As our hilarity faded away, I felt a twinge of guilt. How could I be laughing with Mo so recently dead? *Because life goes on,* I told myself. *Because one event has nothing to do with the other. Because I could feel Mo laughing with me.*

• • •

The Wentworth event planner, Sarah Collins, met us in the lobby. She was effervescent.

Her smile was bright and constant. She chatted about everything with ease in one long run-on sentence.

"Follow me . . . I checked availability, and we have one suite available the days you're looking for . . . I'll take you through the lobby so you can have the full experience. I'm so glad it worked out that I could meet you today . . . Did you notice the grounds? Don't you love autumn in New England? The colors . . . although I love lobster and steamers . . . I was just thinking that I'm in the mood for some . . . the chef here does a wonderful thing with steamers . . . his secret is garlic and vermouth. So here we are!"

The hotel had been restored to its former glory, and it truly was spectacular. High ceilings with plenty of gilt, huge crystal chandeliers, and cushy rugs. The Eastern Turret Flag Officer's Suite had a double shower, a whirlpool tub, and a fireplace in case the nights got chilly.

We booked it for three nights, starting on our wedding day, Thursday the twenty-first.

"It's only six thirty," I said. "How about dropping me at home so I can pick up my car? If you don't mind doing a grocery run, I can do a last-minute check at the office. I should be home by seven fifteen or so."

"Why don't I just drop you at work and pick you up after I'm done shopping?" Ty asked.

"Even better!"

"Any chance you'll make grilled chicken, with your mom's special barbecue sauce?"

The sauce was dark and rich, tangy, and sweet, and spicy hot.

"That'll work if you don't mind a late dinner. I have some of the sauce stashed in the freezer. The chicken only needs half an hour to marinate, then boom, it's on the grill."

He said he'd get us a nibble as a starter and dropped me at Prescott's front door.

Everyone had left for the day, and the building was dark, except for the night-lights, low-wattage ceiling lamps inside and harsh white lighting aimed at the front door and loading dock.

I stepped into the office, entered the code to turn off the alarm, and pushed open the heavy door to the warehouse. Motion sensors activated a few overhead lights, throwing eerie shadows along the cement floor and shelving. It wasn't bright enough to see much detail, but it was more than adequate to find your way to wall switches for additional lighting if you wanted.

Upstairs, I checked my email. Wes had sent instructions for completing his justice-of-the-peace reference. I agreed with Maggie that Wes would be terrific at taking depositions. The directions said it would take eight to ten weeks for a decision. I did the math. Wes would hear right around Thanksgiving. I was certain he'd be approved, which meant there'd be something else to be thankful for this year. I completed the form and wrote two paragraphs in the comments section stating that I'd known Wes for a dozen years and that he was detail-oriented, hardworking, and ethical. I sent him a copy and submitted the form.

I'd hoped to find a good-news email from Fred telling me he'd tracked another one of the 1930 Martin guitars, but he hadn't written anything. There was nothing from Sasha about Mo's print, either. No one knew better than I did that appraisals took however long they took, and that there was no way to rush the process, but that didn't mean I had to like it. I checked my voice mail. Gertie Joan hadn't called back from Mississippi. Sometimes no news represented good news. Nothing bad had happened, or a bad situation hadn't gotten worse. This was not one of those times. I swiveled to face my window, suppressing my impatience. The sky shone with a soft pink blush as the sun sank below the trees and the autumn-ripe foliage trembled and glimmered in the breeze. As I sat there, twilight faded to dusk.

I brought up the notes I'd scribbled for Mo's eulogy and typed my remarks like a script. I read it to myself, then read it aloud, making eye contact with Mo's print as if it represented the congregation, tweaking it both times. I read it aloud again. It was good. I printed it and turned off my computer. Positioning Mo's woodblock print in clear sight of my desk had served its purpose, helping me connect with her. I was ready to deliver my eulogy, which meant the print could go back to the safe. I switched off my desk lamp, but there was enough light filtering in from the outside lamps and the warehouse night-lights for me to unearth a protective cover, essentially an acid-free, oversized padded envelope, from the supply closet behind my desk and make my way to the easel. I found the gloves I'd placed behind the print, put them on, slipped the print into the envelope, and removed the gloves.

I was three steps from the exit when a close-by clunk, metal on metal, made me jump and spin around. It was loud, too loud to be from the street, the sound floating in the air. I tiptoed to the outside wall, staying clear of the window, and listened carefully. With the window closed and the ventilation system humming, I barely heard the evening sounds, and no traffic, yet I was certain I hadn't imagined the grating thump.

I sidestepped to the left of the window and peered into the night. Bright white light emanating from the rear, where the loading dock was located, illuminated a slice of parking lot on my side of the building. Between that and the rising moon, I was able to see an acorn skitter across the asphalt and a few leaves sweep by, but nothing else. I edged forward to peek the other way, but it was so dark I couldn't even make out shapes. A truck rolling by on Ellerton had hit a rock or a branch, and the cargo, pipes, maybe, crashed into one another. That was as logical a conclusion as any.

I was halfway across the room when the lights flickered, then went out.

"Whoa!"

I was standing in total darkness. I waited for the generator to kick in. One Mississippi, two Mississippi. Five seconds. Ten. Twenty. Thirty. It never took longer than half a minute for the generator to spring into action.

Another metallic clank, this one louder, followed by a sharp, metallic grinding, a sustained metal-on-metal rasping. *A metal ladder.* Someone had perched a ladder against the wall leading to my office. They'd cut the electricity and sabotaged the generator.

It wasn't even seven o'clock. *Why would someone break in so early?*

Scuffing, the sound heavy boots make on metal.

Think.

I could probably make it downstairs before they got in, but then what? When the electricity went off, the doors to the high-end auction venue, tag sale room, loading dock, front office, and safe latched automatically, a fail-safe redundancy. The good news was that the alarm company would be automatically notified. A real person would contact me via office phone and cell within a minute, hoping to hear our safe word. We'd have a good chuckle at the random power outage. If I didn't pick up or they didn't hear the word, they'd alert the police that someone was burglarizing Prescott's, or that we were otherwise under attack.

Another sound, this one more a clomp than a scuff. The intruder was closing in.

The phone rang. It went immediately to voice mail, our night message. My cell would vibrate momentarily. It did so, and a soft light emanated from my tote bag, resting on my desk.

I needed to do something. Go downstairs or stay. Hide or fight. With the doors locked, if I went downstairs, I'd be trapped, a sitting duck. I owned a gun, a Browning 9 mm pistol, and I was a good shot, but it was at home, in my bedside table, so it did me no good here.

Still holding the print, I scooted across the room, grasped my tote bag, dropped to my knees, and crawled under my desk. I positioned the covered print against the modesty panel, centering it so it blocked the view under part of the middle section. If the intruder looked down, he'd see what appeared to be a to-the-floor modesty panel with tapered openings on the sides, not a woman's foot. I felt around in my bag for my phone, saw I had voice mail from the alarm company, and texted 9-1-1: *Break in @ Prescott's. My office. Help.*

Glass shattered, and the thunderous roar was so loud I ducked as if the fusillade were directly overhead. It took all my self-control not to shriek.

My phone! If it vibrated again, the intruder might hear it. I could turn it off, but I might need it. I tapped twice to stop the vibrating. Knowing that the screen would still illuminate, I poked it down to the bottom of my tote bag. I pulled my knees to my chin. My heart battered my ribs. My mouth was arid, and I kept swallowing to fight the urge to cough.

More glass broke, tinkling this time. I pictured little pieces falling to the floor, landing on top of one another.

I opened my eyes and took a breath.

It was happening, and it was happening *now.*

White light shone below the parts of the modesty panel that remained open. A flashlight. More crackling of glass, followed by a heavy thud. The intruder had stepped or fallen over the sill and landed hard. Footsteps crackled until they were at the bathroom door. I scrunched in closer to the modesty panel, trying to make myself invisible, terrified that as the person moved around the light would fall on me.

I peeked.

Someone tall, a man, I guessed, dressed all in black, wearing a ski mask and gloves, stood at the threshold to the bathroom, observing. He stepped back and aimed his light at the open door that led to the spiral staircase, pausing for a moment, perhaps to listen. He walked past the seating area to the far end of the office.

"What the—?" he muttered.

I didn't recognize the voice, but who could from a two-word whisper? I was still pretty sure it was a man, but it could have been a woman with a deep voice.

Wood from my rooster-collection display case cracked. Something tumbled to the ground, porcelain or glass, and shattered. Tears spilled onto my cheeks, and I bit my bottom lip to keep myself from crying out. My rooster collection had started as my mother's rooster collection. If he'd broken one of my mother's roosters, I'd kill him. I'd hunt him down and kill him. I sat hunched over, weak and feckless, weeping silently into my thighs. I told myself to stop crying, to toughen up, to think. I used the sides of my hands to wipe away my tears.

A siren's squeal broke into my futile thoughts. Finally, the cavalry was on its way.

The air grew still, then loud again as the intruder bolted across the shards of glass to the window, an oscillating stream of light marking his path. A moment later, the light went out. I heard his feet hit the ladder, followed by his pounding retreat. Ten seconds later, there was one last cacophony of metal crashing into metal and dragging along asphalt, then utter silence.

I held my breath and listened.

Within seconds, my brain registered the chirr of katydids and crickets, and I exhaled. I didn't move. I didn't trust that it was over. A brisk wind chilled me, but still I didn't move.

Cal, whose hobby was rock climbing, had come for the print. It had to be Cal. Nora, his lover, told him the print was in my office, and he came for it. Or Trish mentioned to Lydia. Maybe it was Trish herself. She knew it was on display, too. Trish was tall for a woman, a world-class athlete. Even in her six-ties, she'd easily be able to climb a ladder and hop a windowsill. But she had no reason to steal the print. Steve did. Steve, who was, according to Lydia, always short of money. He was an athlete, too. He'd seen it just the other day.

I scrambled out from under the desk and stood with my back to the wall, clutching the print to my chest. The darkness was deep and frightening, and there was nothing I could do but wait.

CHAPTER EIGHTEEN

I t looks like a branch fell on a wire," Ellis said, "knocking out the electricity."

"My generator didn't work."

"Someone cut the connection."

We sat on stools on the landing outside my office. The techs had been inside for about twenty minutes. I was hungry and tired and irritable.

"You're saying this was deliberate sabotage?" I asked.

"Yes."

"So the loss of power was a coincidence? Doesn't that seem hard to believe?"

"Not necessarily. Think it through. How long was the intruder inside?"

"It's hard to say. It seemed to last forever, but it was probably only two or three minutes."

"Which means he didn't need the electricity to go off. Our normal reaction time to a call from your security company would be seven to eight minutes. Still, it's a question worth asking, because while the electricity zapping out probably was just a lucky break for him, it did delay our reaction time by about an additional five minutes. The tree branch was lying in the middle of the road, tangled in the downed wires."

"How did you get past it?"

"The guys from your security company were ahead of us, and I followed their lead. We left our vehicles on the side of the road and jogged in. What are the chances that it was an inside job?"

"Zero."

"Your loyalty to your staff is admirable, Josie, but you know better than that. More than ninety percent of art heists are perpetrated by someone who has the key or code or knows his way around the security system."

"No one used a key or security code."

"Still . . . with stats like this, I have to ask."

"My staff is not involved."

"Who, then?"

"Someone after Mo's print."

"Cal."

"That's my guess."

"So you think he's around."

"Don't you?"

Ellis didn't answer right away.

I skewed around to see inside my office. Ty and Eric stood in front of the broken window. Ty held a sheet of plywood in place while Eric pounded nails. Gretchen leaned against my desk watching them work.

Ellis's phone rang, and he took the call. His end was mostly grunts.

Gretchen was number two on the alarm company call list. When I hadn't responded to their calls and texts, they'd called her, and she whipped into action, activating our emergency plan with calm confidence. She called Ty and Ellis to let them know I wasn't responding. She called Sasha, Fred, Eric, and Cara to tell them to stand by for further instructions. She drove to the office to ensure the security company and police were on scene, and she sent me a text saying: *I'm here.*

During the time that Ellis had been consulting with the forensic team, Eric had called Floyd, our glazier. He left a message, and Floyd had called back, promising to be here by nine in the morning to replace the glass in the window and in my display cabinet. Eric assured me he could do the carpentry repairs himself, that the display cabinet hadn't splintered, that only one side panel had broken.

I'd arranged with Russ, our security company's account manager, to station security officers in the parking lot all night, some sitting in cars, others walking the perimeter. I doubted such vigilance was needed, but I'd sleep better knowing the place was secure. He'd already sent over the security camera footage. No one was visible from any of the camera angles. We'd placed cameras to take in all outside access doors and the loading dock, but nothing else. Rocky Point was not a high-crime zone.

My phone vibrated. It was a text from Zoë. She wrote: *Are you ok? Hurry home. Soup is simmering.* I texted back: *I accept!*

I closed my eyes and let a picture of the outside of my building and the surrounding area come into my consciousness.

The generator was housed in a metal shed positioned on a concrete slab on the side of the building farthest from the Congregational church. We'd laid asphalt from the back parking lot to a six-foot-high fieldstone wall that separated the entry to the tag sale from the back. On the rear side of the wall, the unadorned blacktop allowed us access to the shed. On the front side, a flagstone path led from the front parking lot to the tag sale venue door. I'd had the wall built for aesthetic reasons, not for security. An unintended consequence was that anyone working on the generator wouldn't be seen from the front. It simply hadn't occurred to me that someone might sabotage the generator or break into my mezzanine-level office.

A muscle on the side of my neck twitched, and when I realized I was clenching my teeth, I opened my mouth wide. My jaw would be sore in the morning. The intruder had planned the attack carefully. I'd been scared. Now I was angry, but there was no one to be angry at. The best antidote to impotent rage was action. I emailed Gretchen:

This may be a case of closing the barn door after the horse escapes, but let's get bids on adding additional security cameras so we see everything, a 360 view of the building, parking lot, and grounds.

"Maybe," Ellis said, tapping the END CALL button.

I spun back to face him. "Maybe what?"

"You asked if I thought Cal was around. Maybe. How could he have known that the print was in plain sight?"

"Trish might have mentioned it to Lydia. Lydia might have told him."

"You think Lydia is in touch with Cal?"

"I think it's possible. She loves him."

"She insists she hasn't heard from him since the morning of the day Mo was killed."

"Either she's telling the truth or she's lying to protect him. If she's in touch with him, I doubt she would have fessed up. She probably thinks he's being railroaded."

"How else could he have found out?"

"Nora Burke."

"How is she involved?"

"I hate to gossip."

"Telling the truth to a police officer during an investigation isn't gossip."

"I told you about the Colonial Twist. Did you talk to Chester about Cal?"

"Yes."

"Did Nora's name come up?"

"Come on, Josie. Tell me what you know."

"You're right. Nora went to the Colonial Club with Cal. Chester got the vibe that they were more than mere friends. Nora is married." I gave him her address.

"Who else besides your full-time staff, Nora, and Trish knew the print was on display in your office?"

"Steve." I explained the circumstances of his visit.

"How about regular people? You know, the folks you do business with on a daily basis who might have been in your office while the print was in plain sight."

"Like who?"

"Your accountant."

"No."

"Your lawyer?"

"No. Just Davy, our guitar expert. No one else."

"Ty?"

My hackles rose. "No."

"A salesman."

"No."

"A customer."

"No."

"Maybe you want new hardwood and Eric brought up the guy to measure the space."

"No."

"Okay." He stood up and shook out his pant leg. "I have enough for now. Let's plan on talking in the morning."

"I'll be here around eight thirty, or earlier."

Ellis walked into the office to talk to the last remaining crime scene tech. I followed along. Russ leaned against the back wall, ready to escort Ellis and the tech out. No one, not even a police chief conducting an official investigation, was allowed in the warehouse unescorted. I stood just inside the door watching as Ty and Eric finished boarding up the window.

Ty stepped back to assess Eric's handiwork. "Good job, Eric."

Eric flushed, embarrassed at the praise. "It's okay, I guess."

"Thank you—all of you," I said, walking closer.

Gretchen turned at my voice. Her eyes radiated concern. "Are you all right?"

I patted her arm. "I'm fine. Thanks for taking care of everything."

I picked my way to the display case at the end of the room. The damage wasn't as severe as I'd feared. The wood was as Eric described, and only two panes of glass in the display case had shattered. The only rooster that had been broken was a no-name vintage cartoony-looking one I'd bought a year earlier because I'd thought it was cute, but I had no emotional attachment to it. A wooden one had also fallen to the ground, but it wasn't even chipped or cracked.

I squatted and reached into the back of the bottom shelf where I secreted the most valuable of the roosters—my mother's favorites. Her first acquisition, a yellow-and-red ceramic beauty, was among my most cherished possessions. I stroked the rooster's breast and felt my mother's love.

I eased it back into place, then stood and turned around. Ellis and the tech were talking in a low voice. Eric was gathering up his tools. Ty nodded at something Gretchen said. Fatigue weighed down on me. The crisis had passed, and I'd coped well, as always. Gretchen said something to me about covering for me in the morning, and I nodded. People left. After placing Mo's print in the walk-in safe, which Gretchen had offered to do, but which I insisted on doing myself, Ty and I left, too.

Russ semisaluted as we drove toward the exit. I nodded, acknowledging the gesture. I looked to the left, the fast way home. The road was blocked. The utility people didn't seem to have made much progress. Fluorescent orange wooden horses blocked the road. SOUTHERN NEW HAMPSHIRE ELECTRIC was stenciled on the crossbeams in navy blue. Two utility vans sat across the road. Spotlights mounted on the vans' roofs illuminated the road like day. A police cruiser, its rooftop red light spinning, blocked the other side. Ellis's SUV sat nearby. A long, thin, knobby branch lay in the center of the road amid downed wires. The limb was silky gray and spotted with moss. Two men wearing company-branded windbreakers and hard hats stood on the leaf-covered shoulder talking with Ellis.

I dug around in my tote bag for my phone. "Stop for a sec."

He did so, and I jumped out. I walked in front of the SUV and shot a video, panning slowly left to right. I touched the STOP button, then took a few still photos of the men, the vehicles, and the log. I tapped through the options to upload the video and photos to the cloud.

"How come?" Ty asked when I was back in the car.

"Posterity. Trust no one. My dad was a skeptical man, and he taught me well."

"What caught your eye?"

"Ellis said he had to jog through the woods because the branch was in the road, tangled in downed wires. That was two hours ago."

"And you wonder why it's still there."

Ty pulled out, turning right, the long way around.

I closed my eyes and leaned back. I was exhausted, to-my-bones weary.

As soon as we got home, I put on my bathing suit, ready for food, drink, and a long soak in my newly installed hot tub. As I shrugged into my heavy red cotton to-the-ankle bathrobe, a cover-up selected more for warmth than glamour, Wes called. I let it go to voice mail. He didn't leave a message. Instead he texted: *Your break-in is tomorrow's lead. Call me. Or text answers: Is it connected to Mo's murder? Was your security sloppy? Any comments?*

I went downstairs and poured myself a martini from the shaker in the fridge, took a sip, and texted back: *I'm fine, thanks. No, my security wasn't sloppy. You may quote me as follows: "No one was hurt. Nothing was stolen. The police and my alarm company responded within minutes, and I'm very grateful."*

He called again, almost immediately, and this time he did leave a message.

"Josie," he said, his tone both aggrieved and impatient, "you didn't respond to my question about a possible connection to Mo's murder. I have a source saying the intruder never left your office, that he had expected Mo's woodblock print to be there. Is that true? And what about your generator? Why didn't it start up when the electricity went off? Also, my source says that the thief didn't tape the window when he broke it, so it shattered, and there was glass everywhere. Confirm it for me, okay? Broken glass everywhere—I love it! That's a great image! Send me a photo!"

Gretchen, I thought. Eric would never talk to a reporter. He was too shy and too scared of making a mistake. Gretchen was effusive and chatty by nature. It wouldn't occur to her to withhold facts.

I texted back: *I have no reason to think Mo's print was involved, and if you write that there is a connection, you're likely to have to print a retraction. Re: generator—no comment. I can confirm that there was glass everywhere. No photos available.*

An hour later, after I'd finished my martini and decimated a bowl of Zoë's minestrone soup and a gooey grilled cheese sandwich, I was snuggling up to Ty in the hot tub. I rested my head against his chest, and as the steamy water bubbled against my back and neck, I felt myself relax for the first time since I'd heard that metallic scraping hours and hours ago.

CHAPTER NINETEEN

I woke before the alarm went off, momentarily confused about where I was. I sat up, clenching the sheet to my chin. The green luminous dial on the old-style alarm clock next to my bed, a relic from my childhood, read 5:52. I heard water running downstairs. Ty was making coffee.

"Hey," I said as I stepped into the kitchen.

"Good morning, sunshine! I'm going to make you banana pancakes."

"You're a man for the ages. Want to marry me?"

"Too late. The girl of my dreams has already got me latched down."

I poured us glasses of orange juice and slid onto the bench on the window side of my farm-style kitchen table. I fluffed up two of the orange-and-blue-plaid pillows and leaned back into the corner, stretching out my legs.

Ty began pulling ingredients from the cupboard. "How are you feeling?"

Billowy clouds floated in a cerulean sky. I touched the window. The glass was cold. September mornings often started with a shuddering chill.

"Angry. Frustrated. Confused."

"Because of the break-in?"

"Did Cal really think we wouldn't figure out that he was behind the theft? He must think I'm a fool."

"He doesn't think you're a fool. He thinks you're naïve and gullible."

"Thanks."

Ty smiled as he delivered a cup of coffee.

"What a man."

"Just because I poured you a cup of coffee? Talk about a cheap date."

"Does Cal think Chester is naïve and gullible, too? That he could skip out on a six-figure debt and Chester would simply let it go?"

"Maybe he still plans to pay. Didn't you tell me that Chester let him settle his losses over time before?"

"Only because Cal had a viable plan to sell Japanese woodblock prints."

"From what I can tell, Cal's a narcissist, and narcissists have seriously inflated ideas of their own capabilities and importance."

A bantering comment died on my lips as a stunning realization startled me into silence. Chester said Cal sold Japanese prints. Plural. I needed to ask Anita about all sales of prints from *One Hundred Famous Views of Edo*, not only *Meguro Drum Bridge and Sunset Hill*. If I was right, I might be able to find a shop or gallery offering one in the same stellar condition as Mo's and learn the source. If it was Cal, they might have contact information that would lead us to him, especially if they were repeat customers. It was also possible I could find his ad. He might even have one running now. If so, I could respond to it, pretending to be a collector. The clock mounted above the refrigerator read 6:10. I had nearly four hours to wait before my appointment with Anita.

"How long until pancakes?" I asked.

"About an hour, probably. The batter has to rest."

"I'm going to do some research."

I hurried into my study and brought up the *Seacoast Star*'s website. Wes's article read:

Break-in at Prescott's
Police Investigate a Possible Connection
to Mo Shannon's Murder

An unknown intruder shattered Prescott's Antiques & Auctions' mezzanine-level office window at 7:02 p.m. yesterday, according to Russ Barstow, account manager at King Security Corporation (KSC). Josie Prescott, Prescott's owner, was in her private office at the time, but managed to avoid detection. "No one was hurt," Ms. Prescott stated. "Nothing was stolen. The police and my security company responded within minutes." A Prescott's staff member who saw the office after the break-in described it as horrific. "There was glass everywhere."

Southern New Hampshire Electric reports that a downed wire on Ellerton Street, which runs directly in front of Prescott's, caused a widespread loss of electricity, starting at 6:53 p.m. Prescott's was among the nearly 1,000 users who lost service. All service was restored by midnight. When asked why Prescott's generator didn't work, both Prescott and Barstow refused to comment.

A Japanese woodblock print by the celebrated artist Utagawa Hiroshige, titled *Meguro Drum Bridge and Sunset Hill*, which had been owned by murder victim Mo Shannon, was on display in Josie Prescott's private office prior to the break-in. A police source has confirmed that the print, which is valued at more than $25,000, is safe and undamaged.

The police don't know whether the intruder was after that print in particular, but they are working on the assumption that there might be a connection between Mo Shannon's murder and the break-in. "We're pursuing multiple lines of investigation," Rocky Point Police Chief Ellis Hunter said. "It's premature to announce a connection that might not exist."

Anyone with information about Mo Shannon's murder, the downed wire, the nonworking generator, or the break-in at Prescott's Antiques & Auctions is asked to call the police at 603–555–3900.

I emailed my entire staff:

Hi All,

If you've seen today's *Seacoast Star,* you know that Wes is quoting someone on our staff. If you're Wes's source, please let this be the last time you speak to him on or off the record. Please don't speak about Prescott's business to him, or to any reporter—or anyone—without talking to me first. No harm has been done here, but I want us all to remain tight-lipped. Remember the old navy adage: Loose lips sink ships.

Thanks,

Josie

I shut my eyes for a moment. Running a business was so complicated. I shook off the momentary apprehension that threatened to distract me, opened my eyes, and got back to work.

I Googled "Buy original 100 Famous Views of Edo print" and got more than 300,000 hits. I went through the first three pages of listings. Despite my search criterion specifying an "original," every one was a repro.

I visited the three largest art auction sites but found no ads for original Hiroshige prints.

I navigated my way to all ten of *Antiques Insights'* most recent "Best of Asian Art" dealers, auction houses, and galleries. I thought I was onto something when I read the promotional copy from a gallery in Zurich offering a near-perfect print, but it was a false alarm. Their "near-perfect" wasn't even close to the vibrant colors found in Mo's print.

I slapped my chair arm, frustrated.

Dealer-to-dealer sales were, universally, the largest component of the antiques market, yet evidently, Cal hadn't gone in that direction. Why not? Probably because he figured he had a better chance of pulling the wool over an amateur collector's eyes than he would a professional dealer, and he wouldn't have to offer any discounts. That made sense.

If I wanted to sell an original Hiroshige for top dollar, I'd advertise on *Antiques Insights'* website. It was expensive, but it was worth it. I opened their search box and asked for an original Hiroshige print. Nothing was available.

I frowned at my monitor, racking my brain for additional alternatives.

It was possible, although unlikely, since I doubted Cal wanted the world to know about his side business, that he had created a website to sell prints directly to consumers. I typed his name into Google. All the listings were connected to his faculty page at Hitchens and his staff listing at the museum. He did, in fact, have a website, but it was simply a shell, a profile of him and a list of his published writing, with links to Hitchens and the museum.

I was missing something. I leaned back and shut my eyes, thinking.

Could Cal have promoted the offering to collectors of Japanese prints, maybe by sending an email to the Langdon Art Museum's house list? Since he was the assistant director, it was reasonable to assume he had access to that list.

I could call the museum director on Monday or even email him now.

Lots of people checked their work emails over the weekend. I decided to hold off. I couldn't think of a way to pose the question without risking damaging Cal's reputation, and no way would I do that on spec. Maybe I wouldn't have to wait, though. Ellis might know the answer now. I emailed him and asked if in the police search of Cal's various email accounts they found any record of a sale of a Japanese woodblock print, or a negotiation, or even an inquiry. I also asked if they'd checked with the museum about whether Cal had sent a mailing to its list offering a print for sale.

I stared at my monitor, thinking. Had Chester used the plural "prints" as a figure of speech or a slip of the tongue? Maybe the sale to Mo had been Cal's one and only deal. No. Chester was clear—Cal had spoken about avoiding flooding the market, which meant Cal had more than one print to sell. If I were Cal, how would I go about selling one or more additional prints without making waves, while still maximizing my take?

I remembered Mo's exhilaration at acquiring her print. If a year later Cal approached her saying he'd found another print from the *One Hundred Famous Views of Edo* series, she would have snapped it up. Cal didn't need to advertise if he could go back to satisfied customers.

Assuming he had some, how could I locate them?

I searched *Antiques Insights'* archives and found that fourteen prints from the *One Hundred Famous Views of Edo* series had sold during the last year. I scrolled through the list. Only two were described as originals in perfect condition. *New Fuji Meguro,* number 24, sold in January. The seller was a California gallery. The buyer, who paid $22,750, lived in New Mexico. The second one, *Benten Shrine, Inokashira Pond*, number 87, sold in late June. Both the seller's and buyer's names had been redacted. Typically, galleries and antiques dealers wanted their names to show—it was good for business. Individual sellers and collectors usually did not. Sometimes they were trying to avoid the tax man. Other times they didn't want to alert thieves to where they could find valuable art. The sales price was listed at $24,000.

I had a contact at *Antiques Insights,* Cormac McKenna, known as Mac, who could look up the redacted information, and if I came up with a good enough story, he might pass along the name, but he wouldn't be at work on a Saturday. Still, it couldn't do any harm to email him. Mac might be one of those people who stayed connected to his work email 24/7.

I drafted a subject line that I hoped would get my email read right away:

Urgent. "Benten Shrine, Inokashira Pond," #87

For the text, I wrote:

Hi Mac,
I'm sorry to bother you on the weekend, but I'm investigating a potential fraud case. It's urgent that I know who sold the print "Benten Shrine, Inokashira Pond," #87 listed in your archives.
Thank you,
Josie

I reread it, my finger hovering over the SEND button, fretting that Mac would hesitate to respond to what might be a police matter. Then I realized I had no reason to think he would shy away from doing the right thing any more than I would, and sent the email on its way.

I opened a new document and began writing my own ad. After several false starts, I ended up with *Wanted: Any original print from Utagawa Hiroshige's "100 Famous Views of Edo." Must be original in perfect condition. Will pay top dollar.* I created a new Gmail account, using "HiroshigeFan" and some numbers as my name. I also opened a new *Antiques Insights* account. Before posting my ad, though, I needed a phone.

I called Shelley, in New York City.

"'lo."

"Shelley? It's Josie."

"God, Joz. What time is it?"

I glanced at my monitor. It read 6:50. "Oh, Shelley, it's ten to seven. I'm *so* sorry."

"What day is it?"

"Saturday."

"Have you gone insane?"

"I need a favor. I didn't even look at the clock."

"You've got to get out of New Hampshire, Josie. It's not healthy to be up this early."

I laughed. "Early birds catch worms, Shelley. That's me, an early bird."

She groaned. "Go away, Josie. You just called me a worm. I was out dancing until four. Call again at noon. Or better yet, one."

"That's definitely something I miss about New York. Dancing till four. Where'd you go?"

"Same old, same old. We started at the Flamingo, then went to the Roadhouse."

"Big band, then country. You've got to come up here sometime, Shelley. We have a fabulous country-dancing joint, twice as big as the Roadhouse. The Diamond Cowboy."

"You're such a card. Can I go now?"

"It's urgent. I need a phone. A throwaway with a New York City area code. I'm hoping you'll buy it for me and send it overnight. Use the post office—they deliver on Sundays."

"Okay. Good night."

"The post office closes at one. I'll send you a text to remind you."

"Come for brunch. You can buy it yourself."

"I wish I could. You come for brunch. You can bring the phone with you."

She laughed and hung up.

Shelley was a peach, and I missed her. I sent the text summarizing my request, adding that our next brunch was on me, then, with my ad on hold until I had the phone number, I thought about what I should do next. I might not be able to post my ad, but I could prepare for my talk with Anita.

I used the photo of Cal I'd found on the Hitchens University faculty page and got one of Nora from her church newsletter. I cropped the photo so only Nora showed. Just for good measure, I decided to include a photo of Lydia, too. Her professional headshot from the Technology Transfer Department's Web page was flattering. She looked self-assured and determined, not harsh or ruthless. I downloaded all three images to my phone.

Mac emailed back. He wrote:

Hi Josie,

Good to hear from you.

As you know, we take all cases of fraud extremely seriously and we work hard to ensure that people buying from our site can do so without concern. We vet every ad. In this case, the description of the print, the seller's guarantee, and the price were all in line. What information do you have and what do you hope to learn? Maybe it would be easier if we spoke. 917.555.8762. Now is good for me if it's good for you.

Regards,

Mac

I dialed his number.

"Thanks so much, Mac, for making yourself available on a Saturday—and so early."

"When you have a two-year-old, this is late."

"I didn't know you had a child. That's wonderful! Boy or girl?"

"A boy. Sam. Sam the Man. So . . . Josie . . . what are you saying about this print?"

"I need to learn who sold it. I think it might be a gambler who sells repros as originals to pay down his debt."

"Are the police involved?"

"Yes, but they don't know I've contacted you."

"Will they have to?"

"No. They may need to contact *Antiques Insights,* but no one will know you and I spoke."

"Thanks. If the situation warrants contacting the seller or the buyer about the potential fraud, will you let us do that?"

"Yes . . . with the same caveat. I can't speak for the police."

"That's fair. The seller was Pat Durand." He read off a Gmail address. The phone number started with a 207 area code, Maine. "The buyer is Michelle Michaels." Mac gave me her contact information, an AOL email account and a Kansas City address.

I thanked him again and promised to keep him posted.

I reviewed my options: tell Ellis about Michelle Michaels and Pat Durand, ask Mac to get Michelle to contact me, or ask Wes to check them both out. There was no choice, not really. Ellis had to know.

I emailed Ellis with an update, keeping Mac out of it, and asked him to let me know what he learned.

There was nothing else I could do until Branson Wills opened at ten.

I was halfway out of my chair when I realized I hadn't watched the video I'd shot last night. I opened the file and hit PLAY.

"Oh, wow," I whispered.

I raised my eyes from the screen and stared unseeingly into the woods. I watched the video a second time, horrified at what I was seeing.

After a moment, I brought up the Home Depot's website.

A minute later, my questions answered, I texted Ellis: *Call me. Urgent.*

CHAPTER TWENTY

llis called me two minutes later.

"Thanks for calling so quickly, Ellis. Can you meet for a minute?"

"I'm on the porch now."

"I'll be right there."

I stuck my head into the kitchen. "I'm going to talk to Ellis. I won't be long."

Ty held up the coffeepot. "Want a refill?"

"Good idea."

Steaming mug in hand, I slipped on a sweater coat and walked across the driveway to Zoë's porch. Hazy mist rose from the fields, and dew glimmered on the white aster and late-blooming purple flowering raspberries.

Ellis was half-sitting on the railing drinking coffee from a thermos.

"Thanks for meeting me so quickly," I said. "What did the utility people tell you happened last night?"

"A branch took the wires down. They had to wait for a supervisor to assess the conditions before they could begin repairs. Power was fully restored by midnight."

"Did you look at that branch? I mean really look at it?"

"It's about ten feet long, slender, with smaller branches and twigs running along the whole length of it."

"But no leaves. That branch was covered with moss. It didn't break off a tree—it's been lying on the forest floor for months, probably years. Have they thrown it away yet? It might help prove that someone tampered with the power lines."

"We've got it."

"You knew?"

"I wouldn't say I knew. I'd say we're thorough. Keep in mind, it might be nothing more than some kids who thought it would be fun to create a blackout."

"I think the same person who broke into my place took down the wires."

"Pretty risky."

"Not so much if you wear rubber gloves and stand ten feet away."

"Downed wires can ricochet."

"I don't know whether he got lucky or what; I just know he did it."

"Who's he?"

"Probably Cal."

"Wouldn't he worry about someone driving by and catching him in the act?"

"There's not much traffic at night. This was a deliberate act, Ellis. Someone found the branch and whacked at the wires until they fell. He had a clear plan. First, he disconnected my generator. Second, he knocked down the wires. Third, he broke into my office."

"Fourth, he got away. How?"

"The scraping sounds I heard were from a telescopic ladder being extended. He had to have a ladder, and this model is easy to carry. You can buy one that weighs less than forty pounds at the Home Depot for less than two hundred dollars. He parked at the Congregational church and used the trees as cover. It's only about a hundred yards from my building to the tree line, then a quarter mile on an easy-to-follow path. Figure a minute to collapse the ladder. If it were me, I'd bring a sturdy backpack to carry it—much less unwieldy and much quieter. Add a minute to pack it up and swing it into place. Thirty seconds to pass the tree line, less if he sprints, and another five minutes to reach the church, less if he jogs. Soup to nuts, it wouldn't have taken him longer than seven or eight minutes once he hit the parking lot. As long as he was in the woods, he was safe. It was an audacious and clever plan."

"What happened after he got to the church?"

"He tossed the ladder in his trunk or in the backseat and off he went. Oh! I don't know if the church has security cameras. Do you?"

"Do you think he had a partner?" Ellis asked, ignoring my question.

"No. He didn't need one, not with the generator out of commission. Remember, he thought he had the whole building to himself."

"Could it be a woman?" Ellis asked.

"Sure. I carry things that weigh more than that all the time. I bet you're examining the branch for touch DNA."

"Which I doubt we'll find."

"How about bits of rubber from the gloves?"

"Unlikely, but possible."

"Examine my parking lot and the path—you'll find shards of glass. He walked on them. With all the rain we've had, there may be footprints."

"Good idea."

"You'll check the church for security cameras, too."

Ellis smiled and sat in one of a pair of Adirondack chairs. "Have a seat and tell me what else I'm going to do."

I laughed and sat down. I drank some coffee. "I suggested that you check Cal's emails for references to the Japanese prints."

"Already done. Our computer forensic team tells me no emails about Hiroshige or any Japanese woodblock print have been found on any of Cal's accounts or computers."

"Of course, if Cal used a different device and a new email address, we'd have no way of knowing what he's up to. Will you contact the director of the Langdon Museum and ask if Cal had access to their house list? Mailing the museum members might be a good way to drum up business."

"That's a smart idea. Why did you ask me to look into that buyer, Michelle Michaels?"

"The easiest way to sell another print would be to approach a satisfied customer. Presumably, she is one."

"How did you get her name?"

"I'm reviewing ads offering Japanese woodblock prints going back a year. I think Cal is using that name I wrote you about, Pat Durand."

"Thanks, Josie. I'll follow up."

"I'm going to place a 'Hiroshige print wanted' ad. I'll let you know if I get any nibbles from Pat Durand or anyone else."

"You'll let me know *before* you follow up."

I smiled. "Of course."

We sat in companionable silence for a few minutes. When my mug was empty, I told him good-bye and went home to eat pancakes.

Rocky Point Congregational Church's pastor, Ted Bauer, and I were pals. I frequently walked through the woods that separated our properties to stretch my legs and get some air. Ted was an avid gardener, and in nice weather, I often found him working in his rock garden. Ted's wife, Peg, a tag sale regular, was a nurse. Their routine had her dropping him off at the church en route to her job at Rocky Point Hospital. Her shift started at seven, so I wasn't surprised to see him kneeling on a gray foam pad beside a clutch of lavender phlox. He leaned back on his heels when he heard a vehicle turn into the parking lot, and when he saw it was me, he smiled and stood. Ted was about five-nine and stout, probably thirty to forty pounds overweight. His blond hair had long since turned gray.

"Don't tell me you're getting rid of that beautiful phlox."

"Perish the thought! I'm dividing and moving some of the clusters. Spreading the wealth, as it were."

I scanned the gutters, then turned to the light poles. "Ted, do you have any security cameras I'm not seeing?"

"No, why?"

"My place was broken into last night. I think there's a chance the thief used your parking lot."

Ted's brows drew close together, and he reached out a garden-gloved hand as if to touch me. "Is everyone all right?"

"Yes, thank you. And nothing was stolen."

"Is this related to the power outage?"

"I think so."

"So this was no casual break-in." His eyes emanated caring. "Is there anything I can do?"

I smiled. "No, thanks, Ted."

"We talk sometimes about installing cameras."

"It's hard to decide what's best."

"Please let me know if we can do something."

I thanked him again and walked to my car. By the time I was buckled in and ready to leave, Ted was already back in his garden, hard at work.

* * *

I sat at a worktable in the warehouse and talked to each of my key staff, one at a time, reassuring them that I was fine, that the break-in was an aberration, and that repairs would be completed shortly. I asked Eric and Gretchen to pass the news along to the part-timers.

Everyone reacted as expected: Sasha listened without comment, twirling her hair nervously; Fred got angry, wishing he could have a few minutes alone with the intruder as soon as he was caught; Eric was anxious, shuffling in place, while nibbling on his bottom lip; Cara was worried about everyone and everything, eager to help in whatever way she could; Gretchen was more concerned about my emotional well-being than the break-in per se.

Gretchen took two steps toward the front office, then stopped. After a moment, she marched back.

"It was me. Wes called me and asked so many questions, some of them so awful . . . you know . . . lurid. I had to stop him."

That sounded just like Wes. "Like what?"

Tears glistened on her long lashes. "He asked if any of us used your office for a little nooky when you aren't there. Isn't that horrible?"

Rage, which had fired up as soon as I heard the panes of glass break, and which had been simmering all night, began bubbling to a boil.

I forced myself to speak calmly. "That's unbelievable, actually. A new low, even for Wes."

"I was shocked, completely shocked. I told Wes no, of course not. Then he asked how I could be so certain." Gretchen raised her chin. "I know I should have ignored him, but I couldn't. I simply couldn't. I said maybe his wife expected to find him there with a sweet young thing and broke in to check."

I laughed, my anger dissipating in an instant. "Well done, Gretchen! What did he say to that?"

"He chuckled as if he'd just been razzing me and I'd landed a winner. After that he started asking questions about what was taken and who had keys and so on. I was so relieved he stopped trying to create a scandal, I said too much."

I stood up and patted her shoulder. "Thank you for telling me. It looks like there was no lasting harm done, and you've learned an important lesson: Don't take the bait. Not that I blame you—Wes is a champion baiter."

"Thank you for understanding. I promise nothing like this will ever happen again."

As soon as she was gone, I set off to the tag sale venue. I'd bought the nineteenth-century building, which had started life as a manufacturer of canvas products like sails and duffle bags, for its bones and location, but every inch had to be upgraded, from the electric and the plumbing to the foundation and the roof. I walked through the warehouse to the inside access door and stepped into a different world. I'd brought the tag sale venue up to code and expanded it, but I'd kept the nostalgic rustic feel. Our warehouse was modern and efficient, the auction venue was luxurious, and the tag sale venue exuded country charm.

After a quick walk-through to confirm that Eric had done his usual capable job setting up the displays, which, of course, he had, I met our newest part-timer, Melissa Sayers. Melissa was new to Rocky Point, the wife of a doctor who'd just accepted a job at Rocky Point Medical Center. She was tall and thin, somewhere around forty, with medium brown hair, cut short. She wore a maroon Prescott's polo shirt and khakis, as we all did on tag sale days. She had the residue of a deep tan and dark brown eyes.

Before leading me up to her, Eric whispered that she'd gotten tired of selling men's suits, which had been her last job, and loved antiques. She'd passed her background check with flying colors and seemed eager to learn. Today, she was scheduled to shadow Eric.

I loved that Eric and Gretchen had taken the initiative to hire her, and I hoped she worked out, as much for their sake as for mine.

Sasha was booting up a laptop in the Prescott's Instant Appraisal booth. I told her she could plan on me staffing it from noon to two, and left.

At nine fifty-seven, I turned into the Murphy's Interiors parking lot. When I reached the Branson Wills boutique, Anita was sitting at her desk, typing into her computer.

She greeted me warmly and invited me to sit.

I brought up Cal's photo and slid my phone across the desk to Anita. She swallowed, twice. Her recognition was apparent.

"You know him."

"Yes. He's a customer."

"This is Cal Lewis, the man I mentioned who sold the print to my friend, Mo. You said you didn't recognize that name. What name did he give you?"

"I'm sorry, Josie, but I'm just not comfortable talking about my customers."

"And I hope you know I feel the same. I'm not asking you to gossip. I never gossip. I hate gossip. This is part of an appraisal that I'm afraid might lead to an investigation into fraud."

"You suspect him of misrepresenting a print?"

"I'm afraid so. Did he buy a Hiroshige print?"

She didn't reply for several seconds. "I hate this."

"So do I. It's important, Anita. You know I wouldn't be asking if it wasn't."

She kept her eyes on my face, thinking it through. "He said his name was Pat Durand."

"Thank you." I took a notebook from my bag. "What did he buy, and when?"

She tapped into her computer. "He's purchased two twentieth-century Japanese woodblock print reproductions, both from *One Hundred Famous Views of Edo*. The first was sold on June nineteenth: *Benten Shrine, Inokashira Pond*, number eighty-seven. He bought the one you asked about, *Meguro Drum Bridge and Sunset Hill*, number one hundred eleven, on August twenty-third. He paid eighteen hundred fifty each time, cash."

"What's his address?"

Anita turned to her computer for a moment, then read off a Rocky Point post office box number, 156.

"His phone?"

"None given. I have an email address, though."

She called it out, the same Gmail address I got from Mac.

"I think Cal is ready to sell some more prints. He's gone into hiding, and I'm afraid he's deputized someone into helping him. Can you tell me when you last sold one of these prints?"

"Actually, a woman bought one yesterday, Hiroshige's *Flower Pavilion, Dango Slope, Sendagi*, number sixteen, also for cash, the same price, eighteen hundred and fifty dollars."

"Did she seem agitated?"

"Not so much agitated as . . . I don't know . . . unengaged. I asked her a bunch of normal questions, you know, was she trying to match a color scheme? Was she a fan of all Asian art? She didn't want to talk at all. She wasn't even aware that this portfolio encompassed four seasons, and when I told her, she didn't seem to care. She merely flipped through and picked one in what seemed a random fashion."

"What's her name?"

"I don't know. She didn't want to be on our mailing list."

I brought up Nora's photo on my phone and handed the unit to Anita. "Is this her?"

Anita shook her head. "No. I've never seen this woman before."

"Are you sure?" I asked, surprised. I'd been certain that Nora was Cal's co-conspirator. I swiped the screen to reach Lydia's photo and gave the phone back to Anita.

She stared at the image, then shook her head. "No. I don't recognize her, either."

"Thank you, Anita." I glanced at the ceiling. "Are there any security cameras?"

"Only in the back office. Murphy's isn't concerned about shoplifting. It's up to each of us to decide if we want to install a security system. Cameras are on my list."

"So there's no photograph of her."

"No."

"Can you describe her?"

"Not really. She wore a bulky coat, so I have no sense of her body shape. She wore a hat, black felt with a big brim."

"What color was her hair?"

"I'm sorry. I didn't notice."

"Eyes?"

She opened her palms. "I wish I could be more helpful. I was busy, and she was in a hurry. She was in and out of here in about two minutes. I just don't remember."

I thanked her again and started for the front, then paused. "Did I hear you right before—you bought an entire portfolio."

"Yes. A lovely set, probably from the 1930s. I've been selling them one at a time, mostly to decorators."

"Did you have the portfolio appraised?"

"No, it didn't seem worth it. You know it's more profitable to break the book."

I hated that some dealers embraced a policy of cutting art prints from bound editions, but I understood it. A nondescript nineteenth-century book in decent condition that included ten illustrations of anything from flowers to medical devices might sell for fifty dollars. If the dealer sold each of the prints individually, he might garner a hundred dollars each, netting a thousand.

"You're right, I do understand. The economics are hard to ignore. May I see the prints you have left?"

Anita swiveled toward an oak architectural cabinet, the kind used to store oversized drawings and blueprints. She opened the third drawer and flipped through some plastic-encased images, selecting half a dozen Hiroshige prints. She fanned them out on her desk facing me.

"I have more, but this is a representative sample."

The prints were the same size as Mo's, with the same distinct and spectacularly vibrant colors.

The third one grabbed me, number 76, *Bamboo yards, Kyōbashi Bridge*. A man standing on a wooden boat punted down a nearly deserted river. He was passing under a bridge. A dozen people walked overhead, none of them aware of him any more than he was aware of them. The blues were spectacular, ranging from a deep navy blue in the shadowy water under the bridge to cobalt glistening in the moonlit sky. Hiroshige's prints took my breath away. I looked up. Anita was watching me.

I smiled. "Hiroshige knocks me out."

Anita smiled back. "I could look at them forever. It's the storytelling."

"And the quiet."

"And the colors."

"And the detail."

"All that."

"What makes you think they're from the 1930s?" I asked.

"There were many reproductions featuring this level of craftsmanship created during that period."

She was right. But it was also possible she was wrong.

"Did you ever consider that they might be authentic?"

Anita looked down at the prints. "Do you think it's possible? The colors are so vivid."

"I know. You almost never see it, but 'almost' is the operative word in that sentence. When I finish appraising Mo's print—her heir asked my company to appraise it—I'll let you know what I learn."

"Thank you. That's very generous of you. Do you think I should hold the others back?"

"I would." I laid the print back down. "You know the importance of provenance, Anita. You also know I would never poach one of your sources. That said, I'm hoping you'll tell me where you got the portfolio."

"You're asking a lot."

"I know."

"Only because you're you, Josie." She swiveled toward her monitor, scrolled down to read something, then turned back to me. "Eli bought the collection from a dealer in Winslow, England, Richardson Antiques."

She gave me Richardson's contact information, and I thanked her.

As I walked out, I considered my next steps. Five paces from my car, a glimmer of an idea came to me with a thud, and I stopped short.

A horn blared. I was blocking traffic.

I mouthed "Sorry" and continued to my car. I leaned against the hood and stared into the middle distance, considering ways and means. The sun warmed my face, and I shut my eyes, enjoying the sensation.

"Okay, then," I said aloud.

I sent two identical emails, one to Ellis and one to Wes:

I have confirmed that Cal is using the name Pat Durand and P.O. Box #156.

I emailed Sasha, too:

It looks like Cal bought Mo's print from Anita Wills. Eli bought a complete portfolio from Richardson Antiques in Winslow, England. Anita thinks the set is a repro from the 1930s. Please contact Richardson's for more information.

I added the antique shop's contact information, reread the message, and hit SEND.

I tossed my phone in my bag and drove back to work.

CHAPTER TWENTY-ONE

I was standing in the front office sipping coffee, getting ready for my stint staffing the Prescott's Instant Appraisal booth, when Cara told me a woman named Gertie Joan Mays was on the line. I nearly pounced on the guest-table phone.

"Gertie Joan! I'm so glad to hear from you."

"I hope it's okay that I'm calling on a Saturday. I hate to disturb you on the weekend."

"I'm thrilled you called. Tell me you have good news."

"I have good news."

I sat down, dragged over a pad of paper, and extracted a pen from the Prescott's mug in the center of the table.

"I'm ready when you are."

"Ricky Joe McElroy purchased that guitar on June second, 1973. He paid twenty-eight thousand three hundred and ten dollars. That's a lot of money."

"It sure is. Did you find the receipt or an entry in a general ledger, or what?"

"Both. I found the receipt, then matched it up to the general ledger."

"Gertie Joan, you're a treasure and a half."

"That's nice of you to say. Gil Paul, that's my brother, bought the guitar on March fifteenth, 1971. So he had it just sitting on the shelf for more than two years. I trailed that one from the receipt to the general ledger, too."

"How much did he pay?"

"Ten thousand five hundred. That makes him look kind of sleazy, doesn't it? Charging Ricky Joe nearly three times what he paid."

"Paying a third is standard in the antiques business," I said. The direct and indirect costs of acquiring, appraising, cleaning, marketing, and merchandizing objects add up quickly. "Who did he buy it from?"

"A woman named Marianne Dowler. There's a note on the receipt in Gil Paul's handwriting that reads 'granddaughter of Estelle Mae Bridges, friend of Rbt. Johnson.' There's an address listed, but no phone number."

Gertie Joan called out the address. In 1971, Marianne Dowler lived in Clarksdale, Mississippi.

"Fabulous. Did you find any other documentation? Notes, maybe, about provenance . . . you know, the trail of ownership?"

"Nothing like that. Only purchase and sales records."

"Thank you again for looking. I'm so appreciative. I hate to ask you to do more, but I'm going to need the original documents, or at least good clear copies of everything."

"I can't let the originals go, but I'm glad to send you copies. As it happens, I'm one step ahead of you! I took photos with my smartphone and emailed them to you. Is that good enough?"

"Let me check that they came through. May I ask you to hold on for a minute?"

"Sure."

Gretchen wasn't at her desk, so I commandeered her computer, logged into my email account, and downloaded the photos.

"Gertie Joan?"

"I'm here."

"The two sales receipts are perfect. The general ledger shots are a little wiggly, though. Can you get someone to press down on the pages so the writing near the binding is visible?"

"Let me do that now. I'll call you when I send them."

Gertie Joan was a woman of action. Ten minutes after we hung up, two completely legible photos arrived. While I was waiting, I composed an email for her to send me, confirming that she had the original documents in her possession, and that these photographs represented an accurate and complete record of Abbot's involvement with the 1930 Martin OM-45 Deluxe guitar, serial number 45317. I sent it to her, then called to thank her for retaking the photos and ask her to cut and paste my content into an email to me. She opened it then and there, read it aloud, and said it was fine. I had the email less than a minute later.

"Gertie Joan, what's your favorite flower?"

"You're going to send me flowers?"

"A lot of them. A huge bouquet."

She laughed, a tinkling happy sound. "Instead of a big bouquet, I'd like an orchid. I've always wanted one, and now I have the time to take care of it. I understand they're tricky to grow."

"I can make this happen, Gertie Joan. Do you have a certain species in mind? Or a color?"

"Nope. You pick. Make it flashy." She laughed louder. "Just like me."

I was still chuckling as I returned to the tag sale venue. Gretchen was working at one of the cash registers.

I waited until there was a momentary lull. "I need you to investigate orchid options for a novice who lives in Florence, Mississippi. Get her one she can't kill. Better yet, get her lessons on how to keep an orchid alive. She wants a flashy one."

Gretchen's eyes glinted with excitement. This kind of project was right up her alley.

"I'm on it."

It was eleven thirty-five, which meant I had enough time to begin the hunt for Marianne Dowler. No Dowlers lived in Clarksdale, but hundreds of Dowlers lived in the South. At eleven fifty-five I threw in the towel. I emailed Fred Gertie Joan's photos and asked him to find Marianne Dowler but not to contact her until we'd spoken. I turned off Gretchen's computer and went to start my turn in the Prescott's Instant Appraisal booth.

I spoke to Fred, taking an early lunch, en route. "I just sent you an email. We're making progress. How's Davy doing?"

"Good. He's at his hotel doing some research."

"Did he give you any hints about what he thinks?"

Fred smiled. "What do you say when a client asks you that question?"

I grinned. "I tell them an appraisal is a process."

"That's what he told me when I asked, almost word for word. I know he wants to confirm some of the materials, specifically whether all 1930 Martin

OM-45 Deluxe guitars' backs and sides were made with Brazilian rosewood and topped with torrefied Adirondack spruce. He's also checking out the gluing techniques."

"I hate waiting."

"Me, too."

I ran across the warehouse and reached Prescott's Instant Appraisal right at noon.

A man named Finn sat across from me in the Prescott's Instant Appraisal booth. He was in his seventies, short and thin, with scraggly gray hair and leathery brown skin, the kind you get from years of outside work. He told me he was a retired roofer, and his wife was pestering him to divvy up some of their collectibles among their grandkids.

"Once you get on Harriet's radar, the only thing you want is to get off."

"That's why you've brought this Coca-Cola Barefoot Boy tray in for appraisal."

"Exactly. I'm hoping it comes in at something around fifty dollars. My granddaughter Allie likes it a lot, but her sister Naomi got the miniature watercolor Harriet and I picked up on the Isle of Wight in the 1980s. It's a cute little thing, about two by two, a picture of a church. I saw one just like it for sale in the church gift shop the last time we were there for thirty-four dollars. That was three or four years ago now, so I figure with inflation and all I'd be on solid ground valuing it around fifty dollars."

"Are you from the Isle of Wight?"

"Can't you tell by looking at my Irish mug? My mum used to say I had a map of County Clare written on my face. It's Harriet's people that hail from the Isle of Wight."

"So where did you get this tray?"

"Darned if I know. Harriet thinks we bought it at a yard sale when we were first married, around 1975, but I just plumb don't remember."

"Let me take a look."

Branded paraphernalia was a popular collectible. This one featured a Tom Sawyer–looking boy lounging against a tree in a bucolic setting. The boy wore chinos and a long-sleeved blue shirt with the pant cuffs and shirt sleeves rolled up. He also wore suspenders, a broad-brimmed straw hat, and an ear-to-ear grin. He was surrounded by grassy fields. He had a white-bread sandwich in one hand and a bottle of Coke in the other. A cute mutt sat facing him, his eyes fixed on the sandwich. The illustration was rimmed by a double border, two inches of red and a quarter inch of gold. The words DRINK COCA-COLA appeared in white script at both the top and bottom of the image. I inserted a loupe in my right eye and examined the tail of the *C* in "Coca" at the top. A tiny all-cap message divided onto two lines read TRADE MARK REGISTERED.

My heart pattered a bit faster than normal. Each letter was distinct. This was no quick-and-dirty knockoff.

I turned the tray over. The back was black. I removed the loupe and handed back the tray.

"Thanks for bringing this in, Finn. To properly authenticate and value this object, we'd need to take some time with it, but based on my instant appraisal—this tray is evidently the 'real thing.' Are you sitting down?"

"With my feet planted."

"Your tray has the right markings in the right places, properly executed. It's in wonderful condition. If it's real, I would expect it to sell for at least a thousand dollars. Maybe twelve hundred."

Finn's eyes popped open, forming perfect little saucers. "That's more than fifty."

"Looks like you'll have some rejiggering to do."

Finn shook my hand enthusiastically and left, carrying the tray as if it were made of pure gold. As he pushed through the outside door, I noticed Frank Shannon standing just inside, his eyes on my face, his expression somber, and I stood up. He jerked his head to the left, silently asking if I could step outside with him. I nodded. The clock over the door told me it was twenty to one.

I turned to the next person in line, a young woman, and smiled. "Someone will be right with you."

I did a 360. Fred was standing near the back, greeting people as they ambled by, offering to answer questions. I raised my arm, caught his eye, and waved him over.

"Cover for me, all right?"

"Sure."

Fred took my place, and I went outside. I found Frank leaning against the trunk of a willow tree, partially hidden by the drooping branches.

"Sorry to bust in on you," he said as I approached. "Trish and Lydia are over talking to Pastor Ted about Mo's funeral. Trish is having a container-load of flowers dropped off Tuesday morning. It's all bull, if you ask me. Mo doesn't need a special send-off to get to heaven. She's already there, standing next to God."

"Oh, Frank." I touched his arm.

"Trish tells me to be quiet, that the send-off is for us, not her. I guess that's right." He turned back to face me. "I stopped by to see that you're all right. I read the *Seacoast Star* article about the break-in."

"Thanks for asking. It was scary, but no harm done."

"Except to a window and a display case."

"Except for that."

"Were any of your roosters hurt when the glass shattered?"

"None I care about."

"Do you think the guy broke in to get Mo's print? Trish told us it was on an easel, in plain sight."

"I don't know."

"Quite a coincidence about the power going out. I hear a branch snapped off a tree. You'd think the power company would do a better job trimming them."

"Where'd you hear that?"

"I don't know. The *Seacoast Star,* I reckon."

"I'm not sure it was a coincidence. Maybe someone wanted Prescott's to be in the dark."

Worry lines appeared on Frank's forehead. "That's quite a thought."

"Josie!"

I looked up. Abby Young, the older woman who'd been part of Mo's book club, was smiling and waving at me.

"Abby! Nice to see you."

"Any *Y*'s for me?"

Ever since the day she found an old wooden figurehead with the letter *Y* carved onto the woman's apron, Abby's been a fan of the tag sale.

"I'm not telling! Finding *Y*'s on your own is part of the fun!"

Her smile faded as she recognized Frank. She patted his arm and walked inside.

"I buy pizza for my staff on Saturdays," I told Frank. "Want to come in for a slice?"

"I'd better not. Thanks, though. Trish wants to play some tennis, to get the kinks out, she calls it. Athletes, even retired ones, can't stay still for long."

"Not golf?"

"Not since the day she retired. She won't touch a club. She can't stand playing with amateurs. I wonder if it'll be the same for me with guitars."

"I doubt it. So she plays tennis. Is she any good?"

"Better than me, which isn't saying a whole lot. Speaking of guitars . . . any news about mine?"

"Not yet. We're making progress confirming provenance, but it's a process. One step at a time."

"Progress is good." He aimed his index finger at the woods on the other side of the parking lot. "I walked along Ellerton to get here . . . but what about that path? Does it lead to the church?"

"Yes. It's about a quarter mile, a nice walk."

He turned to face me. "You ready for your eulogy on Tuesday?"

"Yes."

"Trish will be glad to hear it."

He squeezed my shoulder and set off. I stood under the willow tree watching him trek across the parking lot and disappear behind a screen of bushes and trees.

A moment later, a soft voice called, "Josie?"

I turned. Steve's girlfriend stood nearby. I remembered her name was Kimberly. She wore a Kelly-green crewneck sweater that set off her titian hair, and brown jeans.

"Do you have a minute?"

I smiled. "Sure. Kimberly, right?"

"Yes." She turned around slowly, taking in the path to the tag sale entrance, the building, the half-full parking lot. "What made you decide to open your own business?"

"Why do you ask?"

Kimberly met my eyes. "Envious, I guess. You're so accomplished. Was it a long-term dream?"

"Not really. I moved to New Hampshire for a fresh start. I worked in antiques before, so I knew something about the business. Are you thinking of starting a company?"

She stared at her feet for a moment. Worry lines wrinkled her brow. "No . . . but I'm thinking I might need a fresh start. Did you get divorced? Is that why you moved?"

I twirled my engagement ring. "I've never been married."

"What, then?"

I didn't want to talk about that horrible year, my last living in New York City, especially to a stranger. You always hear how whistle-blowers endure contempt and mistrust, and that's what happened to me after I reported my boss's collusion with the competition in a price-fixing scheme. Then my dad died. Two weeks later, my boyfriend at the time, Rick the Cretin, announced I was getting to be a downer, his word, and left me cold. My dad always said when you're at the end of your rope, tie a knot and hang on, and if you can't hang on, move on. I lasted a year before moving to New Hampshire to start a new life. I could no longer recall the details of what those miserable people had said about me in my hearing or even the specifics of what they'd done to make me feel so isolated, but the feelings their shunning had engendered were seared into my soul and would stay with me forever. Living well was the best revenge, and I was living well indeed. I had a thriving business and employees I cared about and trusted; I was engaged to a man I adored who adored me; I was involved with New Hampshire Children First!, work that added meaning to my life; and I had good friends, real friends, friends who wouldn't toss me in a Dumpster like yesterday's trash, no matter what. I couldn't imagine why Kimberly was asking about such old news.

I smiled again, hoping she'd let it go and change the subject. "A bunch of things. It worked. I love my life here in New Hampshire. Where are you thinking of going?"

"I don't know. I have a son, and that makes moving tougher." She dismissed the topic with a wave of her hand. "Never mind. What I really wanted was to ask you about Steve Jullison. Mo's ex. What do you know about him?"

I let my astonishment show. "Me? Why on earth would you ask me that?"

"You two seemed close."

"We're not."

"I don't want to make another mistake." She looked around again. "I'm not doing a good job of asking, but I was hoping you would advise me."

Gretchen advanced toward us from the tag sale entrance, stopping twenty feet away, waiting for my signal.

I raised a finger, indicating I'd be with her in a minute. "I'm sorry I can't help you, Kimberly." I glanced at Gretchen, then smiled at Kimberly. "Duty calls."

I left Kimberly standing there, her pretty face framed by the yellow-gold willow leaves.

"Problem?" I asked Gretchen in a whisper.

"Not exactly. It's Wes Smith. He's on line one. He says it can't wait."

"Thanks."

I trotted to the front office. I felt bad for Kimberly, and sad, too. Maybe it was because her relationship with Steve was secret that she had no one she could talk to, no one she could trust to tell her the truth: *Be careful. If a man cheats on one woman, it's not a stretch to think he might cheat on you, too. Steve is a world-class liar.* I could hear the platitudes most people would dump on her: *You've invested so much time in the relationship, what's a little more? Love is always worth fighting for. Don't give up—Ryan needs a dad.* As I entered the building, I glanced back. Kimberly hadn't moved. Her eyes remained fixed on the ground in front of her.

"Kimberly!" I called.

She looked up.

"Come on in—let's talk some more."

She took a step in my direction. "Are you sure? I don't want to be any trouble."

I smiled. "I've got pizza!"

She came on the run.

CHAPTER TWENTY-TWO

I asked Gretchen to make Kimberly comfortable, told them I'd be back in a flash, and dashed to my office to take Wes's call.

"Hey, Wes. It's me. What's going on?"

"You should have called me." Wes sounded huffy. "What do you know about this Pat Durand person?"

"Nothing other than what I told you—Cal is using that name. I'm not holding back on you, Wes. What about the PO box?"

"It's real, and they have security cameras—except they only store the images for ninety days, and guess what? No one's checked the box for the last three months."

"When was the box opened?"

"June eleventh, this year."

Pat Durand opened the post office box three days before he bought the first print from Anita. "No doubt the clerk doesn't remember a thing about him."

"The clerk has trouble remembering his own name. It gets worse. You need two IDs to open a box. One of them was a lease for an apartment at 965 Ocean View Lane. Duh! There is no Ocean View Lane in Rocky Point. The other ID was for a nonexistent Hitchens employee. That one included a picture, but it's still a bust, because all you can see is that the person is white. The photocopy is in black-and-white and pixelated. Between the short hair, long bangs, and bad lighting, you can't even tell if it's a man or a woman. The police are stymied. There are nine full- and part-time workers at Hitchens who have rights to create IDs. They issue thousands of them—all the students, faculty, staff, authorized researchers, visiting professors, select vendors, etcetera, etcetera, but that's not relevant anyway because this one isn't real. Someone jury-rigged the design in Photoshop, adding a photo they probably got off the Internet, printed it out, and laminated it. It's a dead end. Plus which, using a fake name isn't against the law unless you intend to commit a crime like fraud, and the police are a mile away from proving that, even if they can confirm who Pat Durand is or was, which they can't."

"Cal may not be the only person using the name."

"Who else?"

"Someone helping him."

Wes's voice lowered conspiratorially. "Like Nora."

"It's possible. I'm convinced that she knows where Cal is. Do you think she's aware the police are onto her?"

"No. If she has any suspicions, she probably just thinks she's paranoid. When you're having an affair, you're always looking over your shoulder."

"And you know this how?"

"I read a lot. Same as you."

"What about Nora's husband?"

"Kevin. I hear rumors he's the jealous type. Lots of innuendo, nothing specific."

"Who said what?"

"You're asking for my sources?" Wes asked, outraged.

"As if." I laughed. "I'm asking whether people are actually saying things or whether you're reading between the lines."

"Two people told me he keeps her on a short leash, but they both have an ax to grind. One is an ex-girlfriend with a grudge. Kevin dumped her years ago, and she's as bitter now as she was then. The other is one of Nora's co-workers who was hot on her a few years ago and resents her brush-off."

"Are Nora and Kevin happy?"

"I guess. Why?"

"Because if she's happy, it's hard to see why she'd be sleeping with Cal."

"I figure that's just sex, you know? I mean after a few years, sex is just same old, same old, so if you're that kind of person, you go sniffing around. Kevin isn't. Nora is."

"Do you think that's right, Wes? Romance only lasts a few years?"

"Like I said, it depends on the person. For most people, it only lasts a few months."

"That's pretty cynical."

"Nah, I'm not cynical. I'm realistic. I'm a reporter, so I see more of the dark side than you do. You're all about the froufrou."

I started to argue the point, then decided to let it go. "Never mind. Kevin is in construction. Is that right?"

"He's a project manager for Calidale Vista. Do you know them? They're huge."

"Really? I got the impression from Nora that he was one of the guys pounding the nails, not that he was running the show. She told me being an accountant was really tough, that sometimes she wished she was in construction like her husband because nails don't talk back."

"Good one, Joz!"

"Good one, Nora. I'm just repeating what she said. What else have you learned?"

Wes hadn't dug up any dirt. Neither Nora nor Kevin had financial troubles, pending lawsuits, or criminal records. Which didn't mean Nora wasn't having an affair with Cal and helping him commit art fraud any more than it proved Kevin wasn't controlling.

"Have the police talked to that neighbor?" I asked. "The one who was on a business trip to Brazil?"

"Yup. His name is Walter Greene, and he saw two cars parked in front of the Shannons' the day Mo died. One was there when he got home from work about four thirty. He didn't recognize the car, and he didn't see the driver. He can't even say what model or color it was. The second car drove up as he was getting his mail, about quarter to five. That was Cal. Walter knows him by sight. Cal walked onto the Shannons' property. Walter went inside to drop off the mail. He figures the first car drove away while he was inside, because when he went outside again to look around his garden, it was gone. Then a minute or two later, here comes Cal, hustling to his car and leaving. He saw you and Chief Hunter drive up about five to five."

"This is incredible, Wes! We have Cal at the murder scene at the right time."

"I know—it's a definite hot patootie! Cal kills Mo and runs for it. Now we just have to find him."

"I'm stunned. We knew it was possible—and it is."

"It's more than possible. It's likely."

Sadness washed over me. "Cal killed Mo."

"It looks that way. What else ya got?"

"Nothing."

"Okay, then. I'll catch ya later."

I replaced the receiver, then stood, staring at it.

Cal and Nora and Lydia—three such different personalities. Cal was arrogant and narcissistic, with morals so elastic anyone following his play risked whiplash. Nora was smart and methodical, with an unexpected party-girl edge. Lydia was guarded and suspicious, wrapped in a melancholic fog.

I called downstairs and asked Gretchen to load up a tray with pizza and bring Kimberly up.

Gretchen placed the tray on the butler's table. I asked her to tell Fred I was sorry for not coming back to finish my shift, and to let him know I'd try to fill in later in the afternoon.

After Gretchen left, Kimberly reached for a slice of pepperoni. "Thank you for this. And for inviting me in to talk. I've been reading about you and your company for years. I'm a real fan."

"Thank you. I know a little about how hard you work from Mo."

"I'm crushed about her death. That's part of what has me reeling."

"Crushed is a good word for how I'm feeling, too. She was a good friend."

"And a wonderful teacher."

"I know she loved her work. How about you . . . Do you like teaching?"

She patted her lips with a napkin. "Yes."

"I hear some hesitation in your voice."

"You know how it is . . . you can love the work and the schedule . . . but it sure would be nice to make more money. Sometimes I think I should just drive away, to do what you did, to start over."

"Drive away where?"

"That's part of the problem. I love Rocky Point, and I don't want to live anywhere else. I love Steve, too. But if our relationship isn't going to work, I want to know now, not a year or five years from now."

"What does he say?"

"Give it time. Which isn't helpful. It's also hard because I have no one to talk to. Almost no one knows we live together."

"It's hard to make decisions in a vacuum."

"Exactly. What do you think I should do?"

"I don't know." I took a slice of mushroom pizza. "Did you grow up in Rocky Point? Is this home?"

"Sort of. My mom and I spent summers here starting when I was in grade school. We had a cottage on the beach. My dad came up weekends. We lived just outside Boston, so it wasn't that far for him. Then he got transferred to Dayton. That was about five years ago, and everything changed. They sold the cottage last spring. I tried to buy it, but I couldn't afford the fair market value, and they couldn't afford to let me have it for less."

"That's tough."

"Nothing's easy, right? Rocky Point is a great place to be a kid, and I wanted Ryan to have that same experience."

"Isn't he?"

"Not really. It's different when you live in a single-family house on the water." Kimberly smiled, a memory coming to her. "The girl who lived in the cottage next door to us . . . her name was Chelsea . . . she and I did everything together, all summer, every summer. We played beach volleyball. We went spelunking in the salt caves at the end of the beach. We even went clamming right in front of our houses. Ryan doesn't have any of that. We live in a condo a mile from the shore, without a private lawn or anything."

"Those summers sound heavenly. No wonder you want that for Ryan."

"God, I remember it all like it was yesterday. The lock on one of my bedroom windows was broken, so I never had to worry about getting locked out." She laughed. "That was when we were older. We'd go to the beach late at night to smoke and drink beer. All I had to do was shimmy down a tree."

"Does Chelsea still live in Rocky Point?"

"No. You know how it goes. People move away. They change. Chelsea lives in Colorado Springs now, with her husband and three kids. I emailed her about buying the cottage—I thought it would be fun to go in together—but she wasn't interested. She hasn't been back east since she left for college. If she didn't send Christmas cards, I'd never hear from her."

"It's hard when orbits no longer overlap."

"Is it inevitable?"

"That you lose touch with friends? I think each situation is different. I'm not friends with anyone from Welton, where I grew up. I have one good friend from my years in New York. Regardless, it sounds like you're ready for some stability."

"Desperate is closer to the mark. And I'm not sure Steve can handle that." She stood up. "Thanks for the pizza and for letting me vent. I'm sure it will all work out."

I carried the tray downstairs and led the way to the front office.

Cara was on the phone and raised her hand, catching my attention. I placed the tray on the guest table.

She punched the HOLD button. "I'm sorry to bother you, Josie, but this woman bought a pair of bronze bookends at last week's tag sale. Lincoln. She wants more. I checked the computer. We don't have any more in stock. She's asking where we got them so she can see if more are available. What should I tell her?"

"Find out exactly what she's looking for. Bronze bookends? Only bronze bookends featuring Lincoln? Anything Lincoln? Presidential bronze bookends? Tell her we'll let her know when something she wants comes available, but that we never reveal sources. If she pushes, I'll take the call."

Cara smiled broadly. "I can do it."

"Good—but if you need help, that's okay, too!"

I walked Kimberly out. She paused with one hand on her car door handle to thank me again for the pizza and conversation.

"I don't know that I was any help, but you're always welcome to run things by me. I know how hard it is to be on your own."

She thanked me for the offer and drove away.

Kimberly seemed to have a good heart, but it was clear that she was struggling to juggle her own needs with Ryan's and Steve's. I hoped she'd figure it out.

As soon as I walked back inside, I stopped thinking about Kimberly and started thinking about Marianne Dowler, who'd sold a guitar in 1971.

If Marianne paid taxes, the Mississippi Department of Revenue would know it, and if it was public information, Fred's contact would tell us, but that call would have to wait until Monday. I sent Fred a quick email with the suggestion.

I returned to the tag sale venue, thanked Fred for covering for me, and took over for him at the instant appraisal booth. Afterward, I texted Ty that I wanted to go to the Colonial Twist for dinner. I asked him to make a reservation. I added that he'd need to wear a tie and jacket. Then I got back to work.

Davy Morse, our guitar expert, called around four, saying he was leaving for New York, had some details to confirm, and hoped to get us his report by midweek. I told him that was fine and resisted asking for an interim update.

CHAPTER TWENTY-THREE

T y and I got to the Colonial Twist about seven thirty. We were all buffed up. I wore a short-sleeved cherry-red dress. It had a fitted top and a swirly skirt, and when I wore it, I felt pretty. Ty wore a brown suit with an off-white shirt and a green-and-brown-striped tie. He didn't react to the white-helmeted doorman or the heavy wooden door, but two steps into the lounge, he stopped short.

Every chair in the lounge was taken. A couple stood by the mantel, laughing.

Ty turned to look at me. "Can you believe we didn't know this place existed?"

"Can you believe it's this successful without Chester promoting it?"

"How did he do it?"

"He found himself some well-heeled gamblers, and word of mouth did the rest."

"Too bad. I thought maybe he'd found an elixir and we could help him bottle it. We'd make a million dollars before morning."

We made our way to the bar.

Chester came toward us, hands extended. "Josie! The Colonial Twist is honored."

"You're very kind. Chester, this is my fiancé, Ty Alverez. Ty, Chester Randall." As the two men shook hands, I added, "I see we were lucky to get a reservation."

"I can always make room for friends. Why don't you order a drink? It won't be too long."

The bar was almost as crowded as the lounge, the happy rumble of conversation sprinkled with laughter. I waited by the side wall while Ty elbowed his way to the elephant railing.

As I'd anticipated, all the men wore jackets or blazers and ties. I felt a bit underdressed because most of the women wore evening attire, the little black dresses and sparkly tops you see at cocktail parties. I didn't recognize a soul.

Chester joined me. "A table should be ready in about ten minutes."

"Perfect."

Chester leaned in close to my ear so he wouldn't be overheard. "I was going to stop by on Monday. I heard about the break-in on the news. Are you all right?"

I kept my voice low, too. "Yes, thank you. I'm fine. It was pretty frightening, though."

"You don't know who did it?"

"No."

He cast his eyes around the room, keeping a professional watch on the servers and his guests. "So . . . do you have any news regarding the whereabouts of our mutual acquaintance?"

"No. How about you?"

"I thought so, but no. I followed his lady friend after she left work yesterday. She drove to a cobbler on Islington. Why does anybody go to a cobbler five miles from her condo, and farther than that from her job, when there's a shoe repair shop a half mile from where she lives? Do you know that stretch of Islington? Down by Hatchett Street? The neighborhood is solidly working class, a little long in the tooth, maybe, but decent. Nora stayed about an hour."

"I can't see Cal living in a working-class neighborhood. He's too proud."

" 'Pride goes before destruction, a haughty spirit before a fall.' When vermin is under attack, it does what's necessary to survive."

"Where did Nora go next?"

"Straight to her condo."

"And you went back to check out the shop."

"That's right. As far as I could tell, it's just a shoe repair shop. I figure she waited while they replaced a heel and gave her shoes a good shine."

"An hour is a long time for that."

"I know."

Ty walked up carrying my martini and a glass filled with amber liquid. Chester said he needed to check on something and walked toward the restaurant.

I took a sip. The drink was cold and thick, creamy. "Yum. You don't drink beer out of a glass very often."

"This isn't a drink-from-the-bottle kind of place. Plus, they have Allagash White on tap."

"Really! Allagash White. I'm stunned. You're not serious!"

"Sarcasm doesn't become you."

"I wasn't being sarcastic. I was celebrating with you."

"Oh." He raised his glass.

I clinked and said, "Here's to us."

"And to silver light in the dark of night." He touched my glass, then drank. "Ahh! Allagash White. Life is good."

The hostess, another attractive woman in a black dress and pearls, led us to a table in a corner. The cloud-white tablecloth was soft and supple. I could see myself reflected in the silver flatware. Delicate yellow blossoms drifted alongside a tea candle in a shallow bowl of water. To my left, I could see the entry to the casino.

I turned my attention back to Ty. "If I ask nicely, I bet Chester would show you the casino."

"Not tonight. Tonight I just want to be with you."

"You're so romantic."

"I'm in love."

I raised his hand to my cheek and closed my eyes. "Me, too."

The waiter appeared. I chose Mama's lasagna. Ty went for the lobster alfredo primavera. We decided to share a Caesar salad.

The food was wonderful, and the service was even better, there when you wanted it, but unobtrusive. We sat and talked about nothing in particular. It was, all in all, a perfect evening.

"What do you think?" I asked Ty as soon as the waiter cleared our plates.

"Delicious. Next time, I'll try the steak."

"Me, too."

Chester beamed when we told him how much we'd enjoyed ourselves.

I had a new favorite restaurant.

• • •

Shelley came through. The disposable phone with a 917 area code arrived just before eleven on Sunday morning. I texted her a thank-you, not wanting to risk waking her again, then dashed to my computer, entered the phone number into my *Antiques Insights* request for a Hiroshige print in perfect condition, paid the fee, and posted my ad.

At two, I sat on the couch, reading "Poor Sherm," a short story by Ruth Chessman that had been featured in *Alfred Hitchcock Mystery Magazine* as a "classic."

Ty came into the room. "You look deep in thought."

"Relationships are complicated."

"What did I do wrong?"

I laughed. "Not you. You're perfect. I was thinking how fragile life is. Blink twice and you miss it."

"You miss your mom."

"And my dad."

Ty sat beside me and kissed the top of my head. I leaned into his shoulder and let the memories come. From the time I was about six until my mom died, our little family of three spent a weekend a season in Dennis, on Cape Cod. We stayed in a beachfront cabin. My folks got the bedroom. I slept on the couch.

During my mother's final pain-ridden days, we'd gone for one last weekend. It was September, and my mother had insisted that she was eager to go on our annual hayride. My dad, afraid that sitting on hard slats of wood and bouncing along the rough track would be too much for her, arranged with a local farmer for a custom ride. While she napped inside our cabin, Dad and I covered the cart's floor with thick blankets and set up three tranquility chairs, low and cushy. We reclined in style as the farmer drove us slowly along a packed-dirt path that ran alongside his property. My mother kept her eyes on the fire-colored leaves and breathed in the pine-infused scent of fall.

I leaned over and kissed Ty. "Ready for a hayride?"

At three, Ellis, Zoë, her son, Jake, her daughter, Emma, Ty, and I bundled ourselves into hoodies and sweaters and drove to the Allen Farm. We walked along the faux-torchlit path to where an old wagon was waiting, and I took my place next to Ty. For the half hour we rocked along the path, I was young again, and I had my mother near me.

After we got back to my place, I grilled burgers and dogs, and then, as twilight's purple blush enshrouded the meadow like a veil, we sat around the fire pit, watching Jake and Emma play badminton until they could no longer see the birdie.

Later, the kids roasted marshmallows and passed them out to the adults, and as I licked the gooey sweetness from my fingers, I thought I was maybe the luckiest woman in the world.

CHAPTER TWENTY-FOUR

 was first into work on Monday morning. As soon as I booted up my computer, I emailed Mac at *Antiques Insights*.

Hi Mac,
How did Pat Durand pay for his account? What credit card did he use? How did his buyers pay him? Did the transactions go through PayPal? Thanks!
Josie

Mac's reply came quickly.

Hi Josie,
Yes, everything went through PayPal.
Mac

I looked up from my monitor. PayPal linked to a credit card. The police—or Wes—could probably find the record, but that wouldn't help. I was certain that Cal, using the name Pat Durand, had acquired the kind of credit card you prepay in cash and refill as needed. Lots of places sold cards like that, and many of them didn't have security cameras, since tracking buyers would be bad for business. In all likelihood, the post office box had been opened simply because Pat Durand needed an address to get the credit card, but he was paying the bills online. I'd taken one step forward and one step back. I'd learned the details of Cal's operation, but I'd made no progress in tracking him down.

As I began considering next steps, Shelley's phone rang. I grabbed it, then froze with my finger hovering over the ACCEPT CALL button. If it was Cal, he'd recognize my voice. Same with Nora. Same with Lydia. I hoped who- ever was calling would leave a voice mail.

The display said it was an unknown number. A few seconds later, an email popped into my newly created Hiroshigefan Gmail account.

Hello!
I see you're looking for an original print from 100 Famous Views of Edo—I have one. Where are you located?
Pat

I knew how I wanted to reply, but I hadn't considered what name I should use. I swiveled toward my window. One of my best friends in grammar school was named Andrea Brewster. We'd called her Andi.

Hi Pat,
Which one do you have? I'm from New York.
Andi

Hi Andi,
"Flower Pavilion, Dango Slope, Sendagi No. 16" in stock. Do you know it?
Pat

I Googled Hiroshige "Flower Pavilion Dango Slope Sendagi No. 16." The print depicted an exquisite cherry blossom scene. Indistinct figures strolled through the orchard, taking in the astonishing, fleeting beauty.

Hi Pat,
I love it! I want it! Can you send photos?
Andi

Hi Andi,
Will do. I'm on the road right now, so it will be a few hours before I can get them to you, though. Okay?
Pat

Hi Pat,
No problem. I'll be running around all day anyway. Are you a dealer?
Andi

Hi Andi,
Yes. And you're obviously a collector of great discernment!
Pat

I didn't roll my eyes, but I could have. Pat was treating our exchange like a mating dance. I represented fresh meat. Flattery, he assumed, would boost the price. I decided to let him think his ploy had worked.

Hi Pat,
Thanks! I try.
Where are you located?
Andi

Hi Andi,
Maine. But I get to NYC often. Are you in Manhattan?
Pat

Hi Pat,
I live in Manhattan, but I happen to be in Boston for a few days. Where in Maine?
Andi

Hi Andi,
Bar Harbor. Too far. I can get to Boston.
Pat

Time to slow it down, to think, to regroup, to consult Ellis.

Hi Pat,
Let me check my schedule and get back to you.
Andi

Hi Andi,

Okay. Talk soon!

Pat

I checked the voice mail on the phone I was now thinking of as Andi's.

"Sorry I missed you. I'm calling about a fabulous Hiroshige print that meets your specifications. I'll email you now."

"What?" I said aloud, confused.

Pat's voice sounded female. *How could that be?* Anita had identified Cal as her customer, Pat Durand. My brows drew together. It seemed Cal had a partner after all. *Who is she?* It wasn't anyone I knew. She had a faint British accent, as if she'd been reared in England but had lived here for decades.

I called Ellis.

Ellis didn't speak, but he didn't need to. His attitude was apparent from his icy stare.

We sat in a booth at the Rocky Point Diner. We each had a coffee. Outside, the clouds were thickening.

Ellis stretched out his arm, palm up. "Give me the phone."

"Why?"

"I need to have that voice mail analyzed."

"I thought I would text Pat Durand."

"Why text?"

"Whoever is behind this scam might recognize my voice."

His lips tightened. "Yet another reason for you to let us take it from here." He stretched out his arm, palm up. "Give me the phone."

I slid the phone across the table. "I thought I was helping."

"You agreed to consult me *before* you took action." His eyes remained unrelenting. "You don't know what you're getting yourself into, Josie. If Cal or whoever is behind this is a killer, your life may be in danger. Even if he's merely a crook, he may feel cornered and become deadly. These conditions require finesse. To make matters worse, your well-intentioned efforts may chase him deeper into the woods."

I swallowed hard, abashed. "What can I do?"

His hand closed over the phone. "I'll get back to you on that." He relented. "I know you thought you were helping."

He slid out of the booth and left.

I sat in my car and called Max. I explained the situation and asked his opinion. "I know I messed up. How can I make it right?"

"How about if I call Ellis on your behalf and offer your assistance in fielding any calls or texts. I'll make it clear your only interest in this is your appraisal, but that since your interest might run alongside his interest, you're eager to cooperate."

"You make it sound so easy, Max. I'm glad you're on my side."

I was almost back to my office when I remembered Quentin's Spy Shop. I'd passed it each time I visited Anita's boutique inside Murphy's Interiors. I backtracked to Route 1, parked near the front, and went inside. I approached the shop and found my attention riveted to the video playing on a TV just inside Quentin's. A woman was demonstrating how to use a hidden voice recorder built into a lipstick.

Twenty minutes later I was back in my car, the proud owner of a voice-changing machine. One of the settings was a female with a slight British accent. It looked like Cal didn't have a partner after all.

CHAPTER TWENTY-FIVE

F red was hot on the trail of another guitar, so I called his contact at the Mississippi Department of Revenue, Heather Jan Lassiter. She was surprised at my request.

"As I told your associate, we never release personal information. Individual tax records are personal."

"I don't need to know anything about Ms. Dowler's taxes. I just need her address."

"Her address is personal."

"Darn! I really need to talk to her. There's no possible bad outcome. I'm trying to trace an antique."

"I'm sorry, but I can't help."

I thanked her for her time and hung up.

I called the city clerk's office and spoke to another nice woman who, like Heather Jan, refused to release personal information.

"Is there anyone there close to retirement? Someone who would have been on the job in the early 1970s?"

"Why?"

"I have an off-the-wall question about Clarksdale in 1971. I know, I know . . . that's not something you hear every day, is it?" I laughed. "Who do you think I should talk to?"

"You're right, that's not an everyday request. You should talk to Jay Malc. He's an engineer with the county. He's retiring at the end of the year, and he knows everything about Clarksdale from long before I was born."

She gave me Jay Malc's full name, Jay Malcom Curtis, and his extension number, then transferred me.

Jay Malc Curtis answered on the first ring. He had a deep baritone, a radio voice.

"I'm an antiques appraiser calling from New Hampshire. I have a question that will, I suspect, surprise you . . . To complete an appraisal, I need to speak to Marianne Dowler, and I'm having trouble finding her. I know she lived in Clarksdale in 1971, and I know Clarksdale isn't all that large. Since you've been in the workforce since about then, I was hoping you might know her."

"Know Marianne Dowler! Sure I do. She went by Mari Mae. I haven't thought about Mari Mae in years. We went to the same high school. Mari Mae and I worked together on a science fair project our senior year. She was truly special—smart, hardworking, dedicated."

I did a private fist pump. There was nothing as exhilarating as moving an investigation forward. "Did she leave Clarksdale after school?"

"That's right. She went north to college. She got herself a scholarship at Temple."

"In Philadelphia. Where is she now, do you know?"

"I'm not rightly sure. Mari Mae used to come home now and again—I don't know why, to tell you the truth, since she didn't have any family left. I haven't seen her in . . . I'm guessing it's fifteen years, maybe more. She married a Yankee, I know that for certain. He was from Boston, I think."

I crossed my fingers. "Do you recall his name?"

"Rayburn Sanford. She called him Ray. Said he was her ray of sunshine."

"That's sweet, isn't it? What did she study at Temple?"

"Psychology. She went on and got a Ph.D. From New York University, I think it was, but I'm not sure about that."

"You've been very helpful, Mr. Curtis. May I have your home or cell phone number in case I need to reach you again?"

"Sure."

He called out both numbers.

"When did you graduate high school?"

"Nineteen seventy. Can you believe it? I started here with the county in 1975, and I've been here ever since. More than forty years."

I congratulated him on his retirement, then listened as he told me how he and his wife were going on a cruise to Tahiti to celebrate. While he spoke, I Googled "Marianne Sanford" and "Boston."

Marianne and Rayburn Sanford lived in Amesbury, an affluent suburb of Boston. Ray was a psychiatrist in private practice. Marianne was a professor at Rockport University, with three books and more than fifty peer-reviewed articles under her belt.

I thanked Jay Malc and called Marianne's office number. It went directly to voice mail.

"Dr. Sanford, my name is Josie Prescott." I explained who I was and where my company was located. "I have a question about a guitar you sold to Abbot's Musical Instruments in 1971." I gave her my contact information, then added, "I know this must come as a surprise to you. I look forward to filling you in. I think you'll be pleased!"

I walked into the front office. Gretchen was smiling at her computer monitor like a cheerleader facing adoring fans.

"You look like you just won the lottery," I said, grinning.

"I think I've exceeded your expectations." She spun the monitor 180 degrees so I could see it. "This is a vanda orchid. Can you believe that color?"

The blossom was dazzling, a rich blue, closer to purple than turquoise, specked with white. The blossoms were large, four inches or more.

"It's gorgeous!"

"Do you think Gertie Joan will like it?"

"How could she not? Where would you buy it?"

"There's a place in Jackson. They've agreed to give Gertie Joan lessons."

"Perfect!"

Matt Janson, the owner of Janson's Antiques Mall who'd asked me to lunch to discuss his plans to expand his business, was waiting by the Blue Dolphin's hostess stand when I arrived for our twelve thirty date. He greeted me warmly, taking my right hand in both of his and giving it a gentle squeeze.

After we ordered and our drinks had arrived, iced tea for him, hot tea for me, Matt said, "I've been impatient waiting for this lunch."

"Tell me what's going on."

"I want us to be partners."

"You do?"

"You said it yourself—I should open a second location. I want us to do it together."

"You need the money?"

"No. I need you."

I leaned back and smiled. "I'm intrigued. Where are you thinking?"

"Where do tourists go?"

"Rocky Point Beach."

"Too close to my current location."

"You're going to Maine."

"Why not Vermont?"

"Too saturated. York Beach?"

"Too close."

"Wow. Portland. A more populated location lends itself to a year-round business."

"Want to go in with me? Now that you have a TV show, you're a big draw. I've had this idea for a while. I've been working up the courage to approach you."

"Ha, ha."

"I'm serious. I didn't want to come to you with a half-baked proposal. At this point, I'm closer to three-quarters baked, so I feel comfortable pitching it."

"How would it work?"

"We'd call it Prescott's Antiques Mall. It would look like my barn. We share start-up costs. I'll be the COO, chief operating officer. You'll be the CEO, chief executive officer. We split the profits. What do you say?"

"I say maybe. I'm interested. I need to think about it."

"Sure. Take as long as you need. But know this, Josie . . . it would be an honor being your partner."

"Thank you, Matt. I feel the same. All I have to do is look at your place to see what you're capable of. You've made a wonderful business there."

"Out of nothing."

"Don't exaggerate. There was a barn."

"And a field. What do you think—should I add a petting zoo?"

"To bring in families? Don't they already shop there?"

"Yeah. But I've got the land."

"I wouldn't do it. Too labor intensive."

"A tea shop?"

"To bring in more women? Aren't they already your primary demographic?"

"They'll stay longer. Make a day of it. Bring their girlfriends."

"Maybe. But only as a concession."

Matt patted my shoulder. "See. I knew we'd be a great team."

I smiled and raised my tea cup for a toast. "To us."

Marianne Sanford called back at four Monday afternoon.

"I can't remember ever being as astonished as I was listening to your message," she said. "I haven't thought of that guitar in a thousand years. Maybe two thousand."

I could hear a hint of Mississippi in her voice.

"I can only imagine. I think the guitar I'm appraising is the one you sold back in 1971. I'm hoping you can tell me its history."

"Why? What possible reason could there be for you asking that question?"

"Provenance. I need to show an unbroken chain of ownership from the time of manufacture to now. Martin sold fourteen of this model guitar that year, but all the stores Martin sold them to are out of business, and their records are long gone. I can't go forward, so I need to go backward. So far I have traced the guitar to Abbot's Musical Instruments, where their records show you as the seller. To continue the chain, I need to know how you acquired the guitar. What can you tell me about it?"

Seconds ticked by. If Dr. Sanford shut me down, our hunt was probably over.

"I'm sorry."

"I understand this may be asking you to think about something you don't want to think about. If it wasn't crucial, I wouldn't ask."

More time passed, a minute or longer.

"I'm sorry," she repeated. "I'm not comfortable discussing it. I'd better go."

She hung up.

I slapped the desk, frustrated with myself. I knew better. You could have all the antiques knowledge in the world, but if you couldn't read people, you were certain to fail, and I'd just messed up. There was some kind of secret associated with Frank's guitar, and I might have squandered my only opportunity to learn it. I should have read her mood better. I should have been more sensitive. I should have eased into my questions. *Shoulda. Woulda. Coulda.*

Pat Durand emailed a photo of *Flower Pavilion, Dango Slope, Sendagi*, number 16, a stock shot, probably an image she—or he—found on the Internet. I realized that since the voice on the message had been female, I was now thinking of Pat as a woman.

I called Max but got his voice mail. In case you were in the throes of a legal emergency, he invited you to call his cell phone. I didn't want to bother him, and I could easily wait until morning. It was probably a good thing to keep Pat Durand on pins and needles.

I stared at the image. Cherry blossom season in Japan is a time of celebration and joy, and it showed in this print. The trees were lush, the blossoms white, tinged with pink. Unlike the loneliness and isolation shown in most of the prints in the series, several people, though their faces were generically drawn, interacted with one another. Others reclined on benches under the trees, their eyes on the blossoms. The print exuded a soothing and reflective mood, evocative of innocence and a more peaceful time.

I confirmed that Pat only sent the one photo. She hadn't included a shot of the print's back, which any reputable dealer would have done. Not only can potential buyers discover flaws such as foxing or water stains, which might be hard to spot in a busy design, but marks indicating authenticity, such as labels, gallery notations, or signatures, can be examined, and if expected marks are missing, that needs to be noted, too.

Cal was not Pat Durand. Cal would know better. Pat Durand—presumably Cal's partner—was an amateur.

CHAPTER TWENTY-SIX

Tuesday morning, I woke up just before the alarm went off at seven. Ty was organizing a training session at the Portland, Maine, office, and he liked to be at his desk before everyone else, so he left home around six thirty. I stumbled downstairs, poured myself a cup of coffee from the pot he'd left on the burner, and found an I-love-you note on the counter. I pressed it to my chest, to my heart.

At eight, I called Max and got him.

"Your timing is good. I'm just sitting down at my desk with a coffee. How can I help?"

"Two things. I want to run a business expansion opportunity by you and get your read on it, and I got an email from that Pat Durand person. I'd like to arrange a phone call with her—I'm calling Pat 'her' since the voice on the phone is female—anytime tomorrow morning."

"How about you come in at nine and schedule your call to Pat Durand at ten thirty? We can talk about the business thing first. I'll have the police come at ten to get everything set up. Does that work?"

I said I'd bring some of Noeleen's muffins, and I could hear him smack his lips.

At ten, I was in my office. I emailed Pat Durand a thank-you, and asked if she could call me at 10:30 tomorrow morning. Two minutes later, she replied saying 10:30 was perfect.

I'd caught up on emails, and I was deep into reviewing my accountant's latest good-news report when Sasha called to update me on Mo's print.

While she hadn't yet located any verified originals we could use to validate the woodgrain pattern she'd spotted in the print, Richardson Antiques in England had been helpful. They'd given her the name of the portfolio's former owner, a widow. It seemed that the widow had found the portfolio in a trunk after her husband's death, that she hadn't seen it or heard about it in twenty-two years of marriage, and that she had no documentation, so Sasha wasn't hopeful she'd get any useful information, but she planned to talk to her anyway.

"As you suspected from the start, we'll need to send it out for a materials analysis," I said. "I want every *i* dotted and every *t* crossed."

Sasha said she'd get quotes, and I thanked her. The fact that the portfolio had been found in a trunk was encouraging. If the prints hadn't been exposed to light, that might explain why the colors were so vivid.

Dr. Marianne Sanford's class schedule was posted on the Rockport University's website. She was teaching Principles of Social Psychology today from 10:00 to 11:15 A.M. The classroom wasn't listed, but her office was, W-396 in Westover Hall. I checked the campus map and saw that Westover Hall was one of four buildings surrounding a spacious stone courtyard. Parking lot 4 was closest. I glanced at the clock on my monitor. It read 10:20. Rockport was only about a twenty-five-minute drive. Call it a half hour each way and a half hour to talk, I should be back by noon or twelve thirty at the latest. Mo's funeral was scheduled for two. I had plenty of time.

Rockport University was located on a thirty-five-acre campus. The entire place, from the ivy-covered fieldstone buildings and meticulously groomed grounds to the fresh-faced students and courteous staff, seemed unreal, as if it had been staged for a movie.

The parking security guard cheerfully directed me to a visitor's spot. A gilt-edged sign pointed me toward Westover Hall. A wide marble staircase took me to the second floor. A glass-fronted cabinet listed all this semester's psychology courses. At thirteen minutes after eleven, I stood just outside room W-208, an auditorium-style classroom, where Dr. Sanford was finishing up her lecture.

At eleven fifteen exactly, the double doors burst open and scores of students rushed out. I pressed myself against the wall, avoiding the deluge. The river quieted to a stream, then a trickle, then stopped. Dr. Sanford stepped out. She looked just like the photo posted on Rockport University's website. Her chin-length black hair was curly. Her skin was cocoa brown. She had a model's face: prominent cheekbones, a high forehead, a long, slender nose, and a determined chin. She wore a bone-colored cable-knit turtleneck sweater, black slacks, and black leather ankle boots. She carried a red leather briefcase.

I peeled myself off the wall. "Dr. Sanford?"

"Yes?"

"I'm Josie Prescott. I was hoping you had a moment to talk."

"The antiques appraiser."

"Yes. I'm sorry to barge in on you like this, but it's important."

She leveled assessing eyes at me. I didn't waver.

"Follow me."

I walked alongside her down the wide corridor and around a corner to a door with her name on it. She used a key she took from an outside pocket of her briefcase to unlock it.

Books jammed the shelving that lined both side walls. White sheer curtains allowed the light in, and the office was bright. Her desk was messy. Stacks of folders were squeezed between piles of books and an all-in-one computer. Three framed vintage travel posters were mounted on the back wall. One advertised an Eastern Airlines flight to sunny Florida, bragging that it was only a ten-hour flight from New York to Miami. The second one recommended traveling across Australia on the Trans-Australia Railway. The illustration showed a man wearing a duster and a wide-brimmed hat riding a camel. The third featured a cheetah tracking the viewer, its eyes black and piercing. The copy advertised an African safari organized by Imperial Airways.

Dr. Sanford placed her briefcase on the floor and sat behind her desk. "Have a seat."

"You like to travel."

She smiled, and her face was transformed from severe to playful. "More than anything. If I could, I'd never stop."

"What's your favorite place?"

"Jordan for exotic—leaving the airport, I felt like I was walking into the Bible. Bonaire for diving. Paris for romance." She flipped a hand. "It depends. What's yours?"

"I don't have as much experience. I'm on the hunt, though, for the perfect honeymoon location."

"Congratulations. When are you tying the knot?"

"June."

"Beautiful. What do you like to do?"

"Everything. Nothing. I want to gel and swim and snorkel and hike and have nice dinners."

"Go to Maui."

"Maybe. Hawaii's pretty far, though. I hope you don't mind . . . I'm here to ask for information about the guitar."

"Will it be published?"

"If it's ever sold, information about it will appear in a catalogue. But right now the owner simply wants to know how much it's worth—estate planning."

"You're putting me in a difficult position."

"Why is that?"

"I got the guitar from my mother, who got it from her mother. My grandmother went to a lot of trouble to keep the story of how she came to own it private."

"Is she alive?"

"No."

"If the truth became known, who would it hurt?"

"That's a good question." She thought about it for a moment, her eyes on the travel posters. "No one." She refocused on me. "What do you need to know?"

I found my little notebook at the bottom of my tote bag and flipped it open to a blank page. "What is your mom's name?"

"My mom was Lucille Mae Dowler. My grandmother was Estelle Mae Bridges. Want to guess what my middle name is?"

I laughed as I scribbled their names. "Mae."

"How'd you guess?"

"I'm known for my deductive reasoning skills. Plus a man named Jay Malc Curtis called you Mari Mae. That's how I found you."

"Jay Malc! We went to school together. What a great guy he was! Good through and through."

"He said the same about you." This was the moment of truth. "How did your grandmother come to own it?"

"She got it from a boyfriend, Robert Johnson."

"The blues guitarist?"

"Yes. He and my grandmother were . . . well . . . friends."

"When did he give it to her?"

"My grandmother was a proud woman. She never admitted she had an affair with Robert Johnson, though certainly I assumed she had. My brother and I romanticized their relationship."

"She married your grandfather after Johnson's death."

"That's right. He never knew about their involvement. My grandfather was a hard man."

"Hard in what way?"

"He was sarcastic, sniping, but words weren't his only weapon. He was the kind of man who sees you have a sore spot on your foot and accidentally-on-purpose treads on it. I could tell that my mother despised him, that she could barely stand to be in the same room with him, but she never spoke a bad word about him. My family wasn't known for its openness or its communications skills. I knew there was bad blood, but I honored her reticence by not asking any questions about it." She swiveled to face the windows. "Or maybe I just didn't want to know." She spun back and raised her chin, keeping her eyes on my face. "My father died in 1962. My brother died in 1963. My mother died in 1968. I moved in with my grandmother for my last two years of high school. She died in 1970, a month before my graduation. I went through everything my family owned and sold everything I could, including the guitar, to get money to move to Philadelphia. I won a good scholarship to Temple University, but the stipend only covered about half my expenses, to say nothing of transportation."

"That's a lot of loss in a short amount of time."

"Yes."

"What happened to things like photos and papers, you know, birth certificates and so on?"

"I packed them in boxes and left them in a storage unit back in Clarksdale. For decades, I went home every few years, to visit my family's graves, to attend a high school reunion, that sort of thing. The last time, I went for an old high school friend's fiftieth birthday party. After that, I realized I'd changed. Clarksdale no longer felt like home, so I transferred everything into plastic tubs and shipped them to my house."

"May I go through the contents? I assure you I won't damage anything or take anything without your permission. I'll only be seeking evidence related to the guitar's ownership."

"No one but me has ever looked through them."

I met her resolute stare. "Please."

"It's a privacy thing. I don't like the thought of anyone pawing through my possessions."

"I understand. How about if you do the pawing? I'll be a witness."

She paused again, her eyes once again on the back wall. After a minute, she came back to me. "I don't know. I want to talk it over with my husband. Ray sees the world unvarnished."

"Of course."

She stood up. "You probably think I'm being silly. Sentimental."

"I respect your instinct for privacy. I believe that finding the truth is always worth the effort, though, and that hiding the truth is always a mistake. But that's me."

"If you asked me about a theoretical situation, I'd say the same thing."

"I understand. Life isn't a theory—it's your life."

She took a step, then stopped. "I believe in living my values. You can come and help me go through things."

I nearly bounced out of my seat, but I spoke with calm composure. "Thank you. When is good for you?"

"Friday. I don't come to campus on Fridays."

I walked beside her to the door. "What time?"

She suggested ten, and I agreed. I wrote down her street address, email address, and home phone number, thanked her again, and left.

I was in my car, backing out of the space at 12:02 P.M.

I was thrilled that Dr. Sanford agreed to let me search for documents about the guitar, but I didn't much feel like celebrating. Instead, I rehearsed my eulogy the whole way back to Rocky Point.

CHAPTER TWENTY-SEVEN

I stopped at home to change from my chinos into something more appropriate for a funeral, settling on a black-and-dark-green tweed pleated skirt with a dark green blouse, a black blazer, and low-heeled black pumps. I drove myself to the church, arriving about ten minutes early, and parked in a spot near the front.

A representative from the funeral home handed me a program. I stepped aside to read it. After Pastor Ted spoke and we sang some hymns, those of us scheduled to deliver eulogies would be brought up to the stage one at a time. I was delivering the third eulogy, after Helena, the director of New Hampshire Children First!, and Edna, Mo's principal.

The usher led me to an aisle seat near the front. Helena sat on the aisle across from me. We nodded, acknowledging one another. Frank, Trish, and Lydia sat alone in the front pew on the right.

The service started shortly after two when Willa Como, a classically trained pianist, stepped onto the stage and sat at the organ. She played the prelude, Bach's Cantata BWV 147, "Jesu, Joy of Man's Desiring." Ted came up next, then Willa played three hymns. I joined in the singing. Helene spoke about Mo's core goodness. Edna spoke about her work ethic and the lives she'd touched through her teaching. Then it was my turn.

The church was about three-quarters full. Trish held a lace-edged white handkerchief to her eyes. Her shoulders shook. Frank sat next to her, holding her hand. Lydia's eyes were fixed on her thighs. She'd lost weight, and she looked frail. Nora and her husband, Kevin, were seated about halfway back on the right, next to the other book club members. Ellis sat in the last row on the left. Detective Brownley sat two rows in front of him on the right. Wes was seated at about the midpoint, on an outside aisle.

My heart rate doubled and my mouth went dry as I climbed the stairs. I thanked my escort and took my notes from my jacket pocket. I swept my eyes across the church. Steve, Mo's ex-husband, stood at the back, half hidden by a stone column.

"Mo Shannon was my friend."

Kimberly, Steve's girlfriend, stepped into the church. The funeral director approached her. She shook her head and waved him away.

"Which makes me one of the luckiest people in the world, because when Mo was your friend, you were set for life."

Kimberly crept forward, her eyes on the crowd, angling her head to see around people.

"Mo only saw the good in people, the potential. She believed that people were essentially decent. She didn't merely mouth the words, she lived the life."

Kimberly sidestepped toward the right. Steve kept his eyes on my face.

"She worked with children, both in her job as a teacher and as a volunteer. You've heard of those successes. I witnessed some awe-inspiring moments, like the time she knelt beside a little boy so scared and hurt after enduring years of abuse, he could barely communicate. She whispered to him, always smiling, a portrait of tenderness and devotion. She comforted him enough to trust her, and he let her place him on a horse, his first time. I watched his frozen expression, the face of silent suffering, soften into a smile of wonder and delight. They set off, Mo leading the pony around the indoor ring, an image of an angel. Mo loved children, and children loved her."

My eyes filled, and I paused. Kimberly turned her head and spotted Steve, pinning him with her eyes. She walked slowly, deliberately, toward him. Steve leaned against the column. As far as I could see, Steve had no idea Kimberly was in the nave.

"Mo loved Japanese woodblock prints. I asked her what it was about them that spoke to her. She said it was the duality. Muted colors that communicate vibrancy. Isolated settings packed with life. Two dimensions communicating a three-dimensional narrative. This duality could be seen in Mo herself. Mo was reserved and introspective, yet when she walked into a room, people gravitated toward her, wanting to know her. Mo was quiet yet lively. She

delved into the dark corners of children's lives, yet all she saw was potential."
I paused and looked out into the congregation for a moment. "Mo will stay in
my heart forever, a reminder that when we're patient and kind, we bring out
the best in one another."

As I descended the steps, I took one last glance at the back. Neither Steve
nor Kimberly was in sight.

I waited in line to pay my respects to Mo's family. The temperature had
dropped during the service into the fifties, and the cold got inside me.

Frank embraced me, a bear hug. "Thank you, Josie."

"Frank . . . my condolences."

He gave me a final squeeze, and I moved on to Trish. Her face was gaunt.
Her eyes were swollen and moist.

"I'm so sorry, Trish."

"Thank you for those beautiful remarks, Josie. It helps a bit."

I touched her forearm. Lydia stood two paces away, alone despite the crowd,
as rigid as a fence post. She stared at me.

"Lydia, I'm sorry for your loss."

Pastor Ted walked up in time to hear my comment and Lydia's reply.

"I know."

Before I could formulate a response, Pastor Ted nodded at me and touched
Lydia's shoulder. "I'll stand here beside you, Lydia."

I acknowledged Ted's kindness with a brief smile and walked slowly to my
car, trying to account for Lydia's apparent malice, but I couldn't. She was as
sharp as a porcupine needle and just as cuddly, and that was simply who she
was, at a garden party, viewing art, or at her sister's funeral. It felt personal,
but it wasn't.

"So what did you think?"

I spun toward the voice. It was Wes.

"Hi, Wes. I thought it was a lovely service."

"You got anything for me?"

"No. You?"

He glanced over both his shoulders, then lowered his voice. "I think Lydia's involved."

Incredulity froze my words.

"I know. It's a super-shockeroonie."

"My God, Wes—what do you know?"

He grinned. "Nothing. I'm just thinking aloud." He turned around to face the receiving line. "I mean, jeesh! Look at her. She looks like she's made of stone."

"She's grieving, Wes."

"If your sister was murdered, wouldn't you show a little emotion at the funeral?"

"We shouldn't judge."

"That's what you always say because you're so nice."

I smiled at his backhanded compliment.

Kevin Burke walked Nora to her car. Her eyes were red, and her blond hair was in disarray. She clutched a wadded-up tissue in her hand. Kevin turned her to face him and said something. She wrapped her arms around his shoulders, pressing her cheek into his chest. After a moment, he pulled back and kissed her. She touched his cheek. They looked like a couple in love. Kevin stood beside her car until she belted herself in. As she pulled out of her spot, they waved to one another, and he walked to a pickup truck two rows away. Presumably, they'd driven separately because they came from work. I was about to ask Wes if he had any other news when I noticed Chester's black sedan on the street. With all the traffic, it was easy to miss.

"I have to go," I said.

"Why? What's going on?"

"Nothing. I'll call you."

I jumped into my car and got it started. To distract Wes, I waited for a minute, fiddling with the radio setting, then checking my phone for messages. I gave a quick finger flutter and pulled out, turning left, toward my company. I was six cars behind Nora, and three behind Chester. Vehicles peeled off, and others joined the flow. Soon only one car separated Chester from Nora, and two separated me from him.

A half mile farther on, just after we turned onto Main, Nora sailed through a yellow light. The car ahead of Chester stopped for the red, trapping him. I spun right, turning quickly onto Milo Street, then zipped left onto Lister Road, a residential street that ran parallel to Main. I sped up. At Tapson, I turned left, rejoining Main, only two cars back of Nora. Chester wasn't in sight.

Nora made a right onto Islington. Three miles down, she parked in front of Anthony's Shoe Repair. I drove past her, pulled a quick U-turn, and parked diagonally across the street. I had an unobstructed view of the entrance. Nora leaned her head against her steering wheel, clutching it as if it were a life ring, and wept. After a minute, she sat up and wiped away the wetness with a tissue. Her chest heaved as she inhaled deeply, trying to pull herself together. Another minute passed before she opened her car door.

I slunk down, holding my arm up to block my face while allowing myself a clear view, but it wasn't necessary. Nora was so wrapped up in whatever was going on within herself, she didn't even glance around. She dragged herself into the shoe repair shop as if she were facing the gallows. I agreed with Chester. That Nora used this cobbler made no sense.

The sun slanted off the plate glass window, so I couldn't see inside, but from the steady foot traffic, I could see that the shop was busy.

I waited.

After about ten minutes, I called my office. Cara told me everything was fine and asked about the funeral. Fred, she said, was out meeting with a curator about an unsigned Impressionist-style painting we'd acquired in an estate sale. Eric was outside, overseeing a crew he'd hired to clean the gutters. Cara passed me on to Sasha. Sasha read me catalogue copy for some marbles we'd bought about two years earlier* that were going to be featured in an antique toy auction next spring. I approved it. I spoke to Gretchen next, who gave Melissa Sayers, our new part-time employee, a glowing review. When I was done, I checked the time. Nora had been inside the store for nearly thirty minutes.

I called the Rocky Point Police Department, and Cathy, a civilian admin, told me Ellis wasn't available. She transferred me to his voice mail. "Ellis, I'm at Anthony's Shoe Repair." I gave him the address. "I know how odd this might sound, but Nora Burke went in more than half an hour ago, and she hasn't come out. It's possible she's meeting Cal. Anyway, I thought I should let you know."

---

* Please see *Glow of Death*.

I texted Wes: *Can you find out about Anthony's Shoe Repair on Islington?*

Ten minutes later, phone in hand so I wouldn't miss a response from either of them, I got out and looked around. The neighborhood was just as Chester had described it, solidly middle class, decent but uninteresting. Harvey's Market, a discount grocery store, was two blocks down on Islington. Anthony's Shoe Repair was one of a series of small shops that ran for a block. An Italian deli was on one side, and a small convenience store was on the other. Across the street, two-family houses shared driveways and minuscule front yards. Every house was freshly painted, though. There were curtains on the windows and flowers in the gardens. I locked my car, waited for the traffic to slow, and crossed the street.

CHAPTER TWENTY-EIGHT

A nthony's Shoe Repair looked like every other cobbler's storefront I'd ever been in. Cubbyholes lined the left wall, displaying everything from shoe dye, shoe polish, and shoelaces to umbrellas, rain boots, and plastic ponchos. A cash register sat on the counter toward the rear alongside an old-fashioned cast-iron receipt spike, half filled with pink slips. A short old man with rounded shoulders, wrinkles on wrinkles, and a thick white mustache stood behind the counter. I wondered if he was Anthony.

I eased a red umbrella from the stack and pretended to read the label, half turning toward the rear so I could continue my assessment.

Two raised shoeshine chairs abutted the wall to my right, both empty. Next to them was a door bearing a gold-and-black paper sign, the corners curled with age, that read PRIVATE. In back of the old man, a chest-high counter allowed him to pass items back and forth to a man in the rear. That man was taller and broader than the man in front, and about half his age. He stood in profile, hammering something on a worktable I couldn't see.

Nora was nowhere in sight.

A woman hurried in and placed a pink receipt on the counter. The old man held it close to his eyes, then turned to a shelf behind him and found her bag. She paid in cash, and he added the paper to the stack on the spike. The transaction took about a minute.

Where was Nora?

A man in a gray suit that could have used pressing entered the shop and plodded to the door marked PRIVATE. Without saying a word, he opened it and passed through. I had enough time before the door swung closed to see a flight of steps leading down.

I slipped the umbrella back into place and smiled as I approached the counter. "Hi. I'm looking for Nora Burke."

"Who?"

"Nora Burke."

He shook his head. "I don't know a Nora Burke."

"I saw her come in here about forty minutes ago."

"A customer, maybe. She left."

"No. She didn't come out. Her car is here."

He shrugged and turned his back on me.

"I need to talk to her. It's important."

He didn't turn around.

I looked past him. The man in the back was working a wheel, spinning it forward, then backward. It made a grinding noise, louder when he rolled forward than when he rolled back.

I sidled to the door marked PRIVATE, and with my eyes on the back of the old man's head, I patted the air in back of me until I found the doorknob. I turned it slowly and tugged gently. It opened soundlessly. I crossed the threshold and eased the door closed. To my ears, the latch clicking home sounded as loud as a jackhammer. I was standing in a windowless whitewashed stairwell under a single lightbulb covered by a white glass globe. Muted sounds drifted up from the basement, a chair being dragged across a concrete floor, perhaps, followed by a man's rumbling laughter and rustling papers.

I took a step down, and the wood creaked. I froze for three seconds, then continued, leaning heavily on the railing to mitigate the squeals of old wood. Eight steps down, I reached a half-landing. The staircase turned to the left. I counted six additional steps. At the bottom, I stood on a square landing facing a closed door. I placed my ear against the door, and sounds resolved into words.

Two men were talking, one a baritone, the other a tenor.

"You know anyone who's been to Lake Worth, Florida?" the baritone asked.

"Sure. It's a nice residential area, you know, a little suburban, quiet. My aunt is down there and likes it."

"Then my wife won't." He laughed, the same rumble I'd heard at the top of the stairwell. "My Bea likes a little pizzazz."

"Take her to Miami. South Beach."

"That's what I'm thinking."

I took a to-my-toes calming breath and exhaled slowly through my mouth, opened the door, and stepped into a big room with narrow frosted-glass windows running along the front of the building. A stack of metal pipes lined the floor underneath the windows. The room was as large as a basketball court. The two men I'd heard talking were sitting at a battered round table. One held a copy of today's *Seacoast Star*; the other was busy with a crossword puzzle. The table was the kind used at banquets, set for eight or ten. Without a tablecloth, all its nicks and chips showed.

I counted five doors. The one opposite the windows, to my right, was labeled with the same kind of sign as the door I walked through: PRIVATE. Two doors opposite from where I stood read MEN and LADIES, a nonamusing misalignment—men are men, but women better be ladies. To my immediate left were two more doors, both unlabeled.

The man holding the newspaper lowered it to the table and stood. He was big and burly, and nearly bald. "Can I help you?"

"Where am I?"

His forehead creased. "Downstairs."

"I know that, but what is this place?"

"A social club. Who are you?"

"Josie Prescott. Who are you?"

"What do you want?"

"I'm looking for Nora Burke." I sent my eyes around. "Where is she?"

He took two steps toward me. "You're in the wrong place, lady. This is a members-only club. You need to leave."

I turned to the door marked PRIVATE. "What's in there?"

"Nothing for you."

I walked toward it.

"Stop!" he bellowed.

I stopped and met his eyes, and shivers ran up my spine like a spider. "Sorry." I back-stepped to the staircase door.

"Who are you again?"

"Josie Prescott, an antiques appraiser. I don't want any trouble. I just need to talk to Nora. I thought she was here."

The tenor stood and watched our interaction as if it were a tennis match.

My phone vibrated, and the baritone's gaze shifted to my hand. It was Wes, calling from his office at the *Seacoast Star*.

The man stomped toward me and grasped my arm, rotating my hand palm up so he could see the phone display. "Are you kidding me? You're a reporter?"

"No. I told you. I'm an antiques appraiser. This call is about advertising my company's weekly tag sale."

The baritone snatched the phone. I reached to grab it back, but he kept me at bay with one outstretched arm. I stopped trying to recover it, and he pushed me backward, not too hard or far.

"What's your password?"

"Come on. You want me to go . . . I'll go. No harm. No foul."

"That ship sailed by. What's your password?"

"Six eight two eight."

He tapped the numbers in, brought up my text log, and raised his eyes to mine. "This ain't no ad. You asked a reporter to check out Anthony's." He opened the telephone window. "Are you kidding me? Your last call was to the police?" He turned to the other man. "Tell 'em." As the tenor ran for the door marked PRIVATE, the man holding my phone wrenched my tote bag from my hand. He dumped the contents onto the table. He flipped open my wallet and thumbed my license out. "Well, at least you gave your right name." He tossed my phone onto the pile.

Grasping my arm with a viselike grip, he walked me across to one of the unmarked doors, yanked it open, shoved me in, and slammed it shut. His shove catapulted me into some plastic shelving that lined the back wall. I toppled to the ground as empty plastic storage containers and packages of paper goods rained down on me. The snick of the lock turning resonated like church bells. Struggling to my feet, I grabbed the doorknob and pulled. Nothing. I turned it and pushed. Nothing. I pounded on the panels. Nothing.

"Let me out!" I hollered. "Help! Help! Help!"

Silence.

I was trapped.

I heard people calling out instructions, but the words were indistinct.

"Let me out!" I shouted again. "Help! Help! Help!"

Scraping sounds told me things were being moved around. What if they edged a table under the doorknob?

Help didn't come.

Slender threads of light showed me where the door met the frame. I reached for my flashlight, pulled gently to activate the retractable cord, and examined my prison.

The shelving I'd crashed into was made of hard gray plastic. White plastic tubs on the bottom shelves hadn't fallen. Each one contained a pile of food prep, serving, or eating objects, including shish kebob skewers, spatulas, slotted spoons, flatware, steak knives, and two-pronged corn holders. It took me five steps to walk from the door to the back wall and seven side to side. A fluorescent light fixture was mounted overhead, but there was no switch.

I closed my eyes, then opened them. I had no time for self-flagellation. Later, I could beat myself up, but not now.

The rumblings and rasps from outside continued unabated.

Three cabinet hinges were attached on the inside. I could remove them, and the door would fall forward, held in place only by the lock.

I needed a screwdriver. I opened every drawer and cabinet and found lots of pots and pans and dishes, but no tools.

I tried the skewer first, but the point was too thick. I used one of the prongs on a corn holder, and it fit, but snapped off. I tried another, and it snapped off, too. Tears of frustration welled in my eyes. I tried a regular knife. Too wide. A butter knife. Too rounded. I reached for a fork, certain the tine would be too large and too blunted, but it fit as if it had been designed for the job. It took less than a minute to remove the two screws. I placed them and the two parts of the hinge in a bowl and started work on the middle hinge.

The noise stopped as suddenly as it had started.

The quiet was even more alarming than the noise had been. They'd left me locked in a dark closet. I told myself to keep focused on the task at hand, to work the problem, to not make things worse by succumbing to paralyzing fear.

Five minutes later, I slipped the last hinge and set of screws into the bowl. I tapped the door, once, twice, then pushed harder. It collapsed at a crazy angle, the lock holding the left side mostly in place. On the right, a two-foot gap allowed me to view part of the room. I eased my head and shoulders through and looked around.

The place was deserted. The door to the room marked PRIVATE stood open, revealing another large room, an outside loading dock with the doors ajar, and the alley that ran behind the building.

Using the flats of both hands, I thrust the door forward, and it opened an additional inch. I rammed it with my shoulder, and the wood around the lock cracked. I rubbed my shoulder. I'd have a heck of a bruise in the morning. I kicked the door, hard, and finally it gave and broke away from the lock, taking some of the frame with it. It landed on the ground with a loud smack.

The contents of my tote bag were heaped on the table, just as I'd last seen them. The bag was on the floor. I grabbed my phone to check the time—unbelievably, only fifteen minutes had passed. I swiped my arm across the table, and everything tumbled into my bag. I was about to dial 9-1-1 when I heard footsteps and froze.

I listened hard but didn't hear anything else. I unlocked my phone. Wes had texted *I'm on it,* a simple reply to my request for information about Anthony's Shoe Repair. I started to call 9-1-1 but couldn't think of what to say. There was no emergency. I decided to call Ellis from my car instead. I started for the stairs, then paused to look into the other room.

Six- and eight-foot rectangular meeting tables were positioned in staggered rows. Dozens of standard-issue metal meeting-room chairs were shoved against the walls. Half a dozen had fallen over. Playing cards were strewn across a felt-topped round table. A roulette wheel sat on another round table. The social club was really an illegal gambling joint, and at the thought that the police were en route, the staff and players had abandoned it willy-nilly. Evidently, Nora was more of a gambler than I realized. Or Cal was here and she'd come to visit him.

I took a step toward the open room and stopped short, groaning in pain. Sharp daggers stabbed at my upper back and left shoulder. I took stock. I did a deep knee bend. I rotated my shoulders forward and backward. I lifted my arms, then swung them back. Nothing was broken. Everything hurt. I ignored the pain and continued walking, pausing in the doorway to send my eyes around.

With people adding cheer and energy, the room might have been more appealing, although I doubted it. The walls were empty. The windows were painted black. The overhead lighting was harsh. Big, bulky security cameras dotted the ceiling. Rainbows prismed from a mirrored disco ball, circa 1973, coloring the barren tables and scuffed off-white linoleum floor.

I crossed the room, stepped outside onto the concrete platform, and choked on the stench of garbage emanating from a row of old metal trash cans that lined the wall on the left.

A cold east wind whipped through the alley, and I rubbed my upper arms.

The alley was narrow, barely wide enough to accommodate a delivery van. Two cars were parked a few buildings away, their tires up on the weed-filled shoulder. The asphalt was pitted. Tufts of weeds had sprouted in the cracks.

No one was in sight.

Steps at either end of the platform allowed easy access from the alley to the loading dock. I spotted a door on the right two paces from the stairs. I edged my way along the building, hoping to find a window in the door so I could peek in, but it was solid. I tried the knob, turning it gently. It was locked.

I wanted to see if Nora's car was gone. I considered circling the block but decided it would be quicker to go through the building. I was three steps into the casino when I heard footsteps on the concrete loading dock. I dashed to the side wall, detonating spikes of pain in my thighs. Peering through the open doors, I could see a triangle of platform and alley, but not the door. Lydia, still wearing the navy-blue suit she'd worn to church, her small blue purse dangling from her shoulder, climbed down the stairs and hurried to one of the cars. A few seconds later, a car engine turned over; then a vehicle drove by, hitting potholes and kicking up pebbles.

I backed up to the wall and slid to the ground as I tried to make sense of the images and ideas rattling around in my head.

Lydia was here.

That singular fact had to be explained. Lydia had parked in the alley, which meant she knew about the back door or entered the casino through the loading dock. I glanced around. Streaks of violet and yellow light reflecting off the disco ball mottled the floor. What did Lydia have to do with this dilapidated ersatz grandeur? This place was a dump by any standards, depressing and demoralizing. Why would Lydia come here to gamble when she was a member of the upscale Colonial Club? She wouldn't. Lydia wasn't here to gamble—she was here to see Cal. Maybe Lydia came for solace and found Cal with Nora. I used the wall to heave myself upright.

My squabble with the baritone hadn't felt like an emergency; this did. I rooted through my bag for my phone and dialed 9-1-1. I reported that something was wrong in the basement of Anthony's Shoe Repair, then sank onto a gray metal folding chair to wait. A moment later, I realized that Nora and Cal might be injured. I needed to check, to see if I could help.

I zigzagged my way across the casino, avoiding tables and chairs. A dull ache radiated from my back to my legs, adding a layer of misery to the pricks of pain punctuating every step.

I approached the inside door near the closet, the only one I hadn't identified. I held my breath and listened for ten seconds, hearing nothing but the random clicks and creaks of an old building settling, the whirring of a refrigerator in back of me, and a dog barking somewhere outside. I turned the knob. The door opened silently, and I stepped over the threshold into a dimly lit short hall. A closet door on the left stood open. A man's trench coat hung on the rod. A pair of black wingtips sat on the floor.

Three paces down the hall, I came to a bathroom on the right. The fixtures were old and dingy. Two more steps brought me to the end of the hall and the entryway to a room. I stood on the threshold to survey the space. A bureau rested against the front wall, to my right. Drawers were half open, clothes flung aside. A round oak table stood directly in front of me, with two old ladder-back chairs ranged around it. Papers were strewn across the top, and some had fallen to the floor, including a half-hidden issue of *Antiques Insights*. I recognized the cover and felt a judder of comprehension. That was the issue where Rheingold Gallery had been highlighted in the "Small Victories" column. A mattress lay on the floor in back of the table, the bedding all tangled. Leaning out to see to the left, my mouth went desert-dry.

A river of blood had pooled on the vinyl tile.

Cal lay on the floor, faceup, dead. I swallowed a scream. I clamped my teeth onto my bottom lip. His eyes were open. His mouth was closed. The top of his head was dented and matted with blood. Horrified, I covered my mouth with my hand.

I stepped into the room, one tentative step. There was nowhere to hide, no kitchenette, no extra closet, no oversized cupboards. Nora wasn't here. No one was here. I approached Cal's body and squatted, and a blaze of pain jagged up my back. I took his wrist in my hand and felt for a pulse, just in case. There was none.

I stood, stunned. *Cal is dead.* The words echoed in my brain. *Cal is dead.* I couldn't bear to look at his bloody corpse, but I couldn't look away. *Cal is dead.* It took a minute or more before I was able to think. Seemingly unrelated facts and observations clattered against one another as I stared, unseeing, at his body.

I turned to the clutter on and near the table. The issue of *Antiques Insights* answered the niggling question about why Cal chose Rheingold Gallery. He didn't study his options—he simply scanned the article, saw that Rheingold sold Japanese art, and figured it would serve his purpose just fine. Maybe he visited the gallery's website and discovered its logo was easy to download. He never expected to be challenged because he never expected Mo to appraise the print. I walked around the room, examining every flat surface. I crouched over to see into the open drawers. There wasn't a computer in sight. Lydia hadn't been carrying anything except a small shoulder bag. Someone else had been here and had ransacked the place. Nora?

Someone hammered on the outside door, breaking into my inchoate thoughts.

Before I could decide what to do, footsteps pounded down the stairs, and a moment later, the inside door was flung open. Two uniformed officers I didn't know burst into the hall with their guns drawn, aiming them at my chest.

CHAPTER TWENTY-NINE

Four hours later, just after nine, I sat chin deep in my hot tub grip-ing to Ty about being kept at the police station for two hours. One jet shot hot bubbles at my left shoulder blade. Others were aimed at my lower back and legs. I'd hung scores of miniature Japanese lan-terns along the path from the back door and around the patio and hot tub, and streaks of muted orange stippled the churning water. Ty sat on the wooden deck, his legs dangling toward the lawn, cooling down in the chill night air.

He drank water from a plastic bottle. "Two hours isn't unreasonable."

"Spoken like an ex-cop. I finished my statement in thirty minutes. I looked at mug shots and worked with a sketch artist for another hour. Then they had me sit around and do nothing until I begged to be sprung."

"You refused medical treatment, so they assumed you were okay."

"I was. I am. What does that have to do with wasting my time?"

"They needed you to be available in case more questions came up, and don't forget, you found the body."

I huffed, leaned my head against the rubberized edge, and closed my eyes.

"I can tell the difference between a recalcitrant witness and a weary one." Ty's voice softened. "You're in the weary category. Are you sure you're okay, babe?"

I opened my eyes. "You're so wonderful, Ty. I'm fine." I closed my eyes again. "Weary is the right word, though. Along with a little beat up. Mental note to self: Next time you're locked in a closet, don't use your shoulder to batter down the door."

"Good tip."

"Ellis was surprised that I couldn't ID the thug who tossed me in there."

"Because you couldn't ID him or because he's not in the system?"

"Because he's not in the system. The whole operation operated without any official notice. They're trying to figure out who owns the building and who ran the casino."

"What about the old man upstairs?"

"Anthony. He doesn't know anything about anything, so he says. When I called Ellis saying that Nora had gone into the shoe repair shop and hadn't come out, he sent Detective Brownley to check. Anthony was as uncommunicative with her as he'd been with me. Ellis was asking for a search warrant when I called nine-one-one."

"What's Anthony's problem?"

"Follow the money. I'm sure someone is paying him off to play dumb, and he doesn't want to ruffle any feathers. He has a sweet deal, and he knows it."

"Anthony's Shoe Repair. That's a helluva front for an illegal gambling club."

"You'd think Rocky Point is a hotbed of gambling. First, Chester's non-profit casino, now this no-name place located under a genuine business. What's the world coming to if sweet little Rocky Point has turned into a gambling mecca?"

"Don't be naïve. Rocky Point has always been a gambling mecca. Lots of places are. People like to gamble. Let's start with state-sanctioned lottery games. In Rocky Point, there's Gibbon's Tavern, where you'll find a poker game any night of the week in the back room and bingo run through churches and service clubs four or five days a week. And let's not forget the high-stakes mah-jongg game Liz runs out of her suburban colonial."

"How do you know all this?"

Ty kissed the top of my head. "I know everything."

I pretend-slapped my forehead. "Silly me to have forgotten that."

"I've seen you enjoy a good game of gin."

"So true. It was my dad's game. I never play for money, though."

"Who won?"

"Him. All the time. I am a woman of many talents. Cards isn't one of them."

"You're good at all the important things."

I smiled and opened my eyes. "I bet Lydia's still at the station. I was waiting in the lobby when they brought her in. I didn't notice any blood on her clothes, but I'm not sure I would have spotted anything on that dark material."

"Any sign of Nora?"

"None, and Ellis wouldn't tell me a thing. When I reached street level outside Anthony's, her car was gone. I called Wes on my way to the police station to ask if he knew where Nora was. I'd already asked him to check out Anthony's Shoe Repair. I added the building and the casino to his list."

"What did he say?"

I deepened my voice, mimicking an indignant Wes. " 'What do you mean you didn't take any photos?' "

Ty laughed.

I splashed around a little. "Wes had no idea where Nora was and would see what he could ferret out about the other things. Once we know who owns or runs the place, we'll probably know why Cal was staying there. The answer might be nothing more than opportunistic convenience. Cal was a gambler. He knew the social club had an extra room in the back. He asked for a favor, and the powers that be said sure."

"How do you figure Lydia knew where he was?"

"No doubt they've been in touch all along."

"If she helped him avoid the police, they're going to charge her with obstructing justice."

"They've already got her for murder."

"They'll add it on."

"It's horrible. Worse than that, actually, when you think about it, because if she was helping him stay clear of the police after he killed Mo, the justice she obstructed involved her sister. I know she's cold, but surely she cares about finding Mo's killer—unless she killed her, too."

"It's rare that siblings kill one another."

"But not unprecedented. Lydia saw Mo as an obstructionist to her relationship with Cal. Or maybe Mo found out that Cal had conned her. She warned Lydia she was going to tell the police what he'd done. She would have, too. Mo was that kind of honorable."

Ty lowered himself back into the tub, settling next to me. "And everyone knows that love is blind. If Mo represented a threat to Cal, Lydia would have struck before Mo could follow through."

"I understand. I'd do anything to protect you."

"Would you lie to the police? Hide a killer?"

"Yes."

Ty placed his arm around my sore shoulder and gently stroked my upper arm. "Me, too."

"Good." I snuggled in closer. "One thing Ellis did tell me was about Michelle Michaels, the buyer of the other woodblock print that Pat Durand sold on *Antiques Insights*. I was right—Pat Durand contacted her about buying another print, but she wasn't interested. She said no before Pat told her which one she was selling, so it's just another dead end. It does support the conjecture that both Cal and his female partner were using the name Pat Durand, though. Which is interesting but doesn't bring us any closer to finding her. Ellis also told me that Cal didn't have access to the Langdon Museum's house list. Only the director and the marketing team do. At Ellis's request, the director checked—no mailing has gone out in a month."

"Sometimes knowing what the bad guy *isn't* doing helps you find out what he *is* up to."

"Ellis told me about other dead ends, too. The forensic team didn't find anything significant on the log used to down the wires, and there were so many footprints on the pathway through the woods that they couldn't sort them out. They did find glass shards along the path, though."

"That's something."

"I guess."

We sat quietly for a while. Wisps of misty fog descended on the meadow.

I sank farther underwater, letting the steamy water lap up over my chin. "Maybe Cal's murder has nothing to do with the print. Let's say Lydia hotfooted it to Cal's place immediately after the funeral expecting sympathy; instead, she found him in bed with Nora. Lydia lost it, grabbed something, a baseball bat, for example, and started whaling on him."

"Except there wasn't a bat at the crime scene, and you said Lydia wasn't carrying anything but a little purse."

"It's possible Nora took it away."

"Lydia kills Nora's lover and she helps cover up the crime? Unlikely."

"True," I said. "Maybe Lydia showed up wanting love, and Cal broke up with her."

"Why?"

"He decided he liked Nora better. No, that doesn't fit. Nora was pretty into her husband when I saw them in the parking lot after the funeral."

"She was putting on an act—she has a guilty conscience."

I slapped the water. "Or . . . or . . . or . . . this is all conjecture, Ty. We don't have any evidence of anything. Not a shred. Lydia didn't use a baseball bat. If Cal played softball, he'd have had a glove. There wasn't one."

"You looked?"

"I noticed. I noticed something else, too. There was no computer. Call me crazy, but I can't see Cal going to the public library to check his email. Ellis told me his phone is missing, too."

"Interesting. Was Cal Pat Durand?"

"I guess we'll find out if Andi Brewster's call goes through as scheduled—after all, dead men can't take phone calls." I repositioned myself to allow the steam and pulsing bubbles to hit my neck. After a moment, I continued. "Ellis asked us to move the call from Max's office to the police station so their tech people can try to trace it. He agrees that Cal might have been working with a partner."

"Lydia."

I rested my head against Ty's shoulder. "Or Nora."

"Are you going to be able to handle it—my achy shaky baby?"

"Ha! There's nothing wrong with me that two ibuprofen and a good night's sleep won't cure." I yawned. "Speaking of sleep . . . I think I'm done. I'm getting pruny."

Ty stood up, and water cascaded from his bathing suit. He reached out a hand and helped me onto the deck. He wrapped a towel around me, and I rubbed myself dry. The night noises soothed me, the birds saying their final good nights and soft rustlings from the woods. I slid my feet into my flip-flops. Ty turned off the jets, drew the cover over the tub, and led the way inside.

As I stepped into the kitchen, a thought struck me with the clarity and force of a meteor, and I fell back against the wall. I clenched the towel closer as the implications and ramifications jostled for position in my brain.

Ty walked toward me, his eyes on my face. "You look like you've just seen a ghost."

"Oh, Ty . . . I need to call Ellis right away . . . I just remembered . . . There was a stack of metal pipes in the social club. The murder weapon was right at hand. Talk about an easy way to dispose of a weapon—all you'd have to do is toss it back in the pile."

CHAPTER THIRTY

es called at seven twenty Wednesday morning.

"I've got an info-bomb. Can you meet now? At our dune?"

"Yes."

I got to the beach before Wes. Bundled in my sweater coat, I climbed the dune. I was stiff but not gimpy, and my bruises were colorful and tender to the touch but not debilitating. Nonetheless, I was glad I'd taken some more ibuprofen before I set out.

The day was bright and windless. Golden stars flicked across the dark blue ocean surface. The temperature was just shy of fifty. It would be another perfect autumn day. To the north, a man wearing an anorak walked along the shoreline, his golden retriever darting around a jumble of seaweed. To the south, two older women walked in tandem. One was gesturing wildly. The other was laughing. I wondered what was so funny.

A car screeched to a stop. I turned toward the street and watched Wes step out of his car and shrug into a brown leather jacket as he clambered up the dune.

"Hey, Wes. Nice threads. You look very cosmopolitan."

"Thanks. Maggie got it for me."

"How is she feeling?"

Wes flushed with pleasure. "We had a doctor's appointment yesterday. Mom and baby are perfect!"

I touched his arm. "That's wonderful, Wes."

"Yeah. We're stoked. So you sure landed yourself in the middle of this one, huh?"

"What are you talking about?"

"It looks like Lydia's in the hot seat, and you're the key witness. She's been at the police station all night."

"What evidence do they have?"

"MMO, baby. MMO. Motive: Cal was two-timing Lydia with Nora. Means: It's too early for a definitive analysis, but my police source tells me that the ME found residue from something that might be metal and wood splinters in the wound. The wood could have come from the hardwood flooring, but the metal is foreign to the room, so that means the murder weapon was made of metal or something like metal, and—hold on to your hat—there's a pile of metal pipes at the social club."

Evidently, my late-night call to Ellis had already reaped a benefit.

Wes continued. "Opportunity: You place her at the scene. What more do they need?"

"What is Lydia saying?"

"Nothing. She's lawyered up."

I turned toward the ocean. "I can't believe it. Lydia killed him."

"There's more. Your RFI—I've got it."

"What's an RFI?"

"Request for information. Get with the program, Joz. You asked about Anthony's Shoe Repair, the building, and the social club. The building is owned by a holding company called PDS, Inc. Wait for it . . . PDS owns *all* the buildings on that block. The company is based in Bermuda, a tax haven extraordinaire. The corporate officers are all employees of a Hamilton law firm. They're not talking, natch. There's no way to tell who really owns it. Anthony's Shoe Repair rents that space from PDS through a local property manager. They know nothing except the name of their contact, one of the Bermuda lawyers. They say they had no clue that anyone was using the basement. Ditto PDS. Ditto Anthony, and ditto Anthony's employee, the guy in the back, whose name is Boris. You met Anthony, the old man behind the counter. He identified you from your photo and said you were nosy." Wes chuckled. "In any event, the social club doesn't exist in any formal way. It's not a registered business or charity. The utility charges come through on Anthony's bill. He says he never thought to question it, even though his charges quadrupled after the social club opened about ten months ago. Anthony denies it, but the police think whoever ran the social club was slipping him cash to look the other way to people trooping in and out, and to cover the utilities. Anthony is old school. He doesn't take credit cards, and with an all-cash business, no one, not even a forensic accountant, can verify revenue sources or expenses."

"How can Boris not know something?"

"People only see what they want to see. You know that. You ran into exactly the same issue that time Gretchen went missing.* Employees don't turn in their bosses because you don't bite the hand that feeds you."

I didn't want to believe it, but I knew that Wes was right. "I guess . . . but if nothing else, wouldn't you be curious?"

"Sure, but I'm a journalist. Lots of people think asking questions is just looking for trouble, so they steer clear." Wes extracted his notebook and tugged the pen from the wire casing. He opened to a page marked with a slim black ribbon. "Your turn—fill me in. I want the blow-by-blow. Start with leaving the church after Mo's funeral."

I told Wes everything, including why I was following Nora.

"Describe Cal's apartment."

"It was messy. And sad. There was a chest of drawers, a table and two chairs, and a mattress on the floor, that's it. The drawers were open. Clothes and books and papers were scattered everywhere."

"Like he was a slob?"

"More like someone did a quick search."

"I can't believe you didn't take pictures!"

I gave him an "oh-puhleeze" look, and he sighed, Wesian for disappointment.

"I know you didn't see Lydia whack Cal, but did you hear anything?" he asked.

"Only her footsteps as she left."

He flipped his notebook closed and stuffed the pen back in place.

"Catch ya later!" he said, and started down the dune.

I stood at the top a while longer, watching the frothy waves roll to shore.

I got into work around eight fifteen. I needed to leave for my meeting with Max around quarter to nine, which meant I had plenty of time to check my

---

* Please see *Killer Keepsakes.*

email and read updates from my staff. The first thing I did was say hello to Hank and Angela and refresh their food and water. While I waited for the coffee to brew I booted up Gretchen's computer, so I wouldn't have to go upstairs.

Cal was killed in a building owned by PDS, Inc. No one knew who was behind PDS. I brought up a search engine and typed "Trish Shannon" and "first golf win." The first hit linked to a photo from a 1974 Los Angeles newspaper. A younger Trish stood on a golf course, her arms high over her head in a V, smiling with unadulterated joy. The caption read NEWCOMER PATRICIA D. WERNER CELEBRATING HER FIRST PROFESSIONAL WIN. Trish was a nickname for Patricia, and Trish changed her name from Werner to Shannon when she and Frank married. Trish's legal name was Patricia D. Shannon, which meant her initials were PDS. Trish owned the building where Cal was killed.

I had just poured myself a mug of coffee when the front door swung open and Lydia stepped in.

She looked the worse for wear. She was still wearing the same blue suit she'd worn at the funeral, but now it was crumpled and stained along the hem. Her hair was stringy. Her eyes were red and moist, not as if she'd been crying but as if she were struggling to keep them open.

She closed the door. "I didn't know if you'd be in this early."

"I'm not always."

She drew her hand across her brow. I watched her, my mind racing to guess why she was here.

"Can I get you something?" I asked. "Coffee? Tea?"

"Coffee would be good. Black. Do you have a minute to talk?"

I'd never heard her sound so measured and noncombative. "Sure. Have a seat."

She took the closest guest chair. I poured coffee into a Prescott's mug and brought it to the table.

Lydia cupped the mug, staring through the aromatic steam into the coffee as if she hoped to find answers. After a moment, she lifted her bleary eyes. "The police told me you were at Cal's, that you saw me."

"Yes."

"They're probably going to arrest me for murder. The only reason they haven't is that they don't have the murder weapon and your testimony proves I wasn't carrying it when I left. Unless they think I went back to Cal's place after dropping the weapon and his computer in my car trunk. Can you believe they're that stupid? Who'd go back to a murder scene?"

"Someone who forgot something."

She blinked at me. "Like what?"

"I don't know. Cal's phone. Cash. The coveralls she wore while she killed him."

"You saw me—I wasn't the least bit bloody."

"Thus the coveralls."

"Did you see me carrying coveralls?"

"No."

She lifted a hand. "That's my point." She drank some coffee. "What exactly did you see?"

I was sorting through whether there were any parts I should withhold when she spoke again.

"Trying to figure out a good lie?"

I met her steely glare and looked for signs of grief, but I found none.

"I wish I could help you, Lydia, but I can't. I saw two men in the big room at the bottom of the stairs and you, and that's it."

"Who were the men?"

"I don't know. I couldn't identify them. How did you know where Cal was staying?"

"Why wouldn't I know? Cal was my boyfriend. Of course we were in touch."

"The police must have searched your bag, which means they must have found the phone you used to communicate with him."

"They didn't search anything. I wouldn't let them, and they don't have enough for a warrant."

"You wouldn't be talking so openly about being in touch with Cal if the police didn't know about it. How did they find out?"

She raised her chin, in defiance or a dare, I couldn't tell which, and glowered at me. "I told them. My mother owns the building. I stopped by now and then to check on the place. Sometimes Cal went with me, so when he needed a safe place to stay, he thought of that room. He asked if he could use it, and I said yes."

"Then you knew about the casino."

"No. I haven't been there in a while. I was speechless when Cal told me."

"Who owns it?"

"I have no idea."

"Why didn't you close it down?"

"I planned on it, as soon as Cal left."

"I bet the police were livid with you for lying."

"I don't care. I knew Cal didn't kill my sister, and just because the police ask questions doesn't mean you have to answer them."

"How could you possibly know he didn't kill Mo? He was there. He had a motive. He fled."

"He ran because you were hounding him about that print. For God's sake, he was an expert, but oh no! You knew better. You poisoned Mo's mind with your talk of formal appraisals and insurance riders."

I kept my eyes on her face. She seemed to actually believe what she was saying. Denial, thy name is Lydia.

"You must have seen or heard something," she insisted. "Cal was killed minutes before I arrived."

"I didn't."

She placed her mug on the table and stood. "I shouldn't have come. I don't know what I expected. Mercy, perhaps."

"Mercy?"

"Compassion for my grief, understanding for my need to know." She walked to the door. "Forget it."

As I watched Lydia tramp across the parking lot, I wondered whether she'd fibbed. Despite saying she'd come to hear what I'd witnessed, I thought it was likely that she had a different agenda completely, that she hadn't expected to learn anything new; rather, she'd hoped to confirm that I hadn't seen her kill the man who'd betrayed her.

The lack of blood on her clothing could be easily explained. She could have worn lightweight plastic coveralls, then turned them inside out, rolled them up, and stuffed them into her waistband where they'd be hidden from view by her jacket. I could understand why the police wouldn't formally charge her with Cal's murder until they found where she'd bought them or dumped them, or both, and the weapon she used to kill him, but I bet they were keeping close tabs on her. I peeked out the window. I wasn't surprised to see Detective Brownley drive by in an unmarked car seconds after Lydia left the lot.

I pulled into the little parking lot behind Max's office and backed into a spot by the rear entry.

Every time I stepped into Max's office, I was reminded that people are complex. He always wore traditional tweedy suits and bow ties, yet in furnishings his taste ran to contemporary. Today's suit was gray. His tie was red with black polka dots. His desk was a slab of black granite perched on stainless steel legs. Black-metal-and-stainless-steel bookcases lined one wall. The guest chairs were black leather and slouchy. The carpet was a red-and-gray block print. The art was abstract, mostly oils, all black-and-white geometric shapes or slashes of red or purple or gold.

Max sat at his desk. I sat in one of the comfy leather chairs. I opened the box of muffins I'd picked up en route, and he dove in.

He tapped a yellow legal pad with his fountain pen. "I've reviewed Matt Janson's business plan. Rather than a partnership, I'm going to recommend that you buy Janson's Antiques Mall outright. Offer Matt a good employment contract with a profit-sharing component. He'll work for you, with his first assignment getting the Maine location up and running while continuing to manage the venue he started and overseeing Prescott's. If it doesn't work out or if he quits and cashes out, that's that. You can shake hands and move on."

"I love it . . . but do you think he'll go for it? I'm sure he expects a cut of everything in perpetuity, which he'd have in a partnership."

"Sell it as plenty of profit-earning upside with no risk. He's the one who suggested using Prescott's as the brand."

"You're right. What's my next step?"

"Decide if you want to proceed. If so, we'll get going on due diligence."

"I want to proceed."

"Terrific. I have a good feeling about this, Josie." He finished his muffin.

"If it works, you'll go from one location to two plus one in development in a few months."

"Thank you, Max. You're a treasure."

"You, too. You're an ideal client." He switched off his desk lamp and stood. "What do you say . . . should we hitch up our wagon and mosey on over to the police station?"

I stood. "Hitch up our wagon? Mosey?"

"I can't help it. I just tried out for *Oklahoma!*"

"I didn't know you could act."

"Who says I can?"

I laughed. "Or sing."

"Ditto."

"You're too funny."

"That I am."

He held the door, and we agreed to drive separately. I called Matt en route and left a message saying that I wanted to move to the next step and had some ideas to discuss. I hoped my news would make his day.

CHAPTER THIRTY-ONE

Katie, the police department's IT tech, was ready to go when Max and I arrived. Police Officer Dawn LeBlanc was there, too. Dawn was short and stocky, with shoulder-length medium brown hair, brown eyes, and a sprinkling of freckles across her nose. She worked for a police force in a nearby town and had helped the Rocky Point police with undercover assignments in the past.* Her job was to play Andi Brewster at the meet.

Ellis led us into Interrogation Room Two, and we took seats around the table. An assistant district attorney named Cheryl Tavery fussed a little about the language Max had written absolving me of responsibility and liability for anything and everything, but finally she signed all four copies. After I signed, too, he distributed them, shook hands all around, and left.

Ellis sat at the head of the table, to my left, with Cheryl next to him, across from me. Katie was next to her at the foot of the table, surrounded by computer and electronic equipment. Cables snaked across the table from her computer to the phone. Dawn sat next to me, on my right, pen and pad in hand.

Ellis slid the phone unit from the center of the table toward me. "I assume you're all right with our using your phone and voice changer. Probably we could forward the number to a police cell phone and get our own voice changer, but why risk it? I'll see you get them back."

"Of course." I placed my voice changer next to the phone, attached the cable, and tapped the voice changer's screen to bring up the southern-woman

---

* Please see *Dolled Up for Murder* and *Glow of Death*.

option. "My job is to role-play the call with Dawn, is that correct? I play Pat Durand. She plays Andi Brewster."

"Yes, but let's start with you explaining the antiques aspect to Dawn."

I pushed my chair out, angling it so I faced Dawn straight on.

I described Hiroshige's woodblock prints, showed her a photo of *Flower Pavilion,* and detailed how I'd tried to create an impression that Andi was a bit overeager and naïve.

"I'm certain Pat Durand is not an art or antiques expert," I said and explained how Pat hadn't sent any photos of the back of the print. "Pat is involved in art fraud, though, and maybe murder."

"And as such, should be considered armed and dangerous," Ellis said. "Thank you, Josie." To Dawn, he added, "Any questions?"

"Only one—what if Pat Durand doesn't answer our call?"

I jumped in. "Pat is expecting Andi's call, so if she doesn't answer, I think you should hang up, then call back a minute or two later, sounding mystified that Pat isn't there, explaining that the previous hangup was you, that you wanted to confirm the time, blah, blah, blah. What do you think?"

Dawn made a note on her pad. "My goal would be to set another time to talk?"

"I wouldn't. I'd try to set a time to meet without any intermediate steps."

Dawn looked at Ellis. "Sounds good to me. What do you think?"

"I like it. Cheryl? Any objections?"

"I'm always in favor of hurrying things along. Make certain you don't say anything that could be interpreted as entrapment."

"Of course."

I looked at Ellis, then Cheryl. "Are you sure I can't do it? We know the voice changer works. Why not?"

Cheryl was brusque. "Because it's police business."

Ellis looked at Dawn. "We'd talked about arranging to meet at the gazebo on the village green. The overhang on the roof will allow Katie to hook up her equipment so it's out of sight. But don't mention it to Pat Durand. Get a commitment to meet in Rocky Point tomorrow afternoon around five. Once she agrees, tell her you'll call her back with a location when you know where you'll be." Ellis caught Katie's eye. "We can delay telling her the location until around four or four thirty—does that give you enough time?"

"We'll be done by then. Plus, my assistant, Curt, and I will be wearing Park Department uniforms. We'll cover the gazebo in tarps and put up 'People Working' and 'Wet Paint' signs. Everyone will think we're whitewashing it."

Ellis rubbed his nose. "Good. Josie? Are you ready?"

"Yes. Someone do a ring, ring, beep for me."

"I'll do it," Cheryl said. "*Brrrrng. Brrrrng. Brrrrng.* Please leave a message at the beep. *Beep.*"

I closed my eyes. "Pat, I'm sorry I'm missing you. That hangup you just got—that was me. When you didn't pick up I got afraid I had the wrong number or the wrong day or something. Anyway . . . maybe I wrote it wrong in my calendar. It doesn't matter! I hope you're doing fine. I really love that print! Love it! The colors are so incredible. It turns out I'm going to be in Rocky Point, New Hampshire, tomorrow, Thursday, so I'm hoping we can connect around five in the afternoon. Give me a call, okay? I probably won't be able to pick up, but I'll get the message for sure. I'll bring cash, so if the print is as beautiful in person as it is in that photo you sent, we can do the exchange right then and there. Talk to you soon—or rather, see you soon! Bye-bye!" I opened my eyes and looked around the room. "How was that?"

Cheryl smiled. "Masterful. I'm glad you're not a defense attorney I have to face in court."

I felt myself blush at the compliment. "Thanks."

"Talk about a hard act to follow," Dawn said. She dragged the phone unit closer. "I'm ready to go. I don't need to practice."

Ellis turned to me. "What could Pat say that might trip Dawn up?"

"Nothing I can think of. If Pat asks why you like the print, just talk about the beauty of the scene and the colors. If she uses any technical terms, feel free to giggle with embarrassment and ask what they mean."

"Dawn?" Ellis asked.

"I'm good."

"Okay. Let's do it."

Dawn looked at Katie.

"The tracer is up. The recording is on."

Dawn put the phone on speaker and dialed. After six rings, a robotic voice invited Dawn to leave a message. The sound reverberated through the room.

She hung up. We sat silently for more than a minute; then Dawn hit REDIAL and waited for the beep. She spoke clearly and confidently, parroting my message, her tone warm and excited. When she was done, she replaced the receiver.

"Well done, Dawn!" Ellis said.

"Now all I have to do is actually talk with a southern accent while maintaining that kind of perkiness. I can handle the southern accent, but the perkiness may kill me."

Everyone laughed.

Ellis stood. "Thank you, Josie. I'll walk you out."

"Good luck, everyone."

When we reached the lobby, Ellis stopped. "It goes without saying that you shouldn't talk about this with anyone, and you shouldn't be on the village green tomorrow afternoon."

"You're more than welcome. I'm glad to help."

Ellis grinned. "Thank you. I appreciate your cooperation very much. No offense intended."

"None taken. I won't talk to anyone about this, and I won't go to the village green tomorrow afternoon."

I had a day to find a place where I could see the gazebo without being seen.

I dug my phone and keys out of my tote bag, then locked it in my trunk. Matt had called back saying he was eager to hear my ideas for the new business venture and asking when I'd like to get together. I didn't want to talk to Matt until my mind was clear, so I texted him that I would call him soon to schedule a time.

I crossed the street and climbed a low dune, relishing the warm September sun. The ocean was green today, darker than emerald, lighter than pine. To the north, far from where I stood, a woman rode a gray stallion along the shoreline, and I thought of Mo.

I sat on the sand, letting the breeze tousle my hair, and stared at the horizon. A thought came to me: What if Lydia was telling the truth, that she hadn't killed Cal? The memory of what I'd overheard at the garden party—Frank and Trish agreeing to kill Cal—remained fresh in my mind. I wondered if anyone had checked them out.

I texted Wes: *Do Frank and Trish have an alibi for Cal's murder?*

My phone vibrated. It was Sasha. I took the call. Sasha had news about Mo's print. The prior owner's great-great-grandfather had been a professor of industrial design at Oxford University, specializing in medical instrumentation design. He'd visited Japan as part of a Dutch delegation before and after the country opened to the West.

"Rangaku," I said, referring to a body of knowledge developed by the Japanese through their relationships with the Dutch. "You've done a great job, Sasha."

She also reported on the quotes to test both the paper and the ink. Greyson Chemicals wasn't the cheapest, but we agreed they were the best, so we decided to go with them.

Moments after our call ended, Wes texted back: *Airtight. Why?*

My phone vibrated. It was Cara. Dr. Sanford, the woman who sold the Martin guitar to Abbot's back in the early 1970s, was on the line. She was close by and wondered if she could stop in.

"Tell her I'll be there in ten minutes."

I had almost reached my car when Nora pulled into the lot. I stood until she parked and got out of her vehicle, then walked toward her. Everything about her looked tense. A muscle on the side of her neck twitched. Her knees were locked.

I said hello and asked how she was.

"Okay, I guess. I'm pretty freaked out, actually. I can't imagine why they want to talk to me."

"Probably they think you know what Cal was doing at that social club."

Her lips tightened. "Why would they think that?"

"I saw you at Anthony's Shoe Repair yesterday, just before Cal was murdered."

She tried to smile, and failed. "I didn't kill him."

"I believe you."

Her tension eased, just a bit. "Why?"

"Because of how you hugged your husband after Mo's funeral. I know how a woman looks when she's giving a man she used to love a good-bye hug. This wasn't that. You hugged him like he was your safe harbor." I took a step closer and lowered my voice. "Did you break up with Cal?"

"I went there to play bingo."

"The police know you were involved with him."

"That's crazy!"

"I'm sorry."

"I don't know what you think you know, but—"

She broke off when I held up a hand. "Don't. Folks at the Colonial Club reported that you and Cal were an item."

Nora seemed to falter. She closed her eyes for a moment. After a few seconds, she turned toward the ocean. "I'm such a fool."

"Indiscreet, perhaps; not necessarily foolish."

"I acted like a giddy teenager."

"What attracted you to him?"

"You've seen Cal, haven't you? He was gorgeous!"

"I suppose."

She turned back to face me. "You didn't think he was good-looking?"

"I don't think appearance has much to do with attraction."

She half-smiled. "It does for me . . . at least at the start. And he seemed so urbane, so debonair. So different from Kevin."

"What changed?"

"Gambling. At first, going to the Colonial Club was exotic and fun. I'd make twenty dollars last an hour, but Cal lost hundreds, thousands, so much money, not once, but over and over again. He finger-popped the whole way through, like it was nothing. After a while, I thought it was, well, pathetic."

"Did he ever ask you for money?"

"No. He wouldn't."

"How about the Japanese woodblock prints? Did he ask you to help sell them?"

She looked mystified. "What prints? Like Mo's?"

I ignored her question. "Was Cal alive when you got to Anthony's?"

"Yes. I told him it was over."

"How did he take it?"

"He was philosophical. He said we'd had a good run, but that his luck always did run out. It took two minutes. Three, maybe. He didn't care, not really. I was so relieved. I'd been afraid he'd argue with me, try to convince me to give it another go. Then I went and sat in on a bingo game. In case anyone saw me there, I needed a cover story." She smiled again, a weak one. "I won five dollars."

"Have you told the police?"

Her smile faded. "Just about playing bingo. There are security cameras all over the casino, so I knew they'd know."

"You should tell them the truth. It will help them set the timeline."

"No way. Kevin will find out. I can't believe I went to the Colonial Club with Cal. If I hadn't done that one thing, no one would know, and everything would be all right."

"The police are good at keeping secrets. You have an opportunity to be a hero here."

She rubbed her temples for a moment. "I've made such a mess of everything."

"You made a mistake, that's all."

She aimed her big, frightened eyes at me. "I wish—"

Nora turned without finishing her thought and walked quickly toward the front door.

I hoped she'd take my advice and tell the police the truth, but I doubted it.

CHAPTER THIRTY-TWO

I was sitting at the guest table when Dr. Sanford arrived about twelve fifteen. She wore black jeans with a red sweater and a gold chain belt, casual chic. I told myself not to get excited, that her calling didn't mean she had news about the guitar's provenance.

She didn't want anything to drink, and I suggested going up to my office. She walked beside me through the warehouse, observant and silent, intelligence radiating off her like heat. Upstairs, she settled onto the love seat. I sat across from her and waited for her to speak.

"I know how easy it is to create a website and a social media history on the fly, so I wanted to visit your company without giving you time to fake a persona. I'm convinced—you're for real."

In her position, I would have done the same thing.

"I'm pleased I've passed muster."

"My husband and I spent yesterday evening going through everything I inherited that could possibly be related to the guitar. I know I said that you and I would look together, but the more I thought about it, the less comfortable I got." She extracted an envelope from her briefcase. "I brought you copies."

"Thank you so much. That's wonderful of you. If you made copies, that implies you found something you thought I could use."

"I did. My grandmother kept a diary. She was a hairdresser by occupation, but a poet by avocation. She had big ideas and big dreams, but back then, a black woman in the Deep South, well, her options were limited." She reached into the envelope for an old photograph, which she laid on the butler's table, facing me. "I found this photo between two pages of her diary."

I reached for it, then hesitated. "May I?"

"Yes. You can keep it. As I said, it's a copy. You can publish it, if you want."

I picked it up. "This is Robert Johnson."

"Yes, a studio shot."

I read the inscription: *To my best girl, Robert Johnson.* "The guitar he's holding sure looks like a Martin OM-45 Deluxe."

Dr. Sanford eased a sheet of paper from the envelope and handed it over. "Here's a copy of the back."

I squinted at the blurry red mark. "Cloister Studio. San Antonio." I smiled. "San Antonio . . . Robert Johnson recorded fifteen tunes for Vocalion Records in San Antonio in 1936. If he had a record contract, naturally they'd want some publicity shots."

"It gets better." She removed a sheaf of papers from the envelope and slid them onto the table. "These are copies of Grandma's diary, every page that mentioned Johnson. The Post-it Note flags where I found the photo."

I skim-read the first two pages, then looked up. "They were in love."

"It sounds like he was the love of her life."

"Does she explain how she came to own the guitar?"

"Robert got sick. Speculation was that he'd been poisoned by another girlfriend's husband. My grandmother knew he wasn't faithful to her, and she didn't care. I don't understand that. Do you?"

I thought of Nora. "Love can be so powerful, reason goes out the door. It's irresistible, like a tidal wave, so yes, I do understand that."

"That's lust, not love."

"You may be right, but when you're in the middle of it, you call it love. I suspect it's a walk-a-mile-in-her-moccasins thing. I don't judge."

"Perhaps. My grandmother wrote that she offered to nurse him, but he refused. From all reports, Johnson was a prideful man, and he didn't want a woman he loved to see him weak and delirious. It broke her heart. A friend took him to his house on the plantation where he worked, but Robert left his guitar at her place for safekeeping, saying he'd be back for it as soon as he got better. He died two days later. He was twenty-seven."

"That's tragic."

"My grandmother cherished that guitar because of the man who played it." Dr. Sanford stood. "I give you all this information for my grandmother.

She hid her love for Johnson her entire life. There's no reason to hide it anymore. She's smiling down on me right now, I just know she is."

"If I get to share your grandmother's story, I promise you I'll honor her love for Robert Johnson."

Dr. Sanford reached out a hand as if to touch my arm, then pulled back. "Thank you."

As we walked downstairs, she asked, "How much do you think the guitar is worth?"

"It's too early to speculate. We're still in the authentication phase. On the face of it, this guitar has everything going for it. It's in perfect condition, it's rare, it's scarce, it's been owned by legendary players, and guitars are enduringly popular. It ticks all the boxes."

"Players—plural. Someone besides Robert Johnson has played it, or is now."

"I'm sorry. I can't say."

"When will you know if it's genuine?"

"Soon, I hope. We're working with a New York–based expert. I expect to hear from him any day."

We walked across the warehouse.

"Will you be able to learn how Robert Johnson acquired it?" she asked.

"I don't think so, but that missing link shouldn't hurt the value. People don't always keep receipts, and if they do, it's not unusual that they get lost over the generations. Life isn't a business, after all."

I pushed open the heavy door to the front office.

"Will you let me know its value when you determine it?"

"I can't. The current owner has only asked me to appraise it, not sell it, and appraisals are confidential."

"I understand."

Dr. Sanford offered her hand for a final handshake, and her grip was firm.

I placed the copies of Estelle Dowler's documents on the guest table. While I waited for Fred to finish a phone call, I swiveled to face the window. A gust of wind whipped through the fallen leaves, funneling them up as if they were caught in a twister, then, moments later, releasing them, and they twirled to the ground like confetti. I should begin thinking about the wedding. There were so many details, from designing invitations and selecting the music to identifying a theme and choosing the caterer. I had catalogue copy to review, too, and Matt Janson's business plan to study. I didn't want to do any of that. I didn't want to do anything. I was on edge. *Don't think—do.* My dad repeated that admonition a thousand times in the months after my mother's death when I was rudderless, and later when I was in college and overwhelmed. Action might not cure anxiety, he said, but it sure helps manage it.

Fred hung up. "That was Davy."

"From your eyes, I can tell you have news."

He grinned. "We've got ourselves a real-deal 1930 Martin OM-45 Deluxe guitar."

"Hot diggity!"

He leaned back, a happy man. "Super hot diggity!"

I pointed to the papers on the table. "Dr. Sanford gave me copies of documents that validate the claim that the guitar was owned by Robert Johnson just before his death."

His eyes fired up. "This might really be something."

I held up crossed fingers. "Any leads you're still following?"

"No. I've verified eight extant guitars, and that's as far as I think we'll be able to get. I primed every pump I could find."

"Eight of fourteen . . . that's like a sixty percent success rate, Fred. Unbelievable."

He grinned again, more broadly this time. "Why are you surprised?"

I laughed. "I'm not. I'm awed."

I asked Fred to research whether Cloister Studio kept any records about Johnson's visit, specifically whether he'd brought his own guitar to the photo shoot or used one they had on hand, like a theater prop. If he'd brought the guitar with him, it would go a long way to showing that he'd actually owned it. The odds that Cloister retained records that detailed were remote, but we had to check.

The phone rang. Trish was on line one.

Trish sounded agitated. "May I come to talk to you? It's urgent."

I told her yes and gathered the documents related to her husband's private appraisal into a pile and handed them over to Fred for safekeeping. He placed them in a drawer, out of sight.

• • •

Trish didn't want to go to my private office.

"Can we step outside instead? It's so lovely out."

"Sure." I grabbed my jacket.

I led the way to the bench over by the tag sale venue.

Trish sat with her knees together, her back board-straight, and her eyes fixed on the distant woods. Sunlight touched her silver hair, setting it aglow like a halo. I sat at an angle, my right thigh resting on the seat. Her expression was austere, her jaw set, her neck muscles rope-tight.

"Thank you for seeing me with no notice. I needed to talk to you. I need to explain." She met my eyes. "Frank and I have agreed to a policy of no secrets. Never again will we keep things from one another. Not to protect ourselves. Not to shield Lydia. Never." After a few seconds, Trish asked, "Do you have some good news for us about Frank's guitar?"

Frank told me he didn't want Trish to know about the appraisal, that he didn't want anyone to know. If he'd changed his mind about keeping secrets, he hadn't told me. For all I knew, Trish had found the receipt and was trying to suss out information behind his back.

"I'm sorry, Trish. I can't comment. All appraisals are confidential. I can't even reveal whether we're conducting one or not."

"Really?" I didn't respond, so she added, "It doesn't matter, I suppose. We're leaving New Hampshire. I can't stay in that house. I haven't slept since Mo died. I doze a little, then jerk awake. Frank doesn't even try. He sits in his studio all night, playing guitar or listening to music."

"I'm so sorry, Trish. Where are you going?"

"Mountain climbing to start with. If we get tired enough, maybe we can sleep. We fly to Lucerne in a few days."

I wondered if Ellis knew they planned to leave the country. "Does Lydia go with you?"

"No. I don't know Lydia's plans. She's reeling. We all are, I suppose, but Lydia is less communicative than either of us. So much loss . . . truly, it's almost too much to bear. You know that the police think Lydia might have killed Cal?"

"I heard that, yes."

"She didn't." Trish studied her hands. "It's absurd. Horrifying and absurd."

She raised her eyes and scanned the parking lot. "Well, then . . . you're probably wondering why I'm here. Three reasons. First, I couldn't leave without thanking you for Mo's eulogy, for being such a good friend to her."

"I meant every word. Thank you for including me."

She patted my hand. "We're putting all our furniture we want to keep and most of our clothes into storage. I'm hoping you'll sell everything else, all the outdoor furniture, sports gear, and miscellaneous items, like pots and pans and so on, that sort of thing. Will you take it on?"

"Of course. We can buy the objects outright or you can consign them."

"I don't want to think about them again, so I'll ask you to buy them outright."

"All right."

She paused for a moment. "The third thing I want to say . . . that I *need* to say . . . it's my fault you were attacked at that social club." She raised a hand to stop me from interrupting. "I drove Frank and Lydia to do some terrible things." She paused again, this time for several seconds. "You need context to understand, to forgive me. I was worried about Frank's gambling, so I put him on an allowance. Doesn't that sound awful? This was years ago, before we were married even. His royalties and fees are deposited into a bank account that only I can access. He agreed, but still . . . I dole out money to him as if he were a child. I hate it, but I do it, because it's the smart thing to do. It was a good system, and we've built some impressive holdings over the years, but the system broke down. He needed twenty thousand dollars, far more than his allowance, and he knew I'd demand an explanation before I gave it to him, and he also knew that if he told me the truth, I'd refuse."

She stopped talking, and after a moment, I asked, "Was it a gambling debt?"

"No. Frank told me that he only plays a little nowadays, and that he never loses much. It wasn't that. He couldn't tell me because it was a secret. He'd promised Lydia he wouldn't tell."

"Cal. It was Cal's gambling debt."

"Yes . . . and Frank and Lydia were right—I wouldn't have paid a nickel to help Cal." Trish closed her eyes for a few seconds, then took in a deep breath and opened them. She turned toward me. "I'm asking for your compassion, Josie. Cal owed more than sixty thousand dollars. Sixty thousand! Can you believe it? He lost it in one night at the Colonial Club. Lydia wanted to help him, but her trust is set up to provide periodic payments. She can't touch the principal without my permission. She gave Cal forty thousand dollars, all the cash she had available and all the cash advances she could get on her credit cards."

"Lydia went to Frank for help."

"Never underestimate the devotion of a father to his daughter."

"What does Frank's devotion have to do with my getting hurt?"

"I own that building."

"But you didn't hire those thugs."

"No, of course not. But I've been a hands-off owner. When the cat's away the mice will play."

"Lydia runs the casino."

Trish closed her eyes for a moment. "How did you know?"

"She mentioned she stopped in now and again. No one else would know that the space was available and the owner wouldn't catch on."

"She started it as a fun surprise for Cal, a birthday present. A pop-up casino, she called it. Then it proved so popular, she let it continue."

"Did you know she let Cal stay there when he ran for it?"

"No. I was outraged. I still am." Trish stood. "The point is . . . I wanted to say . . . the attack happened in my building, under my watch, except I wasn't watching, and I sincerely hope you weren't hurt."

"Thank you. It could have been worse." I stood, too. "Do the police know you're leaving the country?"

"Our lawyer plans to tell them today."

We walked to the parking lot.

When we reached her car, she paused. "Can you come today? Now? To take everything away."

"Yes."

As soon as I stepped inside, Fred said, "Cloister Studio is long gone—they closed down in 1958. Their photo archives and business records are at the University of Texas, San Antonio. The librarian was helpful, but of no help. The photo Dr. Sanford gave you is the only one they have of Robert Johnson, and there are no relevant business records. That said, here's my estimate of value."

He handed me a sheet of paper on which he'd written *$500,000+*.

"This is a big number."

"And I'm being conservative."

"That's great news. Get the instrument and the extra case ready for pickup or delivery." I turned toward Gretchen. "Please call Frank Shannon and tell him his appraisal is ready. Ask him to stop by—or I can bring everything to him. I'm going to the Shannon house now. Trish wants to sell some things." I faced Fred. "In fact, Fred, why don't you come with me? Get Eric and a couple of other guys, too. Let's take the truck and plenty of packing materials." I turned back to Gretchen. "Don't leave a message—speak only to Frank." As Fred headed into the warehouse, I congratulated him on his thoroughness, then turned to Sasha. "Where are we with Mo's print?"

"Greyson Chemicals expects to finish their materials analysis by the end of business today."

"Good."

I sat at the guest table. Hank sauntered over, jumped into my lap, and curled up. The sounds of a normal workday combined with Hank's soft purr soothed me.

Gretchen hung up. "Frank isn't home—I reached him on his cell. He says he'll be here at three."

Fred and I drove in my car. The part-timers rode with Eric in the truck. Fred and I video-recorded everything outside and in the shed, and the marked items inside, as per our protocol. While Eric and his team loaded the truck, I met with Trish in the living room.

"Until I've done an appraisal on some of the more valuable objects, like your golf clubs, I can't determine actual value. All I can do is offer you a third of what I expect everything would sell for at the tag sale, and I know that's going to be far less than what things are actually worth. I encourage you to let me appraise things first."

"Thank you, Josie. I appreciate your frankness. As I said, though, I just want everything gone."

I did the calculations, Trish approved the number, and I asked Gretchen to prepare the paperwork. When it arrived, Trish signed the e-forms.

I left the men to their work and drove back to the office.

*   *   *

At three o'clock sharp, Frank thanked Gretchen for the escort to my office and sat on the love seat. I chose the wing chair.

"You didn't need to come up."

"Trish told me about your conversation."

"She said you're going to Switzerland."

"Yeah. It was Trish's idea, and I think it's a good one. Better to work our bodies for a while, then light somewhere new."

"How's Lydia?"

His lips folded together, and he shook his head. "Not good. It's killing me, watching her suffer. When you love someone, their pain is your pain, except more so because it's doubled. You feel it as if it's happening to you, and you see it happening to them."

"You're okay leaving before Mo's killer is found?"

"It's not Lydia, if that's what you're asking."

"I wasn't."

"If there was anything we could do . . . if Lydia wanted us or needed us, we'd stay."

"It's a mess."

"A big one. Life keeps on coming at ya, that's for sure. So what do you have for me about my guitar?"

"Good news. We have great confidence that the guitar is genuine and that it was owned by Robert Johnson. I've documented ownership from you back in time to a woman who had a long-running affair with him. She kept a diary. One entry specifies that Johnson was sick, deathly ill, and that he gave her his guitar for safekeeping. So we have it in his hands, then hers. The only missing link is how he came to own it. That gap won't hurt the value, though."

"That's incredible work, Josie. Lay it on me—what's it worth?"

I smiled. "Five hundred thousand dollars, or more, largely because of the associations with star blues players—you and Johnson."

"Hot damn." Frank grinned. "You've made my day."

"We aim to please, and sometimes we can."

Frank stood and extended his hand. "Well, I guess this is good-bye, then."

I didn't stand, and I didn't take his hand. I kept my eyes on his face. "Before you go, there's something I need to tell you."

His eyes grew wary. He lowered himself to the love seat, perching on the front half of the cushion.

"I know you broke into my place to steal Mo's print, Frank."

"Whoa, girl. You can stop right there."

"Forget the fact that Trish as good as told me—saying you needed twenty thousand dollars to help Lydia settle Cal's debt and asking for my compassion. I knew anyway. You trained as an electrician, which means you knew where to hit the power line to cause an outage without frying yourself. You also knew how to sabotage my generator."

"Trish told you no such thing. She was upset you got attacked in her building, that's all. As to the rest, you've got an active imagination, Josie. Anyone could have mucked with the power."

"You're the only person who asked if my roosters were okay. How could you know the glass in the display case had been broken if you hadn't seen it? That wasn't part of any news story or broadcast. Your plan was slick, Frank, but I'd already removed the print from the easel, and my security company and the police got here before you could finish looking around. I know you did it. You probably justified it by telling yourself that Mo would have been glad to help her sister. You're a the-ends-justify-the-means sort of guy."

Frank walked to the window. He stood for several seconds staring out over the trees.

"I rely on Trish to take care of this sort of thing," he said, his back to me, "apologies and whatnot. It's not in my nature. I just don't have it in me." Frank turned to face me. "That said, I hate the thought of your place being burglarized. I'd like to pay for the damage."

"You can't." I stood. "Glass can be replaced easily and for not a lot of money. Trust can't be bought at any price."

"I'm sorry."

"For doing it? Or for getting caught?"

Frank didn't comment, and his expression didn't change. He didn't look sorry or ashamed or worried or anything in particular. He just looked like Frank, a man more used to adoring fans than paying the piper.

"Come on. I'll walk you out."

CHAPTER THIRTY-THREE

I sat at the guest table thinking that nothing gelled. Disparate facts whirled in my mind's eye like dust particles in the sun. I couldn't stop thinking about trust and betrayal, and about money: earning it, inheriting it, losing it, spending it, protecting it, and gambling it away. And the people. Everything pointed to Lydia as Cal's killer. Mo's, too, really, when you considered that Lydia was on the scene and faced a myriad of issues with her sister. I considered alternatives, experimenting with combinations of people and motives, seeking out patterns, looking for clues in the mundane. People kill because of lust, more than love; revenge, more than hate; and greed, more than longing. The question was who fit that profile, and in one fell moment, the pieces snapped together like a child's puzzle, and I gasped.

"Josie?" Gretchen asked, concerned. "Are you all right?"

I blinked myself back to the here and now. "I'm fine. Thanks."

I allowed myself to sink back into the haze of reflection. Mo had been both a failed romantic and mawkishly sentimental. She viewed the world as she wished it were, with selective vision, whereas Cal had been a realist, astute, intuitive, manipulative, and a deft liar. Mo had loved heedlessly, with all her heart. Cal had been too self-centered to love. Mo had a gentle, trusting soul. Cal had no soul. Steve betrayed Mo, then proceeded to dicker about the terms of their reconciliation. Cal betrayed Lydia, then asked her to bail him out. And she did. Lydia trusted her father. Nora wanted out. The answer was so obvious, I couldn't understand how I could have missed it for so long. *Lust. Revenge. Greed.* Put those three motives together, and a witch's brew of murder boils over.

I knew who killed Mo, and why.

And I thought I knew how to prove it.

I grabbed my tote bag, called out a general "Bye" to my staff, and drove straight to Branson Wills.

I sat in the Murphy's Interiors parking lot searching for a headshot to show Anita. It took less than five minutes to download and crop an appropriate image.

Anita was standing on a low stool twirling an elegant artificial vine around a decorative column. I waited until she stepped down to speak.

"I have another photo to show you."

She took my phone and stared at the photograph, then raised her eyes to my face. "I hate this."

"I know."

"That's the customer who bought *Flower Pavilion,* number sixteen."

I felt like cartwheeling out of the place.

Ellis was on the phone when I poked my head into his office just before five. He pointed at the blond-wood table by the front wall, and I sat facing the window.

"That's right," he said. "Seven o'clock . . . two people . . . thanks."

"You're going out to dinner."

He joined me at the table. "You're some deductive whiz."

"Tonight's Wednesday. What's the occasion?"

"It's sort of a celebration."

"You're blushing."

"Police chiefs don't blush."

"Should I mind my own business?"

"Yes, but I know you won't. It's Zoë's and my 'I love you' anniversary."

"Tonight's the anniversary of the first time you told her you loved her."

One side of his mouth shot up. "And she told me."

"So you're taking her to dinner. That's maybe the sweetest thing I've ever heard. Is it a surprise?"

"No. I told her I think we ought to celebrate more. Life is so busy, it's easy to get into a rut. Better to celebrate the small things."

"I love that, Ellis. I really do."

"Thanks. Dinner isn't a surprise . . ." He reached behind him for a small maroon box. It was from Blackmore's Jewelers, the finest jeweler on the Seacoast. ". . . but this is. What do you think?"

"I think it's fabulous."

He laughed. "Open it."

I lifted the lid. A gold bangle embedded with diamonds rested on a white satin pillow. "Oh, my God, Ellis! This is magnificent!"

"Do you think Zoë will like it?"

I touched his wrist. "I think she'll love it."

"Thanks." He closed the lid and placed it back on the desk. "So, back to business. What can I do for you?"

"I have information about Mo's and Cal's murders."

His tone sharpened. "Talk to me."

"At first, Mo's murder seemed inexplicable. Shift your perspective, though, and the answer is apparent." I explained what I knew, what I suspected, and what I concluded.

"Thank you, Josie. This is incredibly helpful."

"Are you going to let the meet with Pat Durand go forward as scheduled? At five, in the gazebo?"

"Yes. I'll need to verify your information and talk to the DA about a search warrant, but I don't anticipate any problems. Will you be able to help me out tomorrow after the meet? I may need your expertise when it comes to the woodblock print."

I assured him I would, and left.

Fred was alone when I got back to the office around six thirty.

He was reading from a thick sheaf of papers. He handed me a note Sasha had written before she left for the day.

Mo's woodblock print is a fake. A clever fake, but a fake nonetheless.

I raised my eyes. "Have you read the report?"

Fred nodded. "Yes. The ink is good. The production methodology is consistent with known originals. The woodgrain appearing on the paper is accurate—but there were no lees."

I leaned against the table. "No lees means no wood."

"Right."

"So instead of using a woodblock made of cherry or whatever, someone transferred the real woodgrain pattern onto plastic or Formica or something, and printed from that. What about the paper?"

"It's wrong."

I slid into a guest chair.

"The nuclear residue found in the paper fibers proves that the paper was produced in Japan—but during the years following World War II." He tossed the papers onto his desk. "Why would a counterfeiter think it was worth so much effort?"

"Greed. Let's do the math. All the effort is in the preparation. Once I have the plastic or whatever, I can print at will. Just for the sake of argument, let's say I printed a hundred and twenty copies to start. I keep my inventory out of the light and only sell a dozen prints a year, one a month or so. At twenty thousand dollars each, we're looking at nearly a quarter of a million dollars a year. Each year. For ten years. When I run out, I print more."

"What are you going to tell New Hampshire Children First! about the print's value?"

"Nothing. We'll send this print to the tag sale, priced to move. What do you think? Fifty dollars?"

"It's so beautiful . . . maybe seventy-five."

"That's fine. Work with Sasha to buy us a genuine print in perfect condition." I laughed. "Make certain it comes with an unimpeachable pedigree. New Hampshire Children First! gets a valuable print, and we'll all put this episode behind us."

"That's really great of you, Josie. We'll get started tomorrow."

I thanked him, elated that my business was doing well enough that I could fund the contribution to New Hampshire Children First! I dashed off a note to Anita, telling her that the copy of Hiroshige's *Meguro Drum Bridge and Sunset Hill* that she sold was a fake, and I explained why. I suspected the prints she had held back would be back on the shelf first thing in the morning. I also suspected that she wouldn't change her pricing strategy. Why should she? She was selling them as decorative accessories, in the same way some antiquarian booksellers sell rare books by the yard, not for the content but for the colorful leather bindings.

I wrote Mac at *Antiques Insights*, too.

Hi Mac,

You asked me to let you know the outcome of our appraisal of the Japanese woodblock print I told you about, Hiroshige's "Meguro Drum Bridge and Sunset Hill." Based on a materials analysis, we have concluded that it's a counterfeit. Specifically, the apparent woodgrain is nothing more than a visual effect—there are no lees. Further, the paper, while Japanese, was produced after World War II.

This print was sold by Cal Lewis (who is, apparently, partnering with someone using the name Pat Durand) to my client. While I have no knowledge that other objects sold by Cal Lewis or Pat Durand are fakes, it would seem prudent to have everything he sold under either name appraised. I should mention that Cal Lewis died recently. He was murdered, a crime currently under investigation by the Rocky Point police. You may be hearing from them.

Thanks again, Mac.

Josie

I was sorry to open up such a hornet's nest, but it had to be done.

Ty texted that he was running late; he was about to leave work and was in the mood for Italian. He wanted to know what I thought about going to Abitino's and suggested we meet at eight thirty. I replied that was fine. I took advantage of the time to stop by Rocky Point Paper Palace. I parked across from the village green and went inside.

Racks of greeting cards ran the length of the shop, samples of specialty papers hung on rods against the walls, and binders of special occasion options rested on a long wooden table at the back. At Prescott's, we used Rocky Point Paper Palace for all our invitations and special announcement cards. They were expensive, but their attention to detail and the quality of their workmanship were unparalleled.

The shop's owner, a voluptuous blonde named Brenda Cragan, was a former rock 'n' roll singer who'd traveled with cover bands throughout Asia in her twenties, then quit and used her savings to set herself up in business in Rocky Point. Now, twenty years later, her shop had been featured in national magazines and on lifestyle design TV shows. I'd asked her why she hadn't capitalized on the publicity to expand, and she said she loved her life just as it was.

The shop was busy, even at seven thirty. Brenda was just finishing up a special order at the back.

"Josie!" She leaned forward for a butterfly kiss. "What can I do for you?"

"I need help, Brenda." I felt suddenly shy. "Ty and I are getting married."

"Oh, Josie! That's wonderful. You need wedding invitations."

"Party invitations. We're going to have a very small private ceremony, followed by a very large party."

"Nice. Tell me what you're thinking."

"Something simultaneously elegant and casual. I know that's an oxymoron."

"How do you want people to feel when they open the invitation?"

"Oh, golly, I don't know. Like it's going to be fun! But, you know, not silly. And not stuffy, either." I laughed. "In other words, I have no idea." I took a moment to gather my thoughts. "I want something they haven't seen before, yet more on the traditional end of the spectrum than cutesy."

Brenda reached for a book on a low shelf and flipped through to the back. She peeled back a plastic protector and eased out a sheet of parchment with a deckled edge.

I stroked it. The pale yellow paper was luscious, butter soft, and thick enough to sleep on. "It's gorgeous, but parchment feels too formal."

She flipped forward, pausing at a pale ochre sheet, embossed with flowers. "This might be perfect for a June wedding."

"Too . . . I don't know . . . fussy."

I didn't like a pink flax paper with laser heart-shaped cutouts, either. Or a blue-and-beige-marbled paper.

"I don't want to keep you, Brenda. Maybe I should just flip through."

"It's my pleasure to float ideas, Josie, but if you'd prefer looking on your own, let's do that."

"You know me well."

I started at the beginning and quickly discovered it was easy to eliminate options. What wasn't simple was finding any I liked. At ten after eight, five minutes before I needed to leave to meet Ty, I found the perfect paper. I looked over my shoulder, and as if Brenda could feel my excitement, she turned and met my eyes.

I held up my choice, translucent vellum decorated with a border of miniature poinsettias.

"I want tiger lilies and hydrangeas instead of poinsettias," I said as she walked up.

"I love it. It's exactly what you described, traditional yet welcoming."

"Do you have a sample I can take? I want to show Ty."

"Of course. Take this one. I have spares in the back." She slipped the vellum into a white envelope. "I'll have a mockup for you in a few days."

"Sounds good!"

As I drove around the village green heading for Abitino's, I passed Ellie's Crêpes,* one of my favorite restaurants. Ellie's was located directly across from the gazebo and would serve as a perfect vantage point to watch Dawn meet with Pat Durand. If I got there by four, I'd have no problem nabbing a window seat.

---

* Please see *Glow of Death, Ornaments of Death, Blood Rubies, Lethal Treasure,* and *Deadly Threads.*

CHAPTER THIRTY-FOUR

I woke the next morning, Thursday, at six. Wrapped in my favorite pink chenille robe, I yawned my way downstairs and joined Ty for coffee.

He poured me a cup. "You're up early."

"My brain is busy. I get to start planning the merger with Janson's Antiques Mall today."

"What's your first step?"

"Studying his business plan and coming up with a list of questions."

"Are you comfortable taking on a project this big?"

"Yes. Even if we move to D.C., it'll work out fine. Max pointed out that by acquiring Matt's company, I'll be acquiring a top operations guy."

"What do you think about moving to Washington?"

I drank some coffee. "I think I had enough trouble choosing that vellum paper to make any decision bigger than that right now. Except for buying out Matt. That feels like a no-brainer. How about you?"

"I like our life in New Hampshire, but I never want to turn my back on an opportunity."

"If they offer the job and it has to be based in Washington, we can decide then. What's their timeline?"

"Soon."

I reread Matt's business plan just after lunch. Assuming we could come to terms on a buyout, I didn't see how we could lose. He'd thought of everything, from personnel needs to marketing plans and from construction timelines to financing options. He recommended appointing or hiring a general manager for each location to handle the day-to-day, with him overseeing everything. His plan called for me to step back from operations and work more on high-level strategy and promotion. For instance, he thought I could—and should—write a monthly column for *Antiques Insights* magazine, with each article focusing on demystifying some element of the antiques appraisal process. I stared across the room. I would begin by writing about the difference between rarity and scarcity.

I saw the time on my computer monitor—3:30—and leapt out of my chair. I'd been so immersed in Matt's ideas for expansion, I'd completely lost track of time, but there was no way I was going to be late to Ellie's.

I got to Ellie's just before four and found Detective Brownley sitting at the table closest to the front window, reading something on her smartphone.

"Detective . . . may I join you?"

Her eyes showed neither surprise nor annoyance. "Sorry. This is Ellis's table. You'll have to ask him."

"Okay." I glanced around. The place was empty. "Where is he?"

"I don't know."

A favorite waitress, a young French woman named Juliette, stood near the kitchen chatting with a cook. I walked to join her.

"Hi, Juliette. Would it be all right if I moved a table near the window? It's so beautiful out—I want to enjoy the view."

"Of course. Will anyone be joining you?"

"No. Just me today."

Juliette selected a table next to the brick wall and rolled it to the front. Detective Brownley looked up but didn't say anything. I carried a chair and ordered a cappuccino.

My view was perfect. The gazebo, which was draped with plastic, was directly across the street. WET PAINT signs had been taped to the tarp.

Ellis arrived half an hour later, spotted me, and stopped short.

I smiled at him and tapped my forehead. "Great minds."

He met my eyes for a moment, then turned to the detective. "All set?"

"We're good to go on all fronts. Katie's upstairs."

Ellis walked to the back and said something to Juliette I couldn't hear. She opened a door on the side, revealing a staircase I hadn't known existed. Ellis crooked his index finger at me, and I joined him, carrying my cappuccino.

We climbed a steep flight of steps. I paused at the top to look around. The room was set up as a living room, so I inferred that we were in Ellie's home. I hadn't realized she lived above the restaurant.

Katie, the police IT expert, sat at a card table near the front. She wore oversized headphones. A stack of equipment rested on the table. Yellow and blue lights flickered on the bottom box. A man I didn't recognize stood by the window. A Nikon camera hung from a leather strap around his neck. A video recorder rested on a tripod. A pair of earbuds sat on the table.

Ellis pointed to a chair at the far end of the table. "Have a seat."

"Thanks." I sat.

Ellis took another chair and turned it around. He sat backward, resting his forearms on top of the backrest. He lowered his voice. "I told you to stay away."

"You told me to stay away from the village green. I haven't been near the village green all day."

"You're quibbling."

"I am not. More to the point, no one knows I'm here, or as far as I know, that I have any reason to be here."

"Good."

"Did you talk to Anita?"

"Yes. She confirmed what you told me, and we got the search warrant." Ellis's phone rang, and he glanced at the screen, then back at me. "Don't move."

"Why would I? This is the best seat in the house."

He walked toward the staircase and leaned against the wall. I couldn't hear what he was saying. I dug around in my tote bag for my phone to check the time. It was twenty minutes to five.

Katie tapped the microphone clipped to her collar. "Go inside, Curt. Tell me whether the paint is dry."

A lanky man in his forties with sandy hair and a goatee appeared from behind a tree and sauntered to the gazebo. He found a separation in the tarp and climbed up and in.

"The paint is dry."

Katie spun a dial. "Good. Talk to me."

"The paint is dry. The paint is dry. Oh why oh why is the paint so dry?"

"Stand by."

Katie spun around and dipped her head, trying to catch Ellis's attention. He got the message and nodded. A moment later, Ellis finished and returned to the worktable.

"We're ready," she told him.

"Good. Dawn is going to touch base with Pat Durand now, confirming the time and telling her the place. She'll call as soon as they connect."

Katie spoke into the mic. "Curt? You can leave the gazebo."

Ellis leaned against a front window frame. Curt stepped out from behind the plastic and ambled along the path. When he reached an old oak, he stretched. He looked for all the world like a worker on a break.

Sun filtered through the trees. Two men in suits walked across a fresh layer of crunchy leaves and sat at one end of a wooden-slat bench. An older couple sat on the other end, their shoulders touching. A young woman pushed a baby stroller along a distant path.

Ellis's phone rang. He swiped the display to accept the call.

"Hunter . . . Good . . . Thanks, Dawn." He tapped the END CALL button and looked at Katie. "Dawn has confirmed the meet."

Katie pushed a button on her microphone. "Curt?"

"Standing by."

"Open it up."

"Will do."

Curt trotted back to the gazebo. He tugged the tarps and down they came, one section at a time. Curt laid them on top of one another and rolled the pile into a bulky ball. Two minutes after he began, he was finished and out of sight.

"Curt, I'm going quiet."

"Got it."

Katie flipped a switch and turned another dial. "Can you hear me, Curt?"

There was no reply.

"Detective Brownley?"

"Loud and clear."

Katie continued her checks.

"Daryl?"

"I'm good."

I couldn't see Daryl. Or Griff when she checked in with him. Or Officer Meade, a tall ice-blonde I'd met before.

The cameraman used a remote to activate the video camera and leaned into the viewfinder to tweak the alignment.

Ellis sat at the table, rightwise now, crossing his long legs, his left ankle resting on his right thigh. His eyes were fixed on the gazebo.

Katie kept her eyes on her equipment.

I leaned in close to Ellis. "How was dinner last night?"

He smiled but didn't move his eyes. "Perfect. Thanks."

Ellis picked up the earbuds, then turned to Katie. "Do you have regular headphones?"

Katie reached under her chair and came up with a set of over-the-ear headphones.

"You just happen to have them ready to go?"

"I have two additional pairs available, too. And two more pairs of earbuds. Triple redundancy, a good cop's best friend." Katie slid a switch embedded in the headset band to the ON marker and handed them over.

Ellis slid the earbuds toward me. "You okay with earbuds?"

"Yes. Thank you." I lowered my voice. "You're being awfully nice to me."

"I'd rather have you in sight than in trouble."

I eased the earbuds into place. "I never get in trouble."

"Of course you don't."

At one minute to five, Dawn, wearing jeans and a navy-blue windbreaker, strolled along a cross path. The photographer raised his camera and started taking pictures, the clicks a steady staccato beat. Dawn climbed the gazebo steps and stood in the center. After a few seconds, she walked to the far railing and leaned against a column, her back to us. The photographer continued snapping.

At three minutes after five, a woman wearing oversized sunglasses and a black canvas floppy hat that blocked most of her face walked slowly toward the gazebo, looking every which way. She carried a large padded envelope, just the right size to safely transport the Japanese woodblock print.

Dawn spotted her and smiled, a 1,000-watter. "Pat!"

I could hear the south in that one word.

"Andi?"

"That's me, happy as a lark, and rarin' to go."

The woman calling herself Pat climbed onto the gazebo. "Nice to meet you."

"You, too."

Pat patted the envelope. "Here's the print."

Dawn clapped like a schoolgirl. "Yay!"

I bit my lip to keep from laughing. Dawn was one heck of an actress.

Dawn peeked inside, squealed with delight, and slid the plastic-encased print out of the envelope.

"Oh, it's gorgeous, Pat. Look at the colors. They're even bolder than I'd expected. Where did you get it?"

"I can't tell you that, I'm afraid. The previous owner wants confidentiality."

"Really? I'd sure like to know."

"Sorry. I wish I could, but I can't."

"No harm in asking, right?" Dawn tilted her head, faux-thinking, then smiled. "Sold!" She reached into her purse and extracted a large plain white envelope. "Here's the cash."

Before the woman calling herself Pat had time to do more than open the flap, Detective Brownley and three police officers charged the gazebo. Dawn leapt off the platform, landing in a squat on the grass. She jogged out of the way. Pat tried to follow, but before she reached the edge, all three officers surrounded her.

"No!" she screamed.

Griff grasped her arms from behind her and held her fast. I wished they'd turn her around so we could see her face.

Detective Brownley, wearing plastic gloves, grabbed the white envelope containing the cash. "We need you to come with us to the station."

The woman thrashed in all directions, struggling to get away. "No! No! No!"

It was chilling to watch. A few passersby paused, taking it in, followed by a trickle of people who came off the street. I saw two people holding up their cell phones, video-recording the scene.

The detective dropped the money into a plastic evidence bag and sealed it. She got close to Pat and raised her voice. "Please listen. I can arrest you as a material witness or you can cooperate. We have a search warrant for you, your bag, and your vehicle."

Pat stopped struggling. "Oh, God!" she whispered, as despair overtook panic.

A patrol car pulled up and double-parked, its blue-and-red dome lights spinning.

Detective Brownley said, "We need to check you for weapons. I'm going to ask Officer Meade to remove your hat and sunglasses, then we'll check your person."

Pat stiffened but didn't object.

Officer Meade snapped on plastic gloves. She pulled the hat straight up and the glasses straight off. She slid her hand under the hat brim and felt all around the crown. She ran her fingers along the glasses' earpieces.

"Nothing."

Detective Brownley extracted a jumbo clear plastic evidence bag from her pocket and shook it open. Officer Meade dropped the hat inside. The sunglasses went into a smaller bag.

Officer Meade did a thorough pat-down. Pat wasn't armed.

Detective Brownley searched the woman's tote bag. After a moment, she whirled a silver key ring over her head like a cheerleader shaking a pom-pom, then tossed the keys to Officer Meade. "Find the car."

Officer Meade jogged toward the street, pushing the UNLOCK button on the fob.

Detective Brownley slipped the woman's tote bag into another evidence bag.

Officer Meade spoke into her collar mic. "We've got the car. It's parked in front of Parlor Ice Cream."

Detective Brownley told the two other officers, Griff and Daryl, "Take her in."

The woman began crying as the officers led her down the gazebo steps, her feet dragging. Once they reached the grass, we had her full face, her eyes round with terror.

The woman we'd known as Pat was, as I'd expected, Kimberly Larson, Steve's secret live-in girlfriend.

As Kimberly shuffled alongside the officers, tears streaming down her cheeks, a thousand pricks of sadness stabbed at me. Kimberly's face was ashen. Reality was setting in.

The things we do for love.

CHAPTER THIRTY-FIVE

I sat on the wooden bench in the Rocky Point police station lobby waiting my turn to be interviewed. I'd been there about twenty minutes when Steve entered with Officer Meade.

His hair was disheveled. His polo shirt was half untucked.

Officer Meade nodded at me, then turned to Steve. "Have a seat. It won't be long."

Steve sank onto the bench beside me. "Jeez, Josie . . . do you have any idea what's going on?"

"I'm not sure about anything. What did you hear?"

"Nothing. The police just showed up with a search warrant, and now they're crawling all over my condo. Have you seen Kimberly? That detective told me she was here."

"I think she's in the back. Is Ryan okay?"

"Yeah, I left him with a neighbor." He leaned back against the hard bench. "I have a bad feeling about this."

Kimberly hobbled in from the corridor on the right as if she couldn't lift her feet. Daryl hovered near her elbow. Kimberly's eyes were puffy and rimmed in red. Her lips were chapped.

Steve shot up, his mouth falling open.

Kimberly saw Steve and moaned, deflating, sinking to her knees as if someone had pulled the plug on a blow-up doll. She keened, a guttural sound of unendurable pain.

Cathy, the admin, leapt up from her desk, her eyes filled with fear. Griff charged out from behind the counter.

As Daryl hoisted Kimberly to her feet, she broke away, hurtling herself toward Steve.

Steve stepped back, gawking.

I swung my feet up onto the bench. I needn't have worried—she only had eyes for Steve.

Daryl tackled her. Griff held her thrashing legs in place.

Between the two officers, they got her upright and half walked, half dragged her down the corridor on the left, toward the interrogation rooms. She didn't speak, but her mewlings continued unabated and echoed in my mind long after she was out of sight.

Detective Brownley came into the lobby and asked Steve to join her. He touched my shoulder as he left, following her down the right-hand corridor.

Moments later, Lydia stepped into the lobby.

She looked better, as if she'd had a long sleep, a hot shower, and a big meal. She marched to the counter without looking left or right, so she didn't notice me. Cathy asked how she could help her.

"I'm Lydia Shannon. I want to see Chief Ellis."

"He's in a meeting right now. I'm his assistant . . . Is there anything I can do for you?"

"No. It's urgent. I must see him."

"Have a seat. I'll give him the message." Cathy picked up the phone.

Lydia turned, saw me, and approached. She stood in front of me, her displeasure patent in her stance and frigid glare.

"I heard on the news that someone involved with Cal in some kind of art fraud scheme has been detained. Who is it?"

"I haven't heard anything official."

"Tell me unofficially."

"No." I got up and crossed the room to the Community News Bulletin Board.

Lydia spoke to my back. "Your sanctimony falls on deaf ears."

I continued reading the announcements and notices until Lydia's name was called and she followed Detective Brownley down the corridor on the right.

No one came for me until just before seven.

Ellis and I stood side by side in front of the one-way mirror in the police station's observation room. Kimberly sat on one side of the long wooden table, staring at her clenched hands. Officer Meade sat in a corner, watching her.

Ellis arched his back, flexing his muscles. "Kimberly isn't talking."

"She hasn't asked for a lawyer?"

"Nope, and she signed the Miranda waiver. If you can get her talking about the woodblock prints, that might be a start."

"She has a son, Ryan. Steve told me he left him with a neighbor. Is he all right?"

"The neighbors are keeping him overnight. Steve called Kimberly's parents, and they're flying in from Dayton in the morning."

"Poor kid."

"He has a lot of people who love him."

"Did you find other woodblock prints when you searched Kimberly's car or house?"

"No, just the one she had in her possession. We searched her classroom, too. Her principal opened it up for us. Nothing."

"There has to be evidence that explains her connection to Cal."

"We have a phone we found in her bag. Katie's team is working on it now, and another one turned in by Nora. Nora told me you spoke to her, so I can share that she turned over the phone voluntarily. All she's asking is that we keep her name out of the papers, and I think we might be able to do it. Wes is on board."

"You got Wes to agree to hold back news?"

"Nora's involvement isn't germane to the investigation. It's gossip."

"That may be true, but agreeing to sit on a story doesn't sound like the Wes I know."

Ellis grinned. "I promised him an exclusive."

"That explains it. What does Kimberly say about why she has that phone in her purse?"

"Other than commenting that possessing a phone isn't a crime, nothing."

"She has a point."

He glanced at his watch. "It's been a couple of hours. They might have something." Ellis picked up a wall-mounted phone and punched in four digits. "Katie, where are you with those phones?" Ellis listened for almost a minute. "Okay. I'll take what you've got."

"Where did the phones come from?"

"Kirby's, a mom-and-pop electronic store in Elliot, Maine. The buyer purchased four phones, a voice changer, and a laptop in a cash transaction the day Mo was killed and Cal disappeared. The store can't help us ID the buyer because they only keep their security camera footage for seventy-two hours, and the clerk doesn't remember a thing about it."

"I bet Cal bought everything, kept one phone, and gave the others to Kimberly, Nora, and Lydia."

"I'm with you on that. The question is, where are the computer and voice changer now?"

"What does Lydia say?"

"Nothing. Unlike Kimberly, Lydia did call her attorney, and he instructed her not to answer any questions."

"Any news on the pipes in the social club?"

"Just another dead end. It was a good lead, and thank you again, but we heard from the property manager that they're getting ready to update the gas line. We've confirmed the delivery with the vendor. All pipes are accounted for, and none contains forensic material. None has been wiped or cleaned in any way."

Katie stepped into the room and handed Ellis a thick folder.

"Thanks, Katie. Anything I should know that's not in this printout?"

"The top sheets are texts and emails from the phones, followed by a list of numbers called."

Ellis ran his thumb down the lists, thanked her for her quick work, and told her she could go. "There are dozens of calls on both of these phones from one of the missing units. That must be the one Cal used." He continued reading. "The emails support that, but they're all from generic addresses and are unsigned." He placed the documents back in the folder. "Ready?"

"Yes."

"Keep it simple. Stick to the print and how she got involved with Cal."

I followed Ellis ten feet down the hall. We paused at the heavy door that led to Interrogation Room One.

Ellis stood at the head of the table and pointed to a chair across from

Kimberly. I nodded at Officer Meade, sitting near the back wall, and sat down. Kimberly didn't react. A human-sized cage stood off to my right, and I shifted my chair so I wouldn't see it. Three video cameras were mounted high overhead.

Ellis took a remote from his shirt pocket and aimed it at each video recorder. One by one, pinpricks of red light appeared.

"Ms. Larson, as I've explained, we record all interviews. I've activated the recorders." Ellis stated the date, glanced at his watch, and added the time. "You'll recall that I'm Police Chief Hunter. I've asked Josie Prescott to join us. She's an antiques expert, and I'm hoping she can help me understand the transaction you just participated in. Do you collect Japanese woodblock prints?"

Kimberly didn't move. I had no sense she heard him.

Ellis nodded at me.

"Kimberly?"

She raised her eyes to my face. She still looked worn and upset, but she didn't seem panicky. She wasn't shaking or sniveling or, as far as I could tell, showing any emotion at all.

"As Chief Hunter just explained, the police asked me for help. I can't believe you did this, Kimberly. I know you wanted to earn more money, but selling fraudulent art is no way to do it."

Kimberly's eyebrows pulled together. "What are you talking about? The woodblock print is real."

"How do you know?"

"I know where it came from."

"Where?"

Kimberly raised her chin. "You know better than to ask me that."

"Come on, Kimberly. Let's talk turkey. If it's real, why the fake name?"

"I guess you've never worked in a top elementary school. You're supposed to devote every waking moment to the job. If my students' parents found out I was moonlighting, my principal would never hear the end of it, and neither would I." She pushed her chair back and stood. We all followed suit. "I don't want to talk to you about it. I know you mean well, Josie, but all I did was sell a beautiful woodblock print." Kimberly turned toward Ellis. "I'm leaving."

"Not quite yet."

"Then I've changed my mind. I want a lawyer."

"Certainly."

Ellis announced to a video camera that he was suspending the interrogation, then turned the machines off. Officer Meade escorted Kimberly out to make the call.

"Sorry," I said.

"You did your best."

"Now what?"

"I'll point out to her lawyer the advantages of cooperating with us. He'll raise a ruckus, and we'll let her go. We know Cal was involved in fraud, and that she helped him sell the print, but until we can prove intent, we don't have enough evidence to hold her."

He walked me to the lobby, thanked me again for helping, and headed back inside.

CHAPTER THIRTY-SIX

t eight o'clock Friday morning, I stood with my mouth agape. I was staring at one of Trish's golf club bags, disbelieving what I was seeing.

All the objects we'd bought from the Shannons were in a cordoned-off area of the warehouse awaiting appraisal. I'd brought over two standing work lights and video gear to begin sorting through the objects. Not every piece was worthy of a full appraisal. Each of the three golf bags contained fourteen clubs. From watching an occasional golf game on TV, I knew there was no minimum number of clubs a pro golfer could carry, but the maximum was fourteen. Frank told me Trish hadn't played golf in twenty years, and from what he said and what I could see, once she'd quit the game, she hadn't cared for them anymore. The bags weren't covered, and she'd left them in a non-climate-controlled shed, so I wasn't surprised to see a layer of dust on the heads. What was stunning, though, was that one of them, a driver, was pristine.

I ran to a worktable and brought up the video I'd taken the day before. I captured a still shot of the bag containing the undusty club and blew it up. Looking at the clubs carefully, the distinction between the clean driver and the other clubs was unmistakable. I emailed the image to Ellis, then called him.

I got his voice mail. "Ellis, I just sent you a photo." I explained why I had Trish's golf bags, then added, "I can't help but wonder if I'm looking at the murder weapon."

I sent my staff an email telling them not to touch anything in the Shannon section.

I felt shaken and confused. Trish couldn't have known. Using one of her golf clubs to kill Cal pointed right at Lydia, so Trish never would have sold them to us.

I wanted some air. Outside, the sky was thick with ash-gray clouds, and darkening by the minute, so a walk through the woods to the church would be in the near-dark. Instead, I drove to the ocean and parked in the Rocky Point police station lot. A walk on the beach sounded good. First, though, I walked into the station.

Ellis wasn't in. I left a message saying I'd be on the beach for a while, in case he came in.

The ocean was black and churning. Diagonal lines of white foam surged toward the beach. I watched for a few seconds, then walked along the shore. After about ten minutes, I turned around. A gusty wind blew in off the water, and I shivered. When I reached my car, I felt better, stronger, more like myself.

I walked back into the police station. Ellis was in.

"I just left you a message," he said. "I wanted to speak to you before I sent Detective Brownley and a tech team to your place to get the golf clubs."

"Let me text Cara that it's okay." I did so, and she texted back immediately, saying she'd prepare the receipt. "All set." I looked at him. "Are you all right? You look like you haven't slept in a week."

"That's about how I feel."

"Is Kimberly still here?"

"No. Her lawyer showed up around nine thirty last night, and we let her go about ten."

"Now what?"

"I bring the clubs in for forensic analysis, and I think of more questions to ask people, starting with the Shannons. On the off chance the golf club is the weapon, I need to know who had access to them."

"I was at a party there not long ago, and the shed was unlocked."

"So someone could walk onto the property, take a club, use it to kill Cal, clean it, bring it back, and no one would notice."

"That sounds about right. I have another suggestion, too . . . two, actually. First, ask Kimberly about blackmail."

Ellis leaned back and rubbed his nose. "Tell me."

"The only reason Kimberly would conspire with Cal was if she had to. Sure, she wanted more money, but it would never occur to her to do something sleazy. She walked the straight and narrow until she couldn't anymore. Everything started to unravel that day in the faculty lounge when she came into the room and saw Steve hang up the phone. That could only mean one thing—he'd made a call he didn't want her to know about. She assumed he'd called Mo. She hit redial, and sure enough, Mo picked up. She taught in the room next to hers, so she'd know her voice. Kimberly went to Mo's house after school to confront her, to stake her claim. Cal was there to meet with Mo and me. He arrived early, and he saw Kimberly arguing with Mo. Cal witnessed Mo fall. He threatened Kimberly, saying he'd tell the police he saw her push Mo."

"Did she?"

"I don't know. Maybe. Regardless, I can see Cal blackmailing Kimberly. It's just his style of slimy. If you can get her talking about how she was the victim, maybe she'll come clean. My other idea . . . about covering your clothes if you're going to beat someone with, say, a golf club, and you don't want to end up covered in blood. Rain gear would work, and guess where they sell it? Anthony's Shoe Repair. Talk about convenient."

"These are good ideas, Josie." He stood. "Thanks for coming in."

As I crossed back to the beach, I toyed with texting Wes to ask if Anthony's sold any rain gear in the hours before Cal was killed, but I didn't. I suspected getting Anthony to cooperate would be a delicate operation, one requiring Ellis's deft handling, not Wes's bludgeoning.

The sky was steel gray now, and the air was thick with moisture. The swells were growing and breaking hard, slapping the water with a deafening roar. I didn't want to think about blackmail or the kind of emotional anguish that drove someone to kill. I wanted to do something optimistic.

I called Matt Janson.

"Do you have any time today to talk?" I asked. "It won't take long."

"I'm meeting a friend in Rocky Point for a late breakfast. Can I stop by afterward? Around eleven thirty?"

"Perfect!"

As I pulled into my parking lot, Wes broke into the regular radio program with a news flash. "Kimberly Larson is apparently missing. The police are asking for help in locating her." She wasn't at her teaching job, and she hadn't called in sick. According to Wes's police source, Kimberly had been released from police custody at ten last night, and she hadn't been seen since. She didn't go home. She didn't stay in a hotel. She simply vanished.

I pulled into a spot and called Ellis. "What about Ryan?"

"Steve took him to school. He's fine. We pulled him from class and have him safe. Her parents should be here soon. Why?"

"Because I doubt she'd leave without him. She's up to something, Ellis. Something local. Kimberly's parents owned a summer cottage, which they sold last spring. Since it's September, maybe whoever bought it isn't using it. She told me there was a broken lock on her old bedroom window that she used to come and go when she was a teenager. If it's empty, and the new owners haven't fixed the lock yet, it would make a perfect hideaway."

He thanked me so brusquely, I suspected he was already accessing the state tax records for the address. I grabbed my iPad and found it in two minutes by looking up recent sales on a real estate website. I drove directly there.

The cottage was picture-book charming, with weathered dove-gray siding, a terra-cotta roof, a white picket fence covered with red climbing roses, and a wraparound porch. A red maple grew on the left. The place looked deserted, but I wasn't fooled. It was a perfect lair, and I was convinced Kimberly was there, or had been overnight. There was a one-car detached garage.

I parked half a block away and texted Wes to give him a heads-up.

Five minutes later, Ellis drove up in his SUV, followed by a van filled with uniformed officers and technicians. Ellis pretended he didn't see me, but I knew better. Ellis saw everything. I got out and leaned against a streetlamp to watch them work.

Ellis pressed the doorbell, waited ten seconds, rang the bell again, waited some more, then pounded on the door.

Officer Meade and a uniformed officer I didn't know, a young man with red hair, walked up the driveway to the garage. Officer Meade tugged on the door, without luck. She went left and he went right, circling the small structure. They paused at windows and peered in. Ellis said something to two men who were balancing a tall metal ladder on their shoulders, and he pointed toward the beach.

Wes arrived a minute later. He took in the scene at one glance, then hustled toward the ocean. I followed more slowly. By the time I reached the sand, Wes was video-recording the action. I stood in back of the garage, far enough away so I wouldn't interfere with the police, but close enough so I wouldn't miss anything.

The two men wedged the ladder into the sandy ground, then leaned it up against the house. One man held it in place while the other scrambled up. When he reached a second-story window, he pressed his nose against the glass and cupped his eyes so he could see inside. After a few seconds, he tried to lift the window, but it didn't budge. He came down the ladder. They moved it to the next window and repeated the process with the same result. One by one, they made their way across the back of the house. When they reached the side window by the red maple, the man on the ladder easily slid it open. He straddled the sill, then disappeared.

Ellis hurried to the front, and I followed.

A minute later, the front door opened from the inside, and Ellis stepped in. Officer Meade followed him, reappearing a few seconds later with what looked like a gold-colored key on a silver ring. She used it on a lock built into the garage doorjamb, and the male officer hoisted the rolling door. They both put on gloves. She reached in and flipped on the light. I could see that no one was inside. Tools hung from a big sheet of brown pegboard along the left wall. A workbench was positioned at the rear. Two big green plastic trash cans stood on the right.

A rumble of thunder exploded overhead, startling me. I'd been so certain Kimberly was here, and I was wrong. Ellis stepped out, talked to Officer Meade, and drove away.

When I got back to my company, I went to my office and sat facing my window, trying to think about what Kimberly was doing. She said she dreamed of just driving away. Maybe she had. I would have thought she'd take Ryan with her, but maybe I was wrong about that, too.

Wes texted: *Thx for the tip. Kimberly's car found in Rocky Pt Mall parking lot. No sign of her. Any ideas?*

I didn't have a clue, so I didn't text back. Instead, I checked email.

Mac at *Antiques Insights* had written thanking me for the update and letting me know he was working with the Rocky Point police to unravel Pat Durand's crimes.

I had just finished a private meeting with Gretchen, explaining that Ty and I were going to hire a wedding planner, and asking her to help manage the details on a consultant basis for extra pay, when Cara called up to tell me that Matt had arrived.

"Thanks, Cara. Bring him up." I turned back to face Gretchen. "As you can tell, Ty and I know a lot of what we want, but we're wrestling with some things. If you create a timeline with what needs to be done and when, you'll be able to coordinate with the wedding planner, and we'll be certain we don't miss anything."

Gretchen stood, her emerald eyes gleaming. "Thank you for your confidence in me, Josie. I won't let you down."

I listened to the click-clack of her stilettos reverberating through the cavernous warehouse, followed moments later by the steady, sturdy sound of boots. Cara escorted Matt in.

We shook, and I pointed to a guest chair.

"Thanks for coming in, Matt. As I said in my message, I'm interested in proceeding. I've finished reviewing your business plan. It's a winner on all fronts."

Matt leaned back and grinned. "Thanks."

"If you're still of the same mind, I'd like to make an offer to buy you out, then hire you."

He cocked his head. "No partnership?"

"No. Our roles would be as you describe, though. You can have a contract of any length." I smiled. "The terms will be favorable, including a profit-sharing arrangement."

"I'm amenable to discussing it, but I make no guarantee. I've been pretty focused on a partnership."

"I understand. Can we see what develops as we proceed?"

"That's fair. Let the due diligence begin. Do you have someone in mind to run this location?"

"Yes. Our first confidence—I'm trusting you not to repeat this."

"You can. I won't."

"Gretchen. Our office manager."

"That's quite a leap—office manager to general manager in one step."

"She'll be great. Gretchen is one of the most organized and trustworthy people I know. She's confident and poised, and she never pretends to know something she doesn't."

"I wish we could clone her. I'll have to hire from the outside."

"I want to introduce you to my key staff."

When we reached the front office, I waited for Cara to finish her call. "Everyone . . . excuse me for interrupting."

Cara smiled. Sasha and Fred looked up from their computer monitors. Gretchen, who was standing at a file cabinet, turned toward me, a manila folder in hand.

"Do you all know Matt Janson? He owns Janson's Antiques Mall. I visit it periodically and often find hidden gems. Matt, this is Cara, our receptionist and database manager. Sasha is our chief antiques appraiser. Fred is also an antiques appraiser. Eric, our facilities manager, isn't here."

I looked at Gretchen.

"He's meeting with Montgomery's Landscaping Service," she said. "I thought he should visit their headquarters before we signed the contract. One last check."

"Good thinking, Gretchen!" I looked at Matt. "And this, obviously, is Gretchen."

"Nice to meet you all," Matt said, smiling around. He turned to me. "I'll be in touch."

I walked him out, and we shook hands, our eyes meeting, honoring the moment.

CHAPTER THIRTY-SEVEN

Wes was nothing if not thorough. By one, his news reports included a phone interview with Annie Briscoe, a New York City–based dermatologist, who had bought the beachfront cottage from the Larsons last March. The police had alerted Dr. Briscoe earlier that morning that they'd applied for and received a search warrant. She was devastated that her house could have been used by a fugitive. I could admire Wes's journalistic acumen, but her shock and a dime didn't tell us where Kimberly was now.

Ellis stopped by as I was finishing a salad I'd ordered in for lunch.

"Thanks again for the tip about the cottage."

"It was a bust."

"Most tips are. The golf club, on the other hand, that's the real deal."

"Oh, wow."

"The ME matched the shape of the club head to the shape of the wound. The materials found in the laceration appear to match the graphite and persimmon wood in the club's shaft and head. We have to wait for forensic testing, but Trish confirmed the clubs were made of those materials, and she hasn't cleaned them since she retired. This one club was doused with bleach."

"They can do DNA testing on the wood."

"If they need to."

"Was the shed locked?"

"According to Trish, it's never locked."

"I can't believe it."

"Did Kimberly know about the shed?"

"I saw her in it earlier this month. She opened the door and walked in. I wonder where she is right now."

"I can tell you where she isn't—anywhere requiring a ticket or a passport. She hasn't used her credit cards, an ATM, or her phone. I liked your idea—she'd go somewhere familiar and comfortable, and the cottage sure qualified. Are you sure she didn't mention anywhere else that might fit the bill?"

I thought for a moment, reviewing our conversation. "She said she dreamed of just driving away."

"We found her car, so that's out."

"Maybe she bought a new car."

"With what? According to Steve, she doesn't carry a lot of cash."

"Cal did. He funded her purchase of the woodblock print. It's possible he was flush and she cleaned him out."

Ellis tapped a speed-dial button on his phone. When his call was answered, he said, "Check if any car dealers sold a car to Kimberly . . . Describe her . . . She might be using another name. The dealer might have picked her up at the Rocky Point Mall." He pushed the END CALL button and smiled at me. "Another good idea. Thank you."

"Spelunking."

"Excuse me?"

"She and her friend Chelsea liked caves."

"What caves?"

I recounted Kimberly's comments.

"What's Chelsea's last name?"

"I don't know. She lives in Colorado Springs with a husband and three kids. Kimberly exchanges Christmas cards with her."

Ellis called Detective Brownley and told her to pull Steve from his class. "Find that Christmas card list."

According to Chelsea Cox, Kimberly's old friend, their favorite cave was Salt Pearl Cavern at the end of Rocky Point Beach.

As soon as Ellis had that information, he thanked me and left. I waited for him to pull out of the lot, told Cara I didn't know when I'd be back, and drove to Clinton Lane, across from the beach. I parked behind a silver Ford Escape. I took my phone and keys and left my bag in my trunk.

I knew of Salt Pearl Cavern, but I'd never been inside. I didn't like the dark. I'd never thought of my disinclination as a phobia, or even a fear; rather, I simply didn't like the dark. I always left a light on when I left home so I'd never have to enter a dark house, and I'd made certain Prescott's night-light setting was more than cursory. I couldn't imagine wanting to hike into a cave.

I followed a rocky trail inland for about a quarter mile, then pushed through a dense stand of holly, laurel, and oak. A jumble of four-foot boulders ran from the path to the mouth of the cave. I climbed one and slid down the other side. I sat on pebbly ground, positioning myself so I could see through a crevice between the rocks. I wasn't tempted to contact Wes, knowing his rough-and-ready methods, but I would take photos for him.

The waves pounded the shore, so I didn't hear Ellis and the other police officers arrive. They walked in single file, silently. I opened the camera on my phone and began snapping away.

Ellis pointed to Daryl, then to the left of the cave mouth. Daryl walked quickly to the left, flattening himself against the granite wall. He signaled Griff to go to the right. Griff got in position. The same two men who'd carried the ladder at the cottage held two huge LED flashlights. Officer Meade handed Ellis an old-fashioned megaphone.

"Ms. Larson, this is Chief Hunter." His voice sounded echo-y and unlike him. "I've consulted the Rocky Point surveyor. He tells me there's only one way in and out of this cavern. It's over, Kimberly. Come out now, with your hands up, and let's talk about what's going on."

Ellis tried again, making his request seem reasonable. Nothing. After two more attempts, he said, "We're coming in."

"No! Don't."

Kimberly appeared at the cave opening, her hands cheek high. She didn't look anything like as upset as she had the day before. Her eyes were clear, and her chin was up.

"Are you alone?" Ellis asked.

"Yes."

"Where's your bag?"

She lowered her hands. "Why?"

"I need to check for stolen property."

"It's mine."

Ellis scanned the desolate area. "How did you get here?"

"I hitchhiked, then walked."

Ellis turned to the men with the flashlights. "Take a look inside. Daryl, cover them."

"Don't!" Kimberly said. "It's sacred ground. I came out so you wouldn't go in. I haven't done anything wrong."

"This isn't your private property, Ms. Larson." He waved them in. "We need to talk."

"I'm done talking."

"Then we can wait together while they search the cave."

Thirty seconds later, Daryl appeared at the mouth holding a wheeling suitcase in one plastic-gloved hand. The suitcase was black and sized to fit in a plane's overhead bin. He held Kimberly's tote bag in his other hand.

Ellis snapped on gloves and eyeballed the insides. He pulled out a set of keys and read from the red tag attached to the ring. He looked up. "Daryl, call Detective Brownley and tell her to check with Milkin Cars." He tossed the keys to Griff and said, "Find the car."

Kimberly took a step toward him.

"Why did you leave your old one in a shopping mall parking lot?" he asked.

She didn't reply.

"Why did you lie just now about hitchhiking here?"

"It's not a lie when someone asks a none-of-your-business question."

Ellis reached back into Kimberly's bag and extracted a narrow blue plastic binder. I saw a logo on the front and some text.

Ellis said, "Greenfield Travel Agency." He opened the binder and flipped through the papers. "Kosovo. Tonight at eleven from Boston's Logan Airport. You and Ryan. Why are you leaving Rocky Point?"

"You keep asking me about things that aren't crimes. So what if I want to take my son to Europe? The only crime I see is searching a woman's bag without her permission."

Ellis didn't comment. He lifted a manila envelope from the bag and opened it. "What have we here?" He pulled out a bundle of cash. "How much is it?"

Kimberly didn't comment.

Ellis turned to Daryl. "Open the suitcase."

"This is outrageous!"

Daryl reached for the zipper. "It's locked. A small padlock."

Ellis looked into the envelope containing the money, then unzipped a side pocket inside the tote bag and poked around. He zipped it back up and unsnapped a change purse. He shook a small key into his palm and handed it to Daryl.

"Am I under arrest?" Kimberly demanded.

"Only if you insist. We have evidence that Cal committed fraud and that you were involved. Your plan to leave the jurisdiction will convince a judge that you had knowledge of your wrongdoing, and that's enough to prove intent. I don't want to arrest you on that charge, though. I think you're a victim here, Kimberly. I think Cal was blackmailing you."

Kimberly began to cry, and she covered her face with her hands. Ellis nodded at Daryl, and he unlocked and unzipped the suitcase. A shiny laptop sat on top of a neatly folded pile of clothes.

Griff hustled along the rocky path. "The key opens a silver Ford Escape parked on Clinton."

The two men with the flashlights reappeared and talked to Ellis. I couldn't hear what they said. After a minute they left.

Ellis turned to Daryl. "No one goes in this cave until the forensic team gives an all clear."

"Got it."

Ellis touched Kimberly's elbow, and she trudged down the path beside him. Griff followed close behind. I kept taking photos until they rounded a corner and disappeared from view.

I slipped my phone into my back pocket and used footholds on the boulder to heave myself up and over. Daryl's eyes widened and he took a step forward when I landed on his side of the rocks, but he didn't say anything, so I didn't either.

By the time I reached my car, the Ford Escape was already hooked up to a police tow truck. I took some more photos, then started emailing them to Wes. I was still at it when the truck drove off. As soon as I finished, I texted Wes. Before I had the car in gear, he called.

He asked where I was, and I explained about Kimberly's connection to Salt Pearl Cavern.

"I can't believe you didn't tell me about it."

"You're welcome for the photos."

Wes sighed.

I ignored his unspoken disapproval. "The last ones show her new car being towed away."

"What new car?"

"Apparently, Kimberly decided to start over somewhere. She needed to figure out the logistics of getting a new identity, so she bought a car for cash. I'm certain she used a different name. The temporary plates are good for twenty days, plenty of time."

"Car dealers require ID."

"Maybe she paid extra . . . you know . . . cash money. Some dealers would be happy to make up a name and address for you, maybe even jury-rig a fake ID they could photocopy for their files. By the time the DMV catches on, she'd be long gone."

"The dealer's going to get in big trouble."

"Possibly. They'll both deny it—he said, she said." I told Wes about discovering the laptop in the suitcase and the plane tickets to Kosovo. "Maybe she'd planned this for a while, and already had a new identity, a passport—you know, a new name for a fresh start."

"Why Kosovo?" Wes asked.

"No extradition treaty."

"Why would Kimberly buy a car on the down-low if she planned to fly to Europe right away?"

"I suspect she wanted time to think things through and get her plans in order. Evidently, she was ready to face the fact that her relationship with Steve was over. If Lydia was arrested, Kimberly might figure she could come back. If she did, the car would be waiting for her at the airport, and off she and Ryan would go. If she decided to stay in Europe, oh, well . . . she lost a little money on the purchase."

He soft-whistled. "She was cooking on all burners, huh?"

Thunder cracked overhead.

"A storm's coming," I said.

"More than a storm! A nor'easter—we're in for it! Rain starts by six, then the temperature plummets. We may get snow."

"Why do you sound so happy?"

"Because Maggie and I are going to hunker down all weekend."

"What a great idea, Wes! Maybe Ty and I will do the same."

He asked for more details—what Kimberly was wearing and how she looked, did Ryan's name come up, or Steve's, and how did she explain having so much cash—and when he ran out of questions, he gave his usual "Catch ya later" and was gone.

A jagged bolt of lightning illuminated the yellow-gray sky, and I drove back to work.

CHAPTER THIRTY-EIGHT

Ty and I spent the weekend at his house. My place was cozy. His was expansive. He once told me he bought the house because of the view from the living room. We sat on the oversized sofa in front of the wall of windows gazing into the forest. By leaving the outside deck lights on, we had a 180-degree view of the crimson, gold, and orange leaves, their colors as true as fire. By the time darkness descended, the rain had picked up, and all I could see was black. We turned out the deck lights and closed the curtains, insulating ourselves from the outside world.

I stacked kindling and logs for a fire while Ty made martinis. I lit it and watched the flames tickle the bark, then sat on the rug and leaned against the double-wide ottoman. Ty placed a tray on the floor and sat beside me.

He kissed my cheek. "We need to decide on the timeline for selling this place."

"Never."

"Do you want to live here for real?"

"No." I poured us martinis from the silver shaker and handed his over. "I want us to have a home we choose together, but this fire! That view!"

"Do you want us to live at your place?"

"Short term, yes. It's next door to Zoë, and it has a spiffy new hot tub."

"Long term?"

"Once you know whether we're moving to D.C., we'll figure it out."

"Good." He took a sip. "Guess what I did today?"

"You signed up to train as an astronaut."

He laughed. "Where did that come from?"

"I always wanted to be an astronaut."

"Really?"

"Sort of."

"You're a woman of many aspects."

I snuggled into his shoulder and watched the flames leap and curl, a perfect end to a difficult day.

"What did you do?"

"I confirmed our reservation in a gorgeous suite for three nights starting on our wedding day, Thursday the twenty-first."

"Eastern Turret Flag Officer's Suite."

"You have a great memory."

"For some things. For others, I have Gretchen. I've asked her to help us organize the wedding."

"That's a smart idea. I also put twenty sleeping rooms on hold for out-of-town guests ... and ... drum roll, please ..."

I pitta-patted my thighs.

"You said you wanted a honeymoon that offered cosmopolitan amenities and a quiet beach and from-the-shore snorkeling. I've booked us a house on Seven Mile Beach on Grand Cayman Island. We fly out on Wednesday, June twenty-eighth, for ten days."

I sat up and spun around. "The Cayman Islands? That's fabulous!"

Ty grinned like a ten-year-old with a hot new video game. "It's a single-family house and comes with a cook, a housekeeper, and a gardener. The gardener also takes care of the pool. The property includes a full acre of private gardens, winding paths lit by tiki torches, and a twenty-foot-high waterfall."

I placed my glass on the tray and kissed Ty full on the mouth. "Oh, Ty. It sounds heavenly. Magical."

He placed his arm over my shoulder and drew me close. The orange flames curled around and over the logs. Sap crackled and popped.

I leaned my head against his shoulder. "I can't wait."

"Me, too."

"Why do we leave on Wednesday?"

"I know you. After the wedding weekend, you'll want to check in at work for a couple of days."

I smiled. "It's perfect, Ty. Thank you."

•   •   •

I kept checking the *Seacoast Star*'s website all weekend and all day Monday, but there was no new information about Kimberly. The first news came from Ellis, who stopped by my office Tuesday morning.

"I thought you'd want to see this." He handed me a printout of the Rheingold logo. "We found this on the laptop in Kimberly's bag. From fingerprints and the contents of emails, there's no question it was Cal's."

"Was it password protected?"

"Yes. Katie was able to circumvent it, though. Why?"

"If Kimberly couldn't access the computer, she wouldn't have seen the email making Pat's phone date with Andi. Not that it matters whether she knew or not. She couldn't have kept the appointment anyway, since she was teaching. I bet she planned to take the computer to an IT service company and pretend to be so ditzy she forgot her own password."

He laughed. "We found the phone Cal used in Kimberly's suitcase, too."

"More evidence of intent. Anything of interest on the phone?"

"Cal sent a text to the disposable phone that we think went to Lydia. From the time stamp, he sent it during the funeral." Ellis read it aloud. " 'Is it as awful as you expected? See you soon. I miss you.' That helps set the time of Cal's murder."

I touched the printout. "Cal created the Rheingold receipt."

"And the fake Hitchens ID, and the phony lease that was used to open the PO box."

"You're building a case."

"One fact at a time."

After Ellis left, I sent Sylvia Rheingold an email explaining that the Rocky Point police had discovered who created the fake invoice, and that since the perpetrator was dead, there was no reason to think there'd be a repeat performance. I was glad I could provide her with some closure.

Wes and I met at our dune just before two thirty. Last weekend, we had a nor'easter. Today we were in the middle of a mini heat wave. The temperature had soared to nearly eighty. The sun sparkled, and the ocean was bright blue and calm.

Wes pulled out his notebook. "So talk to me. How did you know Kimberly was the killer?"

"I remembered something Ty said years ago—there's always a motive for murder. Always. Even if the motive doesn't seem logical to you, it makes sense to the killer. In this case, the only person who wanted Mo out of the picture was Kimberly. She was petrified that Mo and Steve were going to get back together."

"Were they?"

"Maybe. Kimberly was so desperate to find out, she even approached me to ask—after Mo was dead."

"That was kind of dumb of her, huh? Calling attention to herself for no reason."

"She didn't really call attention to herself, at least not directly. She asked about starting fresh in a new location, which makes me think she'd already half given up. You know how that goes . . . Your rational self knows a relationship is over, but your emotional self doesn't want to let go. Her rational self was asking why I moved to New Hampshire, how I set up a business, and so on. Her emotional self clung to the hope she wouldn't have to leave, that the murder cases would go cold, and Steve would propose, and all would be well with the world."

"Stupid."

"Not stupid. Deluded."

"Whatever . . . So you never bought the idea that Lydia was the killer?"

"Not once I thought about Kimberly's motive. How is Lydia doing?"

"Who knows? She talks, but she doesn't say anything worth listening to. She plays her emotions close to her chin."

"I hope she finds her way."

Wes made a note. "Do you think Kimberly killed Mo on purpose?"

"I don't know that it was premeditated, but it's not like Mo simply tumbled over the wall. Remember what the ME said—Mo's death wasn't an accident. Have you heard whether Kimberly has admitted it?"

"Not yet, but smart money says she'll take a deal. She's already admitted she stole Cal's computer, phone, and voice changer. She insists the cash they found in her purse—fifteen big ones, thank you very much—is hers fair and square. She says that she won it from Cal at poker. That's possible, right? Anyway, what she can't explain away is the rain gear she bought at Anthony's. My police source tells me that checking their sales of rain gear was your idea. You nailed it, Joz! Anthony was in the restroom when Kimberly came in, and Boris made the sale. They found the receipt for one pair of booties and one poncho. Boris picked Kimberly out of a photo lineup. According to Boris, the transaction occurred at the right time—just as the funeral was ending. They've got Kimberly cold."

"What does she say?"

"That Boris is wrong, that it never happened."

"And of course she denies taking the golf club."

"Yup."

"It's not going to be an easy case to win."

"They're retracing her steps after leaving the social club. Maybe they'll find the bloody boots and poncho. Most grocery stores and shopping malls have security cameras aimed at their Dumpsters. That's funny, isn't it?"

"Trash removal is big business. Using another guy's Dumpster saves you money. Cameras discourage the practice."

"Back up for a minute . . . Why did Cal need someone else to buy the Japanese woodblock prints for him, anyway? He was doing fine on his own."

"He was doing fine because he was only selling one fake every few months. After he lost so much money, he needed to sell three or four prints right away to cover the debt. He got Lydia to help, but still needed to raise twenty thousand dollars, and that would simply get him caught up. It wouldn't pay her back or help him finance his lifestyle going forward. He had a choice—risk raising a red flag by flooding the market or find a proxy to do it for him."

"And since what he was doing was illegal, he couldn't simply ask a friend to help him out."

"Nor could he hire it out."

"Why did Kimberly go ahead and sell the print after Cal was murdered?"

"Why not? She had a buyer ready to go."

Wes closed his notebook. "The one thing I can't wrap my head around is that you figured everything out because the ink in Mo's print was too blue. Did I get that right?"

"Not just that . . . but, yeah."

Wes's phone vibrated. He read the message and chuckled. "Guess what? The police found security camera footage showing Kimberly tossing plastic cover-ups in the Dumpster behind Harvey's Market, the one that's closest to Anthony's. The timing is right. Their case is no longer hard to prove."

Even though I wasn't surprised, I was horrified, and I let it show. "Oh, Wes."

"Yeah . . . it gets you thinking, doesn't it? What else ya got for me?"

"Nothing."

"Catch ya later!"

Wes walked-slid down the dune. I stayed for a while, watching the waves slide to shore.

Kimberly would be found guilty of murder and sentenced to life in prison.

Ryan would move to Ohio to live with his grandparents.

Lydia would get a slap on the wrist.

Life would go on.

I pulled into my parking lot around three thirty and saw Steve leaning against the hood of his car, tapping into his smartphone.

I parked two spaces away. Steve looked up. He wasn't smiling, but neither did he look angry or upset.

He slipped his phone into his pocket. "Hey, Josie."

"Hey, Steve."

"I waited to stop by to thank you . . . I know it seems silly to talk about it now, but I heard your eulogy for Mo. It was beautiful. It meant something to me."

"Thanks, Steve. How are you doing with all this?"

"Worse than I expected. I knew I was going to have to leave Kimberly, whether Mo and I got back together or not. I wasn't happy, and it had been dragging on too long. Sometimes you've just got to rip that Band-Aid off."

"Do you think she sensed it, or was she in denial?"

"Complete denial."

"And then there's Ryan."

"Thinking about what he's going through kills me. I know he'll be okay, but you know . . . How do you get over something like this? He's heading to Ohio at the end of the week."

"You'll miss him."

"A lot."

Sadness enveloped me, and for a moment, I struggled to speak. Murder was always horrible, but some crimes seemed especially malevolent.

"What do you think . . . Will Kimberly plead guilty?"

"Beats me." Steve paused for a moment. "The other reason I came by . . . I'm looking for jobs in Florida. The Sunshine State. I could handle a little sunshine right about now. So I wanted to say good-bye."

"Everything is happening so quickly." I extended a hand. "Good luck, Steve."

We shook. I stood by my car and watched him drive away. His world had rocked a little, but after the initial shock wore off, he would go on his merry way, unscathed.

Late that night, Ty and I were relaxing in the hot tub.

We sat quietly for several minutes.

Ty took my hand. "What are you thinking about?"

"Cause and effect."

"Versus coincidence. How come?"

I tried to think how to express what I was feeling. "Have you ever thought about the way so many incidents link back to one singular event? You know, if I hadn't taken that train, I wouldn't have sat next to that person. If I hadn't sat next to that person, I wouldn't have heard about such-and-such a book. If I hadn't read that book, I wouldn't have known that x-y-z was possible. And so on. Have you ever done that?"

"Sure . . . it's kind of fun."

"Exactly. Except sometimes it's not so much fun. Cal came up with the idea to steal Mo's inheritance the minute he heard about it. Isn't that horrible? That one despicable act led to fraud, blackmail, and murder. If Mo's godmother hadn't left her twenty-five thousand dollars, she'd be alive today."

Ty raised my hand to his lips and kissed my knuckles. "You're right. Sometimes it's not so much fun."

EPILOGUE

MAY

Zoë picked the Sunday of Memorial Day weekend for my shower, thinking that guests would feel less rushed if she scheduled it in the middle of a three-day weekend. I'd asked her to keep it small, and she did.

The theme was "Island Loving," in honor of Ty's honeymoon choice. Nine of us sat on her deck drinking mai-tais and mojitos: Zoë; Gretchen; Sasha; Fred's wife, Suzanne; Cara; Eric's girlfriend, Grace; Helene, the director of New Hampshire Children First!; my cousin Becca,* who'd flown in from England; and me. Zoë had arranged for lunch to be prepared by a catering company that brought its own grill and smoker. We planned on doing the same for Sunday's hoedown, so I was glad for the opportunity to test them out.

I raised my glass. "I have a toast."

Everyone lifted their glasses.

"To Gretchen, the new general manager of Prescott's flagship location!"

We clinked and drank, and people asked for details. I sat back and listened to Gretchen's clear and concise explanation of her new position and its genesis. Suzanne proposed another toast, to me, for the expansion, and we clinked and sipped again.

Sasha leaned forward. "Has Ty decided whether to take the national director position?"

"Yes—he will, and we don't have to move. He was able to negotiate basing the position here."

Applause rippled around the room, and another toast was proposed.

---

* Please see *Ornaments of Death*.

"To Ty's success," Sasha said.

Zoë added, "And to your staying in Rocky Point."

Later, Gretchen sat on my right, notating who gave what gift. Zoë was on my left, handing them to me one at a time. I'd asked Zoë to request donations to New Hampshire Children First! in lieu of gifts, and she had, sort of. I thought her wording was clever:

Josie's asked that instead of a gift, you bring a donation to
her favorite charity,

New Hampshire Children First!

I suggest you do both!
In addition to your donation, bring her something small
to mark this special day.

The gifts were uniformly thoughtful, from monogrammed glasses to a set of rare teas, and from a string of mini-palm-tree outdoor lights to a small silver picture frame. Gretchen gave me a copper watering can. Zoë gave me a white satin-and-lace heart-shaped pillow. She'd had it custom embroidered. The message read:

Josie & Ty
Fairy Tales Do Come True

Zoë handed me the last box, a big one.

"What's this? I thought we were done."

"Shelley couldn't come from New York, but she sent this."

I ripped open the turquoise water-patterned giftwrap. Inside the box was a grass skirt. I laughed, shook it out, and stepped into it, lifting my sundress to my waist. Gretchen began humming a hula tune, and I started dancing, shimmying my hips, holding my dress up with one hand, my other arm undulating to the side, an amateur's attempt at hula. I turned slowly, laughing. Photos were snapped and a thirty-second video recorded.

After a minute, I sat down, still wearing the grass skirt. "Shelley embraced the island theme, I see. Hawaii ... the Caymans ... it's all the same, right?"

Zoë handed me the box again. "There's more."

I opened a tissue-paper-wrapped package. Inside was a set of ice-blue lingerie, a French lace strapless bra and matching low-cut panties. "Wow. Look at this." I held the set up for everyone to see, then examined the labels. "They're my size. How could Shelley possibly know my size?"

Zoë grinned. "I raided your underwear drawer."

I laughed again, then picked up a white envelope. Inside was a check made out to New Hampshire Children First! and a handwritten note, which I read aloud:

Dear Josie,

I wish I could be there. (Ha!)

I hope you're having a wonderful day. I got you "something blue" in case you didn't have that yet. Very cool idea, asking for donations to your fav charity.

Love, Shelley

"Shelley is prescient," I said. "I didn't have the blue yet."

"What are you doing for the rest?" Cara asked.

"I'm wearing my mother's wedding ring on a chain around my neck. That's something old. My dress is new. Zoë's going to lend me her gorgeous bangle." Zoë lifted her arm, showing off the gold-and-diamond beauty Ellis had given her last fall. "Now I have something blue."

Becca stood. "In England, we add a bit at the end: 'Something old, something new, something borrowed, something blue, and a sixpence for your shoe.'" She handed me a silver coin. "I brought you a sixpence."

"Oh, Becca! That's wonderful." I hugged her, and as I did, I whispered, "I'm so glad you're here. Thank you for coming."

"I wouldn't miss it—or your wedding."

I gave her shoulders a last squeeze before backing up. I sent my eyes around, including everyone in my comment. "I can't tell you how much it means to me that you're all here, including Shelley, in absentia. Thank you."

We ate, and drank some more, and I did one final hula before calling it a day.

"We raised more than a thousand dollars!"

Ty and I were in the hot tub. I'd told him about the delicious barbecue, demonstrated the hula in my grass skirt, and showed off the gifts, except the lingerie, which he wouldn't see until our wedding day. He congratulated me on my fund-raising success, admired the gifts, and leaned back, resting his head against the bumper and closing his eyes.

I placed my hand against a jet, relishing the pulsating water. "I've changed my mind about our wedding."

He opened his eyes. "What did I do?"

"No, silly! Not about whether to get married, about who to invite. You know I wanted it to be just the two of us on the beach. I've rethought that decision."

He shut his eyes again. "Good."

The next Tuesday, Ty and I walked out of the Rocky Point Community Theater after seeing *Oklahoma!*

He handed me his program. "Max was pretty good."

"I thought he was great. He's a man of many talents. He looked like he was having a blast."

"Any update from Gretchen about the wedding?" he asked.

"The Blue Dolphin is confirmed for catering the luncheon reception, and she's organized chandeliers for the tent."

"Chandeliers?"

"Fancy crystal chandeliers. Hey, you wanted elegant, big fella, you're getting elegant."

"Sweet."

JUNE

My wedding day began with tears. I slept fitfully and was up by seven, gripped by hollow misery. I was burningly upset that my mother couldn't see me in my wedding dress. I was crushed that my dad couldn't walk me down the aisle. I went for a walk in the woods and talked to the sky, to my parents. I told them about Ty and our love and our life together, and by nine, when I got home, I had myself under control.

Zoë arrived a few minutes later and made us scrambled eggs, but all I could do was pick at them. I was jumpy.

At ten, Zoë helped me attach the net veil to the lilies-of-the-valley wreath that sat on the top of my head.

I met her eyes in the mirror. "I wish my parents were here."

She took my hand in hers and squeezed. "They are."

My eyes moistened. "Thank you."

She spread the veil over my shoulders and had me stand. She took a step back and looked me up and down.

"Turn around."

I did so.

I wore a pale peach to-the-ankle sleeveless silk slip dress with a scoop neckline. My sandals were strappy and high-heeled. Becca's sixpence was taped to the bottom of my right shoe.

"I can barely walk in these sandals," I fretted. "If I do a facer in the sand, I'm going to cry."

"I'll be beside you the whole way, and if you fall, I'll pick you up. But how about taking them off once we reach the beach?"

"I'll be barefoot."

"Yes."

"I got a pedicure."

"You're all set, then." She finished her examination. "Oh, Josie . . . you're going to take Ty's breath away."

I smiled.

The limo pulled into the driveway at ten thirty. The driver loaded Ty's and my suitcases into the trunk; then Zoë and I climbed into the back.

Zoë glanced at her watch. "Ellis is picking up Ty at this very minute. Gretchen will meet us at the beach with their boutonnieres and our bouquets. The wedding planner is already at the Blue Dolphin making sure everything is set for lunch."

"It's pretty eccentric for the bride to skip her own wedding luncheon."

"It would be eccentric if the bride skipped it while the groom attended.

But since you and Ty both plan on skipping it, I don't think it rises to the level of eccentricity."

I patted her hand. "Thank you, Zoë. Thank you for reassuring me. Thank you for being you."

The limo rolled to a stop along the sandy shoulder next to the dune where Wes and I regularly met. Gretchen was waiting by the tall grass. Zoë got out to coordinate the flowers. I stayed seated.

Through the tinted window I counted twenty-three people, ranged in a loose half circle. Ellis and Ty were already there, their blue-and-orange boutonnieres in place. I didn't see Shelley. Oh, well. Wes stood next to Ty. This would be Wes's first marriage as a justice of the peace.

Zoë opened the door, and I stepped out. The flowers were perfect, blue hydrangeas and orange tiger lilies, their stems stripped of leaves and wrapped in peach satin. I accepted the bouquet from Gretchen, and tears filled her expressive eyes. She kissed my cheek and hurried to join Jack and her toddler, Johnny.

Zoë touched my arm. "Ready?"

"Yes."

As soon as we reached the sand, I slipped off my sandals. The ocean was jade green today, flecked with gold. The ragged line of guests closed in. Out of the corner of my eye, I saw a woman a hundred yards away, running like a demon toward us. It was Shelley. When she reached the group, she eased herself into the line of guests.

Ellis and Ty approached, and from that moment, I saw nothing except Ty. I was mesmerized by the love in his eyes.

Wes came forward, a black leather portfolio in hand. He opened it and began to read: "Friends, we are gathered here together to join this man and this woman in holy matrimony . . ."

We exchanged our vows. After the kiss that marked our marriage, people applauded.

Gretchen had stashed a cooler behind a dune, and she and Cara poured everyone a plastic champagne glass full of bubbly to toast our happiness. After the first round of toasts, Shelley ran up to greet me and meet Ty.

"I'm so sorry I was late, Josie. I got lost—it turns out all dunes look alike."

I hugged her, and she hugged me back, and we rocked from side to side.

"You came!" I whispered. "I can't believe you came! You're in New Hampshire!"

"I guess the cows came home after all, huh?"

I laughed, and we linked arms, and I turned to face the group. "Everyone . . . this is Shelley!"

When we'd finished our drinks, Ty whispered, "Ready?"

"Yes."

I kissed Zoë's cheek, then waved good-bye to everyone, and we left. The limo driver offered congratulations, and we set off, heading north, toward Wentworth by the Sea.

Ty leaned over and kissed me. "You got married barefoot."

"While your toesies were in foot-prison."

He lifted his right leg a few inches to show off his handsome cordovan slip-ons. "They may be in prison, but you've got to admit, these puppies are good-looking."

"True, but I bet your toes are jealous."

Ty leaned forward to speak to the driver. "Would you pull over for a minute?"

The limo eased onto the shoulder and stopped. Ty stepped out, and I followed.

"What are we doing?" I asked.

"I thought a brief walk on the beach—barefoot—was in order. Toe-parity."

I laughed and kicked off my sandals, and Ty removed his shoes and socks. He took my hand, and we picked our way through the dunes to the soft, warm sand.

We walked for a hundred yards or so; then Ty leaned over and kissed me. "My toes are happy."

"What a relief."

We walked back to the limo, hand in hand, our shoulders touching.

As I slid into my sandals, I took one last look back, memorizing the panoramic view, the dunes with the tall grasses trembling in the breeze, the pink rambling roses, and the sun-specked water, and I knew that glorious image would stay emblazoned in my head and in my heart forever.